THE
SILENT
TRUMPET

THE SILENT TRUMPET

A RADIC & MULROY MYSTERY

BILL GORMLEY

First published by Level Best Books 2025

Copyright © 2025 by Bill Gormley

This novel is entirely a work of fiction. The names, characters and incidents portrayed in it are the work of the author's imagination. Any resemblance to actual persons, living or dead, events or localities is entirely coincidental.

Bill Gormley asserts the moral right to be identified as the author of this work.

First edition

ISBN: 979-8-89820-025-1

Cover art by Level Best Designs

This book was professionally typeset on Reedsy.
Find out more at reedsy.com

Contents

Praise for The Silent Trumpet

"*The Silent Trumpet* delivers a dazzling kaleidoscopic view of contemporary Pittsburgh with a large cast of police officers, jazz musicians, drug runners, and community activists. The story follows the fallout from the murder of a crooked cop and explores the twisted motives, fractured alliances, and crumpled dreams exposed by the investigation led by relentless detectives Branko Radic and Kathleen Mulroy. Author Bill Gormley handles the sprawling cast with a deft hand, keeping the pace fast and the dialogue lively. This is a police procedural with style, soul, and heart."—Delia Pitts, author of the Vandy Myrick mysteries and winner of the Shamus Award for Best Original Hardback P.I. Novel

"As a Western Pennsylvania native, I can attest to Gormley's gift for establishing a sense of place. He's also a devotee of the late Joe Wambaugh's dictum that a cop story should be less about how the cops work on the case than how the case works on the cops. *The Silent Trumpet* is a worthy successor to Too Many Bridges."—Dana King, Shamus Award-nominated author for the Nick Forte novels and the Penns River procedurals

"Packed with suspense and characters you will want to root for, Bill Gormley's *The Silent Trumpet* is a perfectly crafted mystery. This is a new detective series to watch."—K.L. Murphy, author of the Detective Callie Forde mysteries and the Detective Cancini mysteries

Cast of Characters

Pittsburgh Bureau of Police

- Branko Radic, Senior Detective, Homicide
- Kathleen Mulroy, Junior Detective, Homicide
- Anthony Scuglia, Senior Detective, Homicide
- Mike Turley, Junior Detective, Homicide
- John O'Neill, Patrol Officer
- Charles Stilton, Lieutenant, Homicide
- Fred Vinson, Chief, Internal Affairs
- Sean Reilly, Chief of Police
- Gino Gardenia, Senior Detective, Narcotics
- Frenchy Frobisher, Senior Detective, Homicide
- Mark Atwood, Junior Detective, Homicide

The Mabry Family

- Larry Mabry, Jazz Trumpeter
- Gary Mabry, Drug Dealer
- Ernestine Mabry, Mother of Larry and Gary
- Dorothy Mabry, Larry's Daughter
- Wanda Charles, Larry's Ex-Wife

Gary Mabry's Entourage

- Khalif Wilson, Gary's Friend and Chief Deputy
- Bradley Gibbons, Member, Gary's Army
- Marvin Casper, Member, Gary's Army

The Radic Family

Sara Radic, Branko's Mother

Bert Radic, Branko's Father

Close Friends

- Lexie Davodny, River Rescue Unit
- Jake Jacoby, School Bus Driver and Kennywood Park Employee
- Lucas Renfert, Retired Carnegie Mellon Criminology Professor

The Political Establishment

- Walter Graham, Mayor of Pittsburgh
- Phil Hodges, Manager, Mayor's Re-election Campaign
- Cecile Arceneaux, the Mayor's Wife
- Hugh Benjamin, Head, the Mayor's Drug Task Force

Other Characters

- Father Cyrus Buckley, Pastor, St. Martin de Porres Catholic Church
- Bart Fielding, Manager, Muscle Mania
- Jorge Menendez, Drug Trafficker
- Carlos Almazan, Pitcher, Altoona Curve
- Saroja Prakash, Allegheny County Medical Examiner
- Evan Kobosky, Reporter, Pittsburgh Post-Gazette

Chapter One: A Little Night Music

Although nominally a bouncer at a jazz club in downtown Pittsburgh and blessed with a bouncer's physique, Marv didn't have to do a lot of bouncing. Mainly, he handled odd jobs, while reminding audience members at Con Alma to talk softly during a performance. As a reward, he got to hear some amazing musicians, like trumpeter Larry Mabry.

Tall, Black, muscular, and handsome, Mabry cut a dashing figure on stage. He often bent his knees while performing, as he reached for higher notes. Even without his music, he was someone you would notice. With his music, he was charismatic and compelling.

Larry brimmed with self-confidence as he soloed to the jazz standard, "Caravan." At times, he played at lightning-like speed, weaving arpeggios into a motif that sounded like a train hurtling through a tunnel. At other times, he savored and stretched every note, with bleats and growls.

The sidemen laid back when Larry was really cooking. Marv could tell that this was one of those times. In lieu of a walking bass, the bassist opted for pedaling, creating more space for Larry's solos. The drummer was content with soft, lateral brush strokes on a snare drum. The piano player chimed in with occasional punctuation marks. The full ensemble grew more vibrant when Larry played the head one last time. They ended with a triumphant flourish.

The audience responded with clapping, a few hoots and hollers, and one "Amen, brother."

Larry flashed a boyish grin. "Ladies and gents, I hope you enjoyed our set. Our kind of jazz is not smooth, like a baby's butt. It's bristly, like a porcupine. A dash of Coltrane, a sprinkle of Monk, a gram of Miles Davis. We call it straight-ahead jazz. It's not for everyone. But we know y'all are sophisticated enough to ride with it. I'm Larry the Lip Mabry, and you've been listening to the Rough Riders. Stick with us for another set."

The audience rewarded the Rough Riders with more applause.

Placing his trumpet on a portable stand, Larry hopped off the stage. Hal Hirsch, the club manager, caught him as he headed toward the kitchen. "Great set, Larry. Some killer solos."

"Thanks, man."

"Hold up. A guy wants to see you. Says it's important." Hal motioned towards a heavy-set, swarthy man standing by the door. He was nursing a drink and seemed to be smirking. "Know him?"

Slowly nodding, Larry rolled his eyes. "Yeah, I know him."

"Everything okay? You want Marv to escort him outside?"

"No, man. He's police. I can handle it. Tell Barbara I'd like a cheeseburger, well done. I'll be back in five."

Hal waved Marv over. "Something doesn't feel right about that guy. Larry says he's a cop. So, don't cause any problems. But make sure *he* doesn't cause any problems either."

"You got it, boss."

Unobtrusively, Marv edged his way over to Larry and the cop, hoping to eavesdrop.

"You have a lot of fans, Larry," the smirking cop said.

"What do you want, man?" Larry asked. "You're messing with my business."

"We have something to discuss."

"I can give you five minutes. Let's step outside."

Marv peeked through the window and watched as Larry and the cop crossed the street, stopping at a sycamore tree, just leafing out as spring weather kicked in. He was tempted to step outside—in case Larry needed backup. But Hal had warned him off. He stayed put, observing the two men every minute or so. He opened a window a crack, but couldn't hear much, only raised voices.

After five minutes, Marv remembered that he was needed elsewhere. Larry was a spitter, which meant Marv had to mop the stage between sets. He also needed to replace four water bottles and check the lights. His work was interrupted by shouts from outside.

Sprinting to the window, Marv saw Larry sprawled face-down on the sidewalk. The cop was cuffing him, while Larry cursed and squirmed.

Marv ran across the street. "What's going on?" he asked.

"Police. Stay away, big guy. You don't want to be interfering here."

Larry was bleeding from the mouth. His crisp brown slacks were dirty and torn, revealing a nasty wound near the right knee. As for the cop, he had no visible scratches and his shirt was still tucked in.

"What happened, Larry?" Marv asked.

Larry started to speak, but reconsidered.

"The prick took a swing at me," the cop said.

"Is that true, Larry?" Marv asked.

Larry said nothing.

"You're busted, pal," the cop said.

"But the second set is about to begin," Marv objected.

"Tough shit," the cop responded. "You're gonna have to get by without Larry here."

Larry nodded slowly to Marv, who reluctantly backed off. "You want me to call anyone, Larry?"

Larry thought for a moment. "Call Radic. Let him know what went down."

"And who is the officer who's spoiling our second set?"

"Gardenia," the man replied. "Detective Gino Gardenia, Narcotics, PBP. And don't bother to call Radic. I'll tell him myself."

* * *

Detective Branko Radic was down on his hands and knees in his Mexican War District apartment on the North Side of Pittsburgh.

He had just returned from an evening jog, and Ralph wanted him to know how pleased he was to see him, after the painfully long forty-five-minute interlude. Ralph, a rescue puppy, was smothering him with kisses.

At thirty-eight, Radic was finally settling down. A steady girlfriend, a shrinking mortgage, and now a growing dog. He was living the dream. Until the phone rang.

"Radic here."

"Branko, it's Marv from Con Alma."

"What's up, Marv?"

"Hey, I'm sorry to bother you at home so late."

"Don't worry about it. What's going on?"

"Well, it's the Lip. He got into a scuffle with a cop outside the club."

"Is he hurt?"

"It looks like he took a hard punch to the mouth. And he's heading to jail."

"Who's the cop?"

"Gardenia. Gino Gardenia."

"Shit."

"He seemed to have it in for Larry."

"Did anyone see what happened?"

"Gardenia claims that Larry started it."

"What does Larry say?"

"He doesn't. He clammed up."

"Okay, I'm on it, Marv. I appreciate the call."

Two minutes later, despite Ralph's protests, Radic was out the door, heading to Wood Street. As he drove, he thought back to when he met Larry at a jazz club four years ago. Radic was mesmerized by his performance and showered him with compliments after introducing himself between sets.

In that brief conversation, he learned that they both competed in the annual Tough Mudder competition—a muddy obstacle course that leaves participants soiled, bruised, and happy. Sometimes, they car-pooled to train together, as they prepared for another round of blissful mayhem.

As he and Larry became friends, Radic concluded that Larry was destined for greatness. Larry had his sights set on New York City and jazz clubs like the Village Vanguard or Birdland. As Radic saw it, it was only a matter of time.

When Radic arrived at a police substation on Wood Street, Larry was being booked.

"Well, look what the cat dragged in," Gardenia sneered.

Radic took in the scene. Larry's upper lip was puffy, bruised. His pants were torn at the knee, blood congealed just below. His hands and arms showed numerous scratches.

Gardenia, in contrast, looked none the worse for wear.

"Are you okay, Larry?" Radic asked.

Larry shrugged. Uncharacteristically reticent.

Radic turned to Gardenia. "Have you charged him yet?"

"Just about to."

"What's the charge?"

"Assaulting a police officer. Resisting arrest."

"Is that true, Larry? Did you assault Detective Gardenia?"

Larry said nothing.

"Do you want a lawyer?"

Larry shook his head.

"Satisfied, Radic? Now, let me take care of business."

"Not so fast, Gardenia. Has Mr. Mabry received medical attention?"

"We cleaned him up a bit. He'll live."

"That's not enough. His lips are his living. You know that, of course. He needs stitches and he needs them now."

"Well, he's going to spend the night in jail. If he needs medical attention, we can decide that tomorrow."

Radic motioned to Gardenia to step outside the booking room.

"Gino, I don't know what went down, but you're out of line here. I know Larry. There's no way he took a swing at you."

"His word against mine."

"Well, this isn't the first time this kind of thing has happened. You want me to report you to Internal Affairs?"

"You wouldn't."

"Try me."

"He's gonna spend the night in jail."

"If you want to play it that way, okay. But he needs medical attention right now. I'll take him to Mercy Hospital myself. Then I'll bring him back after he gets stitched up."

Gardenia wavered.

"Look at it this way, Gino. If he can't play the trumpet after this, you could be facing a lawsuit. Deliberate indifference in the face of a serious medical need. Do you want that, on top of all your other troubles?"

"What do you know about my other troubles?"

"Word gets around."

"Right. Well, okay. I don't need the aggravation. You sign him out and take him to Mercy after we get his prints. Make sure he's back here after that. If not, I'm the one who'll report *you* to Internal Affairs."

"You're a sweetheart, Gino."

"Yeah, you too."

Chapter Two: My Brother's Keeper

Gary Mabry did not recognize the caller ID, but he immediately recognized the caller's voice—a voice he was trying to forget. His spine stiffened.

"How's it going, Gary?"

"I thought we agreed you would not be calling me anymore."

"No, Gary, we definitely did *not* agree to that."

"I want out."

"That's what you keep saying, but it's not as simple as that."

"Yeah, it *is* as simple as that. Just leave me alone."

"Well, Gary, I was thinking of doing that, but I thought you might appreciate a news flash."

"What news is that?"

"It's about your brother, Larry."

Gary said nothing for several seconds. "What about my brother?"

"I thought you'd want to know that he was arrested this evening. Charged with assaulting a police officer and resisting arrest."

"I don't believe it."

"Which part don't you believe?"

"Larry wouldn't do that."

"Well, believe it or not. He's in custody, even as we speak."

"Who's the arresting officer?"

"That would be me."

"Fuck you, man. You can't get away with that."

"We'll see about that, Gary. But if you and I come to a little understanding,

I guarantee you Larry will be released tomorrow."

"You've gone too far. Stop messing with me and my family!"

"Or what, Gary? Or what?"

"Or you'll regret it."

Gardenia laughed. "I have few regrets, Gary. So, I don't think so. Oh, by the way, Larry's not going to be playing his trumpet anytime soon. Seems like he injured himself while resisting arrest. Have a nice day."

* * *

After receiving Gardenia's call, Gary did what came naturally. He reached for a pill. It promised quick relief, an end to the throbbing in his brain.

But something made him reconsider. It was a memory from grade school. Gary was walking to school, not paying much attention, when two boys came up from behind and tripped him. Gary fell to the ground. Both boys started pummeling him, for no apparent reason. He kicked as best he could, but the boys were strong and vicious. He started to cry, which only made matters worse.

Suddenly, an angel of mercy appeared and started thrashing the two boys. It was Larry. "That's my brother," Larry told them. "Don't you *ever* touch my brother again."

The boys ran away. Larry wiped some blood from Gary's face and gave him some water. He escorted him to school, even though his own school was in the other direction.

Gary looked at himself in the bathroom mirror, a glass of water in one hand, a pill in the other. His good looks were returning, after years of bright red pimples and dull, vacant eyes. His mother had remarked on the change, and she was right.

Gary flushed the pill down the toilet and drank two glasses of water instead. He reached for his cell phone and called one of his friends. "Man, we gotta do something about Gardenia. He's out of control."

They agreed to meet that evening.

Next, Gary reached out to a *Post-Gazette* reporter he had met while volunteering for Mayor Walter Graham's re-election campaign.

After identifying himself, he got down to business. "You interested in a story about a corrupt cop?" Gary asked.

"What's the guy done?" the reporter asked.

"He's extorting money from drug dealers."

"You got proof?"

"I got proof."

"You gonna give me a name?"

"Not over the phone."

"You free to meet?"

"It's gotta be somewhere private."

"How about the Starbucks on Liberty Avenue? At noon?"

"There's nothing private about a Starbucks at noon."

"Okay, what did you have in mind?"

"How about Schenley Park, four o'clock? The Schenley Bridge."

"I'll see you there."

Gary looked at his watch. 11:00 a.m. He had five hours to kill. Maybe a good time to visit Father Buckley. He needed his advice on something important.

* * *

Detective Kathleen Mulroy received flowers at work from time to time. Her boyfriend, Jake Jacoby, a school bus driver and Kennywood Park employee, sent her roses on Valentine's Day and a bouquet of wildflowers on her birthday. Although they had only been dating for a year, Mulroy was sure that he was the one. A super nice guy with a great sense of humor and a big heart.

When Mulroy received flowers in April, she smiled happily, assuming they were from Jake. Then she saw the note: Thank you for being such a great mentor! Yours, John O'Neill. Mulroy's smile faded.

Physically and temperamentally, O'Neill, a new recruit from Mechanicsburg, Pa., reminded Mulroy of a younger Tom Hanks—eager, earnest, sincere, with a goofy grin.

There was only one catch—he had an obvious crush on Mulroy, his field training officer, or FTO for short. It was evident from the way O'Neill beamed whenever Mulroy appeared. It was evident from the way he hung on her every word. And now the flowers.

An attractive blonde, with blue eyes and a winning smile, Mulroy was accustomed to receiving advances from men. She took it in stride and usually bantered to defuse the situation.

But puppy love at work was outside her comfort zone. O'Neill was twenty-four, Mulroy was thirty-one. Mulroy was in a steady relationship with Jake. Besides, she wouldn't dream of fraternizing with someone at work, whatever his age. It was all a bit ironic. She had just convinced O'Neill to stop calling her ma'am. Now she had to keep him from calling her sweetheart.

So she gently explained to O'Neill that a simple thank-you would be better than flowers. Without attributing any feelings to O'Neill, she said that the gesture might be misunderstood by others, including Jake. O'Neill took the reprimand remarkably well. A decent fellow, still learning the ropes.

As the youngest member of the homicide squad, Mulroy had reconciled herself to getting assignments beyond the normal confines of the homicide division, like the FTO assignment that made her O'Neill's mentor. Due to staff shortages, everyone had to pitch in when other divisions were overworked.

As assignments go, mentoring was fairly enjoyable, even if it seldom involved a homicide. Mulroy genuinely liked O'Neill and thought he had potential.

O'Neill did whatever Mulroy asked and did it well. If she told him to prepare a report on a DUI, he wrote it up, quickly and accurately. If she told him to take fingerprints to the Medical Examiner's office, he was there in ten minutes, back in thirty minutes, eager for another assignment. If she told him to hose off the squad car, he did it with all the gusto of a detailer hustling for tips.

But O'Neill often went too far. After learning that his traffic citations would be tallied at the end of each week, he became the department's poster child for handing out tickets. From that point on, he wielded a radar gun with the unbridled joy of a hitter with a baseball bat.

On one of their routine expeditions, at the corner of Forbes and Murray, O'Neill decided to impress his FTO by ticketing a motorist for not yielding the right of way at an intersection. Mulroy felt compelled to intervene and told him to issue a warning instead.

"What are you saying, Detective? He made a left turn as soon as the light turned green, without waiting his turn. Didn't I do the right thing?"

"Did you notice that the lead car from the other direction was okay with the guy's left turn, even though *he* had the right of way?"

"That's not relevant, is it, Detective? The Pennsylvania driver's manual clearly states: If the drivers arrive at the intersection at the same time, the driver making a left must yield the right of way to the driver going straight."

"I don't care what the manual says, O'Neill. Haven't you heard of a Pittsburgh left?"

"A Pittsburgh left?"

"A Pittsburgh left is a time-honored tradition. It may not be state law, but it's part of the city's cultural code. If you're at an intersection and the car facing you wants to make a left, you let him do it, because otherwise he has to wait forever to turn left, and all the cars behind him have to wait forever just to go straight. It's the public-spirited thing to do."

"But the lead car that wants to go straight should get to go straight. Isn't that what the law says?"

Mulroy groaned. "It may be what the law says, but it's not what the people of Pittsburgh say. Ever since the Model T was invented, Pittsburghers have honored left turns at intersections. It's the way we are. It's in our DNA."

"But what about the driver's manual, Detective?"

"If you find yourself in Philadelphia and someone turns left, despite oncoming traffic, throw the book at him. If you find yourself in Mechanicsburg and someone turns left, go for it. But, so long as you're in Pittsburgh, you've got to respect common courtesies, like a Pittsburgh left. The people of Pittsburgh have spoken!"

O'Neill paused. "What if he turns left without signaling?"

Mulroy smiled. "Without signaling? Now that's a criminal offense!"

Chapter Three: Difficult Conversations

Lieutenant Charles "Cheesy" Stilton never liked dealing with lawyers. Especially on a Monday morning. And especially when the lawyer was threatening to sue one of his former Homicide detectives, now with Narcotics, if his client, Larry Mabry, wasn't released immediately.

He picked up the phone. "Gardenia? In my office."

Two minutes later, he was facing Gardenia.

"Just like old times, sir, except now I report to someone else."

"Gino, I hope this isn't another excessive use of force situation. Because you need that like a hole in the head."

"He was resisting arrest."

"What is your body cam going to tell me?"

"I was off duty. I didn't have it with me."

"Very convenient, Gino. So, where did this happen?"

"At Con Alma, downtown."

"What were you doing there?"

"Having a drink. Listening to jazz."

"I didn't know you were a jazz fan."

"I thought I'd check it out."

"Did you clear it with Lieutenant Carson?"

"He gives me a lot of rope. Unlike some people."

"Too much rope, if you ask me. And Larry Mabry?"

"His brother's a drug dealer. I thought he might help us with our investigation."

"So, not exactly off duty. What did you do to him, Gino? His lawyer says he had to be taken to the ER."

"Well, that's where it gets complicated. I didn't think he actually needed medical attention. But Radic showed up. He offered to take him to Mercy. I let him do it."

"What interest does Radic have in this case?"

"I gather he's a friend of Mabry's."

Stilton stood up and approached Gardenia. He observed his face, neck, arms, and hands, while Gardenia stiffened under his gaze.

"Where are your injuries, Gino?"

"I dodged a couple of punches."

"No injuries at all?"

"Well, my neck's a little sore."

"Gino, I'm going to look into this carefully. And I'll talk with Lieutenant Carson. If I find that you used excessive force again, I'm going to write you up. And then we're going to release Mabry."

"Do what you have to do."

* * *

"Free at last. Free at last. Thank God Almighty, I'm free at last." Larry's grin of relief, standing outside the county jail, quickly turned into a grimace. He wasn't meant to smile just yet.

Larry gently massaged his lips, hoping it might help. "You got some Tylenol on you, man?" he asked.

"No Tylenol, bro," Gary answered. "Something stronger?"

"No, it can wait."

"You gonna be able to play Thursday night?"

"No, not until the stitches come out."

"When's that?"

"A few days."

"What are you going to do?"

Larry sighed and stopped walking for a moment. "I'm going to see if the

Drake can pinch-hit."

"For how long?"

"I don't know, man, as long as it takes. I don't think I could play Mary Had a Fucking Little Lamb like this."

"You got screwed, bro. I'm really sorry about this."

"Not your fault, man." Then he paused and looked directly into Gary's eyes. "We gotta figure out a way to get Gardenia off your back."

Gary returned his gaze, with a look of steely resolve.

"No, not that way," Larry said. "Some other way."

"I have some thoughts," Gary said.

"Okay, let's go sit somewhere. Let's figure this out."

* * *

Radic hated to leave home at six a.m. on his day off, especially with Lexie in bed beside him. Sexy Lexie, one of his colleagues, had called her. But that didn't begin to describe her allure.

Lexie was a sprite—mischievous, adventurous, and luscious. Like a creature from a parallel universe—magical and spell-binding. She was the cure for his doldrums, the love of his life. She was joyful ninety percent of the time, and her joy was contagious.

Radic had no wish to leave Lexie, this morning or any other morning, but he had no other choice. He had to head home, to Butler, to deal with an emergency.

His father's dementia had been worsening in recent months. Memory lapses, repetitive comments, and aimless wandering.

Bert Radic was in good spirits most of the time. No obvious signs of depression yet. That, at least, was something to be thankful for. Radic's mother, Sara, was in good health, and she had quit work to stay home with her husband.

But the wandering had gotten much worse. Because the Radic home was rural and near the Succop Nature Park, there were many different ways to get lost.

When a typical wandering episode occurred, Sara would notice her husband's absence, get in the car, and go find him.

On other occasions, a neighbor would spot him, invite him in for a cup of coffee, and discreetly call Sara.

But sometimes it didn't work out that way. Three days earlier, Bert got hopelessly lost two miles from home, while Sara was getting her hair done. A stranger noticed odd behavior—wandering around in circles—and called the police.

An overzealous police officer had arrested Bert after encountering "belligerent" behavior. He then called Social Services before Sara could intervene, triggering an unwelcome series of inquiries that the family had hoped to avoid.

Radic had never met the arresting officer, but he knew Butler's chief of police. After a frank phone conversation, charges had been dropped, and his father was released with a warning. But the Social Services investigation would continue, and the problem could only get worse. A day of reckoning might well be at hand.

Despite Radic's glum thoughts, his mood brightened for just a moment as he pulled into the familiar gravel driveway. The crunching sound under the tires transported him to a simpler, happier time. Pausing, he remembered experiences he and his older sister Petra had shared together before she left home for the Peace Corps, never to return.

Radic tugged reflexively at the silver hoop earring on his right ear—one of Petra's, which he wore to ensure that he would never forget.

Petra's murder, in Guatemala, when Radic was still in high school, had been a crushing blow to the Radic family and to Radic personally. For his parents, it was devastating and deflating. For him, it was devastating but also energizing in an unexpected way. It was Petra's murder that convinced him to become a police officer and continued to motivate him to this day.

Outside of his family, Lexie, and a handful of good friends, few people knew about Petra's tragic death. Radic was basically a private person who didn't like to divulge his innermost feelings or personal experiences to casual acquaintances. None of his colleagues knew either, except for

Mulroy. Radic felt comfortable sharing confidences with her, and she with him.

The familiar aroma of cherry scones greeted Radic as he walked through the front door. Clearly, he was not the only family member who had gotten up early. The scent was welcome because it reinforced his hopes—his mother was a fighter and an optimist. If there was a path forward, she would lead the charge.

Bert, seated on the living room couch, greeted him warmly, as if nothing had happened. Perhaps he had forgotten much of it. After embracing his father, Radic poked his head into the kitchen and kissed his mother. "How bad is it?"

"Let's save that till later, Branko. I've made you a nice breakfast."

"I can see that, Mom. I ought to come home more often."

"You come home when you can. Your father and I know that. And we appreciate it."

A relaxed conversation over eggs, scones, orange juice, and coffee felt just like old times. Bert still enjoyed a good story and was happy to hear about the latest developments at work. He also wanted to know when his son's training for the next Tough Mudder mud run and obstacle course would resume.

"It never stops, Dad," Radic replied. "Calisthenics every morning. Short jogs weekday nights. Longer jogs weekend mornings."

"Does Lexie join you for your jogs?" Mrs. Radic asked.

"Yes, for the short ones, if she's around. And if Ralph allows it."

"You two, you're spoiling that dog," Mrs. Radic admonished.

"Well, he's just a puppy. We can't leave him alone for long stretches at a time."

A neighbor, Frank Masten, appeared just as they were finishing breakfast. He eyed the remnants of their meal. "I should have come earlier."

"Don't worry, Frank, I'll warm up some scones after you and Bert have had a proper walk."

"Sounds good to me. Ready, Bert?" Masten asked.

"Ready as I'll ever be."

After the two men left, Radic helped his mother clear the dishes, and they migrated to the Adirondack chairs on the front porch. It was a beautiful spring morning, the fragrant smell of honeysuckle wafting through the air.

"I've only been here an hour, but he seems pretty good to me."

"He is, most of the time."

"Does he ever get violent?"

"No, never."

"Does he ever get agitated?"

"Yes, of course. When the Pirates are in a slump, he gets agitated. When the number of raisins in his box of Raisin Bran declines, he gets agitated."

Radic laughed. "He really ought to switch to a different cereal. When's the last time he went wandering, before the most recent episode?"

"Two weeks ago."

"What happened?"

"He got a notion to head down to the pond. Unfortunately, he headed in exactly the wrong direction."

"Were you here?"

"Yes, but he snuck out before I could catch him."

"Have you urged him to check in with you when he wants to leave the house?"

"In one ear and out the other."

"Okay. Have you thought about having a sitter when you have to leave the house?"

"We do some of that already. I can rely on Frank and Martha. Elaine and Joe. Trudy. Margaret."

"Do you pay them?"

"Are you kidding? They wouldn't hear of it."

"Is there someone you could pay? A teenage boy? Someone from church?"

"What's the point?"

"Well, here's the thing, Mom. I was able to talk the chief of police into dropping the disorderly conduct charges. He's embarrassed by the whole thing anyway. But Social Services, that's a different story. They might want some sort of good-faith gesture, a quid pro quo, before they drop their investigation."

"And you think hiring someone would do the trick?"

"It's a start. But let's forget Social Services for a moment. Maybe this is a wake-up call. Are you worried about Dad's safety? Are you having more scary moments with him?"

Mrs. Radic sighed. "I thought old age would be different from this."

Radic reached out and clasped his mother's hands together inside his own. "Is it getting to be too much for you? Should we be thinking about assisted living?"

"No! Anything but that. I can manage."

"Well, Mom, if anyone can manage, it's you. But if Dad's wandering about on his own, that could easily lead to something bad."

"I know. I know. But I'm not ready to give up yet."

"Okay, so let me visit the folks in Social Services. Can I tell them that you'll pay someone reliable to look after Dad whenever you leave the house?"

Mrs. Radic nodded, fighting back tears.

"Is it okay if they check in on him every month or so?"

His mother squirmed.

"If they insist?"

"If they insist."

"Okay, Mom, you've been a big help. And you're doing a great job. Dad is lucky to have you in his corner."

"I just hope it doesn't get any worse."

"Me too. Now, let me see what I can do. Tell Dad I went on an errand. I'll be back to say good-bye."

Chapter Four: A Plague of Snakes

Detective Mulroy's day was looking good. O'Neill was off to an orientation session. His absence might give her some breathing room. Also, Radic should be working today. Maybe he needed a hand.

Once at work, Mulroy checked her messages at a desktop computer. From Radic: Off today, back tomorrow. Oh, well. From Lieutenant Stilton: Come see me immediately! Uh-oh.

Stilton looked vexed. His normally calm expression was gone, replaced by a frown. He was pacing, back and forth, behind his mahogany desk. "Sit down, Mulroy," he said. "Do you read the Bible?"

"Yes, I do, sir."

"Then perhaps you've read about a plague of snakes."

"Not recently, sir."

"Well, we have a plague of snakes. Right here in Pittsburgh. In Brookline, in fact."

"Is that a metaphor, sir?"

"No, Mulroy, it's an actual plague of snakes."

"Well, there's some parks in Brookline. You might see some brown snakes or a few rat snakes every now and then."

"Just so, Mulroy. But an African puff adder? A rhinoceros viper?"

"In Brookline?"

"Yes, and in a residential neighborhood, not a park. Seaton Street."

Mulroy took out a small notebook and jotted down the name of the street. "It sounds like a case for Animal Care and Control, sir. Have you called them?"

"Yes, they've disposed of the snake carcasses."

"So they're no longer a threat, sir?"

"Well, the neighbors are very upset. A dead snake one day, a live snake the next day."

Mulroy found herself doodling. A big snake with puffy cheeks. An even bigger snake with fangs. "So, you want me to investigate, sir? Why not a patrol officer? Why me?"

"Well, given our staff shortages, we all have to pitch in. And you have a track record, Mulroy. You solved our runaway chicken case rather nicely last year."

"With all respect, sir, chickens are chickens and snakes are snakes. I'm not sure I'm cut out to handle a plague of snakes."

"Don't be modest, Mulroy. You have a good head on your shoulders. I know I can count on you. See if there are any other snakes lurking about. We want to reassure the neighbors."

"Right, sir. Just me, sir?"

"Just you, I'm afraid, Mulroy. Radic is taking a personal day. O'Neill is at a training session."

"Will I need any special gear, sir?"

"Well, I hadn't thought of that. But, sure, check with the HAZMAT folks. Maybe they can come up with some boots and a suit. I left a report on your desk, with what we know so far."

Forty-five minutes later, in a small county office on the South Side, Mulroy was wearing a bright orange outfit. A pretty good fit, but more appropriate for Halloween than for a snake patrol, she thought.

"I'm not sure I want to knock on doors, dressed like this," Mulroy said.

The HAZMAT guy laughed. "You'll be glad to have the protection if a snake strikes. Just sign out here. We like to keep track of our suits."

Mulroy signed the form.

"Oh, and Mulroy?"

"Yeah?"

"You look great in orange!"

"Ha, ha. Just for that, I'm gonna make sure I come back with a tear. A tear that's hard to fix."

"Be my guest. Knock yourself out. But these suits are practically indestructible."

From the written report, Mulroy gathered that the snake infestation, such as it was, originated on Brookline's east side. Two carcasses had been discovered in the backyard of a private home on Seaton Street. The Macklers. They were very upset.

From a quick Google search, Mulroy was intrigued. A rhinoceros viper was a truly rare breed, not typically found in the U.S. Someone must have brought the snake to the city, illegally.

The African puff adder was equally rare, though some sightings were reported in upper Michigan and northern Wisconsin. Unlikely that they would have wandered voluntarily all the way to Pittsburgh.

Before leaving the office, Mulroy established that certain venomous snakes could be kept as pets in Pennsylvania, but only after the state Fish and Boat Commission granted a permit.

She contacted the Commission and asked for records of all Pittsburghers who possessed such a permit. They promised a list before the end of the day.

Next, Mulroy reached out to the Mackler family. Yes, Sadie Mackler would be home. And yes, she would be more than happy to tell Mulroy the slimy details of what it was like to discover two snake carcasses in her backyard.

Mulroy tossed her orange costume into the back of the car and headed across the river to Brookline.

Chapter Five: Stood Up

It was a rainy Thursday night. Homicide Detective Mark Atwood was not crazy about late-night meetings in isolated places. But Gardenia said it minimized risks.

Gardenia usually stood just in front of the shuttered factory on Sandusky Street on the North Side. No sign of him there, even though he had just called twenty minutes earlier.

Atwood checked his phone messages. No update. And no text message. He looked at both ends of the building, protecting himself from the rain with a battered umbrella.

"Gino?" No answer.

He walked to the side entrance. The door was ajar.

"Gino?"

He got out a flashlight and stepped cautiously inside. He pointed the flashlight in multiple directions. Seeing nothing, he walked farther inside, to where an assembly line once churned out pop bottles. That's where he saw the body.

Gino Gardenia lay sprawled on the cement floor. His head was badly battered and bruised and rested in a pool of blood. Atwood checked but felt no pulse.

"Shit." Atwood was about to call 911, but reconsidered. Donning gloves, he checked Gino's pockets. He found a set of car keys, some crumpled Kleenex, some Vaseline lip balm, and a wallet. No notes with names or phone numbers to worry about.

Nearby, he saw a satchel that contained a gleaming golden trumpet, with the name Mabry on masking tape. He recalled reading an article about trumpets in the newspaper just the other day. It had mentioned that Vaseline was used to lubricate them.

After a moment's thought, Atwood put the wallet, keys, and Kleenex back inside Gino's pockets. He opened the tube of Vaseline and smeared some on Gino's forehead, then applied some to the trumpet. With a clean rag, he extracted some blood from the floor and smeared it on the trumpet, which he then placed inside the satchel, to be stored in the trunk of his car.

Feeling satisfied, Atwood removed his gloves and called 911. Then he called Lieutenant Stilton, after thinking carefully about what he wanted to say.

* * *

Larry was sipping some lukewarm coffee and chewing on a banana—the only breakfast he could handle with his sore lips—when he heard a knock at the door of his Shadyside apartment.

"Larry Mabry? It's the police. Open up."

Larry wiped his lips gently with a napkin and opened the door.

Two officers he didn't know stood before him, both with guns drawn. One looked like a young marine, the other like an aging linebacker.

"Raise your hands up high. You have the right to remain silent. Anything you say can and will be held against you."

"What the fuck have I done now?"

"You're being arrested for murder, you son of a bitch."

"Who the hell did I kill?"

"Detective Gino Gardenia."

"Oh, shit. Oh, shit."

* * *

The man who appeared at Larry's cell door was Black, wearing a charcoal suit, a crisp blue shirt, and a red silk tie. He sported a horseshoe mustache, and his gaze was intense. He introduced himself as Darius P. Larkin, Esq., in a strong, authoritative voice, and shook Larry's hand, looking grim. He explained that he was a partner at the law firm where Larry's usual lawyer worked.

"Did the police explain why you've been arrested?"

"Because I'm Black?"

"Did they say that?"

Larry shook his head.

"What exactly did they say?"

"That I have a history with Gardenia, that I've argued with him in public."

"Is that true?"

Larry nodded.

"What else?"

"They say an eyewitness saw me at the scene of the crime."

"Is that true?"

"No way. I was at home all night."

"Anything else?"

"They kept asking about my trumpet."

"What about your trumpet?"

"It's missing."

"Why do they care?"

"They say I used it to kill Gardenia."

Larkin was pensive. Then he spoke. "When the police come in to interrogate you, I want you to say absolutely nothing. You hear me?"

Larry nodded slowly. "Can I ask questions?"

"No questions. Unless it's to ask for a glass of water."

"Can I talk to my brother?"

"I would advise against that."

"Why?"

Larkin stared intently at his client. "I know more about Gary than you might think, and most of it is not good. You reach out to Gary, the cops will jump to conclusions. Bad conclusions. So, don't reach out to him. Or anyone else. Only me."

* * *

Approximately two hundred citizens crowded into St. Martin de Porres Catholic Church in the Hill District. Most were young, most were male, most were Black. And most were very angry.

Detective Mike Turley eased into a back pew. He was pleased that Lieutenant Stilton had asked him to attend the event. As a Black homicide detective, he was not inclined to sugar-coat the community's concerns.

Turley recognized many faces at the church—some from community meetings, some from church services, some from jail. No sign of Khalif Wilson, Gary's deputy. Well, he was more on the business side of things. No sign of Jorge Menendez either. Not a very political guy.

Gary Mabry, who had organized the impromptu meeting, held the floor, after being introduced by the popular pastor, Father Cyrus Buckley, a barrel of a man known for his pastoral care and social activism. Gary spoke loudly and passionately, without the benefit of a mic. The crowd responded.

"This is a bogus arrest. You all know Larry. Larry is a lover, not a killer."

"That's right, man!" someone hollered.

"Larry wouldn't hurt a fly."

"Amen!" several people chanted.

"If the police want to find Detective Gardenia's killer, they ought to look within the Blue community, not the Black community."

"You tell 'em, Gary!"

"I don't know about y'all, but I don't think Larry's safe in a Pittsburgh jail."

"You got that right, bro!"

"We gotta organize, we gotta mobilize, we gotta criticize. And since it's Larry, we gotta harmonize."

Gary nodded to Larry's piano player, Wade Newborn, who laid down a few gospel chords on the church's upright piano.

Many in the crowd recognized the chords. "We shall overcome. We shall overcome. We shall overcome someday. Oh, deep in my heart, I do believe, we shall overcome someday."

Men and women, singing in unison, joined hands and swayed back and forth to the music.

"That's right," Gary concluded. "We *shall* overcome. Now let's deal with this situation. Let's get Larry released from jail."

"Praise Jesus."

"I hope to see all of you tomorrow. Freedom Corner. Four o'clock. Bring food. Bring blankets. Bring friends. Bring a righteous spirit. But no weapons, you hear?"

* * *

Although Gino Gardenia was not beloved by all or even most of his colleagues, the prevailing view on the police force was that no one should get away with killing a cop, even a bad cop.

At a Narcotics Squad meeting, two officers passed the hat for flowers, while others sat somberly or talked amongst themselves:

"It's got to be some whacked-out druggie. When they're high as a kite, this is the kind of shit that happens."

"The guy couldn't have been too whacked-out. No murder weapon. No evidence on the scene. It was an assassination, if you ask me."

"Gino had enemies. Something like this was bound to happen sooner or later."

"What do you mean?"

"That's all I got to say."

"Everyone is anti-cop these days. How did we get to be the bad guys?"

"It's what they teach in college. It's what they teach in school. It's what they teach on the streets."

"Is there gonna be a funeral? There's no widow, right?"

"There's an ex. She wants a funeral, but not at church."

"Full honors?"

"A twenty-one gun salute, is what I heard."

"We gotta send a message to the community. This will not stand."

"How do we send that message, man?"

"Enforce the law. Seriously, until it hurts. Make our presence known on the street."

"For Gino?"

"Not for Gino. He was an asshole. For us. For us."

Chapter Six: The Price of a Free Lunch

Lieutenant Stilton and Radic had a good rapport. So, Radic wasn't surprised when Stilton invited him to lunch. He was surprised, though, when Stilton suggested that they meet at noon at Eleven, a chic restaurant on Smallman Street in the Strip District.

Upon arriving, Radic was ushered into a private room. Seated there was Stilton, along with the Chief of Police, Sean Reilly.

The two made an odd-looking pair: Lieutenant Stilton—lean, wiry, with neat graying hair and piercing blue-gray eyes; Chief Reilly—plump, with a generous paunch, a whiskey tan, and oversized eyebrows that seemed better suited to someone else's head.

Radic felt as if he had been summoned to the principal's office. He ran through a list of possible offenses in his mind. Not completing his paperwork in time for Reilly's annual State of the City speech. Not donating enough cash to the Police Benevolent Foundation. Referring to Stilton as "Cheesy" behind his back.

"Sit down, Radic. Sit down," Stilton said. "Have you been here before?"

"No, sir. My idea of splurging is a Pitts Burger at Primanti Brothers."

"Well, we need to work on our detective pay grades, don't we, Chief?" Stilton responded.

Reilly grunted, then turned to Radic. "How do you pronounce your name, son?"

"Rad-itch. Like you need to scratch."

"And do you? Need to scratch?"

"No, that's my dog, sir. He needs to scratch all the time." They all laughed.

Radic had broken the ice.

"Let's place our orders first," Stilton suggested. "And then we can get down to business."

"Fine by me," Radic said. He ordered the prosciutto and cheese omelet, with a side order of hash browns and a Coke.

"You've heard about Gardenia, of course."

Radic nodded.

"Terrible business," Stilton continued. "Do you know anything about the case?"

"Just what I've heard in the squad room, sir. And what I read in the *Post-Gazette*."

"What did you think of Gardenia?"

Radic squirmed. "With all due respect, sir, I try not to talk out of school about a fellow officer. Especially a dead officer who may have died in the line of duty."

"Quite right, quite right," Stilton said. "But confidentially, what did you think of him?"

Radic said nothing.

"It's okay, son," Reilly interjected. "We genuinely want to know your opinion. Whatever you say, it won't go beyond these four walls."

Radic sighed. "Okay, well, I wasn't his biggest fan. He was rough around the edges. He used excessive force in at least two situations that I know of before he left Homicide for Narcotics. Both involved Blacks. And there are rumors that he was bent."

"Corrupt?" Reilly asked. "You're saying he was corrupt?"

"Just rumors, sir. You asked for my opinion."

"Any evidence to support your opinion?" Reilly asked.

"Well, sir, I happen to know that he's under investigation by Internal Affairs. The word is that he's been extorting cash from drug dealers."

"Who told you that?" Reilly asked.

Radic shrugged. "I can't tell you, sir. I have to draw the line somewhere, even if this is a confidential conversation."

Stilton intervened. "Okay, you're a good detective, Radic. I'm not surprised that you sussed that out. Right, Chief?"

Reilly nodded.

Stilton continued. "So, tell me about Gardenia's latest arrest. Larry Mabry."

"What do you want to know, sir?"

"How did you get involved in this case?"

"Larry Mabry is a friend of mine. I met him at a jazz club four years ago. I like him. And he's a hell of a trumpeter. He could make the big time someday. He's that good."

"How well do you know him?" Stilton asked.

"I go to hear him play two or three times a year. We sometimes train together for Tough Mudder competitions. We've gotten to be friends."

"Does he have a violent streak?" Chief Reilly asked.

"He's competitive. He's strong. But he's basically a gentle, respectful guy. You can tell that from his music. And from the way he behaves."

"How so?"

"He's courteous, polite, charming. He doesn't do drugs. And he seldom drinks. If your stereotypical jazz musician is somebody who walks on the wild side, that's not Larry."

"Okay, fair enough," Stilton nodded. "What brought you to the station last Saturday night?"

"I got a call from Marv, the bouncer at Con Alma in the Cultural District. He said a police officer was hassling Larry at the club and that Larry got hurt and was arrested. I agreed to look into the matter."

Stilton nodded. "So you dropped by the substation. Mabry was being booked when you arrived?"

"That's right, sir."

"What did you observe?"

"Well, Larry looked like he had been in a street fight. But Gino? He looked like he had just returned from church. Gino claimed that Larry had assaulted him. It just didn't add up."

"Anything else?"

"Well, there's two things I know about Larry. First, he wouldn't have taken a swing at Gino or anyone else. Like I said before, he's on the up escalator. It's just a matter of time. He wouldn't do anything stupid to jeopardize his career. And second, he's a *very* strong guy. If he had taken a swing at Gino, you would have seen it on Gino's face."

"Okay, got it. So, what made you volunteer to take Mabry to the ER?"

"Larry's lips were in bad shape. He needed stitches. Lips for him are like hands for a piano player. That's how he earns his living. There have been cases where a trumpet player got into a fistfight and never played the same again. Chet Baker, for example. I wanted to give Larry a fighting chance to heal properly and quickly."

"Is he healing? Or is he hurt badly enough that he might retaliate? Do something drastic? Something stupid?"

Radic paused. "We all have a boiling point, sir. I'm sure Larry does too. But Larry should be okay in a couple of weeks, thanks to the stitches. That's what his doc says. And Larry is too smart to risk his career just because some bully of a cop had a run at him. Pardon me for being so blunt.

"Frankly, I'm surprised that we've arrested him for Gino's murder," Radic continued. "What's the evidence to justify that?"

"Telephone logs indicate that Larry Mabry contacted Gino on at least two occasions. Eyewitnesses say they had harsh words at a local gym."

"That's it? Pretty flimsy evidence for a first-degree murder charge, if you ask me."

"An anonymous source says Mabry's trumpet was the murder weapon."

Radic laughed. "That's extremely hard to believe, for all sorts of reasons. Do we have this murder weapon?"

"Not yet. We're working on it."

"I'm skeptical."

"The charges may or may not stick. But we had enough evidence to arrest him."

"Care to tell me more?" Radic asked.

"Maybe later," Stilton said. "Meanwhile, we appreciate your candor. Right, chief?"

Reilly nodded.

"So, how would you feel about being lead detective for Gardenia's murder?" Stilton asked.

Radic looked up, surprised. He hadn't guessed where this was heading.

"With all due respect, sir, I'd rather not. Gino and I had some history, as we've discussed. And one of the suspects is a friend of mine. I'd rather that you find someone else."

"Understood. Understood. But you're one of my finest detectives, Radic. I trust you to leave no stone unturned. To be relentless. Resourceful. Open-minded."

"There's gotta be somebody else, sir," Radic said.

"Well, there's a couple of Homicide detectives who'd love to do it," Stilton said, "including the arresting officers. Frenchy Frobisher."

Radic winced.

"Or Mark Atwood."

Radic winced again.

"There's someone else who's taken an active interest in the case, son," Reilly said.

"Someone else, sir?"

"The mayor. He wants you to take the case."

"The mayor? You gotta be kidding. I don't even know the mayor."

Reilly shrugged. "Nevertheless, Lieutenant Stilton has recommended you for the assignment. And the mayor has recommended you as well. Do you think you're capable of conducting a full and fair investigation?"

Radic felt trapped. If only he had seen this coming, he might have answered a few questions differently.

If this assignment was to be tolerable, he needed to work with someone he liked, trusted, and respected. Someone like Mulroy. Their approaches to detective work differed. Radic was more evidence-based, Mulroy was more intuitive. But they worked well together.

"I'll do it under one condition, sir," Radic said.

"What's that?" Stilton asked.

"That you pair me up with Mulroy."

This time, it was Stilton's turn to be surprised.

"But she's a newly minted detective."

"She helped to solve one of our toughest murder cases."

"True. True. But this is a *very* sensitive case."

"Mulroy is a very sensitive detective."

"Granted. Granted. But think of the politics for a moment. A lot of your fellow officers are howling for blood. A leading suspect is a friend of yours. A tough assignment for you. Maybe even tougher for Mulroy, who's still learning the ropes?"

Like it or not, Radic thought, this is beginning to look like a fait accompli. If so, he should bargain while it was still possible. "One more request, sir."

"What's that?" Stilton asked.

"I would want full access to Gardenia's Internal Affairs file. Unredacted. If other officers are in the frame as possible suspects or accomplices, I need to know who they are and what the evidence is against them."

Stilton and Chief Reilly looked at one another. "Can you excuse us for five minutes, Detective?" Reilly asked.

"Of course," Radic said. "I'll be right outside."

Chapter Seven: Knocking on Doors

Mulroy minded her footwork as she mounted the steps to the Mackler residence on Seaton Street. When snakes are in the vicinity, dead or alive, you can't be too careful.

Admittedly, if she really wanted to be careful, she would be wearing her Hazmat outfit. But she had decided to leave her orange jumpsuit in the car, for her own comfort and to avoid scaring civilians. It was there if she needed it.

Sadie Mackler opened the front door and invited Mulroy to come inside. "I'm fed up," she exclaimed. "Fed up. Where are our tax dollars going if not to protect us in our own homes?"

"I understand how you feel," Mulroy began, in her most soothing tone of voice, but she was quickly interrupted.

"This is supposed to be a peaceful residential community, not the Serengeti plain. What business does an African snake have in my backyard?"

"No business at all, ma'am, that's why I'm here, to …"

"I've read about snakes, you know. They get into people's plumbing, that's what they do. And where does it end? Would you want a snake in your toilet while you're trying to do your business?"

"Well, no, ma'am, I don't think anyone would. But that's why I want to…"

It took a while, but eventually Mulroy persuaded Sadie Mackler to show her the exact locations in her backyard where the carcasses were found. The locations turned out to be very close to a fence, adjacent to a property on a parallel street.

"What street is that, ma'am?"

"Creedmore Avenue."

"Do you know the people who live there?"

"That's the Roziers."

After thanking and reassuring Mrs. Mackler, Mulroy zig-zagged her way over to the Rozier residence and knocked on the door. A middle-aged man with sandy hair and thin-rimmed glasses answered.

"May I help you?" he asked.

"I'm Detective Mulroy from the Pittsburgh Bureau of Police," she said, flashing her badge. "Have you heard about the snake carcasses that were discovered in your neighborhood?"

Rozier laughed. "Come on in, if you like. Sadie Mackler has talked about nothing but snakes for the past few days. So, yes, I think you could say I'm familiar with the topic."

"You don't sound too concerned," Mulroy said.

"Well, I don't mean to be glib," he said. "I'm as concerned as the next person. But I'm not going to go out and purchase an AR-15 to protect my family from a rattlesnake. I see weeds as a more immediate threat. How can I help you?"

"Have you seen any snakes in your neighborhood?"

"Nope."

"Any suspicious activity?"

"Nope."

"Any thoughts on where the snakes came from?"

"Well, it's a bit of a mystery. We're not that close to the woods or a pond or a zoo. It's kind of hard to figure out."

"Does anyone in your neighborhood own any other type of exotic pet?"

"Not that I know of."

Mulroy checked in with a few other neighbors and didn't learn much. She headed back to the office without having seen a single snake.

A list of Pittsburghers with venomous snake permits awaited Mulroy at work. Almost all of the permit holders, she noticed, were men.

Running through the list, Mulroy identified three individuals with a 15226 zip code, Brookline. She circled the three names.

Mulroy's initial impulse was to call all three persons, but then she looked at a map. One of the addresses jumped out—on Eben Street, close to Seaton Street.

Checking her watch, 3:10 p.m., Mulroy decided to make another run out to Brookline. The home on Eben Street seemed normal enough. A two-story Cape Cod, with shutters that could use a fresh coat of paint. Unlike other homes on the block, it did not boast a well-manicured lawn and garden. This sparked her interest.

Instead of confronting the owner directly, Mulroy walked across the street and knocked on one of the doors.

"I'm sorry to disturb you, ma'am. I'm from the Pittsburgh Bureau of Police, and we're investigating some suspicious activities involving snakes in your neighborhood. Have you heard anything about snakes?"

"No, I haven't," the woman replied, introducing herself as Mrs. Saunders.

"We discovered some snake carcasses—exotic snakes, poisonous snakes, a couple of blocks from here."

"Oh, my."

"You haven't heard about that?"

"No. I would have remembered."

"Have you noticed any suspicious activity in the neighborhood?"

The woman's eyes brightened. "Actually, I have."

"What did you see?"

"There's a guy who brought some cages into his home late one night. I told my husband, there's something fishy going on there. Chickens is what I thought at first. But if it was chickens, we would have heard them, right? Or smelled them?"

"Which house is it, ma'am?"

"It's that one over there, next to the corner house," she said.

"Do you know who lives there?"

"It's a gentleman who keeps to himself. I only met him once."

"Do you know his name?"

"He's Chinese, I think. Or Korean. Something like that."

Mulroy looked at her list. "Dong Nguyen?"

"Bingo! That's the guy."

"Have you seen him lately?"

"Not for a couple of days."

"If you do see him, anytime, day or night, would you give me a call?"

Mulroy gave Mrs. Saunders a card and thanked her for her help. Then she walked across the street and knocked on Nguyen's door. As expected, he wasn't home or wasn't answering. Mulroy headed back across the Fort Pitt Bridge to Jake Jacoby's apartment.

Jake's apartment was, in a word, masculine. Two pairs of running shoes by the front door. A small bar between the dining room and the kitchen. A pair of oars in the living room, from his rowing days at the University of Florida. A stationary bicycle in the study, so he could stay fit all year round.

But there were also touches of playfulness from the students he ferried back and forth on his school bus. Stick-figure paintings portraying Jake as a goofy guy eating a candy bar, or carrying a dozen balloons, or trying to steer his bus past an angry bull standing in the middle of the road.

Jake greeted Mulroy at the door with a sexy, bristly kiss, thanks to his thick mustache. "You won't guess how I spent my day," Mulroy said, rolling her eyes.

"Does this call for a drink?"

"At least one."

After two drinks, some braised salmon, roasted potatoes, and green beans, Mulroy was feeling mellow. Mellow enough that she took Radic's call in stride. "Yeah?" "Okay." "Right." "No, not a problem." "Could be." "I'll be there."

"What's up?" Jake asked.

"Seems like I have a new assignment. The snakes are on hold."

"What's the new assignment?"

"Gardenia's murder."

"Just you and Radic?"

"No, Scuglia too. As soon as he can shake loose from another case."

"When do you get started?"

"There's an autopsy at 10:00 a.m."

"Lucky you. Maybe we should go to bed early tonight."

"You're reading my mind."

Chapter Eight: The Power of Vicks

Mulroy arrived at the Medical Examiner's office on Penn Avenue a couple minutes early. Radic was already there, seated on a bench, checking messages. He looked up, offering a half-smile in lieu of his usual banter. Mulroy responded with an exaggerated grimace and sat down.

The Medical Examiner, Saroja Prakash, walked briskly out of the autopsy room, with a movie star's flourish. Even in surgical garb, she was a striking woman, with high cheekbones, full lips, and dark brown eyes. "Radic, Mulroy, nice to see both of you."

"You too, Saroja," Radic said.

"Mulroy, this is your second rodeo, as I recall," she said.

"That's right, ma'am."

"Forget the ma'am, stuff. We're all in this together."

Mulroy nodded appreciatively.

"Did one of you bring some Vicks?"

Mulroy reached into her purse, as Radic reached into his pocket.

Prakash laughed. "You two don't need any coaching. Smear on some Vicks, grab a cap and gown, put on some booties, and let's get started."

As they entered the autopsy room, Mulroy noticed the strong scent of formaldehyde. It made her want to gag. She was tempted to apply more Vicks, but didn't want to draw attention to herself. She would grin and bear it. Even in front of Radic, who would never judge her harshly, she wanted to seem confident and self-assured.

"The protocol will be the same as for any autopsy," Prakash began. "But let's be honest. The victim is a cop. It's a high-profile shooting. I'm going to be as thorough as I possibly can be."

"Understood," Radic said.

"How well did you know him?"

"Pretty well," Radic replied.

"And?"

Radic said nothing.

"Okay. I get the picture. Let's proceed."

Prakash unveiled Gardenia quickly and without ceremony. His face, battered and puffy, was barely recognizable.

Mulroy gasped.

"Take a moment, Detective."

Mulroy took a deep breath, then instantly regretted it. Was there a way to breathe deeply without smelling deeply? Probably not.

Bracing herself, Mulroy glanced at the rest of Gardenia's body. A hairy chest. A beer belly. Cuts on both hands. The key was not to look at his battered face.

After a brief pause, Prakash continued. "Blunt trauma to the face. Repeated blows with a blunt instrument. Maybe metal. Probably not wood, because I don't see splinters."

Prakash extracted some fibers from Gardenia's face and deposited them in small plastic containers. "We might get lucky," she said. "I can tell you one thing. There's some kind of grease or salve on his face. We'll test it. It might be important."

"As for the rest of the body, abrasions on both hands. Fresh wounds on both arms. A distended thumb. I'd say he fought back."

Prakash opened up the body with quick, decisive scalpel strokes and with the benefit of a saw. One by one, she removed his internal organs, weighed them, and took biopsies for analysis.

"Anything I should be looking for, Detective?" she asked, turning to Mulroy.

"To our knowledge, Gardenia was not a drug user. But he interacted with drug users on a regular basis. So that should probably be on your radar screen."

"We would do that in any event, Detective. We'll test the blood, the urine, and the liver. Plus vitreous fluid from one of the eyes. Often, that's the best bet. And I can look for puncture wounds as well. So far, I see nothing like that. What I do see is a broken nose and a broken jaw. Also, severe swelling in the forehead, which probably signifies bleeding from the brain. Whoever did this struck him repeatedly and forcefully."

"Which means?"

"Whoever killed him really hated his guts."

Chapter Nine: The Right to Assemble

Larry Mabry was hopping mad and took it out on his lawyer. "What the fuck do you mean it's still missing?"

"Your friend Wade Newborn visited the jazz club last night. No one could find your trumpet."

"Did he talk with Marv?"

"Is that the manager?"

"He's the bouncer."

"Look, man, I don't know who he talked to. But he said he looked everywhere and it was nowhere to be found."

"Jesus Christ. Do you have any fucking idea what that trumpet is worth?"

"A lot?"

"Twenty K or more. That's how much it's worth. It's a honey of a trumpet. A Monette. It fits my lips like a hand in a glove. Or at least it used to. My lips are swollen. My trumpet's missing. I'm accused of murdering a cop who's probably committed way more crimes than I have. What the fuck is happening to me?"

"Calm down, Larry. It's a difficult time. But we'll get you through this."

"Don't talk to me like I'm some kind of a kid, man. I need to talk with Gary."

"Not a good idea, Larry."

"Well, then, you call Gary. Ask him to go to Con Alma and find my trumpet. Tell him to tear the place apart if he has to. I *need* my trumpet!"

* * *

Twenty-four hours later, Gary clutched a bullhorn at Freedom Corner. He was delighted to see three hundred or so protesters carrying placards: "Free Larry!" "Being Black is Not a Crime!" "Mabry: a Musician, not a Murderer!"

Help me, Lord, he thought. *We need to keep this protest peaceful.* His stomach clenched as he imagined a violent clash with police.

Prodded by Gary, the protesters marched past Duquesne University to Point State Park, where the city's three rivers converged. They paused, as Father Buckley led them in prayer. "Lord Jesus, we ask you to give us the courage to speak truth to power. We have a message that needs to be delivered. We pray that those with power on this earth will understand the limits of that power. We pray that they will release an innocent man so he can return to the bosom of his family."

The chanting protesters marched across the Fort Duquesne Bridge, blocking traffic. Some motorists beeped their horns to show support, while others displayed their middle fingers.

* * *

A dozen police officers equipped with riot gear stood shoulder-to-shoulder, blocking the main entrance to the Western Avenue police headquarters building on the North Side.

"I hope to God this doesn't blow up," Lieutenant Stilton muttered, tugging nervously at his right earlobe.

"Do you want us to clear the crowd, sir?" a rookie patrol officer asked.

"I want you to walk a tightrope. I want you to respect their right to protest peacefully. But if any of our officers are assaulted or if they try to enter the building, you must respond firmly."

"What about verbal abuse?" the rookie asked, gripping his nightstick.

"In this kind of situation, son, there is *no* such thing as verbal abuse. If that happens, you let it go. Understand?"

"Yes, sir."

* * *

Until the protest ended, Radic and Mulroy were officially assigned to a specific police precinct—Zone 4, which included Squirrel Hill and Shadyside. "If something bad happens," Stilton said, "I want you to be somewhere else."

Sidelined for a while, Radic and Mulroy decided to take in the evening show at Con Alma. Larry's quartet would be performing without him. Maybe one of them saw something the other night.

While Mulroy grabbed a couple seats and texted a colleague at headquarters, Radic cornered the bassist, Marius Johnson, a soft-spoken, earnest young man.

"How's it going, Marius?"

"Hanging in there, Detective. Any word about my main man?"

"He's doing okay."

"You know it's bogus. Right?"

"I have an open mind."

"But you know Larry, man. You know he'd never kill anyone."

"The incident with Gardenia. Did you witness it at all?"

He shook his head. "I was having a sandwich. I didn't even know something was up."

"Did you know Gardenia?"

"No."

"Did Larry ever mention him?"

"No."

"Has Larry had any disagreements with any other police officers?"

He shrugged. "None that I know of."

"How about Gary?"

Marius froze at that question. "What are you trying to find out, man?"

"Do you know if Gardenia had a beef with Gary, or if Gary had a beef with him?"

"Hey, I know you and Larry are friends. Maybe I trust you, maybe I don't. But I can't be saying stuff about Gary."

"Not even if it might help Larry?" Radic gazed intently at Marius, hoping that he might guilt-trip him into saying something useful.

But Marius remained unshaken. "This shit is too deep for me. I got to get me a sandwich before the first set. You have any questions about Larry, I'll answer them, cause Larry's got nothing to hide. But Gary…I just shouldn't go there."

Radic nodded. Then he checked in with Mulroy, who was texting with Detective Volcker, a colleague and friend, live from police headquarters.

"About three hundred protesters," she said. "No violence so far. Gary says he wants it to remain peaceful."

"Good. Any word on how long they'll stay?"

"None."

"Keep in touch with Volcker."

"Of course."

"I'm going to talk with the manager. Interrupt if something comes up."

* * *

Hal Hirsch was seated in a small, cluttered office, featuring glossy black-and-white photos of famous jazz musicians from Pittsburgh, including Art Blakey, George Benson, and Ahmad Jamal. He was munching on a pastrami sandwich and doing some paperwork.

"How's Larry? What can you tell me?"

"I can't say anything about the investigation."

Hirsch nodded.

"But I'm optimistic about his trumpet playing."

"He's going to be okay?"

"I think so."

"Any timetable?

"A couple of weeks, maybe."

"I hope so. For his sake. For our sake. He's one of our top draws, you know. And without Larry, the Rough Riders are … well, he's the star, is all I'm saying."

"I know."

"So, how can I help you?"

"We're concerned that Larry's trumpet is missing."

"So am I. I feel just awful about it."

"Tell me what happened."

"Okay. Well, after the incident with that policeman, Gardenia, on Saturday night, I noticed that Larry's trumpet was still on stage. I know how much that trumpet means to him, so for safekeeping, I put it in a cabinet that's hard to access." Hirsch pointed to a small, high cabinet in the corner.

Radic noticed a trumpet case on Hirsch's desk. "The trumpet is not in the case?"

Hirsch shook his head. "No, I removed the mouthpiece and put it in the case. But I decided to hide the trumpet itself. It's Larry's pride and joy, irreplaceable."

"Okay, so when did you notice it was missing?"

"Well, that would have been Friday night, I guess. Wade Newborn came to fetch it. We looked inside the cabinet, and damn it, it just wasn't there."

"Then what?"

"I asked Marv, our bouncer. He knew nothing about it. I asked the wait staff. No one knew where it went."

"Any visitors to your office over the past week?"

"Gardenia, the police officer who started it all. Then later, another police officer."

"Did you get a name?"

"No name. Tall, a buzz haircut, looked like a Marine."

Mark Atwood, Radic thought to himself. "Anybody else?"

"Wade. And Gary."

"Gary was here?"

"Two nights ago. Larry asked him to find the trumpet."

"And?"

"No luck."

"Let's take another look."

"Sure."

Hirsch climbed up on a shaky stool and opened the cabinet.

"Well, I'll be god-damned."

A gleaming, gold-plated trumpet was there.

Hirsch reached inside to retrieve it, but Radic stopped him.

"Don't touch it!" he yelled.

Radic motioned Hirsch off the stool, donned a pair of gloves, stood on the stool himself, and reached gently into the cabinet. He hopped off the stool with the prized trumpet in his hands. But what they saw was disheartening.

"Good God, what's happened to it?" Hirsch cried.

The trumpet was mangled and twisted, with sticky, red splotches.

"I'm going to need this as evidence," Radic said.

"Do you think it's still usable?"

"I don't know."

"Larry's going to be sick over this."

Suddenly, Mulroy appeared at the door.

"Volcker wants to talk with you, Branko. There's been some trouble at headquarters. They've made some arrests."

Chapter Ten: The Stench of Violence

The air reeked of tear gas, benzene, and fire. The sidewalks were strewn with placards, abandoned by protesters as they fled for safety. A few unclaimed backpacks were visible as well.

A police car had been torched and would probably not live to see another day. Most of the crowd had dispersed, though a few stragglers remained behind.

On closer inspection, most of those remaining seemed to have been dazed or wounded in the melee. Officers and paramedics were checking up on them, offering food, water, bandages.

The entry to the parking lot was blocked by two police cars, so Radic and Mulroy parked nearby. Mulroy texted Volcker to let him know they had arrived.

By prearrangement, they would meet in the parking lot. Radic wanted a candid summary of what had happened before he and Mulroy spoke with Stilton.

Volcker wore a rueful expression as he greeted his colleagues. "Welcome to the party!" he said.

"It looks like a battleground," Mulroy said.

"Anyone seriously hurt?" Radic asked.

Volcker shook his head. "No, thank God. Lots of burning eyes. A few other injuries. One guy fainted and had to be rushed to Mercy Hospital. But they say he's going to be okay."

"Arrests?"

"Two young men were arrested for throwing bricks at our folks. Father

Buckley objected. He got arrested, too."

"Any unnecessary violence on our side?" Mulroy asked.

"Could be," Volcker said. "Atwood is being questioned for hassling Wade Newborn."

"Newborn?" Mulroy asked.

"Larry's piano player," Radic explained. "The one who was missing at the club tonight. Did Newborn do anything to provoke a response?"

"We'll see what the body cams say," Volcker responded. "Maybe not."

"And Gary?"

"Gary was a prince. He kept urging the crowd to be peaceful. He urged them to stay calm after arrests were made. And he led the marchers away when the tear gas was used."

"What prompted Stilton to use tear gas?"

"Two guys torched one of our cars."

"We saw out front. Were they arrested, too?"

"They fled. But we have a bead on who they are. It's just a matter of time before we bring them in."

"So, it could have been worse," Mulroy said.

"It could have been a lot worse. We dodged a bullet. Let's hope our luck holds out."

"Tomorrow?"

"Tomorrow and the day after that and the day after that. This isn't just going away."

* * *

After a tense day, Radic was delighted to see Lexie Davodny's car in his driveway as he pulled up to his home. Lexie was an officer with the PBP's River Rescue Unit, which operated two boats on the three rivers.

They had been seeing each other for over a year. Mainly on weekends, but sometimes on weekday nights. Now that Ralph was in the picture, it seemed that Lexie was coming around more often. Which made Radic smile.

50

Lexie was smart, vivacious, and playful. She loved pranks and often played tricks on Radic—like the time she put dog food in one of his sandwiches. He laughed at the memory, though it had not been funny when he had to spit out the wretched stuff.

Lexie was also drop-dead gorgeous. Her black hair was long and lush. Radic took pleasure in releasing her locks from the bondage of a bun she wore while at work.

Her green eyes were seductive, and she was curvy without being plump. She even smelled good. Her perfume was earthy, with a touch of cinnamon.

"I thought you might enjoy some company, after this evening's disaster," Lexie said, kissing Radic on the lips.

"You mean, you thought that Ralph might enjoy some company. Right?"

"Well, that too."

Ralph planted some kisses himself, and he expected belly rubs. Radic was happy to oblige.

"I don't mind playing second fiddle to Ralph. As long as he brings you here more often."

"Well, it did occur to me that we might be running out of dog food."

"Actually, we're running out of people food. As usual, Ralph's food supply is doing better than ours."

"Including his special treats?"

"Including his special treats."

"Then let's go to bed."

"An excellent idea. Without Ralph?"

"Without Ralph. He has to learn boundaries."

"And me?"

"No boundaries for you. At least not tonight."

Chapter Eleven: Unearthing Secrets

adic did his best to dodge questions and gossip as he made his way to his desk. Most of his colleagues liked him well enough to cut him some slack while he handled a very difficult assignment.

A notable exception was Frenchy Frobisher, a fiery bull of a man who sported a dragon tattoo on his right forearm. Although he said nothing as Radic walked by, he pointed two fingers at his eyes. Frenchy and others would be waiting for a misstep.

As he opened his office computer, Radic was surprised to see an e-mail from Internal Affairs, marked "Confidential." They had sent the requested report.

Radic knew he would eventually receive the report. After all, Stilton and Reilly had promised. But he thought Internal Affairs would drag its feet. Maybe he was wrong. Maybe he and Internal Affairs were on the same side of the fence.

Radic was miffed that he hadn't gotten permission for Mulroy to receive the report, too. "She's going to learn what's in it from me, anyway," he had argued. "What's the point?"

Stilton had sighed. "The point is that it officially limits the source of leaks to one person. Namely, you. If any of this stuff surfaces prematurely, Internal Affairs will know the leak came from you, directly or indirectly."

"What if Internal Affairs leaks the report? I still get blamed?"

"Internal Affairs is not going to leak the report."

With all the excitement last night, Radic needed some quiet time. After touching base with Mulroy, placing his laptop in a backpack, and texting

Stilton to arrange a meeting, he left for his hideaway: a nice, quiet cubbyhole on the second floor of the Carnegie Public Library in Oakland.

Situated between the University of Pittsburgh and Carnegie Mellon University, the main Carnegie Library occupies ten acres and houses approximately two and a half million books and other documents. Radic had started using it when he was a student at CMU. For him, it was a refuge when he needed to read carefully, think critically, or pull a rabbit out of the hat. This was one of those times.

Happily, Radic found that his favorite cubbyhole was vacant. He almost ran to claim it, for fear that someone else might beat him to the punch. Eagerly, he started reading the report.

The first surprise was that the investigation had begun more than two years ago. Either Internal Affairs didn't have the goods on Gardenia, or they were casting a wider net, trying to catch other fish.

The second surprise was that some names had been redacted, despite his explicit demand for full disclosure. Radic cursed under his breath. He would have to confront Stilton on this point later on.

At least the name of the report's author was there. Fred Vinson. An ex-homicide detective. Radic knew him and sort of liked him. Maybe Vinson would be willing to answer questions as the investigation continued.

An hour later, Radic closed his laptop. Covering it with his jacket, he stepped outside the reading room and called Mulroy. They arranged to meet for lunch at Ali Baba's on Craig Street.

Radic arrived first, but Mulroy was not far behind. Radic ordered the shish kebab platter, while Mulroy ordered falafel and a tossed salad.

Nursing cold beverages, they caught up on their love lives. Mulroy wanted to know if Lexie, an amateur pilot, had flown any "missions" lately. Radic wanted to know if Jake, an avid sailor, had purchased a new "yacht."

The answers to both questions were strikingly similar: She keeps threatening, from Radic. He keeps threatening, from Mulroy.

Mulroy also wanted to know how Radic's father was doing. "Has your dad wandered off lately?" she asked.

"No," Radic replied, "but he probably feels like he's under house arrest.

My mom watches him like a hawk."

"Does he get that it's for his own good?"

"He gets it and then promptly forgets. It's tough on my mom."

"I can tell it's tough on you, too. It's hard to see a parent in pain. But sometimes I think it's even harder to see a parent slowly fade away. Especially someone as intelligent and thoughtful as your dad."

Radic nodded appreciatively as their sandwiches arrived.

"So what's the big secret that you couldn't tell me over the phone?" Mulroy asked, after their waitress disappeared.

"I got the Internal Affairs report on Gardenia."

"I'm all ears."

"Gardenia was a more complicated guy than you might imagine," Radic began.

"How so?"

"He was married, divorced after five years, no kids."

"Any evidence of domestic abuse?"

"Why do you ask?"

"Rumors."

"One call from his wife during year four. She didn't press charges. But she filed for divorce. A year later, they sold their home and reached a settlement."

"Do you want me to reach out to the ex?"

"Definitely."

"Okay. What else?"

"We know from Prakash that Gardenia was not a drug user. He may have been a heavy drinker once upon a time. But maybe not recently. In fact, the report says he was a bit of an exercise nut. He visited Muscle Mania in East Liberty once a week."

"Get out."

"That surprised me, too."

"He didn't look that fit on the table."

"I agree. We'll follow up on that."

"Any evidence that he was extorting money from Gary?"

"Yes, there's evidence of that. But Gary wasn't his only victim. He's been shaking down drug dealers for at least five years. Almost always dealers connected with a prominent Mexican cartel, Costa a Costa."

"I haven't heard of them."

"Pretty nasty. You don't want to mess with them."

"But Gardenia did anyway?"

"Yes, and it may have been his undoing. They're not too concerned about a little skimming off the top by friendly police officers. But they get concerned when the skimming escalates to the point where other players get pissed off."

"People like Gary."

"That's right. People like Gary. Internal Affairs confirms that Gary has been trying to bail out for at least a year."

"But Gardenia wouldn't let him?"

"Correct, but that may not be what Gary is telling the cartel. He could be blaming Gardenia for his decision to quit the game. The cartel doesn't like to have to retrain someone from scratch. I'm guessing that Gardenia was Gary's scapegoat."

"Anything else?"

"Yes. Gary was in touch with the press. He's been seen talking with a *Post-Gazette* reporter, Evan Kobosky. And if Internal Affairs knows, there's a good chance that others know too."

"Including the cartel?"

Radic nodded.

"So, he's in danger?"

"If I were Gary, I'd be watching my back."

"Does Internal Affairs have proof that Gardenia was extorting money from Gary and other drug dealers?"

"Yes. Though the cash going into Gardenia's bank account is far less than what they believe he's been netting."

"What's he been doing with the money?"

"They don't know yet. Hiding it somewhere."

"Are any other cops involved?"

Radic sighed. "Yes."

"Are you going to tell me who?"

"I can't."

Mulroy looked hurt. "You don't trust me?"

"No, no. The names have been redacted. So I don't know."

"But you can guess?"

"That's right. It's almost certainly one of his former partners from when he was still in Homicide."

"Atwood?"

"Atwood. Or his previous partner."

"Who was?"

"Frenchy Frobisher."

Chapter Twelve: The M.E. Weighs in

Radic answered immediately when he noticed the call was from the Medical Examiner, Saroja Prakash.

"I have some preliminary findings from the autopsy. Do you want to drop by?"

"Can you give me the headlines?"

"Sure. Gardenia died from blunt force trauma. Repeated blows to the head, resulting in a brain hemorrhage."

"Any thoughts on what the blunt instrument was?"

"It was heavy. Or at least firm. With indentations. Not flimsy. Not flat."

"Which could mean?"

"A lamp, perhaps. But without a light bulb. That would have left fragments."

"A baseball bat?"

"Too smooth."

"A computer?"

"Maybe, if it was heavy enough."

"Brass knuckles?"

"Possible."

"How about a trumpet?"

"A trumpet?"

"That's right. Larry Mabry's trumpet was missing. It's just been found. And it's badly damaged."

"Well, I'll have to think about that. How heavy is a trumpet?"

"I don't know. Two to three pounds?"

"Could be. That would be a first."

"What else did you learn?"

"Well, you remember I said there was something greasy on Gardenia's face?"

"Yep."

"Vaseline."

"Vaseline."

"Presumably, it was on the lamp or the computer or the trumpet or whatever was used as a weapon."

"Okay. We can work with that. How about the toxicology?"

"No drugs in his system. And no needle marks. The liver was enlarged. He had a beer belly. Alcohol may have been a problem."

"Any evidence that he's been working out?"

"Is lifting a cold Iron City to your mouth working out?"

"Just asking. Anything else?"

"Purple bruises on the right hand. Fairly recent."

"That could be from when he beat up Larry Mabry."

"A distended thumb. Very recent."

"The day he died?"

"Perhaps."

"Anything else?"

"Two sets of prints from the crime scene. One belongs to Atwood, who was at the scene. The other doesn't match anyone in our database. Beyond that, nothing to report."

"Getting back to the Vaseline, did you find that in one spot or all over his face?"

"All over. Which makes me think it's connected to the weapon."

"Got it. Can you send us the report? Meanwhile, we'll get you the trumpet before the end of the day."

"Sounds good. Always a pleasure."

"Thanks, Saroja. You're the best!"

* * *

Other than reports from the county clerk's office, Radic didn't get a lot of first-class mail at work. So he was surprised when he noticed a small brown envelope with two first-class stamps, his name as the addressee, and no return address.

After opening the envelope, he peered at a months-old article from the *Pittsburgh Post-Gazette*, with the headline, "High School Band Prepares for State Finals."

Radic was about to toss it when he noticed that a quote from the band leader was highlighted in yellow: "Band members learn how to prepare their instruments before every performance. We teach the string players how to tune their instruments. We teach the brass players how to lubricate their instruments with Vaseline."

Radic was stunned. He read the paragraph again, slowly, then read the entire article from start to finish. "Who knows that we're interested in Vaseline?" he asked himself. Two possibilities occurred to him: someone with inside information on the investigation, or someone who wanted to frame Larry.

Chapter Thirteen: A Visitor from Outer Space

Mulroy was about to leave for work when she received a call from O'Neill, just back from a two-day professional development gig. Headquarters had received a call from a Mrs. Sadie Mackler, of Brookline, who needed to speak with Mulroy, urgently.

Reluctantly, Mulroy returned the call:

"Mrs. Mackler, what can I do for you?"

"They're coming to get me. First, it was snakes. Now it's aliens from outer space."

"What makes you believe that aliens are out to get you, Mrs. Mackler?"

"They sent a scout last night. An alien in a spacesuit. In my backyard, of all places."

"Did he threaten you?"

"You mean, did he point his laser at me? No, but wouldn't you say that just being in my backyard was a threat?"

Often, Mulroy took notes when conducting a business call. In this case, she started doodling instead. A spaceship. A creature with two antennae and pointy ears.

"Did anyone else see the alien, Mrs. Mackler?"

"My son."

"Your son. How old is he?"

"Sixteen."

"And what did your son see?"

"The same as me."

"Your son said he saw an alien, too?"

"That's right. And he took a picture."

"You have a photo of the alien?"

"Absolutely. In my backyard."

"Can you send it to me, Mrs. Mackler?"

"I sure as hell can. What number?"

Mulroy recited her cell number and continued doodling. E.T.

Moments later, Mulroy received the photo. It was kind of grainy, in the dark. But, sure enough, it was a man, or a creature, in a spacesuit, or something similar. Maybe Mrs. Mackler was only half-crazy.

"Did the alien say anything to you, Mrs. Mackler?"

"Not to me. But he was talking to someone in his spaceship."

"In English?"

"No, silly. Aliens don't speak English. It sounded like Chinese."

"So, you were visited by an alien from China?"

"No. An alien from another planet, who speaks Chinese."

Suddenly, a bulb lit up. "Mrs. Mackler, I really want to thank you for this information. It's super helpful. Now I know what I need to do. I'm glad you called."

Mulroy phoned O'Neill and told him to get fitted for a HAZMAT suit. She would fetch hers, speak with Stilton, and meet O'Neill at the "Snake Shack" in approximately one hour.

* * *

When Mulroy arrived at Eben St., wearing civilian clothes, O'Neill was already there, dressed in a policeman's uniform. He mentioned that his HAZMAT suit was in the squad car.

Mulroy, in civilian clothes, knocked forcefully on the front door, then rang the doorbell. No response. She and O'Neill then entered the back yard, through a gate.

No snake carcasses were visible, but something definitely smelled, kind of like rotten eggs. The odor was more noticeable as they approached the basement door. Mulroy tried to peek inside, but nothing was visible, thanks to drapes that thoroughly covered the sole window. Mulroy tried the back door, but it was locked.

"What are you thinking, Detective?" O'Neill asked.

"I'm thinking that we have probable cause to suspect a crime—harboring exotic snakes without a license. But no immediate public health threat that justifies breaking the doors down. O'Neill, I want you to go to your car and sit there until the owner returns, or until I return. I'll go to the office and start the paperwork. With any luck, we'll have our search warrant before the end of the day."

"What should I do if the owner returns, Detective?"

"If he returns, I want you to call me immediately. Then tell him that his home is off limits because we have reason to believe that it constitutes a public health threat."

"And if he refuses?"

"If he refuses, arrest him and cuff him."

"More serious than a Pittsburgh left?"

"Much more serious than a Pittsburgh left."

* * *

The key question that Mulroy had to decide, and quickly, was whether to request a search warrant from a state judge or a federal judge.

The presence of poisonous snakes in a residential neighborhood posed a public health threat to the residents of Brookline. A state judge might well be sympathetic, and a state judge might have a smaller backlog of search warrant requests than a federal judge.

On the other hand, it was highly likely that some of the snakes had crossed interstate borders, possibly international borders as well. The interstate commerce clause could justify a search. And a federal court order might be more all-encompassing when it came to a remedy.

Mulroy gave Radic a call. In a recent case, he had opted for a federal judge, and the decision had paid off. She wanted to hear what he had to say.

Radic was adamant: "You need to move quickly. Strike while the iron is hot. A state judge is more likely to say yes quickly. A state judge has plenty of power. Try Judge Belsky."

After getting some drafting advice from Radic, Mulroy composed a two-pager and alerted Belsky's clerk that she would be coming by immediately.

Mulroy located Judge Irma Belsky on the seventh floor of the City-County Building on Grant Street. Belsky was a short, stout, middle-aged woman with a no-nonsense manner.

Mulroy took two minutes to explain the situation. Judge Belsky asked her to have a seat while she looked at the search warrant petition.

"Detective, do you have any evidence that the man in the space suit was in fact Mr. Nguyen?"

"No, your honor, I do not."

"Here's the thing. You can't accuse Mr. Nguyen of a crime because a neighbor saw an Asian man or an Asian American man in her backyard late at night. And as I understand it, you have yet to speak with Mr. Nguyen. Is that correct?"

"He's been very elusive, your honor."

"So the snake carcasses could belong to someone else. Have you made repeated efforts to speak with the man?"

"No, your honor, I'm working a murder case."

"Your department needs to make a reasonable effort to speak with this man and give him a chance to explain himself before you break into his home. Is that understood?"

"Yes, your honor."

"I agree with you that there are reasons to be concerned, but maybe there's a perfectly logical explanation for the odors you've noticed coming from his home. Until you have stronger justification, I can't approve a warrant."

Dejected, Mulroy called O'Neill and instructed him to return to his station. She also spoke briefly with Radic, who asked her to join him early the following morning to pursue a lead. Mulroy called Stilton and explained the situation. He told her to focus on the Gardenia investigation for the time being, but to pay Mr. Nguyen a visit as soon as her schedule loosened up.

Chapter Fourteen: Sweat Shop

Muscle Mania smelled like sweat, but also like soap and deodorant. The two locker rooms were doorless, and clean-up odors mingled oddly with workout odors. It was like being on a dairy farm, where the stench of manure melded with the sweet fragrance of freshly churned ice cream.

Radic and Mulroy parked their squad car and entered the building. It was only 8:00 a.m., but the gym was already quite busy.

A cheery receptionist named Gloria greeted them at the entrance. "May I help you?"

Radic flashed his badge and asked to speak to the manager, while Mulroy took a peek inside the main workout room. The age range was impressive: young men lifting weights, young women using rowing machines, senior citizens riding stationary bikes at a respectable pace.

Mulroy noticed a formidable array of equipment—cardio-deck machines, lateral leg presses, treadmills, rowers. Even glute machines. Also, a large room for group fitness classes, one of which was in progress. "Shake your booties, ladies."

A familiar, steady pulse beckoned everyone to join in. Mulroy recognized the music. A cool techno tune by Chappell Roan. Hot to Go. Mulroy had let her gym membership lapse. Maybe time to re-up at a nicer facility?

Two minutes later, a man appeared. In his thirties, perhaps, but totally bald. He was fit and taut, with bulging biceps. He strutted towards the front desk and thrust a meaty paw in Radic's direction.

Anticipating a strong handshake, Radic responded in kind, with the trademark grip he used in Tough Mudder competitions while clinging to a rail or pole, to avoid slipping into a muddy pool below.

"Bart Fielding," the man said. "What can I do you for?"

"We're here on a police investigation," Radic said, after introducing Mulroy and flashing his badge. "Is there somewhere we could speak more privately?

"Of course," Fielding said. "Come to my office."

Radic and Mulroy hustled to keep up with Fielding, who power-walked to his office.

He pointed to two seats, asked if anyone would like an energy bar, and invited them to sit down.

"What's this all about, Detective?"

"It's about one of your clients. Gino Gardenia."

"I thought it might be. I was sorry to read about Gino's death."

"Can you tell us how long Gino was a member here?"

"We can look it up if you like. Three years. Maybe four years."

"How often did he come here?"

"About once a week."

"What was his usual routine? What kinds of exercises did he do?"

Fielding laughed. "Do you see that bar over there, Detective? That's where we serve shakes, smoothies, energy drinks."

"Are you saying he didn't exercise much?"

Fielding shrugged. "People come here for different reasons. Most come to exercise. Some come to socialize. A lot of people do both. Gino? He was mainly a socializer."

"Who did he socialize with?"

"Lots of people. Guys. Gals."

"Anyone in particular?"

"No one comes to mind."

Radic knew when he was being played.

"Mr. Fielding, I think I should remind you that this is a murder investigation. We need to pursue any and every line of inquiry. Now, if you like, Detective Mulroy and I can come back this evening and tomorrow evening and the evening after that. We can interrogate *all* of your clients and see what they have to say about Gino Gardenia and his acquaintances. Is that how you want to play it?"

Fielding squirmed in his seat. "Detective, there's no need to be that way. Like I said, Gino spent a lot of time with a lot of folks. If there's one person he hung with more than most, I'd say it was probably Jorge Menendez."

"Can you get us an address and phone number?"

Fielding called the front desk and asked the receptionist to give the police what they wanted. He also asked her to see when Gardenia's membership began.

Radic and Mulroy stood up to leave.

"I don't want any trouble here, detective."

"Is there any reason to expect trouble?"

"No, there isn't."

"Then you have nothing to worry about."

* * *

On the drive back to police headquarters, Mulroy brought Radic up to date on inquiries she had made, including a conversation with Gardenia's ex-wife, Connie Simone.

"What's her background?"

"Grew up in Pittsburgh, attended Catholic schools, went to Pitt. Met Gino online. He was full of himself, but he could be charming. He had just made detective on the homicide squad. She was just starting business school. They got married a year later."

"Any kids?"

"No. She wanted to finish her MBA first."

"And then?"

"And then she came to realize that Gino was not the man she thought he was. He had a mean streak."

"Did he hurt her?"

"Not at first. But he was spending way too much time away from home.

Hanging out with some bad people. When she'd ask him about it, he'd brush her off. But if she probed too deeply, he'd flare up. He twisted her arm once. Punched her in the stomach a couple of times. Shoved her now and then. When he finally gave her a black eye, she knew it was time to leave."

"When was that?"

"Four years into their marriage."

"Any inkling that he was a bad cop?"

"Yes. People would drop by late at night. Sometimes cops. But sometimes civilians."

"Drug dealers?

"She suspected as much. Asked him about it several times. Gino would get very angry. She learned not to do it too often."

"What does she make of Gino's death?"

"She says it was just a matter of time. He was greedy. He was reckless. He made enemies. She says he was an accident waiting to happen."

"Does she have any idea who did it?"

"For what it's worth, she says drug dealers. She didn't finger any of our guys."

"Any evidence?"

"Just a hunch. But she did say one thing."

"What's that?"

"Gino was learning Spanish. Now, why would he want to do that?"

"Why indeed?"

Chapter Fifteen: A Reluctant Witness

Arranging an interview with Detective Mark Atwood was nearly as difficult as arranging an interview with a fugitive. At first, Atwood declined an interview request from Stilton, citing the pending Internal Affairs investigation and other unresolved legal matters, including disputes over his role in recent skirmishes with protesters. That led to an impromptu conversation between Atwood and Stilton, which eavesdroppers reported as tense and confrontational. Witnesses reported four-letter words, a desk pounding, and a slammed door.

Eventually, Atwood agreed to an interview with counsel present. Radic and Mulroy would conduct the interview. Stilton would be listening in another room, though he chose not to inform Atwood of that.

The man who stared defiantly at Radic and Mulroy looked like an ex-Marine, though Radic knew that he was not ex-military. According to the rumor mill, he was booted out of boot camp. Too hot-headed. Six feet tall, with a buzz cut, Atwood wore brown leather boots and an American flag on his lapel. He glowered at Radic while pretty much ignoring Mulroy.

That was typical of Atwood, Radic thought. A man who underestimated women. Well, Radic had seen people underestimate Mulroy before—her intelligence, her courage, her tenacity. Let Atwood learn the hard way.

Radic knew from his file that Atwood was thirty-two years old, that he had made detective two years earlier, and that it had been a close call. Today, he believed, Atwood's career was hanging by a slender thread.

Atwood's attorney, probably in his mid-forties, introduced himself as

Howard Draper. As they shook hands, Radic noticed a tattoo on his right wrist. Could be ex-military, he thought.

After a few preliminaries, Radic began the interview:

"Detective Atwood, what were you doing at the R&T factory site on the night of Detective Gardenia's murder?"

"Gino…Detective Gardenia…asked me to meet him there."

"What was the purpose of that meeting?"

"Detective Gardenia didn't say."

"Were you accustomed to meeting Detective Gardenia at a remote location late at night for an unspecified reason?"

"Accustomed? No. But in Narcotics, detectives sometimes meet in strange locations at strange hours."

"But you're not in Narcotics."

"Detective Gardenia was."

"Did you assume that the purpose of the meeting was to discuss a narcotics case?"

"The thought crossed my mind. But Gino and I had worked on some cases together when he was in Homicide. So, it could have been something else."

"Had you ever met Detective Gardenia before at this particular location?"

"No." But his eyes flickered.

Radic decided to move on. "Detective Atwood, we found your fingerprints in multiple locations at the R&T factory."

"Duh. I was there. And I wasn't wearing gloves."

"We found one set of your prints on a side door handle."

"Which I used to enter the building."

"We found another set of your prints on a bathroom faucet."

"Which I used to wash up after seeing Gino's dead body."

"Was that before or after you called 911?"

"After."

"You said that you and Detective Gardenia were to meet at the factory. Was there a third party who was also supposed to be part of the meeting?"

"No. Just Gino and me."

"We found another set of prints at the factory, not yours, not Detective Gardenia's."

Atwood paused. "I wasn't aware of that. But then again, I was taken off the case before I could do much investigating."

"We found the prints on one of the doors."

"Have you tried matching them up with Larry Mabry's prints? Or would that be a violation of his civil rights?" he asked with a sneer.

Radic ignored the question. "We found those same fingerprints in the bathroom that you used. Are you sure you didn't see anyone use the bathroom?"

Draper intervened. "My client has already stated that he used the bathroom, but that he did not see anyone else in the building. Will that be all, Detectives?"

"No, I have some questions as well," Mulroy said. "Detective Atwood, have you ever met Detective Gardenia at a fitness center named Muscle Mania?"

"I don't understand the relevance of that question to your investigation. How I spend my private time is my own personal business."

"You've just told us that you sometimes conducted business with Detective Gardenia in unusual places, to avoid the glare of drug dealers. Was Muscle Mania one of those places?"

Atwood conferred briefly with Draper, then responded. "Yes."

"Do you have a membership there?"

"Yes."

"Did Detective Gardenia recommend that you become a member there?"

"I don't recall."

"Well, Muscle Mania's records are quite clear on that subject. When you applied for membership there, Detective Gardenia is listed as the person referring you. Does that ring a bell?"

"It could be."

"Is that a yes or a no?"

"It's a maybe."

"How often did you and Detective Gardenia meet at Muscle Mania?"

"Well, it depends on what you mean by meet. I would work out there. Gino would work out there. Sometimes our paths would cross."

"Are you sure about that?"

"Sure about what?"

"Witnesses report that Detective Gardenia was not known to work out. Instead, he was known to do a lot of gabbing. Are you contradicting those witnesses?"

"Hey, people join a fitness center with good intentions. Some people do a lot of reps on a lot of machines. Others don't. I don't see that it matters one way or the other. Or why it matters to you."

"During your visits to Muscle Mania, did you ever have any dealings with Jorge Menendez?"

Draper intervened at this point: "I think we've talked enough about a fitness center that my client visited from time to time, at his own expense, on his own free time. Unless there are any more questions on something else?"

Radic was not ready to call it a day.

"Detective Atwood, why did you arrest Larry Mabry for the murder of Gino Gardenia?"

"'Cause he's the fucker who killed Gino!"

"Was there any evidence to support that conclusion before you arrested him?"

"He's been badgering Gino for months now."

"Over what?"

"Over his brother, Gary, a low-life scum, the biggest drug dealer in Pittsburgh."

"How did you know this?"

"From Gino himself."

"What did he say exactly?"

"That Larry Mabry was a royal pain in the ass, and that he had been making it difficult for him to do his job."

"Any other evidence pointing to Larry Mabry as the killer?"

"Mabry had no alibi for the night of the murder."

"When did you determine that?"

"When we visited him in his apartment."

"Did you ask him for an alibi and then arrest him? Or did you arrest him and then ask if he had an alibi?"

"I believe that's all I'm going to say on that subject."

Radic decided to try another line of attack. "Detective Atwood, have you ever been to Con Alma?"

Atwood paused. "Yes. I was there the other day."

"What exactly were you doing there?"

"Gino had just been killed. I expected to be one of the officers investigating his murder. I went there to see what I could find out about Gino's encounter with Larry Mabry."

"Did you go with someone or by yourself?"

"By myself."

"Did you clear this with Lieutenant Stilton?"

"I saw no need."

"Who did you speak with while you were there?"

"The owner, some of the employees."

"Can you be more specific?"

"I didn't get all their names."

"Isn't that a bit unusual? If you were going to be investigating the murder, wouldn't you keep a record of witnesses?"

"It was a stressful time. My friend had been killed. I didn't do that systematically."

"You didn't do that systematically? Or you didn't do that at all?"

Draper intervened. "I believe my client has answered your question, Detective. If there's nothing further…"

"One more question," Radic said. "While you were at Con Alma, did you see a trumpet?"

"What do you mean by that?"

"Just answer the question."

"I didn't see a trumpet."

"Did you ask about a trumpet?"

"Why would I do that?"

"Just answer the question."

"I didn't ask about a trumpet."

"Did you touch a trumpet?"

Again, Draper intervened. "Detective, my client has said that he didn't see a trumpet. Therefore, by definition, he could not have touched a trumpet. I believe we're done here."

Atwood was the first person to stand up. This time, he glared at Mulroy. Mulroy didn't flinch. Instead, she said, "Have a nice day."

Atwood started to say something, but Draper stifled him. "It's time for us to leave, Detective." And with that, they exited the room.

Chapter Sixteen: Big Boy Escapes

Mulroy was deep into REM sleep when her cell phone interrupted a dream in which she was climbing Mt. Everest, wearing a HAZMAT suit and accompanied by a sherpa. The sherpa turned out to be her boyfriend, Jake. He would get a kick out of that when she told him.

Mulroy reached groggily for the phone: "Mulroy here."

"Detective Mulroy, it's Maureen Saunders from Brookline. I'm very sorry to bother you in the middle of the night. But you said I should call you anytime if the snake guy showed up. Well, he's back. And he's up to no good."

Mulroy sat up, suddenly.

"What's he doing?"

"Whatever he's doing, he's causing quite a ruckus. All the dogs are barking."

"Can you describe more specifically what he's doing at this very moment?"

"Well, there's a big moving van outside his house. He seems to be hauling some cages into the truck."

Mulroy heard the sound of shattering glass.

"Uh, oh. Now he's gone and done it. One of the cages just broke."

"Mrs. Saunders, stay where you are and don't go outside for any reason. I'll be there as soon as I can."

Mulroy called O'Neill and told him to bring his HAZMAT suit and meet her on Eben Street ASAP. She splashed some water on her face, grabbed the nearest pair of pants she could find, donned a blouse, slipped into some shoes, no time for socks, and was out the door in four minutes.

Crossing the Fort Pitt Bridge at night was often a treat, especially with virtually no traffic. Mulroy glanced appreciatively at the gleaming office buildings overlooking the Golden Triangle, where the Allegheny and Monongahela rivers converged to create the Ohio.

But the picture postcard view didn't distract her for long. Methodically, she made a mental list of things she needed to do on arriving at what she and O'Neill had come to call the Snake Shack. Check her gun. Confront the accused. Secure the scene.

Somehow, O'Neill had managed to beat her to Eben Street. He was wearing a HAZMAT suit, arguing vehemently with a man who fit Mr. Nguyen's description.

"You're trespassing, sir," O'Neill said. "I need you to step aside."

"Trespassing? It's my property."

"Your home has been declared a public health emergency."

Nguyen snorted dismissively. "I deal with real emergency. I just lost one of my snakes."

Mulroy glanced quickly at the scene before her. Four cages were already stacked snugly inside the van. The remnants of the fifth were scattered on the sidewalk, near the van. Its occupant was nowhere to be seen.

"Where did the snake go?" Mulroy asked.

Nguyen pointed across the street. Slowly but surely, the snake was heading to Mrs. Saunders' house. He looked to be about four feet long.

"Mr. Nguyen, I want you to catch that snake and catch him immediately."

"That's Big Boy. Not easy to catch Big Boy."

"What kind of a snake is he?"

"An African puff adder."

"Will he recognize your scent?"

"He doesn't like me."

"He doesn't like you?"

"Most snakes like me. He doesn't."

"Does he have any favorite foods?"

Nguyen nodded and pointed towards the house.

"Then go get some of that food, fast as you can. And something to trap him with. Something that's not going to break. O'Neill, you go with him. I'll watch the snake while you're inside."

"You watch him?" Nguyen asked.

"Like a hawk."

Nguyen gave Mulroy a skeptical look but scurried to his home nonetheless, with O'Neill in tow. Mulroy followed Big Boy at a respectable distance as he crawled towards Mrs. Saunders' front porch.

Five minutes later—though it seemed much longer—Nguyen and O'Neill reappeared. O Neill, looking like an actual sherpa, was carrying a blanket, a fishing net, a plastic garbage can, and a broom. Nguyen was carrying several dead birds, in his bare hands. *Eww!*

Nguyen approached Big Boy slowly, crouching, speaking softly to him.

"Come to Papa, Big Boy. I have special treats."

He tossed one of the birds in Big Boy's direction, placing the other birds on the ground at his feet.

Mulroy couldn't see Big Boy's eyes in the darkness. But she did notice some movement. An expression of interest?

Big Boy circled his prey, slowly, almost nonchalantly. Then suddenly he pounced.

Mulroy gasped.

Big Boy had his treat and was slowly trying to digest it, which gave Nguyen time to prepare his trap. Positioning the garbage pail nearby, with its lid off, Nguyen grabbed the fishing net. Still crouching, he waved the fishing net overhead like a lasso and swung it towards Big Boy. The snake reared backwards, but Nguyen caught his head and much of his body in the net. Moving swiftly, he grabbed Big Boy's tail and stuffed his full body into the net.

Next, he deposited Big Boy, squirming and unhappy, into the garbage pail, which promptly turned over. Undaunted, Nguyen grabbed the blanket from O'Neill, stuffed Big Boy back into the pail again, immobilized him with the blanket, and fastened the top.

"Hurry," Nguyen said. "We need to get him into an empty cage. Help me."

Together, Nguyen and O'Neill hauled Big Boy back across the street. O'Neill held the pail from the bottom, while Nguyen kept the cover attached, despite Big Boy's thrashing. Nguyen and O'Neill crab-walked their way back into the house, reappearing five minutes later with Big Boy in a new cage.

As the truck door slammed, Mulroy heard applause from several neighbors, clad in pajamas and nightgowns, observing the show. One or two were taking photos with their cell phones. Mulroy paused to share a word with a TV news reporter, whose crew had just filmed Big Boy's last stand.

As she headed for the squad car, where O'Neill had installed Nguyen in the backseat, Mulroy heard a cry from Mrs. Saunders' second-floor window: "Good job, Detective! I knew we could count on you."

Chapter Seventeen: Two Cheers for Gino

Gardenia's funeral was a somber affair, made even more somber by gray skies and steady rain. Several hundred police officers and a smattering of relatives and friends turned out for the graveside service in Allegheny Cemetery.

Gardenia's first partner, Buddy Holbrook, retired, balding, with a generous paunch, gave a speech that put the best possible light on Gardenia's life: "He always let you know where he stood. And in a tough situation, he always had your back."

Lieutenant Carson, his boss, managed a sendoff that seemed honest, maybe too honest if you took him literally: "Gino always wanted to be a police officer. And he made the most of it."

Radic thought it noteworthy that Chief Reilly, though present, said nothing. Perhaps this meant that he would be speaking to the press about Gino sooner rather than later.

Gino's ex, Connie Simone, shed no tears through most of the ceremony. But she seemed moved when Carson presented her with an American flag at the end of the service.

A buffet lunch at the VFW hall on Liberty Avenue attracted mourners who did not have other plans. Radic felt obliged to attend and urged Mulroy to join him. Scuglia, finally available to work on the Gardenia murder case, said he would be there as well.

The revelry had already begun when Radic and Mulroy arrived at the VFW post. An open bar, courtesy of the Police Benevolent Foundation, helped to ensure plenty of liquid refreshment.

Radic and Mulroy loaded up on brisket, ham, potato salad, and green beans and headed outside to some makeshift picnic tables, taking advantage of improving weather. Scuglia, carrying a full plate, joined them a few minutes later.

Scuglia, who had been a sergeant in the Gulf War before joining the Pittsburgh Bureau of Police, was one of Radic's favorite colleagues. His thick black-rimmed glasses, bushy eyebrows, and grayish black goatee gave him an owlish look. Appropriately so. Scuglia was as wise as they come. With an M.B.A. from Pitt, he knew more about finance than any other homicide detective in Pittsburgh.

"What did you think?" Radic asked him.

"You gotta give the devil his due."

"Unless you're Reilly."

"Yeah, I noticed. What's it mean?"

"The next time they talk about Gino, he's unlikely to get a lot of compliments. Reilly doesn't want to have to do a one-eighty when that time comes."

Atwood and Frobisher were among the last officers to arrive at the hall, having served as pallbearers at the service.

Atwood snarled at Radic on the way in and seemed about to say something, but Frobisher intervened and nudged him inside. Although Radic was not an expert lip reader, Atwood seemed to be suggesting that Radic perform an unnatural act on himself.

"Not one of your fans?" Scuglia asked.

"Apparently not," Radic replied.

"I've heard rumors," Scuglia said. "What can you tell me? Are his days numbered?"

It took Radic a few seconds to remember that Scuglia, like Mulroy, was now authorized to know the contents of the Internal Affairs report. His badgering had finally paid off.

"I'd say so," Radic replied. "He's living on borrowed time. He just doesn't realize it yet."

"And Frenchy?"

"He's in the same boat. But he won't go down with the ship. He's the one to watch."

Radic excused himself to make a phone call, which gave Scuglia and Mulroy a chance to catch up.

"Didn't I see you on Wild Kingdom the other night?" Scuglia asked.

"Ha, ha," Mulroy replied.

"Oh, that's right, it was the evening news. Any snake bites?"

"None that I know of."

"Aren't you supposed to wear a HAZMAT suit when you're out wrestling with boa constrictors?"

Mulroy laughed. "It wasn't a boa constrictor. It was an African puff adder."

"I'm impressed. I didn't know we had those in Pittsburgh."

"We shouldn't. Big Boy was here illegally."

"You're on a first-name basis? Is he in custody?"

"Believe it or not, he is. At an animal shelter. They're trying to figure out what to do with him and the rest of the snakes."

"How about the perp?"

"He's a good candidate for a plea. Apparently, the same people who smuggle snakes also smuggle drugs. He might be useful to us."

"What game was he playing, anyway?"

"As far as we can tell, it wasn't to make money. It was kind of like his hobby."

"Couldn't he have collected stamps instead?"

"Where's the thrill in that?"

Radic rejoined them a few minutes later.

"What's going on?"

"Stilton has authorized a trip to Gino's apartment next week."

"Just us?"

"No. We'll be joined by Internal Affairs, since they've been investigating Gino."

"How's that going to work?"

"I don't know. I guess we'll find out."

Chapter Eighteen: A Meeting at Mellon Park

Gary was bone-weary. Between Larry's bogus arrests and the protests and his own difficulties, he was running on empty. He made a mental note to take a break sometime soon. A visit with his mother would be nice. Some chicken soup, some apple cobbler. Gary set the alarm for 10 a.m. and fell sound asleep.

He was awakened by a call at 8:30 a.m.

"Mabry."

"I don't see what the problem is, man. I've been careful. You've been careful. No one's going to find out."

"Can't we do this tomorrow? I hardly got any sleep last night."

"Okay, I'll be there. Mellon Park."

Gary showered and dressed, then wolfed down a piece of toast and some orange juice. He opened up a footlocker and extracted a Glock 19 semi-automatic pistol. He checked to make sure it was loaded. Satisfied, he dropped the gun into a small satchel, adding a jacket to disguise its shape. Finally, he grabbed an apple.

At 9:30 a.m., he was out the door.

* * *

Saroja Prakash was unaccustomed to performing an autopsy on a trumpet. She knew very little about musical instruments, but she sensed that this particular trumpet had once been very special. The grease on the instrument turned out to be Vaseline, as she had explained to Radic and Mulroy, who wanted to know more.

It struck her as odd that the Vaseline was splattered all over the surface of the instrument. She was no musician, but shouldn't the lubricant be inside the valves or the slides? She also noticed cloth fibers whose path coincided, more or less, with the path of the Vaseline smears. It was as if someone had deliberately applied Vaseline to the surface of the instrument rather than to its interior.

The other oddity was the splotches of blood on the instrument. Wherever she found blood, she also found fiber from a cloth. Either someone had tried to remove the blood from the instrument unsuccessfully, or they had planted the blood there in the first place.

Her watch said 9:45 a.m. She reached for her phone and dialed Radic's number. It would be up to the detectives to figure out what all of this meant. On the surface, though, it appeared that someone was trying to frame the trumpet player.

She explained all this to Radic, who was less ecstatic than she thought he'd be. "It's a shame that Larry's silent trumpet can't testify on his behalf."

"But that's where you're wrong, my friend."

"How's that?"

"Larry's battered trumpet still has something to say. When I put the trumpet on the stand, so to speak, he'll be a strong witness for the defense. It's plain as day to me that someone has planted evidence on the trumpet (and probably on Gardenia as well). That will come out in my report."

"So Larry's trumpet isn't silent, after all?"

"When you read my report, you'll be able to hear trumpet music a city block away."

* * *

Shortly after 10:00 a.m., the Allegheny County Emergency Services Department received multiple 911 calls reporting the same thing—a man

83

had been shot dead in broad daylight in Mellon Park.

The first call arrived at 10:03 a.m. A young Black man was shot twice, once in the head. The murderer fled. What did the murderer look like? Spider-Man.

The second call arrived at 10:04 a.m. A man in a sweat suit was shot. Probably dead. The murderer escaped. What did he look like? A super-hero, from the comics.

The third call arrived at 10:05 a.m. A child predator was killed after getting into an argument with another man. The murderer fled the scene. What did he look like? A ninja warrior.

Detective Scuglia arrived at Mellon Park at 10:06 a.m., followed by Detective Turley a minute later.

The scene they observed was horrific. Children of all ages screaming hysterically, mothers trying to comfort them, onlookers talking frantically on their cell phones. Nearby, a young Black man lay spread-eagled on the pavement near a vacant swing set, a puddle of blood surrounding his head.

Scuglia checked the victim's pulse, while Turley kept the crowd at bay. A few moments later, Scuglia looked up at Turley and shook his head.

Donning gloves, Scuglia reached into the man's right rear pocket and extracted a wallet. He flipped through the cards. Then he called the homicide desk.

"This is Scuglia. Is Radic around?"

After a pause, "Well, find him ASAP and tell him he needs to meet me at Mellon Park. There's been a murder that he's gonna care about."

After another pause, "No, he's in jail again. It's his brother, Gary. Gary Mabry."

Within a few minutes, a technician had secured the crime scene, cordoning the area off with yellow tape and placing a tent around the victim's body for privacy. Additional officers were jotting down names and phone numbers of eyewitnesses before they dispersed.

The initial 911 caller, Mrs. Rebecca Carlson, remained nearby, comforting her six-year-old daughter with soothing words and a bag of dried fruit.

After hearing the essentials from Mrs. Carlson, Scuglia convinced her to remain in Mellon Park until Radic arrived, explaining that Radic would probably be the lead investigator in the case. Or so Scuglia assumed. In a case as political as this one, anything was possible.

Radic arrived at approximately 10:30 a.m., sought out Scuglia for a private word, and confirmed that he would be the lead investigator. "Despite my objections," he added.

Two witnesses were waiting to see him. Scuglia briefly covered the essentials. "We need to notify the next of kin. Quickly. Do you want to do that? Or should I?"

Radic thought for a moment. "Gary's single. And his father is dead. That leaves his mother. And Larry. I should probably tell Larry. Can you tell his mom before it leaks?"

"Do you have a name? An address?"

"Ernestine. Ernestine Mabry. In or near Lawrenceville."

"Got it. I'll do that as soon as I brief Turley."

Slowly, reverently, Radic approached Gary, kneeling beside him. The first thing he noticed was Gary's bloody sweatshirt, featuring a stylized image of a jazz quartet and the words, "The Rough Riders." Even in death, Gary was united with his big brother.

Larry was going to be devastated. And angry. Very angry. Radic was angry too. He knew about many of Gary's wrong turns from Larry and, more recently, from the Internal Affairs report. But he also knew that Gary was trying to find a better path. He did not deserve to die so brutally. He did not deserve to die, period.

Shelving these thoughts for the moment, Radic sought out the crime scene technician.

"What do we have so far?"

"No casings yet. That's going to take a while, if there are any to be found."

"I see a satchel. From the victim or the killer?"

"Probably the victim."

"What did you find?"

"A Glock 19."

"Fired?"

"No."

"Anything else?"

"A light jacket, a campaign brochure for Mayor Graham, and an apple."

"That's it?"

"So far."

"Okay. Thanks. I'm going to talk to a couple of witnesses. Then I need to see the victim's brother."

The crime tech nodded as Radic sought out Mrs. Carlson. Turley agreed to look after her daughter to give them some privacy.

"Mrs. Carlson," Radic began, "we greatly appreciate your reporting the crime and sticking around to help us with our investigation. We know this must be difficult for you and your daughter."

"I'll help in any way I can, Detective."

"Tell me, in your own words, what you observed."

"I noticed the victim talking with someone a few minutes before he was shot."

"Can you describe the person he was talking with?"

"Well, he kind of stood out, because he was dressed like Spider-Man. At first, I thought it was some sort of promotional campaign sponsored by the city or some local business. But then I changed my mind."

"Why is that?"

"They weren't together very long before the two of them started shouting at one another. It got to be very heated. That didn't seem like something commercial."

"Did you hear anything they said?"

"Not really. An occasional word."

"What words did you hear?"

"Money."

"Good. Anything else?"

"Drugs."

"Who used the word money?"

"The killer."

"Who used the word drugs?"

"Also the killer."

"Okay, what happened next?"

"Well, Spider-Man started pushing and shoving the victim."

"Did the victim push back?"

"At first, no. But then, when the shoving got worse, he punched him. In the stomach."

"How did Spider-Man react?"

"He got *very* angry. Then he took out a gun and started waving it at the other man."

"What did the other man do?"

"He started yelling, 'There's kids here, man. Don't do this.'"

"And what did Spider-Man do?"

"He shot him, point-blank. Once in the head. Then once in the heart. It was horrible to watch. The shocked look on his face. The blood spurting out of his right eyeball." She shook her shoulders in disgust at the memory.

"And then?"

"And then Spider-Man ran like a bat out of hell."

"In which direction?"

"Towards the old Nabisco plant, over there," she said, pointing to Bakery Square, on Penn Avenue.

"Mrs. Carlson, did you notice anything unusual about Spider-Man's voice when he was talking?"

"He was agitated, angry. And he swore a lot."

"Any accent?"

She paused. "None that I noticed."

"Is there anything else you can tell me about the victim?"

"Well, I can tell you that he was a nice man."

"How do you know that?"

"Here's the thing. I was suspicious of him at first. He was hanging out near the children's swing set. He was Black. He was by himself. It got my attention. He seemed to be waiting for someone. But, hey, you never know."

"You thought he might pose a threat to your child?"

"Yes, honestly, I did."

"What convinced you otherwise?"

"Well, I was focusing so much on this guy that I didn't notice that Emily wanted to stop swinging. When she did stop, she skidded and skinned her knees. The man saw what happened and came over and reassured her. He had a calm, soothing voice. Kind of like a preacher's voice. And he was ever so sweet to her. That's when I decided he was basically a good guy."

When Radic finished the interview, Turley directed him to another eyewitness, Jessica Falcone. In contrast to the previous witness, this one was chafing at the bit and complaining, eager to go home with her four-year-old daughter. As with the first witness, Turley watched her child while Radic conducted the interview.

"Thank you for speaking with us, ma'am," Radic said. "We know this must have been difficult for you and your daughter."

"What is this world coming to? You can't even go to the playground these days."

"Did you observe the shooting, ma'am?"

"No, but I saw the man who got shot before it happened. He was a pervert."

"How did you reach that conclusion, ma'am?"

"He was hanging around the swings, eyeing up the little girls. That was bad enough. But then he got down on his hands and knees with one of them and started patting her on the butt like a sicko."

"Are you sure that's what he was doing, ma'am?"

"Positive. I saw it myself."

"What can you tell me about the killer, ma'am?"

"I didn't get a good look at him. But he looked pretty athletic. Kind of like a Ninja Warrior."

"Did you hear him speak, ma'am?"

"The two men were yelling at each other. I couldn't tell what they were saying. I was focused on getting my Mandy away from both of them. You could tell something bad was going to happen."

"Did you see the one man shoot the other?"

"I didn't see it. But I heard it. Three shots. That's when I called 911."

"Did you see which way the shooter went?"

"Not really. I was too busy looking after my daughter."

"Okay, ma'am. Thanks very much. We really appreciate your help."

As he approached his squad car to leave the scene, Radic noticed a WTAE-TV van on the outskirts of Mellon Park. Nearby, a reporter, Kelly Robinson, was reporting live and was about to interview a Black man whom Radic recognized as Erskine Howell.

"A young Black man has been murdered this morning in Mellon Park. WTAE-TV has learned that the victim of this shooting is Gary Mabry, twenty-six, of East Liberty.

"Gary Mabry was the leader of a protest rally that sought to secure the release of his brother, Larry Mabry, a prominent trumpet player, who is being held for questioning after the murder of Pittsburgh Police Detective Gino Gardenia.

"With us this morning is Mr. Erskine Howell, a community activist. Mr. Howell, how did you learn about Gary Mabry's death?"

"I just heard about it from a friend. Gary was a peace-loving citizen, devoted to social justice. His brother Larry has been unjustly held by the Pittsburgh Police for a crime he didn't commit.

"Gary spoke out against this wrongful incarceration, and he paid for speaking out with his life. I blame the police department for his death."

"Mr. Howell, do you have any evidence to support the allegation that the Pittsburgh Police were responsible for Gary Mabry's death?"

"My evidence is that I've observed how Black people are treated by the Pittsburgh Police. First, they targeted Larry. Then they targeted Gary. Gary's only crime was standing up for the constitutional rights of his brother."

"Do you have anything to say to the Pittsburgh Bureau of Police?"

"Yes, I do. I say: We are watching you. And we will be heard. You can expect to see us on the streets of Pittsburgh until justice is done, for Larry Mabry, for Gary Mabry, and for the Black community of Pittsburgh."

Chapter Nineteen: One on One

Once assigned the Gardenia case, Radic had made a point not to speak with Larry Mabry alone. With so many land mines lying about, he didn't want to jeopardize the investigation.

He and Mulroy had met with Larry twice, but both meetings were uneventful. On advice of counsel, Larry said next to nothing. He was the complete opposite of his usual buoyant self.

Radic found these meetings unsettling. As a friend, he felt empathy, seeing such a talkative individual reduced to monosyllabic responses. Yet, as a policeman, he couldn't help but feel a twinge of resentment that a suspect would invoke the Fifth Amendment. Did he maybe have something to hide?

Radic brushed all of these thoughts aside as he stepped into his friend's cell, alone. Larry had lost some weight since his last visit. He had bags under his eyes.

"How's it going, Larry?"

"How's it look, man?"

"How's your lip?"

"It's healing." He paused. "Thanks. I owe you for that."

Radic simply nodded.

"Of course, I have no trumpet to play."

"I'm really sorry about that."

Larry paused again. "I know you are, man. But that trumpet…it was part of me. It's like losing an arm."

Radic was having misgivings now. Was he really the best person to tell Larry that his brother was dead? How to cushion the blow? Would Larry even be allowed to attend the funeral? If anyone knew how it felt not to be able to attend a dead sibling's funeral, it was Radic.

Radic plunged ahead. "Larry, I have something to tell you."

Larry looked up.

"It's about Gary."

In the end, he couldn't say it. But he didn't need to.

"No!" Larry cried. "No! No! No!" He stood up, grabbed a clock, and hurled it against the wall. It smashed into little pieces, which got the attention of a guard.

"Is everything okay, Radic?"

Radic winced and nodded. "Just give us a few more minutes."

Larry put his face in his hands and wept. His shoulders shook, convulsively. He gasped for breath. Radic asked the guard for a glass of water.

Five minutes later, Larry wiped his face with his shirt. He looked up at Radic, with deep pain in his eyes.

"Where?"

"Mellon Park."

"How?"

"Two gunshots."

"Where was he wounded?"

"One bullet to the heart. One to the head."

Larry covered his face with his hands, again.

"My mother…"

"What about your mother?"

"Will they make him look good for my mother?"

Radic didn't quite know what to say. "I'm sure they will, Larry. They'll do their best."

"I let him down. I let him down."

"No, you didn't, Larry. There's nothing you could have done."

"He was trying to turn his life around."

"I know."

"That fucker Gardenia."

Radic felt he was drifting into no man's land, where the duties of a friend and the duties of a police investigator collided.

"Larry, buddy, you'd better stop there. If you have something to say about Gardenia, I really want to hear about it. But not now. Think about what you want to say. Talk to your lawyer. Mulroy and I will come back later today or tomorrow if there's something you want to tell us."

"I want to talk."

"Okay, but not now."

"Does my mother know?"

"Detective Scuglia is talking to her right now."

"I need to be with her."

Radic felt tugged in different directions again.

"Maybe we can bring her here, Larry."

"No, no, that wouldn't be good. I need to go home."

"It's a new ball game, Larry. Let's see where things stand when the dust settles."

He got up to go. "Is there anything I can get you?"

Larry said nothing for a moment. "Music. I need some good music."

"Let me see what I can do."

"None of that Kenny G shit."

"I wouldn't do that to you, Larry."

"Straight-ahead jazz."

"You got it, Larry. We'll work something out."

* * *

At Lieutenant Stilton's suggestion, Turley agreed to visit Freedom Corner to gauge the community's response to Gary Mabry's murder. He found a crowd of perhaps two hundred and fifty people seething with anger.

Unlike the previous gathering, punctuated by hymns, spirituals, and civil rights chants, this one was rowdier and younger, with boom boxes competing for attention.

Also, unlike the previous assembly, when Gary was in charge, this one was not well choreographed, if indeed it was choreographed at all. The hostility escalated as the mic shifted from speaker to speaker.

Erskine Howell and other activists sought to whip the crowd into a frenzy. A common theme was that it was time to fight fire with fire.

Father Buckley and Wade Newborn were more restrained. They called for peaceful protest, warning that violence could undermine their cause.

As Turley saw it, Gary Mabry was a convenient prop to Howell and his supporters—someone whose death could be used to pursue political ends. In contrast, it appeared that Father Buckley and Newborn were mourning a lost friend. Their grief seemed personal, not political.

It was a volatile situation, as Turley reported to Stilton. Hard to predict how things would turn out.

Anticipating another march on police headquarters, Stilton deployed four dozen police officers to fend off potential assailants. He also sent several officers to join Turley at Freedom Corner, in case violence broke out on the way to headquarters.

The protesters, for all their rage, seemed disinclined to move. They smoked dope, chatted with news crews, hurled occasional obscenities at the police, and scavenged for food. Turley was beginning to think that a leadership vacuum might have certain advantages from a public safety perspective.

At approximately 10:30 p.m., dozens of protesters decided to head home, as recommended by Father Buckley. But others had different plans.

Contrary to Stilton's expectations, approximately 100 marchers headed deep into downtown. With remarkable speed, they made their way to Market Square, where most businesses were now shuttered for the night. A few restaurants and bars remained open.

The mood, Turley thought, was tense, volatile.

The first sign of trouble began with breaking glass, followed by a burst of flames inside a clothing store. Turley guessed that someone had hurled a Molotov cocktail, though he couldn't tell for sure.

Next came a roar from the crowd, then lots of shouts and screams. Within minutes, the crowd scattered in different directions, no longer a moving stream but instead tributaries of a river.

Some protesters hurled rocks at storefront windows, while others taunted the police. Vandals ransacked stores, especially those containing shoes, sporting goods, and electronics.

Some of the protesters donned masks to conceal their identity from cameras. Others took their chances, and a few actually seemed eager to be photographed.

Another store burst into flames, then a third. A storeowner or clerk, still inside the third store, ran screaming into the street, his right pants leg on fire. A marcher used a jacket to douse the fire, as the man howled in pain.

A handful of police officers tried to respond, but most of the force was back at headquarters, prepared for an onslaught that never materialized there.

Turley himself got hit by a rock, which grazed his right cheek and caused some bleeding. Cursing, Turley dabbed the wound with a handkerchief, ducking between two buildings to stay out of the line of fire for a while.

After the first few minutes, sirens could be heard. Two ambulances arrived, then a fire truck. Fifteen minutes or so after the initial violence, about two dozen additional police officers appeared on the scene.

For nearly two hours, a battle raged. Turley noticed Father Buckley in the thick of things, urging restraint on both sides. Then he observed the priest hobbling for safety towards a park bench, after sustaining a blow of some sort.

At around 2:00 a.m., the looting stopped. Fires smoldered, but were under control. Several people had been taken to Mercy Hospital. Several arrests had been made.

The battle of Market Square was over, at least for now.

Chapter Twenty: A Shortage of Evidence

Lieutenant Stilton reached for his third cup of coffee from the office coffee pot, known informally as "swamp water." Normally, Radic thought, Stilton would have fortified himself with a large caffe latte from Starbucks. But he seemed distracted this morning after the late-night looting.

Scuglia and Turley, who had been on the front lines, looked equally weary, or worse. Scuglia, uncharacteristically unkempt, had probably not had a chance to shower or change. Turley sported an oversized bandage on his cheek from the rock that had found its mark in the melee.

In keeping with Stilton's policy, Radic and Mulroy had been barred from the violence downtown. The order, Stilton confirmed, came from the very top. Chief Reilly.

Radic wondered, again, why Reilly was so interested in the Mabry case, now the Mabry cases. The most obvious explanation was that Mayor Graham was interested. Radic made a mental note to get to the bottom of this.

Someone had kindly brought pastries and orange juice to the meeting. The unnamed Good Samaritan could perhaps be forgiven for not having supplied drinkable coffee.

"Okay," Stilton began, "let's get started. Turley, what can you tell us about last night's battle?"

"It started just before midnight and lasted until about two a.m. Gary Mabry's murder has galvanized the Black community. Two or three hundred protesters met at Freedom Corner. Father Buckley urged them to go home after a while, but several dozen people marched downtown instead. Some of them broke windows and stole merchandise from a handful of stores. Some started fires."

"Any preliminary assessment of the property damage?"

"Several businesses will need new storefront windows. Some will need new locks on their doors. The looters made away with a fair amount of equipment from Granger's Electronics. They suffered the worst. Most of the other owners did okay."

"Anyone hurt?"

"Detective Atwood had to be treated for minor injuries at Mercy Hospital. A few of us needed bandages for this or that. One merchant was badly burned and will need skin grafts."

"And the protesters?"

"A few of them got bloodied up when they did something bad. Mainly vandals. Also, Father Buckley."

"Who the hell would be stupid enough to assault a priest?"

"Atwood?"

"Do we have him on a body-cam?"

"Afraid so."

Stilton shook his head.

"How many arrests?"

"As of this morning, eight. Plus, we're still looking for four others."

"Should we expect more trouble?"

"I think you can count on it."

"Who's in charge, now that Gary Mabry is dead?"

"It's kind of fluid. Father Buckley. Erskine Howell. A couple of others."

"Is our community liaison office helping at all?"

"They're doing the best they can."

Stilton sighed. "Okay, we'll need eyes and ears at Freedom Corner. And we'll need a strong presence at Market Square and at headquarters tonight, if that's where the protesters migrate to."

Everyone nodded. "Radic? Let's start with Gardenia's murder. What do we know?"

"Much of what we know about Gardenia comes from Internal Affairs. Do you want me to talk about that?"

"No, not here. That can wait. Unless you have something from other sources."

"We'll be visiting Gardenia's apartment with Internal Affairs. Nothing to report from that yet. But Mulroy spoke with Gardenia's ex."

"What can you tell us, Mulroy?"

"Gardenia's ex is Connie Simone. Age forty-two. Lives in Swissvale. They were married for almost five years. Not a bed of roses. He was abusive. She called for help after he gave her a black eye. After that, they lived apart. They got divorced four years ago."

"Any knowledge of illegal activity?"

"Lots of suspicions. No hard evidence."

"Radic?"

"We also visited Muscle Mania, a gym in East Liberty. Gardenia was a member. He showed up once every week or two. But he never exercised."

"What are you saying?"

"Seems like he met someone there regularly."

"Do you have a name?"

Radic nodded. "Jorge Menendez. He has ties to the cartel, Costa a Costa."

"Have you tracked him down?"

"Not yet."

"Okay, keep me posted. What about Gary Mabry?"

"He was shot twice, at Mellon Park, after an argument with a man in a costume."

"Spider-Man?"

"Spider-Man. Or a ninja warrior. Depending on who you talk to. They had a sharp disagreement. Spider-Man got physical. Then Gary punched him in the stomach. Spider-Man shot him after that."

"Any ideas about Spider-Man?"

"The witnesses say he was tall, lean, athletic."

"Any accent?"

Radic shook his head.

"Anything we can say definitively about who killed him?"

"We can say definitively that Larry Mabry did not kill him."

Stilton looked up. "Is there a point you're trying to make, Radic?"

"If the same person killed Gary Mabry and Gardenia, then it clearly wasn't Larry Mabry."

"But the M.O.s for the two murders were quite different, weren't they?"

"Yes, but we have no real evidence to connect Larry to Gino's death. And therefore no good reason to hold him."

"What about the Vaseline on the trumpet?"

"Well, there's that. But here's the thing. We've been asking around, and no self-respecting jazz trumpeter would use Vaseline to lubricate his trumpet. That's strictly kids' stuff."

"I thought we got a tip."

"We did, but Mulroy and I think it was someone trying to frame Larry."

"He doesn't use Vaseline?"

"Nope."

"What does he use?"

"Hetman's Oil No. 4. Also, whatever lubricant you use, the oil is supposed to be on the inside of the trumpet, not the outside. According to the M.E., the Vaseline on Gardenia's battered face is conspicuous enough that it looks like the person with the trumpet wanted it to be conspicuous."

Stilton shook his head, wearily.

"Has Larry Mabry given us an alibi yet?"

"Not yet. But he's willing to talk with us now that Gary's dead."

"If he gives us an alibi, we can release him. I'd like to release him. It would help us with the community. But we can't tell the press that we're releasing him because he doesn't swab his trumpet with Vaseline."

"Got it."

"We need to hear, straight from Larry Mabry, what he was doing the night Gardenia was murdered. Set up an interview. Now."

"Will do."

"Do we have any other suspects for Gardenia's murder?"

"No suspects. Just leads."

"Okay, you know the drill. The sooner we have credible suspects for both murders, the sooner we can get some sleep."

Chapter Twenty-One: Bittersweet Memories

Ernestine Mabry was a distinguished-looking woman. Her gray-black hair was tied neatly in a bun. Her thick, tortoise-shell glasses framed a small, elegant face with inquisitive eyes. She wore a flowery dress and a pearl necklace.

Her face betrayed grief and sleep loss, but she was composed. She greeted her guests graciously at the door and extended her right hand. Radic clasped both of her hands in his and lingered for a moment.

"Detective Radic, it's a pleasure to meet you. I've heard about you from Larry. He says you keep him from getting flabby."

Radic chuckled softly. "It's nice to meet you, Mrs. Mabry, though I'm terribly sorry about the circumstances."

She nodded.

"This is Detective Kathleen Mulroy."

"I'm so sorry for your loss, ma'am."

"Thank you," she said. "Can I offer you coffee or tea?"

Radic and Mulroy both accepted coffee and sat in the living room, while Mrs. Mabry went to the kitchen. The living room was nicely furnished, with a beige sofa facing a large TV set. An old Victrola record player stood in one corner, an upright Baldwin piano in the other.

On the wall, Radic saw pictures of two exceptionally handsome boys—Larry playing the trumpet; Gary carrying a football.

A large photo featured the entire family—Mr. Mabry, looking dapper and confident in an Army uniform, Mrs. Mabry looking beautiful and happy, and the two boys looking as if they had been up to some mischief.

Mrs. Mabry returned with three cups of coffee. She then produced an assortment of muffins. "From friends," she explained.

Radic nodded. "Mrs. Mabry, we know this is a terribly difficult time for you. But we're eager to catch Gary's killer. And so we have some questions for you. Some of them may not be easy."

"I understand, Detective. There's no one who wants to catch whoever did this more than I do."

"We're going to have to ask you some questions about Larry, too. If you like, we can put those off till another day."

"Let's see how it goes."

"Okay, fair enough. Let's begin with Gary. When was the last time you saw him?"

"Last weekend. Sunday night. He dropped by the day after Larry was arrested."

"How did he seem?"

"Agitated. Upset. Determined to get Larry out of jail."

"How long did he stay?"

"A half hour. An hour."

"Mrs. Mabry, what did Gary do for a living?"

Their host put down her coffee. "Detective, I'm not going to play games. I know that Gary used drugs. And I know that he sold drugs. It's the greatest regret of my life."

"Did you ever speak to him about this?"

"Did I *ever* speak to him about this? Only constantly."

"When did it first begin?"

"When Hubert died."

"Hubert?"

"My husband."

"When was that?"

"Ten years ago. Larry had graduated from high school. He was already playing jazz in Pittsburgh, in Cleveland, in Philadelphia, sometimes in DC.

101

He was very upset when his father died, but he had a career, a reason to live, a network of friends."

"And Gary?"

"Gary was not so lucky. When Hubert passed, he just couldn't accept it. He stayed out till all hours of the night. He got in with a bad crowd. At first, it was marijuana. Then it was cocaine. Really bad stuff. Eventually, we got him into a treatment program."

"Who's we?"

"Larry and me, mainly. Plus Father Buckley at St. Martin de Porres Church."

"How did that go?"

"Not so well. Gary was angry. He had too many demons in his head. He was back on the street soon after they released him from the program."

"That must have been difficult for you," Mulroy said.

"You have no idea, Detective. Does either of you have children?"

They both shook their heads.

"When your child does well in life, there's nothing more satisfying. But when your child stumbles and makes some bad decisions, there's nothing more painful. You blame yourself. You ask a lot of 'what if' questions. You try prayer. You try friends. You try counselors. But sometimes there's nothing you can do. That's hard to accept."

"Did things ever get better?" Mulroy asked.

Mrs. Mabry smiled. "Have you ever been to Kennywood Park, Detective?"

"Many times," Mulroy said.

"Have you ever ridden the Thunderbolt?"

Mulroy nodded.

"That's what living with Gary was like. Riding a roller coaster. Up and down. Up and down. It leaves you dizzy."

There was silence.

"But it also leaves you hopeful."

"Why is that, ma'am?"

"Because my faith tells me to believe in the possibility of redemption. And because Gary had turned a corner. He had decided to give up the life of drugs."

"For real?"

"For real."

"How do you know?"

"A mother knows."

"Can you be more specific?"

"Well, Gary told me he wanted out. Two Christmases ago. He said he had an exit plan. It was only a matter of time."

"What did he mean by that? An exit plan?"

"He never told me exactly. But I noticed things."

"What exactly?"

"He was using drugs less. Much less. His eyes weren't bloodshot all the time. His skin wasn't splotchy all the time. He was clear-headed again. He was funny again. He was sweet again. He was my baby boy again."

At that, Mrs. Mabry burst into tears and retreated into the kitchen. Mulroy followed her.

"We know this is upsetting, Mrs. Mabry. We can come back some other time."

Mrs. Mabry shook her head, blew her nose, took off her glasses, and washed her face with cold water from the tap.

"I want to talk this through, Detective. Just give me five minutes. I'll rejoin you in five minutes."

* * *

Sure enough, Mrs. Mabry returned to the living room a few minutes later, carrying a bag of tissues, a wastepaper basket, and rosary beads. "I'm prepared, Detectives, I'm prepared."

Radic and Mulroy both laughed in admiration.

"You're amazing, Mrs. M.," Radic said.

"Ma'am, I noticed that you have a nice backyard," Mulroy said. "Would you prefer to sit out there? Get some fresh air? It's such a lovely spring day."

"That's an excellent idea, Detective. Let's do that."

After repositioning themselves outside, on folding chairs, Radic resumed the questioning.

"Mrs. Mabry, we're going to need to visit Gary's apartment sometime soon. Do you happen to have a key?"

"I don't. I'm sure Larry does."

"Do you know where Gary did his banking? PNC? Somewhere else? We're going to need to check out his bank statements at some point."

Mrs. Mabry sighed. "Detective, I think I know where you're going with this. Believe me, I've already been there."

"What do you mean?"

"Gary and I used to have a joint bank account. That stopped when I learned that he was selling drugs. I wanted nothing to do with that money."

"Understood. Do you know if Gary left a will?"

"I urged both of my boys to make a will. I'm sure that Larry has one. I don't know about Gary."

Sensing a growing gloom, Mulroy decided to pivot. "Did Gary have any hobbies? Either in the old days or recently?"

Mrs. Mabry brightened at the subject. "In the old days, it was football, football, football. He was the quarterback for Westinghouse High School. The Bulldogs. They made the state championships in his junior year. Didn't win it, but they came really, really close. Then Hubert died in the spring and Gary went downhill. His senior year, he missed so many classes that he got cut from the team. And he dropped out of high school."

"What a shame," Mulroy said.

Mrs. Mabry nodded.

"Did he ever finish high school?"

"He got himself a GED degree. Fairly recently. Like I say, he was on a better path. A path out of the wilderness."

"Any other hobbies?" Mulroy persisted.

"Yes, he's been working out lately. At a gym."

"Which one?"

"Muscle Mania. In East Liberty." Mulroy and Radic glanced at one another, but said nothing.

"Mrs. Mabry, we don't want to keep you much longer, but we need to ask some questions about Larry as well," Radic said.

"You know him, Detective. Do you really believe Larry would kill someone?"

"Mrs. Mabry, I'm supposed to keep an open mind on that subject. Maybe there's something you could tell us that would help Larry out."

"I would love to be able to do that."

"Has Larry ever gotten into trouble with the police?"

"Until this incident, never."

"Has Larry ever used drugs?"

"I'm not going to say never, Detective. Larry is a jazz musician. But he's heard story after story about jazz musicians who've destroyed their lives by using drugs or drinking too much. Charlie Parker. Lester Young. Billie Holiday. He wasn't going to travel that path. So, when I have a glass of wine, he has a Coca-Cola. When his friends have a gin and tonic, he has tonic water. Larry cares too much about music and his career to mess with that stuff."

"Okay, fair enough, that's helpful."

"Has Larry ever hung out with Gary and his friends?"

"Well, it depends on what you mean by that, Detective. If you mean, has he ever met Gary's friends, I'd say yes. If you mean does he stay up partying with them, I'd say no."

"How does Larry spend his spare time?"

Mrs. Mabry chuckled. "Spare time? That boy doesn't know the meaning of spare time. Ever since he was a child, he's been devoted to that trumpet of his. If he's not performing, he spends his time with his trumpet. Or with his band members. Or with his daughter."

"His what? Did you say daughter?"

"You never met Dorothy?"

"No, ma'am."

"Larry became a daddy seven years ago. That child is a blessing."

"Does she live with her mother?"

"That's right. But Larry sees her every week. She's local. He has visitation rights. And he pays child support."

"I didn't know any of that," Radic said.

"Well, Larry doesn't advertise it. But he doesn't hide it either. He's proud of Dorothy. And she loves her Daddy."

"How often do you see Larry?"

"Well, at least once a month. He and Gary come over…he and Gary would come over the first Sunday of every month. Sometimes pot roast. Sometimes chicken. Sometimes a cookout. I guess that tradition is over and done with."

"We're very sorry about that," Mulroy said.

"You know, I'm starting to feel a bit weary."

"Mrs. Mabry, you've been a big help."

"I want to help. I'll talk with you again. I'll talk with you until Larry's out of jail. I'll talk with you until you've found out who murdered Gary. I want justice for both of my sons."

Chapter Twenty-Two: At Last, an Alibi

Darius Larkin, Esq. was sitting next to Larry Mabry when Radic and Mulroy entered the small conference room. Larkin introduced himself; Mulroy and Radic did the same.

"Mr. Larkin," Radic began, "is your client ready to proceed?"

"Yes, he is."

"Mr. Mabry," Radic began, "Where were you on the night of Detective Gardenia's murder?"

Larry looked up. "Detective, I've been reluctant to divulge that information because it might require you to contact my ex-wife. I think you can understand why I might be sensitive on that point."

"Are you saying that you spent the night with your ex-wife?"

"No, Detective, that's not what I'm saying. But my ex-wife knows where I was."

"And where is that?"

"I was with my daughter, Dorothy. At home."

"Can your daughter vouch for that?" Mulroy asked.

"Well, here's the thing, Detective. Dorothy can vouch for me. I'm just not willing to have her do it. So, I've reached out to my ex-wife, through Mr. Larkin, and she has agreed to speak with you. She's not happy about it, and we both agree that under no circumstances are you to talk with Dorothy. But my ex-wife is willing to be interviewed. And she will confirm that I spent the night with Dorothy."

"At the risk of being insensitive, how can we be sure that you didn't leave your daughter at home for an hour while you met with Detective Gardenia on the North Side?"

"Well, first of all, Detective, I just wouldn't do that. If I'm with Dorothy, I'm with her one hundred percent. But second, she had an upset stomach that night. I was the bucket brigade. I was not in a position to go to the 7-Eleven, or to go kill Detective Gardenia, or anything else."

Radic paused the tape, and he and Mulroy left the room. Stilton was standing outside. "Sir, can we get by with this and the ex-wife's testimony?"

Stilton thought for a moment. "How old is the daughter?"

"Seven years old."

Stilton winced. "No one wants to put a seven-year-old kid through something like this. If the ex-wife gives him a strong alibi, that's probably enough to justify his release. But her testimony will have to be airtight."

Radic nodded. He and Mulroy re-entered the room.

Radic turned on the tape. "Mr. Mabry, what is your ex-wife's name?"

"Wanda. Wanda Charles."

Radic obtained a phone number and address and exited the room again, confirming through Stilton that Scuglia would contact Ms. Charles immediately. If necessary, Radic and Mulroy could always re-interview her later.

Radic returned and turned the tape back on. "Mr. Mabry, have you had any personal encounters with Detective Gardenia?"

Larry turned to Larkin, who nodded.

"Yes, I have. I learned from my brother Gary that Detective Gardenia was shaking down drug dealers and pocketing considerable cash for himself."

"Do you have any evidence to confirm that?"

"All the evidence I needed was that my brother told me about it. Gardenia and I had a meeting to discuss it."

"Did Detective Gardenia ask to meet with you, or did you ask to meet with him?"

"I asked for the meeting."

"Where did you meet?"

"He asked me to meet him at Muscle Mania in East Liberty."

"What was said at that meeting?"

Larry sighed. "I explained to Detective Gardenia that my brother was no longer interested in selling drugs and that he was no longer interested in lining the pockets of the Pittsburgh Police."

"What was Detective Gardenia's response?"

"I believe he told me to go fuck myself."

"You're saying he was not amenable?"

"That's correct."

"Did he explain his reasoning?"

"He said that there was no getting off this particular train. I told him that Gary was getting off the train whether he liked it or not."

"What was his response?"

"He laughed and said that Gary could stop using drugs if he liked, but that he expected him to continue to sell drugs. A lot of people were depending on him, he said."

"Did he say who?"

"No, he didn't."

"What did you infer?"

"I inferred that he meant the drug cartel and several police officers, including himself."

"Did he mention any other officers?"

"No, he did not, but Gary did."

"Who exactly?"

"Mark Atwood."

"Anyone else?"

"Pierre Frobisher. Frenchy."

"How did this particular conversation conclude?"

"I told Detective Gardenia that he had two weeks to stop harassing my brother. If he didn't, I was going to report him to his superiors."

"What did he say to that?"

"He got angry. He threatened this and that."

"Any other encounters?"

"The next time I met Detective Gardenia was at the Con Alma jazz club, where I was performing."

"Had you arranged a meeting?"

"No, he simply showed up."

"What happened that night?"

"Detective Gardenia said he had something to tell me and took me across the street. Then he sucker-punched me. In the mouth."

"Did you fight back?"

"No, I did not."

"Did Detective Gardenia continue to assault you?"

"He punched me a few more times, in the stomach and the side, and then he threw me onto the sidewalk."

"Did you fight back at this point?"

"No, I did not."

"Why not?"

Larry paused. "It doesn't go well when a Black man punches a white police officer, even if the police officer punched him first."

"Did Detective Gardenia say anything to you during this altercation?"

"He said that Gary was in over his head and that I was in over my head, too. That's when he mentioned Dorothy."

"What did he say about Dorothy?"

Larry grew visibly upset and paused before continuing. "He said he knew where she lived. He said he knew where she went to school. He said he knew who her best friend was. That's when I decided I wasn't going to finger Gardenia."

Radic suggested a fifteen-minute break, which gave Radic and Mulroy a chance to confer with Stilton and Scuglia. Based on a brief phone conversation with Scuglia, Larry's ex-wife had provided a solid alibi, including confirmation that she had reached Larry on his landline that evening and that Dorothy had been ill. She also said that Larry would do nothing to endanger his daughter or his career.

Scuglia quoted her: "Larry may not be the best husband on the planet, but he's devoted to Dorothy. And he's devoted to that blasted trumpet of his. He always has his eyes on the prize. We split up because that prize wasn't me."

Stilton urged Radic and Mulroy to continue their interrogation. Meanwhile, he would check with Chief Reilly to seek his consent for Larry's release.

Chapter Twenty-Three: Shadows of the Past

Mulroy took the lead when the questioning resumed: "Mr. Mabry, we'd like to shift our focus for a while, from you and your activities to your brother Gary and his activities. Are you agreeable to that?"

Larry nodded.

"For the record?"

"Yes, I am, Detective."

"Can you tell us when your brother first started using drugs?"

"That would be when my father passed. Ten years ago."

"What sorts of drugs did he use?"

"Lots of marijuana at first. Then cocaine. And then opioids."

"We understand from your mother that you got him into a rehab program. When was that?"

"About six years ago."

"How did that go?"

"Not as well as we would have liked."

"Can you explain?"

"Gary stopped using drugs for a while. But the rehab didn't resolve some of the basic issues he was struggling with. A couple of weeks afterwards, he was using again."

"When did he start selling drugs?"

"About eight years ago."

"Can you tell us who he worked with and who his supplier was?"

"Jorge Menendez."

"Is he connected to a Mexican drug cartel known as Costa a Costa?"

"That's my understanding."

"Do you know where Menendez lives?"

"I don't. Gary would meet him regularly, at Muscle Mania.

"You told Detective Gardenia that Gary was ready to turn over a new leaf, to give up the use and sale of drugs. What's your evidence for that assertion?"

"Well, mainly from Gary himself. Usually, my mom and I would raise the subject of quitting, and Gary would shut us down. But two Christmases ago, Gary raised the subject himself. He said he was going to leave drugs behind, because they were leaving him behind."

"And you believed him?"

"Well, not at first. But we began to see some hopeful signs. He wasn't high as often. He wouldn't stare at you with vacant eyes. His complexion began to clear up. His sense of humor returned. He was starting to be Gary again. Not some kind of Zombie."

"Any other signs that he was turning over a new leaf?"

"Well, he was getting more involved in the community."

"How so?"

"He started giving blood. At first, they wouldn't take it because of his drug use. But once he got the drugs out of his system, he would donate blood every three months or so."

"What prompted this?"

"Well, Gary cares about people. Cared about people. That was part of it. Also, he learned that his blood was unusually valuable."

"How so?"

"Gary was born with a blood type that's in great demand. O-negative. It means that his blood can be used for transfusions for lots of folks. It motivated him. It gave him a sense of pride, self-worth. It was wonderful to see."

"Any other community activities?"

"Yes, he's been working for the Mayor."

"For the Mayor...or for the Mayor's re-election campaign?"

"Both. Let's face it, Gary knows a lot about drugs. Gary knew a lot about drugs. He could be a compelling speaker about what drugs do to people, how they destroy lives, how they shatter dreams. He would give talks at schools, at churches. Someone in the Mayor's office noticed him. They asked him to serve on the Mayor's Drug Task Force."

"Really?"

"It's not as crazy as it sounds. Few people could make the case against drugs as strongly as Gary could."

"Did Gary reveal his own connections to the world of drugs to the Mayor's people?"

"Well, I know he was open about having used drugs. I know he talked about rehab. Whether he told folks he actually sold drugs, maybe not. I just don't know."

At this point, Larkin interrupted the interview. "Detectives, I believe my client has been helpful to you. We'd appreciate it if you could give us a progress report on Ms. Charles, before we continue this conversation."

Radic replied: "We've been able to reach Ms. Charles. We hope to have a transcript from Ms. Charles' conversation when we finish up here today."

"And when will you make a decision on my request for my client's release?"

"We hope to be able to give you a response later today."

Larkin nodded and gestured for Larry to continue.

Mulroy resumed the questioning. "Mr. Mabry, do you know if your brother had a will?"

"I hope so. We talked about it two or three times. I urged him to do it. But I don't know for sure."

"Do you have the name of his attorney?"

"I have the name of *my* attorney. That is, my regular attorney. I recommended that Gary see her. You are welcome to contact her."

"Do you know where Gary kept his savings account, his checking account?"

"PNC? Just a guess."

"So he kept all of his funds at PNC?"

"Well, definitely not all. Some of his funds were at Muscle Mania. In a locker."

"Do you know which one?"

"No, but the key is probably in his apartment somewhere. Oh, and one more thing. I remember Gary saying that he had *two* lockers at Muscle Mania. One for the small stuff, one for the big stuff."

"Why two lockers?"

"I don't think he trusted the people he was dealing with. Menendez. Gardenia. He once said, if someone breaks into my regular locker, they'll get a bundle of cash. But that's not where my fortune is. The motherlode is in another locker."

Chapter Twenty-Four: Getting in Shape

Jorge Menendez was proving as elusive as the summer wind. His phone was no longer operative. He had stopped coming to Muscle Mania. No one answered the door at his apartment, on Center Avenue in East Liberty, and his landlord was currently out of town.

Mulroy was frustrated, because she had volunteered to track Menendez down and to follow the money trail that was thought to include him. So far, she had nothing to show for it and no promising leads. Unless…

Mulroy left work early, returned home, changed into something casual, and packed her gym bag. She looked at herself in the mirror. I could stand to lose a few pounds anyway, she thought to herself. With a skip in her step, she sauntered to her car and drove towards East Liberty.

The receptionist at Muscle Mania recognized her from her previous visit.

"Good afternoon, Detective. What brings you here today?"

"Well, guilt, I suppose. And curiosity. I was impressed by your facilities the other day, and your rates seem reasonable. I noticed that you have a thirty-day trial membership. I thought I'd give it a try."

"Wonderful! I'm so pleased. The way it works, you can use all of our facilities for thirty days. If you're satisfied, we'll bill you from when you first came here, today. If not, then there's no charge."

"A great deal. How often do people simply walk away?"

"Almost never. But that's entirely up to you."

After finding a locker and changing, Mulroy decided to warm up on the treadmill, at a modest pace. So far, so good. Then she switched to some squats, with a dumbbell. Ouch! Those muscles needed to be reawakened.

Next, she used a chest machine. More relaxing.

After that, she tried some seated cable rows to exercise her back. Yikes! Those muscles definitely needed some work. Next, walking lunges. Three sets of ten reps.

By 6:30 p.m., Mulroy was flushed and glistening. She showered and was ready to hit the road when she noticed a handful of people at the bar. One, a young woman, was drinking a smoothie.

"That looks pretty good," Mulroy observed. "What's in it?"

"Strawberry, banana, spinach, and avocado."

"Do you recommend it?"

"It's the best."

"As in it's good for you, or it's really tasty?"

"Both."

Mulroy ordered one for herself and sat next to the woman. "It's my first day."

"What do you think?"

"It was fun. I'm glad I came."

"Me too. I always feel virtuous after a workout. More relaxed, too."

As she chatted, Mulroy learned that the woman, Denise, was twenty-six, that she worked for the Pittsburgh Pirates on something called sabermetrics, and that she was between boyfriends. Mulroy was deliberately evasive about her own line of work.

"You ever run into a guy named Jorge here?"

"You know Jorge?"

"A friend says he comes here."

"You got to watch out for that dude."

"Why is that?"

"He's the kind of guy who doesn't take no for an answer."

"He's bothered you?"

"A couple times. I had to speak to the manager about him."

"What did he do exactly?"

"He seemed to be looking to hook up. Thanks, but no thanks. He's not my type. And he was pushing drugs. Pretty openly. I don't need that in my life."

"Did the manager speak to him?"

"He must have. The next time I saw him, he just glared at me. Didn't say a word."

"Have you seen him here lately?"

"Actually, no."

Mulroy got up to go.

"Say, I noticed a twenty-four-hour locker policy in the locker room. Are there any lockers you can rent for a longer period of time? In case you want to come here spur of the moment?"

"I never had the need. But, yeah, there are. I think they're just outside the Pilates room."

"Thanks, I may get one. Hope to see you again."

"Me too."

As she headed to the door, Mulroy almost literally ran into the manager, Bart Fielding. He seemed startled, taken aback. "Detective Mulroy, I'm surprised to see you here. Do we have an appointment?"

"No, we don't. I'm here as a civilian. I thought I'd try out your gym."

She pointed to her duffel bag.

"Oh!"

Fielding's frown turned into a half-smile.

"How did your first session go?"

"Well, I rediscovered some muscles that I haven't thought about in many months. So, I'd say it went very well."

"Good, good, pleased to hear it. Let me know if there's anything I can do to help."

Mulroy was accustomed to people being nervous of police officers. But she thought Fielding had been a little more nervous than most. Maybe a good reason to dig deeper. And definitely a good reason to check out those overnight lockers.

Chapter Twenty-Five: Young Musicians

Larry was touched that his band members had passed the bucket to gather enough cash to buy him a new Yamaha trumpet. It was not the trumpet of his dreams, but it might work as a transition instrument, in conjunction with his familiar mouthpiece. He tried a few scales and was pleasantly surprised. Between the new trumpet and his new upper lip, he hadn't known what to expect.

Larry was also tickled that the Westinghouse High School Band had offered to perform at Gary's funeral. Father Buckley had proposed a variation on that theme: why not a New Orleans-style funeral march before and after the service? School officials had approved a truncated version of the traditional NOLA model. Given logistics, it was decided that the students would perform right after the service.

Freshly released from his Pittsburgh jail cell, Larry had agreed to meet with the student volunteers the day before the funeral to try to whip them into shape.

Band members were jabbering noisily in the gym when Larry arrived. Their laughter and teasing lifted his spirits. But when they noticed his arrival, they suddenly grew silent.

Larry recognized what was happening: When the students looked his way, they saw a man with a trumpet. But they also saw the ghost behind him. The ghost of Gary Mabry.

"How y'all doing?"

A few students muttered a response.

"Who's in charge here?"

One of the students answered: "That would be Mr. Saxby. He just stepped out for a while."

"Mr. Saxby? For real? What instrument does he play? The sax?"

The students laughed.

"Who plays the trumpet around here?"

Several hands shot up.

"Is one of you named Trump?"

The students laughed again.

"Okay. I'm Larry Mabry, Gary's brother. I want to thank you for agreeing to give Gary a proper sendoff. How much do y'all know about New Orleans jazz?"

One of the female students spoke up.

"It's syncopated music."

"Syncopation. Good. A raggedy rhythm. Not Bach. Not Mozart."

"African music."

"That's right. But what *is* African music?"

"Polyrhythms."

"Very good. Polyrhythms. Playing different rhythms at the same time." As Larry gazed appreciatively at the female student, he found himself wondering if this could be Dee ten years from now, playing in a high school jazz band, talking confidently about jazz.

"Why New Orleans?" he asked. "Why did jazz take root in New Orleans?"

One of the male students answered. "Different cultures. Creoles. African Americans. Like gumbo soup."

"Hey, I like that. Gumbo soup. What's in gumbo soup anyway?"

"Everything."

"That's right. Chicken, Sausage, shrimp. The whole kitchen sink. Okay, you guys are on a roll. You know your stuff. But what does New Orleans jazz *sound* like?"

"It sounds like…I don't know…squawks, hollers, meows…like chickens and cats fighting in the backyard."

"Exactly. And those sounds, my friends, are not easy to make. But when you have a trumpet or a cornet or a trombone, that's your best chance to sound like animals messing with each other in your grandma's backyard."

The kids laughed.

"Okay, do you folks know any New Orleans tunes?"

"We can play a couple. When the Saints Come Marching In; and Down by the Riverside."

"Good. Good. That's a start. How about Oh, Didn't He Ramble?"

The students shook their heads.

"Struttin' With Some Barbecue?"

The same student spoke up: "Mr. Saxby said he was going to get us some charts. Maybe they're on the list."

"I hope so. Okay, show me what you've got. Let's start with When the Saints Go Marching In. All together first. And show me some joy on your faces. The music at my brother's funeral should be lifting us up, not dragging us down. My mother has shed enough tears already. I want you to bring a smile to her face. Now let's hear it. A one and a two and a..."

Chapter Twenty-Six: The Mayor's Man

Curiosity had led Radic to suggest Market Square as the venue for a meeting with someone from the Mayor's office. Evidence of the Market Square battle was everywhere. Several storefronts were boarded up. No cars were parked on the usually busy streets. An acrid smell remained in the air. Two or three officers were visible.

Radic found Hugh Benjamin, the head of the Mayor's Drug Task Force, in a booth at the back of a quiet restaurant, sipping a glass of iced tea. Radic ordered an Arnold Palmer and a scone and joined him.

Benjamin was Black, broad-shouldered, and bulky, with the physique of a former prize-fighter now enjoying the good life. When he spoke, his deep bass voice reminded Radic of James Earl Jones.

"Were you here, Detective?"

"No, while I'm running two murder investigations, my boss wanted me to be somewhere else. How about you?"

"No, but I have friends who were."

"What's their take on it?"

"They believe the police targeted the Mabry family."

"Do you believe that?"

Benjamin shrugged. "It wouldn't be the first time."

"Does Larry's release make a difference?"

"It's a good thing. It will buy you some time. But unless you find Gary's killer, soon, the Black community will be very upset."

"That's why I'm here today. I understand that Gary Mabry was a member of the Mayor's Drug Task Force?"

"That's correct, Detective."

"For how long?"

"About a year and a half."

"What was his role on the Task Force?"

"Well, there are no assigned roles for task force members, only for staff."

"I understand. But did Gary make any special contributions to the Task Force?"

"Very much so. He knew the world of drugs in and out. He knew where drugs originate, how they get to Pittsburgh, where people can buy them. He knew which drug dealers are reliable and which are not, which drug dealers are scary and which are not."

"Did you know that Gary was a drug dealer himself?"

"Not at first. Eventually, I started to wonder and had my suspicions confirmed. By Gary himself."

"Did that concern you?"

"Yes and no. There's no question that Gary was an asset to the Task Force. We learned things about drug sales in Pittsburgh that no one else could tell us. Or would tell us."

"But?"

"But we knew that if word of Gary's connections to the drug world leaked out, in the middle of the Mayor's re-election campaign, we would have ourselves a P.R. disaster. Phil Hodges, who heads up the campaign, made that point crystal clear. He said Gary could be an asset or a liability. Our instructions from Hodges were to make sure he was an asset.

"So we urged Gary to keep that side of things under wraps when he was out making speeches. Our students needed to know that he had used drugs and that he had made some mistakes. They didn't need to know that he had been a drug dealer."

"Is there a chance that Gary was still dealing drugs while he was working for the city?"

"It was my understanding that Gary's drug dealing days were over."

Radic nodded. "Who recommended Gary for the Task Force in the first place?"

Benjamin paused. "He came highly recommended by someone close to the Mayor."

"And who was that?"

Benjamin paused again. "Cecile Arceneaux, the Mayor's wife."

Radic whistled softly. "Do you know how he knew her or how he met her?"

"That's above my pay grade, Detective. If you're curious, I suggest that you speak with Ceci yourself. She's expecting your call."

Chapter Twenty-Seven: Clear as Mud

Radic was growing increasingly frustrated with the twin murder investigations. To an outsider, it must have seemed like the police had made little or no progress. To an insider, it felt pretty much the same way.

Radic knew from past experience not to judge himself too harshly during the early stages of an investigation. The tediously-gathered building blocks often laid the foundation for more satisfying discoveries down the road. Still, he was under pressure to get results soon.

It was high time for a fresh perspective—and that meant lunch with Lucas Renfert—his mentor, recently retired from teaching Criminology at Carnegie Mellon. Renfert, who had written articles and books on crime and police procedure, was wise, experienced, and discreet. Maybe he could pull a rabbit out of the hat.

Renfert was relaxing in a dimly lit corner of the Squirrel Hill Café when Radic and Mulroy arrived. A proud Black man, he liked to hide the two-inch scar on his right cheek—a relic of his youth growing up in the Watts neighborhood of Los Angeles.

Scar or no scar, Renfert was looking good. Jogging and tennis kept him fit. Consulting work kept him engaged. His son Norbert kept him motivated.

"It's great to see you, my friend," Renfert said, giving Radic a bear hug.

"It's been too long," Radic said.

"Whose fault is that?"

Renfert gave Mulroy an equally affectionate hug.

"So nice to see you again, Kathleen."

"It's great to see you, Lucas. We've missed you."

The trio placed their orders. Radic asked Renfert about his son Norbert, a good friend and jogging buddy. Renfert asked Mulroy about Jake Jacoby. Any wedding bells? Mulroy dodged the questions artfully, but Radic noticed a rosy blush, which got him wondering.

"So how did you manage to get saddled with two high-profile murder investigations at the same time?" Renfert asked.

"I tried to avoid them, especially Gardenia's," Radic said. "Stilton insisted. And Reilly too."

Renfert raised his eyebrows.

"Reilly is a fan of yours?"

"Maybe, maybe not. Apparently, the mayor wanted me to take the case."

"Really?" Mulroy asked. "I didn't know that. Any idea why?"

"Beats me."

"How about the Mabry case?" Renfert asked. "Why not give that to another detective?"

"The two murders are connected. At least we think so. Right, Mulroy?" Mulroy nodded.

"So what are the ground rules?" Renfert asked.

"The usual. What's spoken in the Squirrel Cage stays in the Squirrel Cage."

"Understood."

"Plus one additional restriction. I've seen a confidential IA report on Gardenia. Mulroy knows what's in it. But I'm afraid I can't share any information that comes exclusively from that report. I've sworn on a stack of Bibles not to divulge anything from that report."

"Whatever you say. You know what's best."

Patiently, Radic summarized the Gardenia case, covering rumors that Gardenia was shaking down drug dealers, Larry Mabry's failed interventions, and Larry's second-hand accounts of Gardenia's interactions with Gary.

"Any hard evidence that Gardenia was engaging in extortion?"

"I have to take the fifth on that question."

"Any evidence that other officers were also on the take?"

"Sorry. I can't answer that either."

"Any useful evidence from the crime scene?"

"Not really. We believe that some evidence was removed from the crime scene, though. Larry Mabry's trumpet, smeared with some of Gardenia's blood."

"Larry's doing?"

"Unlikely. More likely, an effort to frame him for the murder."

"Who discovered the body?"

"Mark Atwood."

"Not your favorite colleague, as I recall."

Radic said nothing.

"Okay, so who do you like for the Gardenia murder?"

Radic shrugged. "The drug cartel is most likely. One of their top dealers wanted out. One of their enablers on the police force wanted a bigger cut. If so, a classic squeeze play. The cartel didn't like the new situation. They responded. Maybe out of anger. Maybe to send a message to other players."

Renfert nodded.

"And you, Kathleen? Do you also like the cartel for the first murder?"

"I'm with Branko on Gardenia's murder. From the cartel's perspective, he was creating problems. They like stability, predictability. The situation was getting wildly unpredictable. They lashed out."

"Who is the face of the drug cartel in Pittsburgh?"

Mulroy sighed. "Well, the face used to be Jorge Menendez. He was the guy who met regularly with Gardenia and with Gary Mabry, at Muscle Mania in East Liberty."

"And where is he now?"

"In the wind."

"Is it possible that he committed the second murder as well?"

"Could be," Radic answered. "We have good descriptions of Menendez, not so good descriptions of Gary's killer. We're just not sure if they match up."

"Okay, so murder number two? What can you tell me?"

Relying heavily on Gary's mother's account, Radic gave equal time to Gary's troubled past and his recent resolve to leave the world of drugs behind. He discussed Gary's interest in politics, his role as an inspirational speaker, and his efforts to free Larry from jail.

"What does the M.E. say?" Renfert asked.

"Gary died of gunshot wounds to the brain and the heart. From a Ruger LCP. No leads on the weapon yet. He was free of drugs, as others have been saying. But there was severe damage to the liver and some damage to other organs, from his years of drug use."

"So who do you like for Gary's murder?" Renfert asked.

"Again, I vote for the cartel," Radic answered. "Gary was roiling the waters. He was jeopardizing their bottom line. He was a threat."

"Kathleen?"

"Branko may be right. The cartel had plenty of reasons to take him out."

"But?"

"Well, I hate to say it, but I think we also have to consider someone closer to home. A member of our police force."

"Why would they kill Gary?"

"They might have believed that Gary killed Gardenia. Or they might have seen Gary as a threat to their steady supply of cash."

"Anyone in particular?"

"We're working on that," Radic answered.

"Any evidence from Gary's apartment on his connections to Gardenia or the cartel?"

Radic sighed. "Believe it or not, we've been denied access to Gary's apartment until Stilton resolves a jurisdictional dispute with Internal Affairs."

"You're kidding."

"I wish that I were."

Renfert took a long sip of iced tea and studied his hands for a moment. "Being honest with you, I feel like I'm being asked to connect the dots, except there aren't that many dots to connect. I'm not sure my imagination is powerful enough to see an image here.

"I'm sorry about that," Radic replied. "We're putting you on the spot."

"I'm not saying I've got nothing. But at this point, I just have a few stray thoughts, not a strong narrative or counter-narrative."

"Any thoughts you have would be welcome," Radic said.

"Okay, let's start with your first murder. I think you're on the right track. Gardenia was a bad cop. And he was asking for trouble when he started tangling with drug dealers. They're ruthless. He should have known better."

"So you agree his murder was drug-related?" Mulroy asked.

"Almost certainly, from what you've told me. But that doesn't necessarily mean the dominant cartel was behind it."

"What do you mean?" Radic asked.

"No drug patch is secure, whether it's Pittsburgh or somewhere else. So continue to look at the dominant cartel. Try to track down Menendez. But be open to the possibility that another drug group is to blame. Maybe it's the outsiders who decided to shake things up and pick up the pieces afterwards."

"Okay. Good advice," Radic said. "We need to look at the bigger picture. We need to find out whether another organization has been coveting this territory. Thank you for that."

Renfert nodded.

"How about the second murder?" Mulroy asked. "What are your thoughts on that?"

"Well, call me crazy, but I think you might be barking up the wrong tree."

"How so?" Mulroy asked.

"The Gary Mabry you've described is very different from the Gary Mabry I've seen on TV."

"In what way?" Mulroy asked.

"The Gary Mabry you've described was seduced by the world of drugs. Then he stepped back from the brink, thanks to strong family support. And then he was murdered."

"You disagree?" Mulroy asked.

"No, not at all. But that's not the guy on TV. The Gary Mabry I've seen on TV was charismatic, articulate, and persuasive. Over the past week, he's become the public face of the Black community in Pittsburgh. That's a remarkable achievement. And it should tell you something about him."

"Which is?" Radic asked.

"Gary Mabry was neck deep in politics. Active in the Mayor's re-election campaign. A member of the Mayor's Drug Task Force. A calm, self-assured leader in a dispute that has threatened to tear the city apart. Plus, the Mayor has taken an active interest in your case. Why? Because of you? Unlikely. You have no real connection to the Mayor. But you do have a connection to the Mabry family. That makes you valuable. That makes you the right person for the job."

"Okay, so what do you suggest?"

"In your first murder case, I say follow the money. See where it leads. Maybe to Mexico. Maybe somewhere else."

"And the second murder?" Mulroy asked.

"In your second case, I say follow the votes. What exactly was Gary's role in the Mayor's re-election campaign? What exactly was Gary's connection to the Mayor? Like it or not, you're in the middle of an ugly political battle. Maybe Gary was, too."

Chapter Twenty-Eight: Staying Out of Trouble

Detective Mark Atwood was not too concerned about his little skirmish with Father Buckley, the meddlesome Black priest. His body-cam would show that he hit the priest on the knee with a baton in Market Square and that the priest crumpled on the spot.

But the same body-cam would show that Atwood had just been hit in the face by a hard object, probably a rock. Blinded for a moment, confused, he could say that he lashed out at the first person he saw, who turned out to be Father Buckley.

He knew that the ground rules for engaging with citizens during a protest demonstration were changing. If you were Black, you could do what you damn well pleased. If you were a white police officer, you were supposed to take whatever they dished out.

But self-defense still applied to police officers, and he had clearly been attacked by someone. He was pretty sure his union rep could get him through this.

In contrast, Atwood was troubled by Gardenia's murder. Gino had been the point guard; Atwood had not, thus far, had any direct dealings with members of the drug cartel. But he knew who they were, and he anticipated that they would reach out to him, sooner or later. The thought made him nervous.

Atwood also feared that his own role in trying to frame Larry Mabry might come to light. At first, it had seemed a brilliant idea to swipe Mabry's trumpet from the crime scene, smash it, smother it with Vaseline and some of Gino's blood, and return it to the jazz club where Gino said he found it.

But for some reason, this had not been enough to justify holding Mabry. Yet another example of growing favoritism towards Blacks.

Atwood also fretted that Gardenia's murder would accelerate the Internal Affairs investigation. He had already been summoned by Fred Vinson for an interview, twice. A poker-faced guy. Not easy to figure out. Did he have a weak spot? Could Atwood call in a favor? If so, from whom?

The best strategy, he concluded, was to lie low for a while and to assume that he was under constant surveillance. That meant no visits to the locker where Gino kept the cash. It also meant that he and Frenchy Frobisher should limit their conversations to calls where they were partnered up. Anything else might look suspicious.

Frenchy was the best partner to have. He didn't put up with any bullshit from Stilton, Internal Affairs, or anyone else. He knew how to turn a negative into a positive, like the time he got decorated for a drug bust that never took place. Suspected of being soft on drugs, Frenchy had placed an old drug stash in a warehouse, called 911, fired a few shots, got rid of the gun, and came out smelling like a rose.

Frenchy was a stand-up guy. Atwood was proud to call him a friend.

* * *

If Frenchy had chosen a partner in crime, it would not have been Atwood. He was a hothead who took unnecessary risks. He created unnecessary complications. He didn't think straight. Sometimes he didn't think at all.

The basic problem was that Atwood was consumed by hatred. Hatred of Blacks. Hatred of gays. Hatred of women. Often, that hatred got in the way of their mutual goals.

Atwood drew attention to himself. And, in the process, he might draw attention to their shakedown scheme. Not a good thing.

Why Gardenia stood up for the guy was a mystery. Other officers were more sensible. Other officers were more intelligent.

Maybe it was because Atwood had one good quality: loyalty. If they were suspected, or caught, Atwood would clam up and stay that way. In a crisis, that was definitely a good thing.

As Frenchy thought about the situation, he needed to get access to Gary Mabry's apartment. And fast. The word was that Gary had kept a list of payoffs to members of the PBP, most likely including Frenchy himself. If so, he needed to get that list before Radic did.

Amazingly, Stilton was dragging his feet on giving Radic access to the apartment. Internal Affairs was gumming up the works. For once, Internal Affairs was doing him a favor. But he needed to get that document, or his career was over.

Would Atwood agree to do it? Definitely. But would he do it correctly? If not, who else might burglarize the apartment? A snitch? A druggie? As he considered the options, Frenchy realized that he needed a special person to carry out this assignment. Someone like Khalif. Smart, cool, level-headed.

He also needed to figure out how to connect with Menendez. His regular phone number wasn't working, and the backup number wasn't working either. Eventually, he would surface. And when he did, Frenchy had a couple of ideas to run up the flagpole. One of them was boats. He knew for a fact that river vessels were seldom searched for drugs, especially at night. Another was schools. With school resource officers being fired, schools were more porous than ever. With Gino gone, Frenchy was ready to step up to the plate.

* * *

Altoona had not been Menendez's first choice for a hideout, but a trip to Altoona was far safer than a trip to Mexico. Flights to and from Mexico City drew extra attention from the authorities. In contrast, the car ride from Pittsburgh to Altoona had been downright boring. In a good way.

Menendez was tempted to return to Pittsburgh soon. He didn't like the idea of leaving eight hundred thousand dollars in cash in an unattended locker. In principle, no one knew which locker was his. But if the police chose to open all of them, he was out a small fortune.

Also, with Gardenia and Mabry out of the picture, it was his job to rebuild the network that linked the cartel to Pittsburgh's drug community. That Frenchy guy might be a good place to start. He had cojones. But where to meet? Another gym, perhaps. Or maybe a boat. With Pittsburgh's three rivers, you had lots of options. If he rebuilt the network successfully, his return to Mexico City would be triumphant. If he didn't, he could face the same fate as Gary Mabry.

Mabry's death was a mystery to him and needed to be investigated. Mabry was getting to be a liability. No great loss. But when a drug dealer dies on your patch, and you don't know who the fuck did it, that's not a good thing.

Menendez pulled into a cantina not far from Route 22. He ordered a Dos Equis with lime and the enchilada plate. He would go underground for a week or two. He needed time to think. He made a mental checklist: a new phone, a new gun, a new apartment.

Chapter Twenty-Nine: When It Rains, It Pours

Mrs. Radic smelled peanut butter. Burnt peanut butter. Not the kind you'd want to spread on your toast.

She looked at the clock, which said 2:23 a.m. Ugh! Then she turned towards her husband. But he wasn't there.

"Bert? Bert?" she cried. Donning a nightgown, she scampered down the steps in her bare feet. The smell was getting stronger, and she saw smoke in the kitchen.

"Bert? Bert?' She found him in the living room, watching television. Except the set wasn't on.

She raced into the kitchen, where the stovetop was on fire. Apparently, Bert had left the burner on and deposited a half-eaten peanut butter sandwich on it.

Thinking quickly, Mrs. Radic grabbed the fire extinguisher from the closet and started spraying. Luckily, the fire had not progressed beyond the stove, and she was able to put it out after several strong blasts. But the stove was a mess, and the kitchen reeked.

Mrs. Radic peeked into the living room again. Bert was still there, blissfully unaware of what was going on.

Returning to the kitchen, Mrs. Radic picked up the landline and dialed her son. "Branko, you'd better come out here. We've had a fire in the kitchen. No, I put it out. But I'm worried about your father. I hate to say it, but I think we need a new game plan."

* * *

It took Radic all of five minutes to get dressed and out the door. He grabbed a sheaf of papers he was supposed to read for the Mabry case, in case he wound up staying a while. Luckily, Ralph was at Lexie's apartment for a couple of days, so he didn't have to worry about that.

As Radic drove to his boyhood home in the dark, with almost no traffic, he felt glum but calm. Truthfully, he had anticipated something like this. Clearly, his father needed more care than his mother could provide. A memory care unit was the logical solution.

The key question was whether his mother should uproot herself and follow his father. If she wished, she could live in a different wing of the same facility. Alternatively, she could remain at home and visit her husband daily.

Knowing his mother, Radic feared that she would feel obligated to follow his father, even though she was still in excellent shape, mentally and physically. A noble impulse, for sure. But it could mean sacrificing her friends, her familiar routines, and her freedom.

After thinking it over, Radic decided to argue that his mother should stay put. She shouldn't feel guilty or disloyal. In fact, Bert would want it that way if he were truly able to weigh in.

When Radic pulled into the family driveway at about 3:30 a.m., he found his mother sitting on the front porch. She rose and gave him a hug.

On entering his parents' home, Radic gagged at the stench. "Let's open some windows, Mom," he suggested. Which they did. "Where's Dad?" His mother nodded towards the living room.

Radic found his father sitting in his favorite chair, watching an empty television screen. "How's it going, Dad?" His father smiled, but said nothing.

"Were you watching TV, Dad?"

Still, his father said nothing.

"I think we need to take Dad to the ER, Mom," he suggested. "Let me check and make sure things are okay in the kitchen. Then we can go together."

Bert Radic was compliant all the way to the hospital and inside the

Emergency Room. Over the course of a half hour, he said exactly two words: Pirates. Losers.

Well, Radic thought, his father hadn't totally lost his memory.

But Radic had never seen his father in such a catatonic state. In fact, that was his unofficial diagnosis. Catatonia. Unable to speak, disinclined to move. The symptoms seemed to fit.

The doctor at the Emergency Department was kind, gentle, and competent. He ordered a CT scan and escorted Mr. Radic into a nearby room, where a staff member conducted the procedure. Meanwhile, the doctor spoke with Mrs. Radic and her son.

"How long has he been like this, Mrs. Radic?"

"He's had some memory issues for well over a year now," she said. "He sometimes wanders off on his own. But this is the worst he's been. He nearly burned the house down, making a sandwich and leaving it on top of a heated stove. He's been watching an empty television screen. And he's hardly said a word since all of this occurred."

The physician nodded. "Is he on any medication?"

"He's on an anti-amyloid drug. Lecanemab."

"So he's been diagnosed with Alzheimer's?"

"Early stage."

"Any other drugs?"

"Anti-depressants."

"Which ones?"

"They started him on citalopram. Then they switched to sertraline after he started acting funny."

"Who's his physician?"

"Do you want the name of his GP? Or the specialist who's been seeing him?"

"Both." Mrs. Radic gave him the names, from memory.

"Has he ever had a CT scan before? If we have a baseline image, we can see if there's been any change in the brain."

"You mean like shrinkage?"

"I didn't want to say that, but yes."

"There was a CT scan when Bert was shaken up in a car accident a few years ago. I have the details at home."

"Was there a concussion?"

"Yes. Grade 2."

"Do you remember if the CT scan was done here?"

"I believe it was."

"And the doctor?"

"Dr. Takota."

"Great! We should have it on file. You've been a big help."

As Radic listened to the conversation, he was impressed by his mother's composure and recall. She was clearly on top of the situation, the old situation at least. But this was a new ballgame. Unless the doctors could perform a miracle, his father was now in need of full-time care.

After a preliminary exam, the physician suggested that they keep Mr. Radic in a private holding area until around 8:00 a.m., when a neurologist was scheduled to begin his shift. The neurologist was the best choice to interpret the CT scan, he explained. He invited Radic and his mother to go home or to stay, as they wished. They chose to stay.

Radic headed to the cafeteria, while his mother got Bert through the processing. When Radic returned with two cups of coffee and four Krispy Kreme doughnuts, his father was said to be resting comfortably. He and his mother found chairs nearby. After two bites of a doughnut, his mother nodded off, while Radic turned to his paperwork. Maybe he could conjure up a fresh perspective on his two murder cases, in this quiet setting, in his hometown, with his mother at his side.

His first thought was that he needed more evidence—evidence that was not in either of his two case files. The missing clues he needed would require better access, better sources, and better information than he had thus far. He blamed himself for some of that. Truthfully, though, his bosses were creating unnecessary obstacles. That would have to change.

To make real progress, it seemed, he needed to make one of the two cases a priority. But which one? His instincts tugged him strongly towards the Mabry case, but he worried that his frosty relationship with Gardenia might be clouding his judgment. He wanted to be fair to Gino, whatever their personal differences.

Maybe it wasn't a question of choosing between the two cases after all. Perhaps it was a matter of knowing where to look for fresh evidence on both cases. And the answer to that question seemed crystal clear—Gary Mabry was the key. If he could understand Gary Mabry better, he might figure out what drew Gardenia to the North Side warehouse and what drew Spider-Man to Mellon Park. At least it was worth a shot.

With that much established, Radic glanced at his mother and decided to follow her example. Tomorrow would be a long day. He put down his case files and tried to get some sleep.

Chapter Thirty: Radic Blows a Fuse

Returning to work after a day off was always the pits. It wasn't just the backlog of meetings, conversations, and paperwork. It required extra effort to be compliant, tolerant, stoic, and understanding, after inhabiting a world where, for the most part, you could be yourself. On days like this, Radic felt like an actor who had forgotten his lines.

When Radic first proposed a search of Gary's apartment, he imagined that he would simply get a key from Larry or Mrs. Mabry. Stilton scotched that idea, saying that he needed time to think through the implications. Internal Affairs would need to be consulted. For the time being, Gary's apartment was off limits.

It soon became clear to Radic that Stilton was caught in a squeeze play between his own Homicide Division and Internal Affairs. In trying to straddle the fence, he was inadvertently hampering both murder investigations.

Radic reluctantly conceded that Internal Affairs had some justification in lobbying for simultaneous access to Gardenia's home. Internal Affairs had been pursuing Gardenia for two and a half years. They might be close to suspending or even indicting two police officers. Also, the joint search had not been the disaster he expected.

But Gary Mabry's murder was different. Although Radic was less inclined than Mulroy to believe that a fellow police officer was responsible for Gary's death, it was a possibility. All the more reason for Radic to visit the apartment soon, before another officer got there.

Once the search was done, Internal Affairs might well make a claim to see some of the evidence. But the search was needed now, and it should be a Homicide search, not another joint search with restrictive ground rules.

Perplexed and irritated, Radic decided to seek out Fred Vinson from Internal Affairs, who, he suspected, was the root of the problem. When he reached Vinson by phone, he found him to be even less forthcoming than Stilton. After some prodding, Vinson conceded that Internal Affairs was fighting his request. In fact, they were even opposed to a joint visit. They wanted sole access to Gary's apartment, in case it contained evidence of Gary's dealings with cops under investigation.

Radic blew a fuse. "How the hell am I supposed to conduct a homicide investigation unless I have access to the victim's apartment? I'm being asked to find a murderer with one hand tied behind my back."

"I sympathize, but you've read our report. We can't allow you or anyone else to compromise our investigation into Gardenia and other members of the police force."

"And who are these other members of the police force?"

"I'm afraid I can't reveal that. It's too sensitive."

"Well, how's this for sensitive? One of those police officers might have killed Gary Mabry. You and I both know that Gary upset their applecart. That's a motive for murder. I need to know who those police officers are. And I need to know about any communications Gary had that might be relevant to his murder."

"I'm sorry, but I just can't tell you anything more than what you read in the report. Even that was a heavy lift. We don't usually share that stuff with detectives outside of Internal Affairs."

Radic hung up the phone without saying goodbye.

Normally, he believed in counting to ten before storming into a superior's office. But this no longer felt like a normal situation.

Radic knocked on Stilton's door and didn't wait for the traditional "come in" to step across the threshold. "I need to see Gary Mabry's apartment. Now."

Stilton sighed and motioned to Radic to take a seat.

"I've been working on this, Radic, believe me. We're almost there. I've proposed a joint search like the Gardenia search. I expect to get the Chief's approval any day now. Until that happens, you need to focus on other aspects of your investigation."

"Without access to Gary's apartment, there *is* no Gary Mabry investigation. Surely, you understand that, sir?"

"Well, I do. But Internal Affairs also has a legitimate interest in Mabry's apartment."

"A homicide should trump an internal affairs investigation."

"Perhaps. But the internal affairs investigation is big. And it could get ugly fast."

"If you want to see what gets ugly fast, just wait and see what happens if we make no progress in finding Gary Mabry's killer. The Black community is tired of hearing that there's no progress on the case. The Mabry family is tired of hearing that there's no progress on the case. I'm tired of making no progress on the case. You're not keeping your promises to me when I agreed to take this assignment."

Radic exited before Stilton could come up with a snappy retort. A few minutes later, in a calmer mood, he considered circumventing Stilton. If asked, Larry would give him access to Gary's apartment. But Larry had enough legal problems without being saddled with that burden. And Radic was reluctant to cross that line himself.

Maybe a conversation with Larry, in lieu of an actual visit? Or maybe Larry could do a reconnaissance mission himself. That was worth considering. Then he thought of another possibility. According to Larry, Gary was going to spill the beans to someone on the *Post-Gazette*. Was he able to do that before he died?

Radic placed a call. "I'd like to speak with Evan Kobosky."

* * *

Radic and Kobosky agreed to meet for lunch at the Porch in Oakland, far enough away from police headquarters and from the *Post-Gazette* building downtown that they would not be noticed.

Radic arrived early enough to enjoy the squeals and giggles of preschoolers riding the carousel in Schenley Plaza. Now that it was May and the weather was nice, the carousel was open for business again.

Kobosky, an investigative reporter for the *Post-Gazette*, arrived on time and greeted Radic cordially. After the two ordered sandwiches and drinks, Kobosky began the conversation. "Usually, I'm the one calling you, Detective. To what do I owe this honor?"

"I'm investigating the murder of Gino Gardenia. And I'm also investigating the murder of Gary Mabry."

Kobosky shook his head in sympathy. "Don't they have any other homicide detectives? That's a lot to put on one person's plate."

"Well, I'm not alone. Mulroy and Scuglia are both working on the case with me."

"Pleased to hear it. You and Mulroy worked really well together on the Carol Sloan case. And Scuglia's terrific. Smart, honest. So, how can I help you?"

"It's my understanding that Gary Mabry intended to meet with you before he died. Did that meeting take place?"

"Yes, we did meet. The day before he died."

"Did he give you enough material for a story?"

"I believe so."

"Do you have a publication date in mind?"

"That will be up to my editor. It could be as early as next week. We're still double-checking the specifics."

"Okay, let me cut to the chase. Did Gary accuse any members of the police force of having committed extortion?"

Kobosky laughed. "You don't mince words, Detective. The answer is, yes, he did."

"Can you tell me which officers?"

Kobosky grew serious. "I have a concern about answering your question. Confidentiality."

"Your source is dead. You have no ethical obligations to a dead source, do you?"

"Yes and no. When sensitive information is revealed, live sources may be suspected of disclosing the information that in fact came from a dead source. I think of that as an ethical problem. The truth is, I'm still verifying the information I've received. Which is perhaps where you come in. As I see it, we can help each other here. I'm willing to give you some names before the story is published, if you're willing to help me get the facts straight."

Radic scratched his chin. "Well, you're not the only one with an ethical dilemma. I have access to information from an Internal Affairs report. I can't share any of that with you. On the other hand, I've also gained information from other sources relevant to both murders. That's more of a gray area. Normally, I wouldn't divulge any of that to you or any other reporter. But, under the circumstances, I might be amenable to a little quid pro quo."

"What are the circumstances as you see them?"

"The circumstances are that we're still struggling to find out who committed the two murders, and we're running out of time. The community is a powder keg."

"Okay, I think I get the picture. So, you'd like me to tell you which cops Gary accused of extorting drug money."

"That's right."

"And I'd like you to tell me whether Gary Mabry was truly out of the game."

Radic laughed, nervously. "You're not making this easy for me."

"Well, Detective, you're not making this easy for me either. If I tell you which cops are under suspicion and you disclose that information to someone who leaks it to one of them, where does that leave me? At best, I might lose a scoop. At worst, they might target me. It's been known to happen."

Radic made a quick decision. "Okay, I'll tell you what I know. Gary wanted out for nearly two years. He was no longer using drugs. And he was no longer selling drugs."

"Are you sure?"

"There were no secrets between Gary and his brother, Larry. According to Larry, Gary was no longer selling drugs, and he was no longer making payments to members of the PBP."

"You've been helpful, Detective. So, here's what I can tell you: Two cops were directly involved in the shake-down. Gino Gardenia and Frenchy Frobisher. A third cop acted as bag man from time to time: Mark Atwood."

"That's pretty much what I thought. Did Gary supply any hard evidence?"

"Yes, he did."

"What type of evidence?"

"A comprehensive list of payments. In writing."

"Were the payments in cash?"

"Totally in cash."

"So his word against theirs."

"Well, not exactly."

"How so?"

"Because he had audio recordings of several meetings."

"Incriminating?"

"Very much so."

"And the audio recordings?"

"I have them."

"I hope they're under lock and key."

"They're in the darkest corner of the deepest vault we have at the *Post-Gazette*, with lots of mousetraps protecting them."

"That's a big story."

"Very big."

"But two killers are still on the loose."

"I hope you find them, Detective. I don't scare easily, but I saw photos of Gardenia after he was murdered. Anyone who would kill someone that brutally…well, let's just say I wouldn't want to meet him in a dark alley."

The two men got up to leave.

"One more question," Radic said. "Did Gary ever mention Jorge Menendez?"

"From the cartel? Yes, he did."

"Do you know how he felt about Gary's decision to turn over a new leaf?"

"He didn't seem to be concerned."

"I'm surprised."

"Don't be. Gary already named a successor."

"And who would that be?"

"Khalif Wilson."

"Gary's Mr. Fix-It. His right-hand man."

"No longer. Khalif is now the leading drug lord in the city of Pittsburgh."

Chapter Thirty-One: The Other Side of the Tracks

T he mayor's home was easy for Radic to spot. He and his wife, Cecile Arceneaux, lived in a charming old mansion in a chic Shadyside neighborhood. The entrance featured freshly painted Doric columns, fronted by two stone griffins. An octagon-shaped gazebo, off to the side, seemed straight out of a storybook.

Though the setting was immaculate in most respects, there was ample evidence of young children. A child's bicycle lay abandoned on the front lawn, next to a battered scooter. A three-foot-tall plastic clown bobbed gently in the wind, waiting to be punched.

Cecile answered the door herself and escorted Radic into a cozy sitting room, next to a spacious dining room, with place settings for an upcoming event. The distinction between public and private space must be very blurry for this family, Radic thought.

Although Radic had seen the Mayor's wife on the evening news, he had never seen her in person. She was a stunningly beautiful woman, with tanned skin, seductive brown eyes, and a warm smile.

She was dressed elegantly but casually, in grey slacks and a Kelly-green blouse that complemented a teal barrette in her thick black hair. If she had not become a public interest lawyer, she could have been a model.

Despite the smile, Radic sensed that Arceneaux was not fully at ease. Her perfect *Elle* magazine eyes were slightly puffy. Perhaps she had been crying. "Ms. Arceneaux, thank you for agreeing to meet with me."

"Please, call me Ceci."

"Okay…Ceci…we're investigating Gary Mabry's death, and we've been told that you knew him."

"You'll have to forgive me, Detective. I'm still processing Gary's death. It came as a shock. And it's going to take me a while to get over it."

"How did you first meet Gary?"

"Well, I'm prepared to tell you, but much of what I have to say is very personal. Can I count on your discretion?"

Radic thought for a moment. "If it relates to the murder, I can't make any promises. But if it relates to you and you only, I see no need to share that information."

"I think I can live with that, Detective. I'm already in a goldfish bowl anyway. But even a politician's wife is entitled to some privacy and, yes, some secrets."

"Agreed."

"Okay, I need to turn back the clock a bit, to set the stage."

"Of course."

"I've been pretty healthy, for most of my life. But in 2018, I experienced some severe stomach pain. At first, I thought, okay, I've been working too hard. Trying to be a full-time lawyer, a full-time wife, and a full-time mom. You know the drill. I tried to take it easy. But the pain didn't go away. So I went to see a local doctor.

"He didn't come up with much. He ruled out a few things: an ulcer, gallstones, kidney stones. And he said that my red blood cell count was low. So, for about a year, I took a drug that's supposed to improve your red blood cell count. Maybe it helped. Maybe it didn't. In any event, I stopped thinking about it.

"Then about a year later, I felt the same kind of stomach pain, but even more intense. I had to take off work. This time, my husband convinced me to go to a fancy clinic, out of town. Meanwhile, this was really bad timing. Walt was on the city council and running for mayor. I was six months pregnant with our second child. I was still practicing law full-time. When it rains, it pours.

"Anyway, I went to this clinic and met with two or three physicians. The team's first thought was cancer. They weren't sure what kind. Maybe Hodgkin's Lymphoma. This scared me to death. I was thirty-two years old and pregnant. Surely, this couldn't be true. They took biopsies of different organs, and came up with nothing. They gave me some medicine to reduce the pain. I returned home, dejected and afraid.

"Jenny was born a month later, six weeks early. She was only five pounds. She had to be placed on a respirator. I felt so guilty, like it was my fault. Walt was very supportive and optimistic. He said everything's gonna be fine. You'll see. She'll be breathing on her own soon. She'll be released from the hospital soon. She'll be breastfeeding soon. And, you know, he was right.

"For the first several months after Jenny was born, I almost forgot about my pain. And objectively, I think the pain subsided for a while. My hormones worked some magic that the medicine couldn't.

"But then, two years ago, the pain returned with a vengeance. That's when I went to see a different local doctor. He asked to see the reports from all the other physicians. And then he asked me a simple question: What can you tell me about your parents? I told him they were from Louisiana and the Caribbean Islands. Then he asked me about my grandparents and my great-grandparents.

"The local doc did some tests and sat me down a few days later. He asked Walt to be there. He said, Cecile, I believe you have sickle cell anemia.

"Sickle cell anemia? I asked him. I thought that was only for Black people.

"He said, I'm guessing that you have some African ancestors on both sides of your family. It would be easy enough to check that out. But the test results are pretty clear. Whatever your ancestry, you have the disease.

"So, I asked him, what's the cure? What should I do? And that's when I learned the grim truth: there is no cure. At least not for me. If you have a healthy sibling with a compatible blood type, a blood marrow transplant is a possibility. But if you don't, you're out of luck. I have a couple of cousins, but for X, Y, and Z reasons, they're not good donors, at least not for me.

"This was really hard to take. But the doc was very understanding. He said:

We can't cure sickle cell just yet, *but* we can reduce your pain dramatically, with regular blood transfusions.

"The catch is that sickle cell sufferers need big transfusions. My blood type is kind of problematic. O negative. If you're O negative, you can only receive blood from other O negatives. And this was during COVID. Blood banks were running low, and doctors were busy dealing with COVID emergencies. My life was becoming a nightmare.

"I went to the blood bank one day, and that's where I met Gary. I thought he was another patient. We stepped outside, to avoid wearing masks for a while. I started pouring my heart out. And he was very understanding. It turns out he wasn't a patient, he was a donor. A really good donor, an O-negative, whose blood can be used by anyone, including me. Gary told me that he was very aware of sickle cell anemia, that it targeted people of color, and he promised to get me the blood I needed.

"I don't know why, but I believed him. And, you know what, a week later, he called me up and said, Ceci, I was able to round up six people with O negative blood, and they've all agreed to donate blood next week. Gary was a lifesaver. Literally.

"I can't tell you what a difference those transfusions made. It was like a miracle cure. They provided instant relief. Of course, I have to go in for blood transfusions every six weeks. But Gary had my back. He organized a donors' group specifically for people who suffer from sickle cell anemia in the Pittsburgh area. I no longer have to worry about where my next transfusion is coming from.

Radic, who had been paying rapt attention, saw an opportunity to learn more. "Who are the donors, if you don't mind my asking?"

"Most of them are from Gary's church. St. Martin de Porres. Most of them are Black."

"Did you ever trace your ancestry?"

"Yes, and it was a revelation. I have African blood on both sides. All told, I'm probably about twelve percent Black."

This piqued Radic's curiosity. "Has this changed your self-image?"

"Well, I always suspected that I had a Black ancestor on my mother's side.

Her parents were from Haiti. My father's side was more of a surprise. And the total percentage was surprising."

"Is this something you've thought about going public with?"

"Walt and I have talked about it. The political consequences, that is. We see it as a potential positive or a potential negative, depending on how it's framed and who does the framing. We've decided that it wouldn't be wise in the middle of his re-election campaign. But after that, under the right circumstances, yeah, we might hold a press conference at some point. It's nothing to be ashamed of. In fact, it's something to be celebrated."

"Getting back to Gary, did you keep in touch with him, after the initial meeting?"

"Of course! Gary and I became good friends. I learned that Gary had his own struggles. He had been a heavy drug user. Cocaine. Crack cocaine. Fentanyl. Dating back to when his Dad died. It was pretty brutal. But he was on the mend. He was turning his life around. I was very proud of him."

"Did you recommend him for your husband's Drug Task Force?"

"Yes, I did. It was an easy call. Gary knew all about drugs, and he could relate to kids, especially Black kids. In a school auditorium, he was absolutely spell-binding. He could have been a politician! Well, in a way, he was a politician. He had a gift."

"Did you know that he was a drug dealer?"

"Not at first. But maybe I suspected it. And, after we became friends, Gary himself told me about it. He was tough on himself. Ashamed. Embarrassed. But he was determined to make lemonade out of lemons. He was determined to use his street knowledge to do some good. Have you ever met a reformed alcoholic? Or a reformed smoker? Sometimes they're the toughest critics of addictive behavior. That's how it was with Gary."

"Did you know about Gary's drug dealing when you first suggested him for the task force?"

"In all honesty, no, I didn't. But was it the right decision? You betcha! Anyone on the task force will tell you that Gary was a mover and a shaker. A natural-born leader. He did more to curb drug abuse in Pittsburgh than anyone else on the task force, with the exception of the director."

"Has Gary been active in your husband's re-election campaign?"

"Yes, he has. Or … was. It was his idea. Not mine. But, naturally, I was thrilled! And my husband is appreciative, very appreciative. We're both in mourning over Gary's death. And very eager to bring his killer to justice."

As Radic reached his car and prepared to leave, another car pulled up. He watched as a mayoral aide brought six-year-old Jenny Graham home. With a glint in her eyes, Jenny raced to the front door, where Ceci awaited her. She jumped into her mother's outstretched arms and gave her a big hug.

Chapter Thirty-Two: A Royal Sendoff

St. Martin de Porres Catholic Church was packed. The smell of incense signaled a solemn Mass. In the front row sat Ernestine Mabry, Larry Mabry, Larry's daughter Dorothy, and her mother, Wanda. Directly behind them sat Mayor Graham, his wife Ceci, their two children, and a security guard.

The presence of the two Graham children came as a surprise, at least to Radic. He was cynical enough to imagine that a mayor running for re-election would pull out all the stops to pay homage to a prominent Black protest leader. On the other hand, he knew that Ceci's affection for Gary was genuine. The presence of two well-scrubbed young children at a funeral struck Radic as a tangible expression of their mother's special connection to Gary.

Radic noted that Mrs. Mabry was carrying a handkerchief and that Larry was carrying a trumpet.

Larry looked different from the broken man he had observed in a jail cell days earlier. The man he had spoken with then was crushed by his brother's death. The man he observed today was calm and reassuring, comforting those who had still not reconciled themselves to Gary's murder. As Radic thought about it, Larry was accustomed to being on stage, and this was a performance, albeit a very special one. What lay beneath that confident exterior was hard to know. Even for a friend.

Grief was evident elsewhere. Dorothy, sitting next to her mother, was sobbing uncontrollably. She looked a lot like Larry, Radic thought. He would like to meet her someday, when this was all over.

Ceci, who had held it together during their private conversation, was struggling today. Like Dorothy, she seemed devastated by a deep and personal loss.

Father Buckley strode to the pulpit after a few introductory prayers. He was wearing a black chasuble and a violet stole. Somehow, he managed to produce a reassuring smile. A mask, Radic thought. According to informants, Father Buckley and Gary had been very close.

"It's often been said that Jesus loved sinners," Father Buckley began. "Gary Mabry would have been the first to admit that he was a sinner. He made many mistakes in his short life, some of them doozies.

"But Gary believed in the possibility of redemption, just as Jesus did. When Gary decided to leave the path of sin behind him, he broke with his past in a big way. He donated blood and convinced hundreds of members of our community to do the same. He got involved in politics, recognizing that there is a lot for us to do here on earth before we receive our eternal reward in heaven. He fought for social justice, including the release from incarceration of persons falsely accused of a crime. He practiced non-violence and did what he could to avoid bloodshed.

"The key to a baseball game is not what happens in the first inning but what happens in the ninth inning. When you think of Gary, I hope you will remember the difficulties he had and the mistakes he made in the early innings of his adult life. But I hope you will also remember the deep reservoir of goodwill and compassion that marked the final innings of his life.

"I see before me this morning Gary's beloved mother, Ernestine, his beloved brother, Larry, and his beloved niece, Dorothy. To them, I want to say this: You can be proud of your son, your brother, your uncle. You can be *very* proud of him. He was a good man who made some mistakes. He was like St. Paul—a sinner who became a saint."

A flamboyantly dressed Black woman whom Radic recognized from one of Larry's gigs, Geraldine Clark, stood up and strode to the pulpit. She wore a black skirt, a flowery blouse, and a black beret with lace. She nodded to Wade Newborn at the piano, who played a few bluesy chords to cue her up.

What a friend we have in Jesus, all our sins and grief to bear.
What a privilege to carry everything to God in prayer.
Oh what peace we often forfeit, oh what needless pain we bear.
All because we do not carry everything to God in prayer.

In the back of the church, two dozen high school musicians stood up, their instruments at the ready. Larry walked down the aisle and joined them. He smiled and played a trumpet fanfare reminiscent of Louis Armstrong at his best.

Then two tubas joined in, followed by three trombones. Next, the rhythm section kicked in: a bass drum, a snare drum, and cymbals. Finally, three saxophonists started playing. The students swayed to the music and exited the church, pausing at the bottom of the steps. Slowly and with dignity, several pallbearers placed Gary's coffin in a hearse. Ernestine Mabry, Wanda, and Dorothy found seats in the car just behind. The mayor's family squeezed into the next car.

As the cavalcade moved slowly down the city streets, the band marched right behind, not dutifully but joyously. With Larry coaxing them, the young musicians did their best to sound like barnyard animals who were having a grand old time.

Occasionally, Larry used his trumpet to quiz his young proteges in a "call and response" fashion.

Sensing the mood, neighbors who gathered along the streets stomped their feet and clapped their hands, swaying to the music. Some joined in the parade, following Larry the Pied Piper.

An hour later, the entourage arrived at Homewood Cemetery, where a grave awaited them. Father Buckley presided over a short, simple burial service. Dorothy placed a rose on the coffin. Ernestine said a final prayer.

As the ceremony concluded, Larry joined Geraldine for a duet. Radic recognized the tune even before he heard the words.

Goin' home. Goin' home. I'm-a-goin' home.
Quiet-like, some still day. I'm just goin' home.

It's not far, just close by, through an open door.
Work all done, cares laid by, goin' to roam no more.

Chapter Thirty-Three: The Big Apple Comes Calling

Larry wasn't sure how his mother would take the news, so he decided to deliver it himself, in person.

He found his mother fixing breakfast.

"No bacon?"

"Dr. Taylor says I need to cut back."

"Sounds like a spoilsport. Didn't he tell you to cut back on sweets, too?"

"That's for my diabetes. This is for my cholesterol."

"I don't know, Ma. I want you to live to be one hundred. But I also want you to *live*. Breakfast without bacon, I'm not sure that's living."

"Don't you worry about that. What brings you here, Larry? Is it something to do with Gary?"

"No, Ma, not really. It's some good news. I got a gig in New York City."

"That's wonderful, Larry. For this weekend?"

"No, it's even better than that. Six nights at the Village Vanguard. For me, that's the rough equivalent of playing at Carnegie Hall. Plus three more weeks in other clubs. One month."

"An entire month?"

"Yep, I'm going to be pinch-hitting for Happy Harlow. He just got sick and is going to be laid up for a few weeks. He recommended me as his replacement."

"What an honor, Larry. I'm so happy for you. This is what you've always dreamed of."

"I know, Ma. But I feel bad about the timing. I know you have a lot on your plate."

"But you'll be back and forth, won't you?"

"I can try, Ma, but it's one gig after another. I'm gonna be there most of the time."

"Oh."

"We can talk by phone if stuff comes up. I'm not going to the moon."

'I know, I know. But don't you have things to do, as executor of Gary's estate?"

"Well, here's the thing, Ma. I'm not sure I want to be executor of Gary's estate."

Ernestine Mabry said nothing for a moment. "Why not?"

"I think you know why not."

"Yes, I guess I do."

"It's a tricky business. Gary made a lot of money. A lot of money. And every penny of it came from selling drugs."

"We've talked about this, Larry. You know I feel the same way. But why not give it to charity?"

"Well, that's pretty much what Gary had in mind."

"So, what's the problem?"

"Well, it's his choice of charities that has me losing sleep at night."

Larry reached into his pocket and showed his mother the list. She read it carefully and put it down.

"Has Father Buckley seen the list?"

Larry shook his head. "I don't think so."

"Wanda?"

Larry shook his head again.

"What are you going to do?"

"That's just it, Ma. I don't know what to do."

"There's a trust fund. For Dorothy."

Larry said nothing.

"Are you going to approve it?"

"I don't know, Ma. What should I do?"

"It's blood money."

"I know."

"But it's for your daughter."

"I know."

"I don't think I can be objective about this. And I have too much going on over the next few weeks. I'm thinking of saying no to the executor thing."

"Can you do that?"

"Yes."

"If you don't do it, who does?"

Larry said nothing.

"Oh, no. Not me."

"You're next on the list, Ma."

"No, I can't. I just wouldn't feel right about it."

"Well, then it goes to the third person on the list."

"Who's that?"

"Father Buckley."

"Do you think he'll agree?"

"Maybe. We can ask him."

"That might be for the best."

"Of course, he has a conflict of interest, too."

"St. Martin de Porres is on the list. I saw."

"But he's a good man. He'll know what to do."

"I agree."

"Why not right now? We can go to the rectory together."

* * *

"Ernestine? Larry? This is a pleasant surprise. Would you like to join me for breakfast? I was about to fix some bacon and eggs."

Larry laughed. "I'm up for it, Father. But you may have to twist Mama's arm."

"Oh, for pity's sake. I'm not supposed to be eating bacon. But it's not a mortal sin if I have a slice or two, is it, Father?"

"Not the last time I checked."

"Then let's sit down together and have some breakfast."

The rectory hadn't changed much since Larry's last visit a few years ago. A statue of St. Martin de Porres in the vestibule, a simple crucifix in the kitchen. The adjacent dining room featured a larger crucifix and paintings of several saints.

A "SHRINE" sign beckoned Larry to a room down the hall. Excusing himself, he walked that way and peeked in. The "shrine" included a Terrible Towel, two autographed footballs, and photos of the "Immaculate Reception" when Steelers running back Franco Harris scored an improbable touchdown to win a key playoff game in December 1972. Larry laughed heartily and returned to the kitchen, comforted by the presence of some secular talismans in the rectory.

As Father Buckley rummaged for a skillet, orange juice, and food, Ernestine and Larry thanked him again for an amazing memorial service.

"When it comes to funerals, Father, you have perfect pitch," Larry said.

"Coming from you, Larry, that's a very fine compliment. And let me return the compliment. You did a wonderful job with the marching band. For a while there, I thought that I was back in New Orleans, where I grew up. It was magical."

The Mabrys and Father Buckley chatted about Gary and the funeral for the few minutes it took to put breakfast on the table.

"So, what brings you here today, folks?"

"Actually, Father, we'd like to talk with you about Gary's will," Larry said. Larry pulled out a piece of paper.

"I already know about the will."

"You do?"

"Gary talked with me about it. And he gave me a notarized copy. Just in case."

"What do you think about it?"

"Well, forgive me, but let me ask you the same question. What do *you* think about it?"

When neither Ernestine nor Larry spoke up, Father Buckley intervened.

"Gary anticipated that you might have some problems with it."

"He did?"

Father Buckley nodded. "Let me try to put it into words. Gary knew you loved him. Both of you. But he also knew you strongly disapproved of how he made a living. He knew you had big reservations about the money he made from selling drugs. He knew you didn't want to think about it or be associated with it. And he knew you might not want to inherit it."

"That's about the size of it."

"So when making out his will, Gary focused on some organizations that he really cared about. The Red Cross. Westinghouse High School. St. Martin de Porres. Do you have any problems with those bequests?"

"Well, yes and no," Larry said. "I'm fine with giving money to the Westinghouse High School Band. I'm not fine with calling it the Larry Mabry Scholarship Fund."

"And you, Ernestine?"

"I'm fine with giving money to St. Martin de Porres. I'm not fine with naming the restoration fund after me."

"How about the contribution to the Mayor's political action committee? Is that even legal?" Larry asked.

"I have no idea," Father Buckley replied.

"I asked my lawyer," Larry continued. "She says it's highly unusual. And it's a huge chunk of change. Nearly a million dollars. It may be contested."

"I understand. And the trust fund for Dorothy?"

"What am I supposed to think about that, Father? I want to help my baby girl in any way I can. But how can I explain to her that she gets enough money to go to a nice college and buy herself a nice home, but the money came from drugs that wound up killing young kids not much older than herself?"

"I understand your feelings. Truly, I do. You're the executor of Gary's estate. What do you propose to do about it?"

"I just can't do it, Father. I'm going to step down."

Father Buckley nodded.

"And you, Ernestine? You're next on the list."

"I can't do it either, Father."

Father Buckley nodded.

"I guess that leaves me."

"Are you willing to do it, Father?"

Father Buckley sighed. "This will was very important to Gary. It's about redemption. It's about making things right. I believe that everyone should have a second chance. This is Gary's second chance. So, yes, if I'm the executor, I will approve Gary's wishes exactly as requested."

Chapter Thirty-Four: Reluctant Testimony

The same receptionist who had greeted Mulroy so warmly a few days earlier was downright frosty when Mulroy strolled into Muscle Mania after work. "What can I do for you, De-tec-tive?" she asked, pronouncing "detective" as if it were a four-letter word.

"I'm back for another workout," Mulroy replied, breezily. "I thought I would get myself a locker."

"I believe you know where the lockers are, Detective."

"Well, I know where the regular lockers are, but I understand that you also have special lockers for guests who want to leave a change of clothing here on a more permanent basis."

The receptionist pointed in the direction of the Pilates room.

"Excuse me, but have I done something to offend you?" Mulroy asked.

The receptionist hesitated for a moment. "I'm sorry, Detective, but if you're here on police business, you should speak with Mr. Fielding. Not with me. And not with any of our other guests."

Ouch! Mulroy was getting the message. "Well, I'm sorry you feel that way. I never truly stop being a police officer, I suppose. But I'm mainly here to get some exercise, as I told you the other day. And if I choose to have a conversation with one of your guests, is that really any of your business?"

Knowing that her movements would be watched, Mulroy marched purposefully to the special locker room, where she noticed perhaps three dozen available lockers, out of maybe one hundred and fifty. Written instructions directed her back to the front desk, which left her exasperated.

Time to reboot, she thought to herself. For the next ninety minutes, Mulroy focused on her hamstrings, her thigh muscles, and her glutes. She forgot about Jorge Menendez, Bart Fielding, and Gino Gardenia. As she lost herself in physical exertion, she began to see the glimmer of a plan.

** * **

Having experienced the Deep Freeze at Muscle Mania, Mulroy decided to try a different tack. By googling the Pittsburgh Pirates, she was able to identify her new friend from Muscle Mania, Denise Wishner, a sabermetrics specialist with a master's degree in Computer Science from Carnegie Mellon. She sent her an e-mail, which began with an apology for not having identified herself as a police officer. Might she be free to meet some evening, though not at Muscle Mania?

Denise replied that she would be happy to meet for a drink at the Pirates VIP Club, immediately after Friday night's game. She also offered Mulroy two free tickets, which she cheerfully accepted. She and Jake hadn't attended a game so far this season. It was time to see whether the Pirates' three-game winning streak was a fluke.

Following the game, which the Pirates managed to win, Mulroy introduced Denise to Jake. Knowing the drill, Jake thanked Denise for the tickets, offered her free tickets to Kennywood Park in return, made an excuse, and promptly disappeared.

"You're lucky!" Denise said. "Why don't I ever meet guys like that? How did you meet?"

"It was on a case," Mulroy replied. "Jake helped us to solve a kidnapping."

"Wow! Good-looking, a nice guy, and he solves crimes too!"

Mulroy laughed. "Well, I don't think Jake would claim that he *solved* the case. But he was definitely a big help."

"Does he have any single friends?"

"Let me see what I can do."

Denise ordered a gin and tonic from the bar, while Mulroy requested a glass of white wine. Denise found a corner where they could converse in private.

Denise began before Mulroy could. "I'm not supposed to talk with you, you know."

"How's that?"

"The receptionist at Muscle Mania noticed that we were chatting. She snitched on me. The next time I showed up for a workout, Fielding, her boss, took me aside and told me not to talk with you again. He said you're stirring up trouble."

"Very interesting."

"Of course, that made me want to talk with you even more!"

"Why is that?"

"Because it must be about Menendez."

"It is."

"And Menendez is a creep."

"Tell me again what you know about him."

Denise reiterated that Menendez had made two or three clumsy passes, which she resisted and which led her to lodge a complaint with Fielding when Menendez crossed a line. After that, he left her alone, apart from a scowl or two.

"Do you remember anything specific he said about his background?"

"Well, he has a sports car."

"Did you see it?"

"No, but he wanted me to."

"Any idea what kind?"

"An Alfa Romeo."

"What color?"

"I never saw it. He just told me about it."

"Anything else?"

"He was definitely from Mexico."

"How do you know?"

"Well, he said so."

"Did he say where?"

"Wapaca?"

"Oaxaca?"

"Yeah, that's it."

"Great, this is really helpful. Anything else?"

"Sorry, that's about it. But you might want to talk with Marilyn."

"Who's Marilyn?"

"Another gym rat."

"Why should I talk with her?"

"Because she almost went out on a date with Menendez."

"Almost?"

"Things got a bit squirrely. She changed her mind at the last minute."

"Does she still come to the gym?"

"No, she stopped coming because of him."

"Do you know how I can reach her?"

"I have her number right here."

* * *

Marilyn Vera's first reaction to Mulroy's phone call was to beg off. She had gone to great lengths to distance herself from Jorge Menendez. The last thing she wanted was to get caught in the crosshairs of a dispute between Menendez and the Pittsburgh police.

When Mulroy explained that Menendez had left town and possibly the country, her position softened a bit. She agreed that Mulroy could drop by her apartment later in the day, but only if everything she said would remain confidential. She did not want Menendez to have any reason to track her down.

Marilyn Vera's apartment in South Oakland was a bit shabby on the outside, but tidy and clean on the inside.

Marilyn herself was a striking woman, with dark brown hair, a shapely figure, and lavender rose fingernails that hinted at a recent manicure.

They sat down in the living room, after Mulroy accepted a Diet Coke.

"I appreciate your agreeing to see me. We're very eager to locate Jorge

Menendez, and Denise thought you might be able to help us out."

"Menendez is a scary guy. I must have been crazy to even consider going out on a date with him."

"How did you first meet?"

"At the gym. Muscle Mania. He came over once or twice while I was on the treadmill. He said he was new to Pittsburgh, and he offered to buy me a drink."

"Do you mean a *drink* drink? At a bar?"

"Yeah, that's what he meant. I said no at first. But he was persistent. Eventually, I said he could buy me a smoothie at Muscle Mania."

"How did that go?"

"Well, it was okay. He was kind of charming in a way. But then, when it was time for me to go, he insisted on walking me to my car. And again he tried to convince me to join him at a bar."

"Did you?"

"No, I had to say no several times. Eventually, he got the message, and I went home."

"Did you see him again?"

"Honestly, it was kind of hard not to. He was a regular at the gym. And he kept chatting me up."

"What happened next?"

"He asked me out on a date. Not to a bar but to a baseball game."

"What did you say?"

"Call me a fool. I said yes. I like the Pirates and I thought it might be fun."

"And was it?"

"Well, that's just it. I never went."

"Why not?"

"Because it was bait-and-switch."

"What do you mean?"

"I thought he was taking me to a Pirates game. But it turns out he wanted to take me to Altoona."

"Altoona?"

"To see a minor league baseball team. The Altoona Curve."

"The Curve?"

"As in the Horseshoe Curve. Where the railroad tracks take a sharp turn?"

"Oh, okay. Got it."

"So, what did you say?"

"I said, no way, I thought you meant a Pirates game."

"And what did he say?"

"He said, what's the difference? The Pirates? The Curve? A friend of his was on the team. He said they were really good."

"Did he mention the name of this friend?"

"No, not really. But he did say they were from the same town."

"Oaxaca?"

"How did you know?"

"Denise remembered."

"Yeah, yeah, that's the place."

"Okay, so then what happened?"

"I told him, there was no way I was going to Altoona with him. He got very angry and started yelling and cursing. At least I think he was cursing. A lot of it was in Spanish."

"What did you do?"

"I ran back inside. I went to see Fielding, the manager. I told him Menendez was harassing me. He came outside, had some words with Menendez. I ran to my car and took off."

"Did you ever see him again?"

"No, I was too scared. I called to cancel my membership. They said okay. And that was that. They even gave me my money back. I guess they didn't want a lawsuit."

"Did Menendez ever get violent with you?"

"Not with his hands or fists. But with his eyes? Yes. If looks could kill, I'd be dead. He was really upset with me. And he seemed like the kind of guy you don't want to have upset with you. The kind of guy who wouldn't hesitate to use violence if he was angry."

Chapter Thirty-Five: Operation Boy Scout

Frobisher was pretty sure his phone was tapped. To reach Khalif Wilson, he used a burner phone instead.

"You sure you have a key to Gary's apartment?" Frobisher asked.

"Positive. What is it you want me to look for?"

"Gary kept a list of all the cash payments to PBP he's made over the past four years."

"I'd say that's your problem, man. Not mine. Why should I care about that?"

"You should care because you handled some of those payments. You could be indicted for that."

"Are you saying my name is on the paperwork? I don't think Gary would do that to me."

"Maybe, maybe not. You willing to take a chance that it isn't?"

"Okay, I get the picture. Any video surveillance at Gary's apartment?"

"We believe so. It's either installed or about to be installed."

"So I could easily be recognized."

"That's where your disguise comes in."

"My disguise?"

"You'll be dressed to look like Radic, the lead detective."

"If he's the lead detective, why does he need to sneak into the place? Hasn't he already been inside?"

"Normally, he would be. But the higher-ups haven't allowed anyone in yet."

"Why is that?"

"Politics."

"So you're trying to get him in trouble."

"That's the idea. We need to tarnish his Boy Scout image. Which benefits you too, because you need Radic like a hole in the head."

"And how do I go about looking like Radic?"

"You'll be wearing a bandana and a cap to hide your face and a police jacket to look like a police officer. I'll drop them by within the hour."

"Anything else?"

"You'll be wearing Nike Metcon 8 training shoes just like Radic."

"I gotta say, the man has good taste in shoes."

"You'll also be wearing an earring just like him."

"An earring, huh? I'm getting a good vibe about this dude."

"Don't get too warm and fuzzy about him. Give him half a chance and he'll bring your drug empire crashing down."

"How tall is he?"

"Six foot two. Just like you."

"Where am I supposed to look?"

"You've been there dozens of times. You tell me. Where does he keep his valuables?"

"There's a loose board under the bed for some of them.

"When do you have in mind?"

"Thursday. 11:00 p.m."

"What if I get caught?"

"You won't. Because I'll be nearby, monitoring the PBP radio all the time. If there's a call to Gary's address, I'll be the first officer on the scene."

"What kind of car will you be driving?"

"A police car. I'll be a block away from Gary's. Euclid Ave. and Rippey St."

"You'll be there for sure? Not some jive-ass mother fucker who wants to arrest me?"

"We're in this together, Khalif. The last thing I want is for you to be arrested."

* * *

Khalif was accustomed to paying cops hush money. Part of the cost of doing business. But he was not accustomed to believing what cops said.

Frobisher was right about one thing—if Khalif's name was on a piece of paper listing payoffs to cops, it would be a shame for that to fall into the wrong hands. So, he was on board with Operation Boy Scout.

But there was no reason for him to do the dirty work. He would find someone else to do it. Someone from out of town. Just in case things went south.

Menendez had a homeboy. What was his name? The baseball player. He would do nicely.

Chapter Thirty-Six: The Six Million Dollar Man

Scuglia was eager to play catch-up on the Gardenia and Mabry murder cases, now that his other murder case was before a jury, effectively ending his involvement. It would be difficult, but he had done it before and could do it again.

The two cases were high-profile, which was a mixed blessing. Everyone from the mayor on down was interested. That meant more resources and more information, but also more interference.

He looked forward to working with Radic and Mulroy, with whom he had a good rapport. He was confident they would make a good team. But he would need to hit the accelerator big time.

Luckily, Scuglia was able to reach Gary's lawyer, Martha Harbison, who was more than willing to talk but who insisted on talking in person. Scuglia agreed to meet her at her downtown office.

Harbison arranged to talk in a plush conference room. She began with a warning: "Before we get started, Detective, you should know that this is the most complex will I've encountered in thirty years of legal practice. On a scale of one to ten, with ten being the most complex, I'd rate it an eleven."

"How so? A lot of bequests?"

"No, it's not that. The will itself is fairly short. The main problem is where the money came from. How much do you know about Gary Mabry's background?"

Scuglia started to sense the problem. "We know he was a drug dealer, if that's what you mean."

"Not just a drug dealer, but a highly successful drug dealer."

"How successful?"

"Have you ever heard of the Six Million Dollar Man?"

"It rings a bell. An old TV series?"

"That's right. Well, Gary Mabry was a Six Million Dollar Man."
Scuglia whistled softly.

"So, are there legal problems with the will?"

"I'm still doing research on that question, so stay tuned."

"What problems do you envision?"

"Well, the basic problem is this: Gary Mabry wanted to give money to some people who are not eager to receive it, and he wanted to give money to other people who may not be allowed to receive it."

"For instance?"

"Well, let's take the eight hundred-pound gorilla first." She handed the will to Scuglia.

"Oh, my God!"

"That's right. Gary Mabry has bequeathed a million dollars to the Mayor's re-election committee, otherwise known as a PAC."

"Can he do that?"

"No, he cannot."

"Then why did you approve the will?"

"Another attorney approved this clause and did so with some justification. According to Pennsylvania law, there are no limits on individual contributions to state and local political campaigns."

"So Gary's in the clear?"

"No, he's not. There are no state limits on campaign contributions in Pennsylvania, but there are local limits. In Pittsburgh, the Ethics Board has decided to follow federal law, which means an individual can contribute no more than three thousand three hundred dollars to the Mayor's re-election committee. My colleague slipped up."

"Oops!"

"But that's not the end of the story. Given this discovery, we need to try to find a legal way to implement Gary Mabry's wishes."

"Is there a legal way?"

"Perhaps. Although federal law places a ceiling on individual contributions to a re-election committee, it places no restrictions on contributions to a super-PAC that operates independently of the re-election committee. If the executor goes along with that idea, that's probably what we'll do."

"Who is the executor?"

"Turn the page."

"Larry Mabry."

"Well, at least that's clear."

"Actually, it's not clear at all."

"Why not?"

"Because Larry has told me that he's unlikely to accept the role of executor of his brother's estate."

"Why not?"

"Well, you should speak with Larry. But I think I can say that he has some ethical reservations about distributing his brother's ill-gotten gains."

Scuglia's head was spinning. "So, if the designated executor refuses to execute the will, what happens then?"

"We go to the next person on the list."

Scuglia flipped a page. "Mrs. Mabry?"

"If she accepts."

"And if she doesn't?"

"Father Buckley."

Scuglia stood up. "I'd better get this information to my colleagues. Will there be a reading of the will?"

"We don't have to do it that way. In this case, I'm inclined to let the executor handle things as he or she sees fit. But first, we need an executor."

Scuglia nodded.

"There's one more thing, Detective."

"What's that?"

"The money."

"The money?"

"That's right. I don't have it. Maybe you can help."

Scuglia laughed. "Me? You think I have six million dollars?"

"No, I don't, Detective. But based on what Gary told me, I think I know where the money is. I'd just like to have police protection when I go to obtain it."

"And where do you propose to go?"

"To Muscle Mania in East Liberty. That's where Gary said the money would be. And he gave me the keys to get the cash."

Chapter Thirty-Seven: Not Quite the Major Leagues

It was a long fly ball to center field. Going, going, gone! Damn. Carlos Almazan slammed his fist in his glove. He had a no-hitter going. Admittedly, it was just the top of the third inning, but still. So much for his dreams of glory and a ticker-tape parade.

After that, the hits just kept on coming. Before he knew it, he had given up five runs to the Akron Rubberducks, and he was unceremoniously dispatched from the game. From the go-to guy to the goat in ten minutes.

Almazan blamed the bad pitch that started the torrent of runs on a phone call from that smart-assed Pittsburgh drug dealer, Khalif Wilson. He wanted Almazan to leave Altoona for a day or two and put his life at risk for some hare-brained scheme that spelled trouble.

He would have to speak with Jorge about it after the game. He had told Khalif thanks, but no thanks, but the guy wouldn't take no for an answer. Acting like he was the king of the jungle, now that the other guy was dead.

Well, who needs this shit? he thought. He had been jailed in Oaxaca four years ago, and it had been no picnic. That time, it wasn't even his fault. This time, it would be his fault. Jail for sure. He might even be deported, baseball or no baseball. There was no way he was going to take that risk.

Almazan showered, saying little to his teammates. After such an atrocious third inning, no one wanted to approach him, for fear of saying the wrong thing. Well, screw them. The next time they wanted a snort of cocaine, they would be on their own.

All he needed to set things right this evening was a cold Dos Equis and a taco platter. Hopefully, Jorge would be around to hang out and explain what the hell this Khalif guy was up to.

* * *

The social scene in Altoona left something to be desired. Like some fucking third-world country, except worse. At least in the third world, you could pay for pussy and no one gave a shit.

It had taken Menendez three or four days to find a chica who was ready, willing, and able. He was much calmer now. Fuck those Pittsburgh gringas who treated him like scum.

Despite his forced exile, it was good to hang out with Carlos and to watch him play. The Altoona Curve reminded him of simpler times when he was an aspiring ballplayer himself. The Curve players, including Carlos, were convinced that all they needed was a lucky break.

Well, he could tell them, that's not the way the world worked. You don't wait for Lady Luck to lend a hand. You take opportunities when you see them. And you create opportunities when you don't see them.

Like right now in Pittsburgh. A new ballgame. New rules. Lots of opportunities. He had high hopes for the new kid. Gary had been great, but he had a soft core.

Khalif, in contrast, was hard. Hard as nails. No one would mess with him, on his turf. Menendez admired and respected that. At the same time, he didn't worry about Khalif, who needed him and his product. Where else was he going to turn?

As for the police, they didn't concern him all that much. The dead guy, Gardenia? A punk. Frenchy? A petty grifter. Those guys thought they were so slick, but they were pendejos. Assholes.

The guy who did worry him was Radic. He had heard about him. Smart. Relentless. Un cruzado. Could he be turned? Probably not. Could he be neutralized? Probably. The question was how.

* * *

From Denise, Mulroy learned that Carlos Almazan was a fair-to-middling minor league player. Destined for greatness? No. Capable of moving up from AA to AAA ball? Perhaps, if he played his cards right and stayed off the drugs.

Denise had spoken with some minor league contacts about the kid, disguising the nature of her interest. They reported that Almazan was a bit of a hot-head. He had been jailed in Oaxaca for petty theft and had hardened after that.

His choice of friends was considered problematic. Jorge Menendez was known to most of the players, especially the Latinos, and was feared by the coaches. A drug kingpin, he posed a direct threat to some of their most vulnerable recruits.

It helped that Menendez was based in Pittsburgh, not Altoona. From the owners' perspective, he was persona non grata. Occasionally, other civilians were allowed inside the clubhouse, but not Menendez. If he was going to corrupt any of the players, it would have to be outside the ballpark.

* * *

As Almazan expected, Jorge advised him to turn down Khalif's invitation. Why risk getting caught for breaking and entering? It could cost you your job. It could cost you your career.

Good advice. But Jorge was surprisingly interested in exactly what Khalif had to say. "When does he want you to break into Mabry's apartment?"

"Eleven o'clock Thursday night."

"And when does he want to give you the stuff for the disguise?"

"The day before."

"Where would you meet?"

"A block away from the apartment."

"What does he want you to steal?"

"A list of drug buys and payoffs."

"Does he know where this list is?"

"He says it's probably under a floorboard. Under the guy's bed."

Jorge sipped a Dos Equis, slowly, and nodded.

"You definitely shouldn't do this," he said.

Carlos nodded.

"But I should."

"What?"

"That list would give me some leverage. I want it. And there might be other stuff in the same place."

"But aren't you worried about getting caught?"

"No."

"Why not?"

"Because I'm going to break in earlier than Khalif's schedule. And you're going to help me set it up."

Chapter Thirty-Eight: The High Seas

Despite all the fuss over who would have access to Gardenia's home, the search revealed precious little of use to any of the ongoing investigations by the Homicide Squad or Internal Affairs.

Dusting for fingerprints confirmed the presence of Frenchy and Atwood in Gino's home, but that was hardly surprising or suspicious. After all, they had been partners and friends.

Of the many pieces of paper seized and analyzed, only one seemed promising—a recent towboat schedule for the three rivers that specified arrival times at Monongahela Locks and Dam 4 in Charleroi for towboats from different companies for two weeks in a row—both in April.

Scuglia's preliminary analysis revealed that several of the barges on Gardenia's list were licensed to companies based in Mexico. Could this be the link to the drug cartel they were looking for? And perhaps an opportunity to interdict drug supplies in the future?

A heated debate ensued over why Gino was interested in barges.

"If Gino was tracking towboats and barges," Radic argued, "they must be involved in Pittsburgh's drug traffic. Otherwise, he wouldn't waste his time."

"But barges?" Stilton asked. "Isn't that a bone-headed way to transport drugs? There's no escape if you're caught."

"Maybe that's the beauty of it," Radic replied. "Who would even think to stop a towboat for drug trafficking?"

"What if the towboats work in tandem with smaller vessels?" Mulroy asked. "If a towboat starts out in Cairo, Illinois, just think of how many cities they could supply drugs to along the way?"

The next question for the group was who should get involved. Homicide? Narcotics? The River Rescue Unit? The Mayor's Drug Task Force? The FBI? The DEA?

Radic wanted to get the feds involved. He noted that at least two PBP officers were suspected of accepting drug money, which made it difficult to speak freely in an atmosphere of mutual trust. He also argued that drug trafficking on the Ohio River was the federal government's jurisdiction.

Scuglia, in contrast, made the case for local control. The advantage of the Internal Affairs investigation, he argued, is that the "bad apples" had already been identified. Keep a tight lid on the operation and exclude the bad apples from all briefings related to the case.

Mulroy found herself supporting Scuglia and recommended getting the River Rescue Unit involved. In brief remarks, she pointed to their impeccable reputation, their knowledge of the three rivers and barge traffic, and their relative independence.

Privately, she saw this as a golden opportunity for Lexie, Radic's girlfriend and Mulroy's chum, to sink her teeth into a career-boosting investigation. She wondered whether Radic was deliberately steering the case away from Lexie, in order to protect her. If so, she understood why he might feel that way. But shouldn't Lexie have the choice?

After much discussion, Stilton resolved the dispute in favor of local control. "Let's give it a try." He asked Scuglia to take the lead on this part of the case.

* * *

Radic was such a notorious homebody that Lexie instantly grew suspicious when he proposed that they go out to dinner in the middle of the week. Still, Lexie always welcomed an excuse to go out. Taking advantage of the warming weather, she changed into shorts and a green blouse that drew attention to her green eyes.

After walking Ralph around the block, they drove to a nice restaurant called The Abbey, in a setting that looked like it had once been a church.

Something was definitely up. A pub, yes. A pub that resembled a church? What might that mean? Surely, Radic was not going to pop the question. They had already discussed marriage at least twice, and both seemed to be on the same page. Definitely a possibility, but not yet.

Radic ordered a draft beer, while Lexie ordered a gin and tonic. They also requested some pita bread and hummus while they waited for their main courses.

"To you!" Radic toasted, with a tip of his glass. "To us!" she replied. "Even better," he said.

Lexie asked if there were any new developments in the two cases. Sometimes Radic didn't want to talk about work at all. At other times, he wanted to talk about nothing but.

"We have theories, we have leads, we have information. But no suspects. Just categories of people who may have committed either crime."

"That's frustrating," she said. "Especially with Gary's murder. I know you'd like to find his killer. For the family's sake. And for the community's sake. Things are still pretty tense in the Black community."

Radic nodded. "I'd welcome a break in either case. They're interconnected, I'm sure of it. If we make progress on one case, we make progress on the other."

"So nothing new at all?"

"Well, we did find something in Gino's home that's generated some talk. In fact, you're likely to hear about it soon. I thought you'd want to hear it from me first."

"I'm all ears."

"It has to do with barges coming into and out of the city. Do you pay much attention to them?"

"Not really. They're pretty predictable, and their trips are well documented. Towboats with barges have to log in to go through one of the locks. It's the other river traffic that keeps us guessing and keeps us busy. Why are you interested in barges, of all things?"

"We're interested in barges because Gino was interested in barges."

"Get out."

"His personal papers include a list of towboats with their arrival and departure times in Pittsburgh for two weeks during April. Handwritten. An expert says it's Gino's handwriting."

"So, what are you thinking? Drugs?"

"Exactly."

"But barges? Who would hitch a ride with a horse and buggy when they could drive a Mercedes instead?"

"We agree with that. It's a puzzle. But is it possible that the drug cartel might see some advantages to transporting drugs via barges?"

"Well, in terms of volume, yes, of course. But in terms of speed, definitely not. And in terms of maneuverability, definitely not. If you're transporting drugs by car, you can alter your route, stop and stay in a motel, do whatever is necessary to avoid getting caught. But if you're transporting drugs by barge, and law enforcement gets wind of it, you're a sitting duck."

"Again, we agree with that. But for the sake of argument, let's say one of the cartels decided to transport their goods by barge. How easy would it be to slip through the net?"

"Well, I'd have to say, very easy. Because there are so many of them. Hundreds every week. And because no one pays any attention to them."

"Exactly."

"So where do I come in?"

"Well, that's where it gets a little iffy."

"Iffy in what way?"

"Iffy as in if you should get involved at all."

"Okay, Branko, just spit it out. You're trying to say something. You're kind of upset. Order another beer and tell me what's bugging you."

Radic laughed. "Okay, maybe another beer would help." He ordered a second beer, and Lexie ordered a second gin and tonic.

"So, let's start from the top. Does Stilton want me to get involved in the Gardenia case?"

"He wants the River Rescue Unit to get involved. So, the answer is yes."

Lexie paused. "But do *you* want me to get involved in the case?"

"Well, honestly, I have misgivings."

"What are your misgivings?"

"Lexie, there's a lot of bad guys out there. That's the nature of my job. And, to some extent, it's the nature of your job too."

"Well, not to some extent. It *is* my job. I'm a law enforcement officer too, even if I don't spend my time chasing down murder suspects."

"Okay, fair enough. I don't want to argue about that. But the point is that in the universe of bad guys, none are more ruthless, more vicious, more lethal than drug dealers. They're the absolute worst. And I, I, I—I just don't want to see you get hurt."

Lexie looked at Radic with affection in her eyes. "That's very sweet, Branko. I know you're coming from a good place on this. And you have every right to be worried or at least concerned.

"But look at it from my point of view. My work is pretty interesting and I enjoy it. But my highs are not as high as your highs, just as my lows are not as low as your lows. From what you're saying, this could be a chance for me to get involved in a high-profile murder case. That sounds absolutely fantastic.

"Now, if I get involved," Lexie continued, "you can rest assured that I will be very, very careful and that I won't put myself in harm's way. I have no intention of getting killed or injured. I don't even want to get a toe blister from this because that would cut into my jogging."

Radic laughed.

"So, I appreciate your concern, I really do. But I hope you're okay with this. Because it sounds like a great opportunity and it's something I'd really like to do."

Radic took her hand and kissed it.

"Is that a yes?"

"I guess it's a yes."

"Wonderful. Let's dig in. I'm starving."

Chapter Thirty-Nine: Familiar Faces
Among the Flowers

Mulroy had visited Phipps Conservatory many times but never in an official or semi-official capacity. She decided to wear a beige pencil skirt and a matching jacket, plus pumps. It felt good to dress up for a change.

The instructions from Stilton were that she should attend a fund-raiser for the Mayor, mingle with the guests, and see what she could find out about the relationship between the Mayor's office and the Mayor's PAC. Yes, it would be fine for Jake to come along. Even better. More natural.

And who would pay? This was one of those undercover assignments that would be handled through petty cash. The PBP would pay the entry fee, one hundred dollars per person, but nothing more.

It was the perfect time to visit Phipps. The middle of May. The displays were carefully curated, the flowers were blooming, and their scents were intoxicating.

An unabashed dahlia fan, Mulroy was captivated by a black red Spartacus dahlia and an assortment of Dinnerplate dahlias—yellow, orange, pink, and purple. She also smiled fondly while tickling some lamb's ears, which felt like their namesake.

The stars of the show were three bears—a Mama Bear, a Papa Bear, and a Baby Bear, preparing to fly a kite, with a carpet of purple lobelia at their feet. At first, Mulroy thought the bears were made of papier mache. On closer inspection, she realized that they were made of tree bark. Imagine the work that went into that!

The hors d'oeuvres were varied and tasty. Mulroy had just snagged a bruschetta when she noticed someone coming their way. A well-tailored man, tall, with an athletic build, maybe of Italian or Greek descent. He had perfect white teeth and a dazzling grin.

"Nice to see you here, Detective."

Mulroy said nothing.

"Oh, I get it. You're here in-cog-ni-to. Don't worry, your secret's safe with me. Phil Hodges, director of the Mayor's re-election campaign."

Mulroy nodded.

"Whatever brings you here, we'd like you to know that the Mayor appreciates the work that you and Detective Radic are doing. If we can help with anything, please reach out to me. Here's my card."

Mulroy took the card.

"Oh, and be sure to try the crab cakes. They're to die for. Sorry, couldn't resist! You being a homicide detective and all."

Mulroy turned to Jake. "Politicians and their lackeys. They get under my skin."

"I understand."

"But he was right about one thing. Let's get some crab cakes before they disappear."

Mayor Graham and Ceci Arceneaux arrived about a half hour after the reception began, beaming and jubilant.

It was hard to believe that this was the same couple that had grieved so openly for Gary Mabry just a few days earlier. It was also hard to believe that Ceci, despite her cheerful demeanor, was, according to Radic, a woman with a very serious illness.

Five minutes later, clinking glasses signaled that it was time for the mayor to give a speech. The man who strode to the lectern was middle-aged, sandy-haired, and self-assured. He seemed at ease, far more comfortable addressing a crowd than Mulroy would ever be.

As Mulroy listened to his five-minute speech, she heard some phrases that she liked. Affordable housing. Food for kids. Treatment for the mentally ill. Was Mayor Graham the real deal or a smooth politician who knew how to spout platitudes? Mulroy was reserving judgment, but his sentiments seemed heartfelt.

Noticing the time, Mulroy shifted her attention from the canapes and the flowers to the business at hand. She saw no point in introducing herself to people at first. Instead, she eavesdropped as best she could.

Mulroy was about to grab another canapé when she noticed one of the guests collapse with a thud. Instinctively, she set down her drink and rushed to his side.

The young man, Black, with a thick beard, was still conscious, but his eyes were fluttering. "What's his name?" Mulroy asked another man, who was crouching over him, trying to get a response.

"Bradley."

"Bradley, can you hear me?"

She got no response.

She repositioned Bradley so he was lying flat on his back. Then she elevated his legs. She noticed that he was bleeding from the back of his head.

"Someone get me some water, please. And a cloth from one of the tables."

Within seconds, someone brought her a glass of water and a large cloth napkin.

She splashed water on Bradley's face, triggering an involuntary response. That was a good sign. Then she began dabbing his wound, gently.

"More water, please? And another cloth?"

At this point, two or three other people were assisting, and Jake was directing traffic away from the prostrate man. Bradley began to stir.

"Bradley, are you okay?"

One of his eyes opened, then the other.

"Any idea what happened?" Mulroy asked the other man.

"He just gave blood. Could that be it?"

"Could be," Mulroy said. Then, in a louder voice, "Could somebody bring me some orange juice?"

Within five minutes, Bradley was sitting up, sipping orange juice. As he held the cup, Mulroy noticed his full name on a name tag: Bradley Gibbons. She also noticed the other man's name—Marvin Casper—and committed both to memory.

Bradley, wide awake now, spotted a large blood stain on Mulroy's jacket and blouse.

"Did I do that?" he asked. "I'm really sorry about that."

"Don't worry about it," Mulroy replied. "We're just glad you're okay."

Mulroy turned to the other gentleman, Marvin, who hadn't said much. "Did you two come together?"

The man nodded.

"You might want to get Bradley some food and then get him to a hospital. He might need stitches."

"Are you hungry, Bradley?"

He nodded.

"Let's see if you can stand up."

With help from Marvin and Jake, Bradley got to his feet. Guests nearby applauded as he did.

"Thank you for your help, ma'am," Marvin said. "I got it from here."

Mulroy and Jake continued to mingle, but the rest of the evening was anticlimactic. She kept Bradley and Marvin in her line of sight. Both were sitting down, and both were eating hors d'oeuvres.

A few minutes later, Bradley and Marvin stood up and greeted a stocky, middle-aged Black man who had come to pick them up. "Well, I'll be damned," Mulroy said to Jake. "It's Father Buckley."

"Who's he, hon?" Jake asked.

"The pastor of St. Martin de Porres. A speaker at Gary's rally. One of the victims at the Market Square protest."

"Sounds like he's everywhere."

"It sure does."

"Is that a good thing or a bad thing?"

"I don't know. But it makes me curious. Very curious."

Chapter Forty: A Look at Locks

The lockmaster, Gus Fabricant, at Lock and Dam 4 in Charleroi, was happy to talk with Scuglia when he showed up unannounced mid-morning. "We're between barges," he said. "You know, you're the second cop to come pay us a visit over the past few weeks," he added.

"Really? Who was the first?"

"I don't rightly recall his name. He was middle-aged, pudgy, maybe Greek or Italian."

"Gino Gardenia?"

"That's right. Are you two working together?"

"No, we're not. In fact, Gino is dead. He was murdered two weeks ago."

Fabricant's jaw dropped. "Lordy, I can't believe it. Did it have anything to do with the questions he was asking?"

"What kinds of questions was he asking?"

"He wanted to know when our barges arrived, what they carried, what our record-keeping was like."

"Did he explain why he was interested?"

"He didn't say a heck of a lot. But, if you ask me, I'd say he was interested in drug smuggling."

"What exactly did he say that led you to believe that?"

"Well, he specifically asked whether we get any towboats from foreign countries, like Mexico."

"What did you say to that?"

"Of course, we do. Not a lot. Most of our shippers are based in the U S of A. But we definitely get shipments from other countries. And Mexico would be at the top of that list."

"Are you expecting any shipments from Mexico today or tomorrow?"

"Well, that's not the way it works. I can tell you who's been here and when. But I can't tell you who's going to come here. You don't have to book a visit in advance. But if you visit us, we like to keep a record of it."

"Okay, let's look at it from that angle. Over the past forty-eight hours, have you had any barges that originated in Mexico?"

"Let's look through the paperwork. Then, if necessary, we can get more information from our computer."

"Thanks."

Fabricant stepped inside a small, cluttered office and produced a logbook. "Okay, here's one from yesterday. I remember it because the captain didn't speak any English. I'd say he spoke Spanish. La Jacinta. That's the name of the towboat."

"And the name of the owner?"

"We can look that up on the computer if you like."

"Please."

Fabricant fired up his desktop computer, typed in a few words, and sat back. "The owner of the tugboat is from Mexico. Gua-de-lah-jar-ah."

"Guadalajara."

"That's right."

"What's his name?"

"Well, I can give you the name of the company. You'll have to get the name of the owner yourself."

"That'll be just fine."

"Exportaciones Internacionales."

"What were they carrying?"

"Gravel."

"Is that unusual?"

"Not at all."

"Did you notice anything unusual?"

Fabricant scratched his chin for a moment. "There were four guys in the cabin, not two. That's kind of unusual."

Chapter Forty-One: Shopping for Shoes

Almazan felt good to be sharing a six-pack of Dos Equis and some take-out with Jorge at his rental home in Altoona. "Did you say Nike Metcon 8 training shoes?" he asked.

"That's what the man said."

"I could use a pair of those anyway. But I doubt they have them in Al-fucking-toona."

"You want me to pick some up when we're in Pittsburgh?"

"Yeah, size twelve and a half. But make sure there's wiggle room for the toes. My toes need room to breathe."

"How will I know whether they're roomy enough for your toes?"

"Wiggle your own toes and see how they feel."

"What if they don't wiggle?"

Menendez thought for a moment.

"If they don't wiggle, get me size thirteen."

The trip to Pittsburgh was slow but productive. It gave them time to rehearse what Carlos would say to Khalif.

"So, one more time. Let's hear it from the top."

"I call Khalif and tell him I'm willing to do it, but I have to do it tonight because we have a night game tomorrow and I'm supposed to pitch."

"Good. What if he says you should call in sick?"

"I say they're very strict about that stuff. No one gets to call in sick, especially the pitcher."

"Good."

"I tell him I have the tennis shoes and I got a mask."

"What kind of mask?"

"A bandana."

"What if he says, that won't work cause it's broad daylight? People will take you for a thief."

"I say, you think I'm stupid? I know that. I wear a COVID mask outside, then I switch to a bandana once I'm inside."

"And then?"

"Then I say all I need is the police jacket and the key to the apartment. ASAP."

"Very good. You're on top of this. It's going to work."

* * *

The man at Khalif Wilson's front door looked familiar. Too familiar. Six foot two. Good-looking. Good muscle tone. He must work out. A silver hoop earring in his right ear. What the…?

"Mr. Wilson, I'm Detective Branko Radic, and this is my partner, Detective Mulroy. May we come in?"

Startled to see the Boy Scout himself at his doorstep, Khalif took an additional moment to size up the man's partner. Blonde, attractive, a good figure, a slight overbite. "What's this about?"

"It's about Gary Mabry. We know you were friends. We thought you might be able to help us."

Wilson opened up the door. "I don't know how I can help, but I'm willing to talk."

"Thank you," Radic said.

* * *

Wilson's apartment, a townhouse in Shadyside, was nicely furnished and cheerful. The living room featured a large fishbowl with exotic fish and a poster of rapper Wiz Khalifa on the wall. The kitchen looked spotless and smelled of freshly brewed coffee.

"Mr. Wilson, I'll be honest with you, we've been working hard on this case, and we don't have much to show for it. Do you have any thoughts on who might have wished to harm Gary?"

Wilson said nothing.

"Look, we know about Gary's involvement in the drug business, and we know about yours as well. That's not why we're here. We are genuinely trying to find his murderer. That's it. Nothing more. We think you might be able to help."

"I don't know what you think about the drug trade, Detective, but it's kind of like a pond or a lake. There's the minnows. That would be Gary and his local crew. Then there's the male betta fish, like the ones you see in the tank. That would be the cartel's local reps. There's also the piranhas. That would be the folks with really sharp teeth back in Mexico. If I was you, I'd focus on the piranhas."

"Anyone in particular?"

Wilson squirmed.

"How about the betta fish then? How about Jorge Menendez?"

"What about him?"

"When's the last time you saw him?"

"A week or two ago."

"Before or after Gary's murder."

"Before."

"Do you know where he is?"

Wilson shook his head.

"Do you know how to reach him?"

Again, Wilson shook his head.

"Do you know his friend Carlos Almazan?"

"I may have met him once or twice."

"Do you know how to reach him?"

"He's a baseball player. You could probably find him at the ballpark."

"Which ballpark?"

"Wherever the Altoona club plays. Somewhere in Altoona."

Mulroy spoke up. "Mr. Wilson, do you know the contents of Gary's will?"

"Not exactly."

"What do you mean, not exactly?"

"Gary talked about it once or twice, but I've never seen it."

"Do you know who the beneficiaries are?"

"I know groups. Not people."

"Which groups?"

"The Red Cross."

Mulroy nodded. "Anyone else?"

"St. Martin de Porres Church."

"Anyone else?"

"Maybe his mom, maybe his brother."

"Not you?"

"I would be surprised."

"Why's that?"

"I don't need a handout from Gary or anyone else."

"How do you make your money, if you don't mind my asking?"

"International commerce."

Mulroy looked to Radic for guidance, to see if she should pursue this, but he seemed to have other ideas. "Any thoughts on how we might find one of the piranhas?"

"I thought you said you didn't care about the drug trade."

"We don't. But you suggested that one of the piranhas is behind the murder."

"That doesn't mean I know who he is."

"Can you give us the name of an organization?"

Wilson shivered. "The less I know about that stuff, the better."

Chapter Forty-Two: The Mexican Connection

The first meeting of the Waterways Task Force included Scuglia, Mulroy, and two officers from the River Rescue Unit—Lexie Davodny and Vicki Morella. Scuglia produced a box of doughnuts, which triggered smiles and a rush to claim the chocolate ones. As his colleagues chomped away, Scuglia handed out copies of Gardenia's towboat schedule.

"Don't get used to the doughnuts," Scuglia warned. "And don't get icing all over the damn papers."

Scuglia began with a PowerPoint that featured Pittsburgh's waterways, with different degrees of granularity—first a map of the U.S. with the Ohio River highlighted, second a map of the Pittsburgh metro area, and finally a more detailed map featuring the river route between Pittsburgh and Charleroi.

"Okay, folks, let me try to summarize what we know and what we don't know about the comings and goings of towboats and barges.

"Based on Gino's notes, and additional information from the Army Corps of Engineers, we believe that at least three towboats from Mexico entered Pittsburgh territorial waters during a two-week period in April. Two of them were carrying gravel, one was carrying coal."

"Do we know whether Gino was interested in these particular shipments?" Lexie asked.

"Actually, we do. You may not be able to tell it from the Xeroxed copies, but Gino highlighted the three Mexico shipments with a yellow magic marker."

"Just those?"

"Just those."

"What do we know about the owners?"

"The two with gravel come from Exportaciones Internacionales, based in Tabasco, Mexico. It's a relatively large firm with annual sales of fifty to sixty million dollars. The one with coal comes from Recursos Energeticos. It's a relatively small firm with annual sales of ten to fifteen million."

"Have we reached out to the Mexican authorities?" Mulroy asked.

"Not yet. And we may never do so."

"Why not?"

"Without putting too fine a point on it, we have no way of knowing who in Mexico's police force can be trusted and who cannot. We don't want to jeopardize our lead by reaching out to someone who's either corrupt or overly talkative."

"Is there a way to use backchannels to get more information? Or to go through the U.S. Embassy?" Mulroy asked.

"We're working on that. For the moment, what we can say is that Exportaciones Internacionales looks kind of fishy. Either they're not well-managed, which is possible. Or they're not reporting all of their earnings, which is also possible."

"How do we know that?"

"Simple back-of-the-envelope calculations. The ratio of income to tonnage shipped doesn't look good at all."

"Okay, so what do you suggest?"

"Our thought is that we want to track the next shipments from Exportaciones to see whether there's anything squirrelly about their behavior. Do they hand off drugs or receive cash as they approach Pittsburgh from the Ohio River, or do they behave oddly in any way?"

"Where do we come in?" Lexie asked.

"The River Rescue Unit can help us greatly with surveillance. But I gotta warn you—it could be long hours, and it could be late at night."

"Aren't you concerned about using a PBP boat to surveil drug smugglers? It's a dead giveaway, isn't it?"

"We don't propose to use a PBP boat."

"Ah ha."

"We propose to use a couple of fishing boats."

"Have you cleared this with our boss?" Vicki asked.

Scuglia nodded. "Subject to certain limits, he's okay with it."

"What are the limits?"

"A limited time period. And limited vulnerability."

"Limited vulnerability?"

"An officer from Homicide or Narcotics will accompany you on every run."

"I don't know whether to be grateful or insulted," Lexie said.

"Try grateful. It's for your own safety. And it's to help ensure that the operation goes smoothly."

"Do we know when their next shipment is coming through?" Lexie asked.

"Well, that's the catch. We don't."

"So how's that going to work? Surely, you don't want us to sit out in a boat for two weeks hoping that one hundred tons of Mexican gravel will suddenly materialize."

"No, we don't. We've established friendly contact with someone at the Corps of Engineers, downriver, in Cincinnati. If one of these shipments goes through Cincinnati, they'll notify us, which will give us time to gear up."

"Do we know for sure that Exportaciones smuggles drugs?" Lexie asked.

"No."

"But Gino thought they did?"

"That's a pretty safe bet."

"Do you think he was teaming up with these guys?"

"Could be," Scuglia replied. "Or maybe he was acting like a good cop for a change. Trying to track down the bad guys."

"Or maybe the Exportaciones folks represent a different cartel than the one that was feeding Gino," Mulroy added. "Maybe he saw them as a threat."

"A clever idea. Is that what you and Radic think?"

"We've discussed it."

"Okay, well, maybe you can bring me up to speed on that later. Meanwhile, any questions?"

"Who's gonna bring the doughnuts next time?" Lexie asked.

"Anyone but me."

Chapter Forty-Three: Unlocking Secrets

Mulroy agreed to give attorney Martha Harbison a lift to Muscle Mania. They were to meet Scuglia there at 1:00 p.m. sharp. "Detective Scuglia says you've actually joined the gym. Working undercover?"

"Well, it's a little more innocent than that. I genuinely wanted to work out. To justify all the doughnuts, you know."

The lawyer laughed. "I admire you for staying in shape."

They pulled up next to Muscle Mania, where Scuglia was already waiting, checking his text messages.

"Okay, detectives, how do you want to play this?" Harbison asked.

"We're going to march in together to see the manager, Bart Fielding," Scuglia explained.

"Don't expect warm and fuzzy," Mulroy warned.

"So he may object?"

"It wouldn't surprise me. But we've already checked with a local judge, to be on the safe side. No warrant is needed. You are Gary Mabry's lawyer and the executor of his estate, Father Buckley, has authorized you to open two lockers and remove all of their contents. End of story."

"And if he objects?"

"That's what we're here for."

Knowing the lay of the land, Mulroy led the charge, giving the receptionist a greeting so cheerful that it might have sounded phony.

Without waiting for Fielding to be notified, Mulroy, Scuglia, and Harbison marched to his office, knocked on the door, and entered.

"Detective Mulroy, I get the impression you're not here for a workout."

"That's correct. This is Detective Scuglia, Homicide, and Martha Harbison, Gary Mabry's attorney. We are here to remove the contents of two lockers that belong to Mr. Mabry."

"Do you have a warrant?"

"We don't need a warrant."

"Well, I'm sorry, Detective, but without a warrant, I don't see how I can help you."

"Actually, you don't need to help us, Mr. Fielding. We have every legal right to recover Mr. Mabry's property. His lawyer, Ms. Harbison, has that authority. And we have a signed, notarized statement from the executor of his estate confirming that she can share what's found with us. Open and shut. We have also spoken with Judge Belsky, to confirm our understanding of the law."

"And if I object?"

"You can object until the cows come home. We're just informing you as a courtesy."

"Detective Mulroy, I must say that I'm very disappointed in you. You came in here under false pretenses and joined my gym. Now you come in as a law enforcement official, using information you obtained as a private citizen. That seems like deception to me."

"You're twisting the facts, Mr. Fielding. There were no false pretenses when I joined the gym. You knew who I was. And I was genuinely interested in coming here. I happen to like it here. And I'm getting fitter by the day. In fact, don't be surprised if I'm back here tomorrow, without a lawyer."

"What if I were to say that you're no longer welcome here, Detective?"

Harbison spoke up. "I would advise you not to play that card, Mr. Fielding. If you were to cancel Ms. Mulroy's membership without cause, she would be within her rights to sue you for discrimination. And it would be my great pleasure to represent her in court. Free of charge."

With that, the trio left Fielding's office, leaving Fielding speechless. They easily located the lockers, and Harbison produced the keys.

"The lucky number is…sixty-eight," Scuglia announced.

Wearing gloves, Mulroy opened it up. Inside, she found a pile of cash and a revolver. Harbison gasped.

"A Smith and Wesson?"

Mulroy nodded.

"Check the chambers."

"All the bullets are there."

"Bag it. And the cash? What would you guess?"

"It looks like hundred dollar bills. Four packets. Forty thousand dollars?"

"Okay, we'll count it properly later. And now, ladies, let's see what we have in locker number…ninety-two."

Mulroy opened this one, too. Inside, she found about a dozen file folders and manila envelopes, maybe more. Each was labeled, handwritten in cursive.

"Can you read out the titles so that we know what we're dealing with?"

Mulroy placed the stack of documents on a table nearby.

"Sure, here goes. Last Will and Testament."

"Can you check the date?"

"March 1 of this year. Does that sound right?"

"Exactly right."

"Red Cross."

"What's inside?"

"Names. Dates. Envelopes with cash."

"The dates. Past? Present? Future?"

"Looks like the future."

"Interesting. The gift that keeps on giving."

"What else?"

"St. Martin de Porres."

"Inside?"

"Architectural drawings. References to a Restoration Fund."

"Cash?"

"Not as far as I can tell."

"Next?"

"The Mayor's PAC."

"Good Lord. What do we have?"

"This is kind of complicated. I don't know what to make of it."

"What do you see?"

"Monthly statements. A bank account at PNC. A list of names, with dollar amounts."

"Do you recognize any of the names?"

"Not immediately."

"Okay, what else?"

"Dorothy."

"What's inside?"

"A baptismal certificate for Larry's daughter, Dorothy. Oh, it says Gary was the godfather. I didn't know that, but it makes sense. And…there's a letter…to Dorothy…it's signed Uncle Gary."

"What else?"

"Bank Accounts."

"Which banks?"

"PNC mainly. Plus, okay, here's one in Zurich. And here's another one in the Cayman Islands."

"I get the picture. What else?"

"Larry."

"Inside?"

"A long letter."

"Next?"

"Mama."

"Inside?"

"A long letter. And a Valentine's card." Mulroy found herself with a lump in her throat, and her eyes glistened.

"Is that a wrap?"

Mulroy nodded.

"Let's take this down to headquarters. Stilton will have to decide who gets what."

Harbison volunteered to take an Uber back to work after telling the detectives to keep in touch.

Scuglia agreed to handle the contents of Locker number ninety-two, while Mulroy agreed to handle the gun and the cash from Locker number sixty-eight. They would converge at the evidence room shortly.

Chapter Forty-Four: Ready or Not

It was a beautiful spring day on the Monongahela River. The sun was radiant enough to imprint images of multiple skyscrapers on PPG Place, made of clear reflective glass.

River traffic was thicker than usual, Lexie thought. With Memorial Day approaching, some recreational boaters had declared an early holiday and could be seen laughing, sipping beers, and engaging in horseplay. Many of them waved to Lexie, who waved back. One of them offered to toss her a beer, which she strongly discouraged with a wagging finger.

Although she was enjoying the day, Lexie found herself distracted. Maybe it was her new assignment, which could kick in at any time. Maybe it was Ralph, who always wanted more attention. Or maybe it was Radic. He was taking the Mabry murder case hard.

Truthfully, he took every case hard, but Lexie could tell that this one was especially tough. He felt strong ties to the Mabry family and didn't want to let them down. He knew he was being closely watched by Stilton, Reilly, and the Mayor. He also knew that some of his fellow officers desperately wanted him to fail.

Lexie admired Radic for investing so much emotional energy in every case. He always brought his A-game to work. But it took its toll. Sometimes it was hard to cheer him up.

Well, there was always Ralph. No matter how despondent Radic was, Ralph could be counted on to bring a smile to his face. In Ralph's presence, he was a carefree little boy. That was the solution. More Ralph time. And maybe more jogging time. For both of them.

Another reveler caught Lexie's eye. He was steering his boat with one hand, clutching a beer with the other. He was also chatting with his friends and not paying attention as he approached another vessel zipping along at a high rate of speed.

Lexie pressed hard on the foghorn button, which produced a deafening roar. Suddenly the playboy noticed what was happening. Dropping his beer, he steered his boat away from the other vessel. Lexie admonished him with a frown and a toot of the foghorn, but left it at that.

Her cell phone beeped. Probably Radic. They had planned on a movie if things worked out. But no, it was Scuglia. Thumbs up from Cincy. C U at 7 pm, your dock. U n me.

Suddenly, Lexie felt butterflies in her stomach. It was truly happening. She was going to do some real police work. Lexie texted her boss, letting him know that she was returning to base and would need to leave early. AOK, he replied. The game was afoot.

Back home in her apartment, Lexie extracted a pair of black leggings and a black sweatshirt from her dresser drawer. She added a black beret to the mix. Who says you can't look stylish at a stakeout?

As arranged, Lexie packed trail mix, cheese, carrots, and crackers—enough for two. Scuglia would bring two thermoses of hot coffee and some Diet Coke.

* * *

Lexie arrived at the dock moments after Scuglia, whose attire included khaki pants and a black parka. He was carrying a duffel bag with provisions.

Scuglia had requisitioned a serviceable motor boat, nothing fancy. Bowing to Lexie's greater expertise in nautical matters, Scuglia invited her to start and steer it. Moments later, they were in a holding pattern on the Monongahela River.

Scuglia got a ping and checked his text messages. His face lit up. "It's from the Dashields Lock and Dam."

"They're near Sewickley. Fifteen miles away. Are the boats through the gates?"

"Five minutes ago. It's show time."

* * *

The towboat appeared over the horizon at 9:03 p.m. The Corps of Engineers in Sewickley said it was pushing three barges, but that was impossible to verify, even with binoculars.

Normally, towboats favored the middle of the river as they passed through the Golden Triangle. Lexie noticed that this one was skirting the shore.

As the towboat reached Stanwix Street, just beyond the entryway to the Monongahela River, she and Scuglia observed something unexpected—a crew member dropped a rubber dinghy into the water and plopped onto it himself. The towboat eased back into the center of the river, while the dinghy headed ashore.

Scuglia reported this to Turley, only a few blocks away.

"Get to the wharf at Stanwix Street as soon as you can."

"What's going on?"

"A possible drug trafficker is about to visit Pittsburgh."

"Okay, I'm on my way. How will I recognize him?"

"If you get there soon enough, you'll see him get out of his dinghy."

"If not?"

"He's medium height, wearing dark clothing and a baseball cap or something similar. I'm afraid we can't say much more than that."

"Okay, ten-four."

Scuglia immediately contacted Radic and explained the situation. "Do you want us to abort and back up Turley?" Radic asked.

"Negative. Stick with the game plan. There may be other drop-offs."

"Roger that. Anything at your end?"

"All quiet here. Pretty boring."

"Hi Branko!"

"Hi Lexie. Stay safe, babe."

"Will do."

"See you in Charleroi."

"You got it."

* * *

Almazan parked the car at the designated spot, a block away from Gary Mabry's East Liberty apartment, and promised to remain there until Menendez returned, no matter what.

As he approached Gary's apartment building, Menendez noticed a camera on a nearby telephone pole. A good thing he was in disguise.

It took all of sixty seconds for Menendez to enter the building, climb the stairs, and open the door to Gary's apartment. Before going about his business, Menendez scanned the ceiling. No evidence of any indoor surveillance. But he was taking no chances. He would remain in disguise throughout.

Mabry's apartment had a musty smell, and a handful of overripe bananas on the kitchen counter attested to the fact that the owner had been away for a while. Out of curiosity, Menendez opened the refrigerator. It was well-stocked.

Menendez peered outside the window. There were several cars parked on the street or in driveways, but none looked suspicious. No pedestrians. The coast was clear.

With that, Menendez turned to the larger of the two bedrooms, upended the bed, and got down on his hands and knees.

The floorboard was easy to spot. Mabry had made no effort to conceal it. Menendez lifted it up without difficulty and used his cell phone flashlight to probe before placing his hands down there. No traps, as far as he could tell.

A metal box, about ten inches by fifteen inches, was the main prize. Unlocked. Inside, Menendez found a bunch of papers, including a list of names, mainly cops, and cash payment amounts. Mission accomplished. He placed the papers inside his jacket and continued to look.

In addition to the metal box, he saw a large envelope with old family photos. No need for those. He also saw an assortment of mementos from Mabry's high school days. No need for those either.

Menendez replaced the floorboard, right-sided the bed, and observed the scene. He straightened out the bedspread. Nothing was amiss. It was as if he had never been there.

Menendez looked out the bedroom window. There was some traffic, but no suspicious vehicles. And no pedestrians.

Looking at his watch, Menendez decided it was time to wrap this up. That was when he heard the soft but unmistakable sound of the front door opening up.

* * *

Luckily, Turley was driving an unmarked vehicle. When he reached Stanwix St., he headed to the wharf and pulled over to the shoulder of the road. A man was deflating a dinghy thirty yards away.

Turley pulled out his cell phone and took several photos. The man, carrying a backpack, certainly fit Scuglia's description. He looked like he could be of Mexican descent, though it was hard to tell for sure.

As soon as he collapsed the dinghy, the man produced a cell phone and made a call. Five minutes later, a car appeared. An Uber, perhaps.

Turley followed the car discreetly as it headed downtown, then into the Strip District, and then into Polish Hill. From Polish Hill, the car headed to East Liberty. The passenger got out at Beatty St., paid the driver, and darted into an apartment complex.

Damn, Turley thought, isn't that the Mabry place?

He called Scuglia. "What's Mabry's address?"

"Which Mabry?"

"Gary Mabry."

"It's in East Liberty. 392 N. Beatty St."

"The dinghy guy is in his apartment building right now."

"Damn it. Call for backup."

"Will do. Then I'm going in."

"Be careful, man."

"Roger that."

209

Chapter Forty-Five: Life on the Monongahela

It was a chilly night, but beautiful. The sky was dark ahead, but if you looked backwards, you could see a half-moon in the west. Except for occasional traffic noise, they heard the steady purr of the boat and the splashing of waves in its wake.

At around 10:00 p.m., Scuglia got a call from Stilton. He put him on speaker phone.

"We've got your burglar. He's been shot in the leg and is being taken to Mercy Hospital."

"What do we know about him?"

"A Mexican national. Jose Castillo. May or may not speak English."

"Turley shot him?"

"No, he surprised another burglar. That's the guy who shot him."

"Another burglar?"

"He got away."

"Did Turley get a good look at the guy?"

"He says it was a cop."

"A cop?"

"Or it could have been someone dressed like a cop."

"What the fuck?"

"We'll sort it out later."

"Do you want us to abort?"

"Definitely not. Stick to your game plan."

"Roger, Lieutenant. Over and out."

Scuglia and Lexie were stunned.

"What does it mean to look like a cop?" Lexie asked.

"Mean? Ugly?"

"Spare me. What are you thinking?"

"I'm thinking Atwood. He's crazy enough to do it. And stupid enough to do it badly."

"Maybe Turley can tell us more."

"I'll give him a call tomorrow to…" Scuglia stopped in mid-sentence, as he noticed an enormous bird flapping its wings and heading towards the shore. The bird chittered and hissed as it descended to treetop level, hovering. "What the fuck is that? It looks like a bird but sounds like a snake."

Lexie laughed. "That's a turkey vulture."

Scuglia shivered. "That is one scary mother fucker."

"Don't worry. As long as you're alive, you're safe. Turkey vultures are like other vultures. Unless you're dead, they have zero interest."

"What if he's desperate?"

"If he's desperate for food, he'll find a dead mouse, a dead chipmunk, or a dead chicken."

They hugged the shoreline as best they could, while the towboat forged ahead in a makeshift center lane. They maintained a respectful distance behind their quarry, using binoculars to observe the captain and the crew every ten minutes or so.

At around midnight, they noticed signs of civilization ahead. They also observed that the towboat was veering towards the shore. They slowed down in response, waiting to see what happened next.

"Two guys are on deck," Scuglia reported, handling the binoculars while Lexie steered the boat. "And they're inflating another dinghy. Any idea where we are? I'd like to alert Radic."

Lexie checked her GPS. "We're running parallel to Route 88. There's a Ford dealership nearby. We're a mile or a mile and a half away from the lock."

"I'll let him know." And he did.

"What should we do?" Lexie asked as Scuglia got off the phone.

"I think we need a diversion to give Radic time to get here. Let's give them something to think about. Full speed ahead."

If there was one thing Lexie was good at, it was full speed ahead.

"Hold on to your hat, Tony. We're going for it."

Not quite ready for a sudden surge, Scuglia actually lost his hat and nearly lost his footing. He held onto the boat for dear life as Lexie raced ahead.

"I didn't say to kill us, Davodny. Slow down."

Lexie slowed down, to forty miles per hour.

"Do you have a megaphone?" Scuglia asked.

"In my backpack."

"Get it out. We're going to announce ourselves."

At this point, they were about fifty yards from the towboat.

"This is the Pittsburgh Police," Scuglia announced. "We need to talk with you."

A bullet whizzed past Scuglia's head.

"Shit."

Scuglia and Lexie both hunkered down.

"Head towards the shore but away from the boat."

Lexie made a sharp left turn and headed for the riverbank.

Two more shots whizzed by.

"We're sitting ducks," Lexie said as she turned off the lights.

Scuglia said nothing. He was clutching his leg.

"You've been hit."

Scuglia nodded, writhing in pain.

Lexie changed course again, creating as much distance as she could between their craft and the towboat.

She called Radic and left a message. "Mayday. Scuglia's been shot in the leg. We're backing away from the towboat."

Two more shots were fired, but they were out of range. "The shooter's on deck. One man on the shore."

Scuglia was losing blood and growing pale. "Stay with me, Tony."

Ignoring everything else for the moment, Lexie turned the boat's lights back on and gently inspected Scuglia's wound. An exit wound in the rear thigh and a bullet hole in the side of the boat suggested that the bullet had missed the thigh bone. Thank God for that.

Lexie grabbed her EMT kit. With scissors, she quickly but carefully removed most of the pants covering Scuglia's left leg. Then she repositioned Scuglia, so his head was resting on a sleeping blanket. Next, she extracted a tourniquet and wrapped it tightly around the wound. Throughout all of this, she chattered away, trying to keep Scuglia calm and alert.

With Scuglia stabilized, she dialed 911. An ambulance would arrive in ten minutes.

Lexie saw two cars pull up near the dinghy's destination. That must be Radic. Then she heard a gunshot. Shaking with fear, she panicked, fearing the worst. But her training kicked in, and she focused on the matter at hand. She needed to get Scuglia safely ashore.

There was no dock nearby, but Lexie spotted a sidewalk close to the water's edge and a fire hydrant. Steering the boat in that direction, she maneuvered as closely as possible, then tossed a mooring line towards the fire hydrant. Bulls-eye.

At this point, realizing that they might still be in jeopardy, Lexie reached for her gun. Removing Scuglia from the boat was a job for two people, not one. She and Scuglia would be safer in the boat than ashore. She doused the lights.

It was hard to tell what was going on one hundred yards away. Neither of the cars was a police vehicle with flashing lights, and visibility was poor.

She reached for Scuglia's phone and pressed Stilton's phone number.

"Scuglia?"

"Sir, this is Lexie Davodny. Scuglia's been shot."

"How is he?"

"Still conscious. He was shot in the thigh. I've called 911."

"And Radic?"

"He's probably one hundred yards away. I heard a shot."

"Hang in there, Davodny. I've already alerted the Charleroi police. They should be there soon."

"Yes, sir."

"Stay safe."

"Thank you, sir."

Despite her training, Lexie found her eyes filling with tears. If this was life in the fast lane, she wanted to be in a different lane. She wanted to be back home with Branko and Ralph. And she wanted everyone to be okay.

Chapter Forty-Six: Watchful Waiting

The Mon Valley Hospital was extremely quiet at two o'clock in the morning. Despite the tension, there was something oddly comforting about the waiting room. Lexie had no idea how good the medical staff was, but she felt sure that Scuglia was in a good place. She started to nod. The day's drama had taken its toll.

She recognized Radic's voice. Was it a dream? Lexie's heart skipped a beat when she saw Radic himself. She knew from Stilton that he was okay, but still, it was comforting to see him in the flesh.

Radic gave Lexie a bear hug and a long kiss after crossing the room. "I was worried about you, babe."

"I was worried about *you*," she said, her eyes glistening. "Especially after the shooting started."

"How's Tony?" he asked.

"He took a bullet in the upper thigh. It'll be slow going for a while. He'll need some PT to get back into shape. But he should be okay. Where's Mulroy?"

"She helped transport one of our suspects to the Charleroi jail."

"One of our suspects?"

"We've arrested four people, including the captain of the towboat."

"Any evidence of a drug shipment?"

Radic nodded.

"It's big enough that Stilton decided to call in the DEA."

"Are you okay with that?"

"I'm more than okay with that. I'd rather focus on the murders and leave the drugs to someone else."

"Are they associated with one of the cartels?"

"Yes, but not the one that's dominated Pittsburgh for years."

"That's kind of what you and Mulroy were thinking, wasn't it?"

Radic nodded.

"And the burglar at Gary's apartment?"

"He's with the same cartel."

"He was injured, too?"

"Yes, but not badly."

A few minutes later, Stilton arrived. Although it was the middle of the night, he looked remarkably chipper and gave Radic and Lexie a V for victory sign.

"This is the break we've been waiting for, eh, Radic?"

"I think so, sir."

He turned to Lexie. "How's Scuglia?"

"I think he's going to be okay, sir. He'll be limping for a while, but there was a clean exit wound. Probably no bone damage."

"He was lucky to have you on board to patch him up."

"Thank you, sir."

"Do we have any ballistics reports on the gunfight at Gary's apartment, sir?" Radic asked.

"Nothing on the second burglar's wounds yet. But we've recovered a pistol from him. We can compare the bullets with those that killed Gary. We have fingerprints from the second burglar and possibly from the first burglar as well."

"Pleased to hear it. So, where does this leave us on access to Gary's apartment, sir?"

"It's all yours, Radic. I'm sorry for the delay. But my hands were tied. I hope you understand."

"Water under the bridge, sir. I'm just eager to search the premises. And obviously, I'm not the only one. How about Internal Affairs?"

"They're unhappy. But we prevailed. Of course, we expect you to make some progress. There's talk about more protests if the Mabry case isn't solved soon. We need to wrap this up!"

Chapter Forty-Seven: A Surplus of Prisoners

An old-fashioned diner in Charleroi had become Radic's home away from home. It was conveniently located just a few blocks from the Charleroi police headquarters, also just a few miles away from the Penn Highlands Mon Valley Hospital, where Scuglia was recovering until he was well enough to transfer to Pittsburgh.

Surrounded by waiters and waitresses who saw him as just another customer, Radic found it easier to think clearly and strategize without the prying eyes and commotion of the police headquarters itself. They also served a good cup of coffee.

After conferring with Radic and Stilton, Charleroi's chief of police decided to charge the four men in custody, including the skipper, with two crimes: reckless use of a firearm and carrying a gun without a permit.

At the same time, police officers from both jurisdictions conferred with the Washington County DA and the Allegheny County DA about the possibility of charging one of the men—the one suspected of having shot Scuglia—with attempted murder.

While munching on a remarkably good cheeseburger, Radic was able to reach Mike Turley at PBP. He had arrested Jose Castillo, shortly after Castillo was wounded by an unidentified intruder at Gary's apartment. Castillo was now recovering at Mercy Hospital but was scheduled to be transferred to the county jail soon.

After congratulating Turley on a job well done, Radic asked about the arrest. "What did you charge him with?"

"For the time being, pretty simple stuff. Breaking and entering, possession of a gun without a permit, and resisting arrest."

"Not murder? Stilton says his prints match the prints in the warehouse where Gino was murdered."

"That's true, though we haven't released that information. Stilton wants you to weigh in before we charge him with murder. When things clear up in Charleroi, of course."

"Can we place him in Pittsburgh at the time of Gino's death?"

"We're working on it."

"Has he lawyered up?"

"You betcha."

"Who did he call?"

"A high roller. Armando Garcia. From Tampa."

"Rings a bell."

"He represents drug kingpins in high-profile cases."

"Is he in Pittsburgh?"

"On his way."

"Any idea what Castillo was looking for?"

"Whatever the other guy was looking for."

"Which was?"

"No clue. But it seems to have been in Gary's bedroom, under a floorboard."

"Did you get a good look at the other guy?"

"A pretty good look. But he was wearing a bandana and a cap."

"What did you see?"

"Well, he was dressed like a cop."

"Which means?"

"He was wearing a PBP vest."

Radic whistled softly. "Those things are hard to come by."

"I know."

"So maybe someone on the inside was lending a helping hand."

"That's what we think."

"Anything else?"

"He was wearing some upscale tennis shoes. Brand new. We got prints."

"What type?"

"Nike Metcon 8."

"Seriously? That's what I wear."

"He was also wearing an earring."

"Hold on a second. He was wearing a PBP vest. Nike Metcon 8 training shoes. And an earring."

"Yeah."

"How tall would you say he was?"

"Tall. Six foot one. Six foot two."

"So, about my height."

"Yeah, I guess so."

"I don't mean to sound paranoid, but it seems like the guy was trying to look like me."

"Why would he do that?"

"It's well known within the department that I was denied access to Gary's apartment until Stilton could work something out with Internal Affairs."

"Yeah, I heard about that."

"So, for some reason, someone wanted to burgle the place *and* make it look like I was the burglar."

"Shit. I hadn't looked at it that way, but I think you're right."

"Maybe he thought we had video surveillance there."

"Do we?"

"Not as far as I know. But nothing would surprise me. In any event, I'm convinced that the first burglar was trying to shift the blame to me."

"Makes sense. You have any enemies on the force?"

"At least two."

"Frenchy?"

"Yep."

"Who else?"

"Atwood."

"I might have guessed."

"See if you can account for their movements over the past couple of days. They know they're being watched, so you'll have to be careful. But do your best. I smell a rat."

* * *

When Radic returned to his apartment after forty-eight hours in Charleroi, he reeked of sweat, seaweed, onions, and French fries. Nevertheless, he received a royal welcome from Lexie and from Ralph, who ran around excitedly until he barfed on the living room rug and was banished to his cage.

Lexie allowed Radic the luxury of a thirty-minute shower before a makeshift dinner consisting of hamburgers, pasta salad, and green beans. Radic didn't have the heart to tell her that he had consumed approximately six hamburgers over the past two days. "The perfect meal!" he beamed.

Having just returned from a visit to Allegheny Hospital, Scuglia's new home, Lexie offered assurances that he would recover fully and that he was in good spirits. "He might even get a medal," she added.

"I hope he does."

"Stilton is beside himself with excitement over all of this."

Radic laughed. "I'm glad we were able to make his day. How's it going with you?"

"I'm due back at River Rescue tomorrow."

"How do you feel about that, babe? Now that you've had a taste of life in the fast lane."

Lexie sighed. "Honestly, Branko, I don't know how you do it, day in and day out. It's too stressful for me. Scuglia is going to be okay, but he came within an inch or two of a shattered kneecap. That's not where I want to be. A life without jogging? A life without walks in the park? It's way too risky."

"Do you regret doing it?"

"No, I don't regret it. It was thrilling and we got a really good result. But I think I'll treat it as something I can tell my grandchildren about."

"Grandchildren?"

Lexie laughed. "Just hypothetical ones."

Ralph began whining in the background.

"Shall we release him?" Radic asked.

"Not just yet. You've showered, and a shower is a terrible thing to waste."

"I can't quarrel with that."

"I'll race you to the bedroom. While we both still have good kneecaps."

Chapter Forty-Eight: Bright Lights, Big City

In New York City, Larry felt like a little boy in a candy shop. The glamour, the glitz, the razzle-dazzle. The neon lights in Times Square, the pulsating rhythms of the subway, the hustle and bustle, the parks, the high-line, the tantalizing aromas in Chinatown, the pizza fumes in Little Italy. It was almost too much to take in.

Unlike Pittsburgh, jazz in New York City ended late. That was fine with Larry, who was a night owl anyway.

Another difference that was easy to like was an audience of jazz aficionados. In Pittsburgh, most people came to a jazz club to eat; the music was secondary. In New York, it seemed, most people came to a jazz club to hear jazz; the food was secondary.

Admittedly, there were musical challenges at first. Larry was the undisputed leader of the Rough Riders. Not so in the Big Apple. The other musicians treated him respectfully, even cordially, but he had to fight for airtime and make the most of it.

The music was less predictable as well. Standard chord changes were the default option, but sometimes band members favored their own chord changes, which required everyone to stay alert. Larry greatly admired the bass player, who adjusted to these alterations with ease and grace.

He also came to revere the piano player, the de facto leader in Happy Harlow's absence. Whatever Larry did, the piano player adapted to fit the spirit of his solo. The connection was uncanny, given that they had never played together before.

By the third night at the Village Vanguard, as the jitters faded, Larry felt that he had died and gone to heaven. The band members were in sync, the audiences were appreciative, and the pay was good. Larry even snagged a good review from a prominent reviewer:

"Trumpeter Larry Mabry played inspired solos, especially for up-tempo numbers. His horn is full of mischief and humor, like that of a young Dizzy Gillespie."

Privately, Larry would have been tougher on himself. His lip was doing remarkably well, but he was struggling to hit the high Cs. Oh well, give it time. On balance, he was playing better than expected, given his injury. And he had not yet exhausted his supply of ChapStick.

After gigs, some of the musicians hung out at a nearby bar or at the piano player's apartment, drinking, smoking dope, and snorting cocaine. Larry begged off after the first night. The wounds of Gary's death were still raw. Anything having to do with drugs set Larry on edge.

Larry was crashing with a friend who lived in Greenwich Village and who worked on Wall Street. Given their hours, they didn't see much of one another, but the friend would be taking in one of Larry's sets on Saturday night. Something to look forward to.

The best time to call Dorothy was usually late afternoon, when she was home from school and hopefully doing a bit of homework. He tried to call every other day. Dorothy was fine, at first, but she grew quiet and sullen when Larry told her that she could not hang out with him for the next three weekends. Hadn't Wanda already explained that? Apparently not.

The other issue gnawing at Larry was hard feelings from his bandmates when he announced that he would be away for three weeks. When they had brainstormed about getting a gig in New York City, they pointed out, the dream had always been to go there as a group.

Well, that was his dream too, but this was a different reality. Happy Harlow's illness created a spot for a trumpeter, not an opportunity for the whole band. That was the way the world worked.

The shared dream issue, big as it was, was not the only irritant for his bandmates. Larry was the main draw, and it was he who handled their bookings. With Larry away for three weeks, the band would be struggling for work and for cash.

For all these reasons, Larry could not share his triumphs on stage with the Pittsburghers who best knew what jazz meant to him. His mother was thrilled, of course, but even she would rather see him in person for dinner than talk over the phone about a glowing review.

After a triumphant week at the Village Vanguard, Happy Harlow's group switched to Smalls for a week. Although not as famous as the Vanguard, Smalls had a great rep with jazz musicians. The acoustics and sound system were great. Fewer seats, so less revenue, but they still paid well.

At one of the Smalls sessions, a highly-regarded drummer took in the second set. Backstage afterwards, he lavished praise on Larry and asked if he might be interested in joining his band for a world tour after his New York dates were through.

Larry could hardly believe his good luck. Let me think about it, he said coyly. But in his heart of hearts, it was an easy choice: Of course, I'll go!

That, at any rate, was his thinking until he received a call from Radic.

"How's it going, Larry?"

"Livin' the dream, man. Livin' the dream. The band is tight. The audiences adore us. And the pay's not bad either,"

"Wonderful! I'm really happy for you, Larry. Just make sure it doesn't keep you from training for the Tough Mudder competition. Have you found a good place to jog?"

"Two places. If I have the time, I take the No. 1 subway from Christopher Street to Columbus Circle. Then I do the Reservoir Loop in Central Park."

"That's a cool place."

"If I don't have the time, I run across the Williamsburg Bridge, about a mile from my friend's place. I call it the Sonny Rollins Loop."

"Why's that, Larry?"

"'Cause that's where Sonny played his sax when he was trying to get his mojo back. Sometimes sixteen hours a day."

"Amazing. You ever tried playing your trumpet on the same bridge?"

"Don't need to, man. I still have MY mojo."

Radic laughed.

"So is this a social call, Radic? Or do you have something on your mind?"

"Larry, I thought you'd want to know that there was a story about Gary in this morning's *Post-Gazette*."

"What kind of a story?"

"It's complicated, but the gist of it is this: Before he died, Gary met with a reporter from the *Post-Gazette* and gave him a detailed list of payoffs he made to local cops."

Larry thought for a moment. "You and I knew that was going on. Why should I be concerned?"

"Well, I don't know, Larry. It's kind of like when you're trying to put the two ball in the corner pocket, but you wind up putting a few other balls in other pockets."

"What the fuck are you saying, man? Just spit it out."

"This story confirms something that wasn't widely known—that Gary was a drug dealer for the past eight years. That's going to be very embarrassing for the mayor, in the middle of a re-election campaign."

"Well, Gary would be upset by that. But I'm not political, man. It doesn't bother me one way or the other."

"It's also going to be very embarrassing for the Pittsburgh police."

"It should be."

"There's also a good chance that this will lead to indictments against two sitting police officers. Maybe more."

"It should."

"I'm not disagreeing, Larry. But you gotta understand this—over the next few weeks, Gary's every word, every step, every activity is going to be under a microscope. Your mother is likely to get unwanted calls, and some reporters may come to the house. Dorothy may get the evil eye from teachers and get teased by classmates. Gary's will is likely to be closely scrutinized."

"Do they mention the will in the newspaper?"

"They don't yet, but the reporter knows about it. It's only a matter of time."

"Damn it, man, I don't know what to say. I've finally made it to the Big Apple. All of our shows are sold out. We got a nice review in the *New York Times*. Skippy Pike wants me to go on tour with him. I can't deal with this shit now, man."

"Larry, I hear you, and I'm not telling you what to do. I just thought you should know."

"Okay, man, you're not telling me what to do. But what is it you think I *should* do?"

"For the moment, maybe nothing. But some people you really care about are going to be hurt by this story. You need to keep in touch with them. Even if you don't come back to Pittsburgh, they need to hear from you, they need your advice, they need you in their lives."

Larry sighed "Father Buckley. Maybe he can sort this out."

"He's an amazing man. He'll do what he can, I'm sure of it. But there are some things that only you can do, Larry. You may have to make some difficult choices."

"I'll think it over, man. I appreciate your call."

Larry looked outside the window of his friend's apartment. The weather had changed for the worse. The skies had darkened, rain was pelting down, and people were scampering for cover. But it wasn't just the weather that had changed. Larry picked up his trumpet and found himself playing "Here's That Rainy Day." It's amazing what one phone call could do.

Chapter Forty-Nine: A Lucky Break

It was rare for Radic to receive a call at home at midnight, even in the midst of a murder investigation. He was a bit groggy as he reached for the phone.

The caller was a young trainee handling phone calls for Homicide. "I'm sorry to be calling you at home so late, Detective, but we just received a call that could be relevant to your murder investigation."

"Which one?"

"The Gardenia murder."

"You're sure this isn't a crank caller?"

"Pretty sure, but judge for yourself. The guy's at a warehouse near where Detective Gardenia was killed. He goes there maybe once a month and happened to be there tonight. He says there's been a break-in."

"Was anything stolen?"

"No, nothing stolen, as far as he can tell. But there's some stuff there that doesn't belong."

"Like what?"

"Binoculars."

"Someone left a pair of binoculars behind, after breaking into a deserted warehouse? Why should I care?"

"Well, there's also some blood."

Suddenly, Radic sat up. "Where's the caller, son? Is he still at the warehouse?"

"Still at the warehouse. He said he's willing to meet you there now, or sometime tomorrow morning."

"Give me his name and phone number and location. Tell him I'm on my way. It's not far from where I live. I'll be there in ten minutes."

"Will do, Detective."

"And thank you, son. You were right to wake me up."

Radic didn't need GPS to locate the warehouse. It lay kitty-corner to the warehouse where Gino Gardenia had been bludgeoned to death.

As he approached his destination, it occurred to Radic that it would be wise to call for back-up, either Mulroy or a patrol officer. But Mulroy was running on empty, like Radic himself. Better to give her a good night's sleep.

A battered Ford truck with Pennsylvania plates sat directly in front. Radic notified a dispatcher when he arrived and gave her the plate number, just in case there was any funny business.

As soon as he slammed the car door, a man emerged from the dimly lit building. He was a redhead, with a pale complexion, wearing jeans and a flannel shirt.

"Detective Radish?"

"Yep, that's me," he replied, not bothering to correct the pronunciation.

"I'm Mark McCool," he said, extending his hand. "I'm the manager of Walsh Electronics. We use this place for storage when we run out of space at our store."

"Where's your store?"

"Oakmont."

"Have you touched anything inside?"

"A light switch. And the binoculars. Sorry about that. Also, I touched some bloody rags, to make sure it was blood."

"How do you know it's blood?"

"It smells funny. And it's attracted some maggots."

"Let's have a look. But first, I'm going to have to frisk you. Are you okay with that?"

"Sure. I get it."

After patting the man down and finding nothing, Radic asked McCool to lead the way.

The warehouse was not very big, maybe five thousand square feet. It gave off a musty smell, and Radic noticed some rodent droppings on the way in. The light illuminated one section of the warehouse, but the rest of the building remained dark.

"Are there other lights you can turn on?" Radic asked.

"Sure. No problem."

McCool walked deeper into the warehouse and flipped a switch, illuminating rows of boxes that seemed to contain small appliances and other odds and ends.

Meanwhile, Radic noticed a table with binoculars and some blood-stained rags. Something smelled funky. Brain tissue, perhaps.

"Does anyone else have a key to this place?"

"My boss, Miles Jackson. But he almost never comes here. It's up to me and my crew to store stuff and to retrieve stuff when necessary."

"How often do you come here?"

"About once a month."

"When was the last time you were here?"

"Probably a month ago."

"Before or after…May 6?"

"I'll have to check."

"Why did you come here tonight? And why so late?"

"Normally, I would come here during the day, with a crew. But we just got an order from one of the universities for a bunch of microwaves for one of their dorms. I wanted to confirm that we have enough of them in stock, and this is the first chance I've had to check."

"Have you ever heard of Gino Gardenia?"

"I don't think so."

"He was a police detective."

"Is that the guy who was killed somewhere near here?"

"That's the one."

"Do you think…?"

"I don't know what I think yet. But this could be a crime scene. We'll get started tomorrow morning."

McCool thought for a moment. "What about our microwaves?"

"When do you need to fetch them?"

"Sometime this week."

"I think we can make that happen. But in the meantime, I'm going to ask you to give me your key. I'll get you a copy tomorrow."

"And tonight?"

"You and I will lock the place up. Then we'll have someone guard the premises overnight. The fun begins tomorrow."

"I don't know what to say."

"No need to say anything. But we appreciate your reaching out to us. Whatever happened here, we need to get to the bottom of it."

* * *

The following morning, Radic briefed Mulroy on what he had learned from his midnight visit to the forgotten warehouse.

"Do you like Castillo for Gino's murder?" Mulroy asked.

"I do. How about you?" Radic replied.

"It depends on what the M.E. says. Is the blood on the binoculars Gardenia's?"

"That's what we need to find out."

Radic called Saroja Prakash, explaining the new twist in the Gardenia case. He promised to get her the binoculars and the bloody rags ASAP. Then he cut to the chase. "Could binoculars have been the murder weapon?"

"How much do they weigh?"

"Two to three pounds."

"Made of metal?"

"Aluminum, I would guess."

"With the right amount of force, they might have been heavy enough to kill Gardenia. Is there blood on the binoculars?"

"Yep."

"That's good. Blood on the glassy part?"

"Yep."

"That's very good. Glass is a good surface for prints. What's your timetable?"

Radic said nothing.

Prakash laughed. "Okay, fortunately, it's a light week. Get me the evidence and I'll get on it right away."

"You're the best, Saroja."

"That's what I like to hear."

* * *

On a whim, Mulroy decided to visit Dong Nguyen, currently awaiting a court hearing on his possession of poisonous snakes. She brought with her several photos and asked whether he recognized any of them.

To Mulroy's delight, Nguyen immediately identified Castillo as someone who was on hand when he received his snake shipment for cash. He remembered him as "mean and nasty." When she asked where the hand-off occurred, he said a warehouse on the North Side.

At Mulroy's request, he produced an address from a text message. It turned out to be the warehouse where Gino Gardenia was murdered.

Mulroy called Radic, excitedly reporting the news. Before the close of business, Radic was able to extract a brief report from Prakash: fingerprints on the binoculars belonged to Castillo, blood and brain matter on the binoculars belonged to Gardenia.

Radic took the information from Prakash and Mulroy to the D.A., who quickly agreed to charge Castillo with the murder of Gino Gardenia. The first murder case was as good as closed. At long last, they could focus their full attention on the murder of Gary Mabry.

Chapter Fifty: Gary's Army

Scuglia was seated in a leather Barcalounger in the family living room—his bandaged left leg propped up and a sheaf of papers on a sturdy wooden table to his left, a large glass of orange juice and two bottles of pills on a smaller wooden table to his right.

"This is just what I needed," he said enthusiastically, as his wife Louise escorted Radic and Mulroy into the living room. "It's great to be back in the hunt."

"He's been so wrapped up in these papers that he hasn't had time for anything else," Louise confided, before leaving the room. "He didn't even watch the Pirates last night."

"Okay, Tony, what have you got for us?" Radic asked.

"We have two lists—a blood donor list and a PAC contributor list. We also have cash to be distributed to people on the two lists through December of this year."

"Alright, let's start with the blood donor list. What can you tell us?"

"We have thirty-six people on that list. All guys."

"How much are they paid?"

"Twenty-five hundred dollars a pop.

"And how often are they paid?"

"Every three months."

"That kind of makes sense. The Red Cross says a donor should wait at least two months before giving blood again."

"I'd say they're complying with that."

"Do we know whether it's legal for people to be paid to donate blood to the Red Cross?"

"I'd say we need to investigate that."

"Okay, so how about the PAC contributor payments?"

"Well, we have twenty-four people on that list. Also all guys."

"Any double dippers?"

"Yes! About half of the people on the blood donor list are also on the PAC contributor list."

"What are they paid?"

"Three thousand, three hundred dollars per person."

"Well, that makes sense. If I remember correctly, the F.E.C. says you can only contribute thirty-three hundred dollars to a PAC."

"So they're in compliance then."

"Hold on a second," Mulroy interjected. "On the surface, when John Smith donates thirty-three hundred dollars to a PAC, he's complying with the ceiling. But that's Gary's money. In effect, Gary is violating the law by donating huge amounts of money to one PAC. Just because he's working through surrogates doesn't take him off the hook."

"Does that mean that the nominal donors are also violating the law?" Scuglia asked.

"We'll have to leave that to the lawyers, but probably," Mulroy replied.

"Do we have addresses for these folks?" Radic asked.

"Yes, we do," Scuglia replied. "And they're very interesting. Many of the guys on both lists live in the same apartment complex on Bigelow Boulevard. I don't know what to make of it, but it can't be a coincidence."

"Excellent. Great work, Tony. This really moves the ball downfield."

"So what comes next?" Mulroy asked.

"I'd say we have a lot of homework to do," Radic replied. "First, we need background checks on all the young men linked to Gary who donated blood or who donated money to the Mayor's Re-election Committee. Tony?"

"Can do."

"Second, we need to investigate campaign finance laws at the federal, state, and local levels. Mulroy, you majored in political science at Duquesne, right?"

"Go Dukes! Happy to do that."

"Third, one of us needs to visit Bigelow Towers and find out more about how it got to be the boot camp for members of Gary's Army. I'll do that as soon as we wrap things up."

"Sounds good."

"Finally, Mulroy, I want you to take the list of blood donors to the Red Cross and find out if these folks are still donating blood now that Gary's gone."

"You got it."

* * *

The Bigelow Towers was privately owned, but it had all the charm of a seedy public housing complex. Grimy, dusty, with cobwebs in corners, pop bottles and beer cans that hadn't been picked up, and occasionally the odor of urine.

Still, Radic had seen and smelled worse. In the hallways, there was little evidence of rampant drug use. And many of the doors were decorated with wreaths, pictures, or welcome signs.

Radic rang the buzzer for apartment 1C, the first on his list. No response. He knocked. Still no response. Next, he tried 2D and 2F, using the same strategy. No answer there either.

As he headed towards the third wing of the complex, Radic noticed a large "Office" sign. He rapped on the door.

An elderly Black woman with a friendly smile introduced herself as Harriet Jones and invited Radic to step inside.

Reluctant to get into the details, Radic explained that he was trying to reach several young men who had donated blood to the Red Cross.

Radic shared the full list of names, which Ms. Jones examined for a minute or so. "Any of them late in paying their rent?"

"Well, some of them, some of the time. I'm not saying it never happens. But the people on your list are better than most."

"Why's that?"

"Because their rent is paid for by a third party."

"Really? Who is the third party?"

"St. Martin de Porres Church."

"You're kidding."

"No, the church rents out a number of apartments for young men who, shall we say, have had some difficulties in the world. Their rent is paid for, consistently. And if we ever have any problems with them, we can just call Father Buckley at the church."

"How long has this been going on?"

"Oh, I'd say two, three years."

"Thank you, Ms. Jones. You've been very helpful."

* * *

The waiting room at the Red Cross reminded Mulroy of other waiting rooms she had visited over the years. Some visitors looked bored, others looked nervous. Mulroy explained to the receptionist that she was there on official police business. Within a minute or two, the office manager appeared and ushered her into a private office.

"How can I help you, Detective?" she asked.

Without divulging all the details, Mulroy explained the essentials.

"Did you know Gary Mabry?" Mulroy asked.

"Gary was a legend here, Detective," she explained. "We depend on word of mouth for new volunteers. In Gary's case, we hit the jackpot. He was bound and determined to get us a steady supply of donors, especially donors of color. We'll be forever grateful for that."

"Any idea how many people Gary recruited to give blood?"

"I can't be precise, but I would guess close to a hundred. Maybe more."

"That's a lot of donors."

"Gary was a godsend to us. It's no exaggeration to say that several people owe their lives to Gary's generosity and, of course, the generosity of the people he sent our way. We call them members of Gary's Army."

"Did you interact directly with Gary to schedule the donors?"

"Most of the time. He was pretty hands-on."

"And if not Gary? Who was his second in command?"

"I don't know if he had a second in command. But sometimes I would deal with a guy named Hodges."

"Hodges? I know that name."

"He has some sort of connection to the Mayor."

"Yes, he does. Was he as helpful as Gary?"

"No one could be as helpful as Gary. Or as personable. He was a sweetheart."

"And Hodges?"

"I don't know. I got the impression that he was doing what he had to do. I never detected any passion for the cause. He didn't donate blood, for example."

"Did you ever ask him?"

"I believe so. I ask everyone."

"What did he say?"

"Nothing much. He just shrugged it off. Not for me. Or something like that."

Mulroy reached into her purse and produced two sheets of paper. "I have a list of blood donors who had a continuing relationship with Gary. Do you recognize any of the names?"

The office manager looked over the document. "I recognize most of the names. But why is this important?"

"Well, for one thing, we'd like to talk with two or three of these people. Do you know if any of these folks are scheduled for a visit over the next week or so?"

"We might be able to help with that. But can you tell me what it is you want to know? Maybe I can help you without you having to bother them."

"I'm afraid we do have to talk with a few of them to understand things better."

"Are you saying between the lines that one of them might have some knowledge of Gary's murder?"

"Not necessarily," Mulroy replied. "But to be honest, we have reason to believe that some members of Gary's army were paid to donate blood. Does that concern you?"

The office manager winced. "Actually, that would concern us, Detective. Our working assumption has always been that most of the members of Gary's army are people of faith. A disproportionate share of them worship at St. Martin de Porres Church. We've always assumed that this was an act of charity for them, as it is for almost all of our other donors."

"Do you ask people to disclose whether they have been paid before accepting blood from them?"

"No, we ask a bunch of other questions—whether they've traveled abroad recently, whether they have any infectious diseases. Our policy is that we don't pay for people to donate blood. It never occurred to us that someone might be paying on our behalf."

"I get it. So can you help us with our request?"

"I'll have to check with my boss, Detective. But I will recommend that we cooperate, because we really want to know if some of our donors are being paid to donate. Paid blood samples and unpaid blood samples are supposed to be labeled differently. If what you say is true, our system isn't working the way it's supposed to, and we need to fix that."

"Did any members of Gary's army ever fail to show?"

"Never. They were thoroughly reliable."

"Unusual?"

"Very. People back out for lots of reasons. They forget. They have other things to do. They get cold feet. But not Gary's army. If they were booked to come in, they came in for sure."

"How do you explain that?"

"Well, until today, I would have said the spirit of giving. But after talking with you, I'm starting to think it wasn't that simple."

Chapter Fifty-One: A Call from Home

Larry was between sets at Smalls, munching on some fish and chips, when he saw the familiar phone number on his cell phone.

"Hey, Dee, how you doing, baby?"

"Larry, it's me, not Dorothy."

"Wanda, why are you using Dee's phone? Is something the matter?"

"Well, yes and no. She's fine. She's not hurt or anything. But she's struggling with some stuff. We need to talk."

"I'm grabbing a bite, due back on stage in fifteen minutes. Let's talk tomorrow."

"Larry, you and I both know that if I call you tomorrow, on my own phone, you're not going to pick up. We need to talk now."

Larry sighed. "Okay, Wanda, what's on your mind?"

"I had to go see the principal at school yesterday. Dorothy has gotten into a couple of fights."

"She what?"

"Some kids have been hassling her ever since that damn article appeared in the *Post-Gazette*. They say stuff like, 'Your uncle was a druggie.' They say, 'Tell us where to score some dope.' They're being real mean to her and she finally had enough."

"Did anyone get hurt?"

"They stopped it before it got real bad, but you know how these things can be. It's not the last of it."

"What did the principal say?"

"She was pretty understanding. Dorothy's a good girl. First offense. But the principal wants me to rein her in, and that's hard with you being away and all."

Larry was silent for a while. "Do you want me to talk to her? To talk to Dee?"

"Yes, I want you to talk with her, Larry, but that's not enough. She's struggling right now, babe. With Gary's death. With you leaving town all of a sudden. She needs you back in her life."

Larry looked at his watch. Five minutes to go. "Wanda, I really gotta go. But I promise I'll talk with her. I'll call her after school tomorrow."

"She adores you, Larry. You know that, don't you?"

"I adore her."

"Well, what does that mean? If you adore her so much, what the fuck are you doing in New York?"

"We've been through this before, Wanda. This is a once-in-a-lifetime opportunity for me."

"I know, I know. But your precious baby girl is in a bad place right now. She needs her daddy. And a phone call just ain't enough."

"I'll talk with her. I promise."

"Oh, and there's one more thing. Dee wants to take piano lessons."

"Piano lessons? Really? With whom?"

"With you, you knucklehead. With you. She's reaching out to you, Larry. That's why I'm reaching out to you. It's hard for me to do this. Do you understand that?"

"I guess so."

"Well, think about it. Do something about it. Sort out your priorities. Don't harden your heart. What you see in New York is a once-in-a-lifetime opportunity. What I see every day is a little girl whose life has suddenly been turned upside down. That's an opportunity too."

* * *

Jimmy Russell, the piano player, sought Larry out when their second set ended just before midnight. "You seemed a bit distracted tonight.

Something on your mind?"

"I was hoping you wouldn't notice, man. Was I that bad?"

"Not at all. It's just that you're usually scorching. Tonight, you were just damn good."

"It's stuff going on at home, in Pittsburgh. I try not to think about it, but sometimes it's hard."

"Maybe you want to join me and the boys for a while. Take your mind off things. What do you say?"

Larry agreed and hopped into a cab with two of the other band members. Their destination—Jimmy's apartment.

Larry began with a beer, which dulled the pain but wasn't enough. He enjoyed the banter and smoked a blunt with the other musicians.

At about 2:00 a.m., Jimmy brought out some cocaine, which he snorted in full view of the other musicians. Jimmy looked quizzically at Larry.

Before he realized what he was doing, Larry snorted some cocaine himself. Pure bliss. It was as if a cloud had been lifted.

An hour later, he did it again. It wasn't until 7:00 a.m. that someone called a cab and sent him home.

When Larry awakened, at about 2:00 p.m., he was groggy, disoriented, nauseous. He noticed blood on his pillow.

Larry staggered into the bathroom and stared at himself in the mirror. The face that stared back at him was a distorted version of himself. His eyes were unfocused, and there was a bruise on his forehead that he couldn't remember or explain.

In his confused state of mind, the face Larry saw in the mirror was not his but Gary's from several years ago. Larry shivered at the thought. All the sacrifices he had made to achieve his dream of jazz stardom in the Big Apple. All the sacrifices his mother had made for Gary and himself.

Larry wondered whether his mother could handle the shock of another drug user in the family. And he wondered what Dee would think if she heard rumors about her father's habits. Well, damn it, that just wasn't going to happen.

Larry retreated to the kitchen, where he brewed some coffee and made some toast. Then he reached for his phone.

242

Chapter Fifty-Two: The Curve vs. the Sea Dogs

Mulroy and O'Neill were relaxing in the homicide squad room, after an early evening talk with Stilton.

"I'm going to be a Grasshopper?" O'Neill asked.

"No, you used to be a Grasshopper," Mulroy explained. "A Greensboro Grasshopper. You've just been called up, from A to AA."

"That doesn't sound like a promotion to me. I used to play AA ball, for Harrisburg."

"We know. That's why you're perfect for this assignment."

"Okay, so what am I now?"

"A Curve."

"An Altoona Curve?"

"That's right."

"And what is it you want me to do?"

"Get close to the pitcher, Carlos Almazan."

"Menendez' friend?"

"That's right."

"You think Menendez is in Altoona?"

"Either that or Almazan knows where to find him."

"Will I get to play?"

"That's up to your manager."

"Does he know what's going on?"

"The owner is a friend of Stilton's. He's told the manager to play along for two or three games. He'll do what he's asked to do."

"But I'm out of shape."

"You don't look out of shape to me."

"I'm out of baseball shape. My reflexes aren't what they used to be."

"We don't expect you to hit a grand slam, O'Neill. We just expect you to play if you're asked to play and to keep your eyes and ears open."

"Got it. Well, it's pretty exciting when you think of it."

"It's also pretty dangerous when you think of it. So I want you to keep in touch with me every step of the way."

"Where will you be?"

"The same motel as you. Or at the ballpark."

"It's a home stand?"

"Yep."

"Who are we playing?"

"I like that, O'Neill. You're already talking like a Curve."

"Well, who *are* we playing?"

"The Erie Sea Wolves."

"Cool. I've played them before."

"How did you do?"

"Would you believe a walk-off home run?"

"No, not really."

"Well, look it up. It was a walk-off home run."

"You have that good a memory?"

"It was my only walk-off home run, ever. There are some things you never forget."

* * *

It was Brews and Boos night at the ballpark. Mulroy had paid for a seat near the home team dugout, just in case her protégé got into trouble. She was enjoying a Curve Burger and fries, along with a Diet Coke. The beers looked tempting, but she needed to stay alert.

Mulroy had never attended a minor league baseball game before this week, and she kind of enjoyed the playful atmosphere. Her favorite part was the beginning of the game, when the announcer had a bit of fun at the opposing team's expense.

Announcer: And now for the visiting Erie Sea Wolves, batting first, the shortstop, Bob Szekeley.

Curious Fans: Who?

Announcer: Bob Szekeley.

Disappointed Fans: Oh.

Kind of mean, but it got the fans into the game.

Despite the light-hearted atmosphere, Mulroy was feeling like a nervous parent. It's one thing to put your life on the line. It's another to put your child's life on the line. O'Neill wasn't her child, but sometimes it felt that way. Also, if she ever doubted it, Scuglia's injury reminded her that a misstep could have serious consequences.

Another reason to be nervous was that she didn't really know what Menendez looked like. Denise had given them a serviceable artist's sketch to point them in the right direction. Menendez was dark, muscular, and mean-looking, with a thick mustache, a ponytail, and a mole on his left cheek.

But Menendez was reportedly into disguises. He might or might not have a mustache. He might or might not have a ponytail. Thank God for the mole on his left cheek. That was likely to stay.

O'Neill's first night as a Curve had been uneventful. He took batting practice before the game, but his only time on the field was as a pinch runner. Mulroy felt sorry for him. She knew that he was hoping to play, to really play, and to get a hit. Once a ball player, always a ball player.

So far, O'Neill was doing really well as an undercover agent. He reported that Almazan was a bit of a recluse, which ironically made it easy to befriend him. O'Neill knew a couple of Mexican ballplayers who had made it to the major leagues, and Almazan seemed eager to hear about them.

Mulroy followed Almazan home after the game and noticed nothing out of the ordinary. As far as she could tell, Almazan was by himself.

Tonight, O'Neill was hoping to really play for an inning or two. And, sure enough, he got his chance, starting in center field. Mulroy felt a gush of pride as her protégé fielded a routine fly ball like a pro. "Way to go, O'Neill!" she yelled, hoping that he heard her.

O'Neill's debut at the plate was less auspicious. With runners on first and second and one out, O'Neill hit a ground ball to the shortstop, who promptly turned it into a double play. Poor O'Neill. Mulroy knew how disappointed he would be.

As Mulroy surveyed the stands, she didn't spot anyone who looked remotely like Menendez. Most of those in attendance were families, including kids. Almost all were Anglo. And most of the adults were too busy laughing and drinking beer to look sinister.

O'Neill was benched after three innings. Mulroy noticed that he sat next to Almazan for the rest of the game. Way to go, O'Neill. He was going to be a good cop.

When the game ended, Mulroy headed to the parking lot. Her plan was to wait there until O'Neill called.

A half hour later, O'Neill sent her a text: We're going for drinks, Knickerbocker Tavern. Mulroy found the address, only two miles away. She decided to head there immediately and wait.

A few minutes later, Mulroy saw Almazan pull up in a Ford Bronco. O'Neill appeared shortly thereafter. The two headed for the tavern, opting to sit outside. Mulroy decided to stay put and observe.

It took the two ballplayers a while to relax, but after a half hour and a couple of beers, the conversation seemed to be improving. Both men were gesturing and laughing. O'Neill produced a baseball from a backpack, and Almazan seemed to be giving him tips.

Wondering where this lovefest was going, Mulroy noticed that Almazan took a phone call. Abruptly, the mood changed. Almazan tossed a couple of bills on the table and took off after saying goodbye.

Seconds later, Mulroy's phone rang. "He got a call from a friend."

"Did he say who?"

"No, but he spoke entirely in Spanish."

"Okay, I'm going to follow him. You follow me."

"Will do."

The trio didn't have far to go. Ten minutes later, Almazan pulled up outside a private home with an Alfa Romeo parked in the driveway. He got out, walked to the front door, knocked, and was ushered inside.

Mulroy caught a quick glimpse of the man who let him in. No mustache, but the man otherwise fit Menendez's description. At any rate, he had a ponytail. She couldn't tell whether there was a mole or not.

Not wishing to arouse suspicion, Mulroy continued to drive by. O'Neill did likewise and reconnected a half block away.

"I think we've got our man, O'Neill. But we've got to tread carefully. This isn't our turf. I'm going to call the Altoona PD. They already know we're doing this. But they'll want to be involved."

"Whatever you say, Detective."

Mulroy reached the chief of police at home. He said he would send out two patrol officers immediately.

"We just have to sit tight for a while, O'Neill. Did you learn anything useful?"

O'Neill shrugged. "He's not a bad guy, as far as I can tell. He's really into baseball. He doesn't think the other players like him all that much."

"Did he say anything about Menendez?"

O'Neill shook his head.

"Did he say anything about Pittsburgh?"

"He said he was there the other day."

"Doing what?"

"He got some new tennis shoes."

"Why go to Pittsburgh for tennis shoes?"

"You got me."

A police car arrived sooner than expected. Mulroy got out of her car and beckoned to the Altoona cops. They got the message and drove past the residence, stopping at Mulroy's car.

Mulroy introduced herself and O'Neill and briefly explained why Menendez was of interest. "How do you want to play this?" she asked.

"It's your call, Detective," one of the officers replied. "The chief said we should just give you support."

"Okay," Mulroy said, "Barnett, you come with me to the front door. Marchese, you cover the back door. O'Neill, you stand near your car. If Menendez tries to run away, follow him on foot. If he tries to drive away, follow him in your car, and we'll catch up as soon as we can."

"Are we after one guy or two?" Barnett asked.

"We're after Menendez. The guy with the ponytail. The other guy is unlikely to go anywhere. Questions?"

"Armed and dangerous?"

"That should be your assumption. Put your body cam on, O'Neill. Just in case. I'll do the same."

"We don't do that here, Detective," Barnett said.

"That's fine. But we do in Pittsburgh. This way, we'll have a visual record."

Mulroy and Barnett gave Marchese enough time to situate himself near the back door and O'Neill enough time to retrieve his police jacket and activate his body cam. Then Mulroy and Barnett marched to the front door.

"Open up, it's the police."

Mulroy and Barnett heard two men talking rapidly, in Spanish. The conversation stopped, and someone spoke up from inside.

"Give me a minute. I'm going to open the door."

"We'll give you ten seconds. Then we're coming in," Barnett said.

The door opened, and Carlos Almazan appeared.

"We're looking for Jorge Menendez. Where is he?"

"He's not here right now."

"Have a seat, Mr. Almazan, while we verify that," Mulroy said.

* * *

One advantage of O'Neill's vantage point was that he noticed a light go on in an upstairs bedroom. Moments later, Jorge Menendez opened a window and eased out onto the roof.

O'Neill didn't know how agile Menendez was, but he saw an opportunity for escape and feared that Menendez saw it too. Next to the roof was an elm tree with sturdy limbs. With a modest amount of effort, Menendez could shimmy down the tree. Judging from his movements, that's what he intended to do.

O'Neill licked his lips and swallowed hard. He patted his revolver. Then a thought occurred to him. He reached into the back seat of his car and retrieved a baseball.

"Put your hands up and stay where you are!" he yelled.

Startled, Menendez lost his footing briefly but recovered it. Not waiting to see what Menendez would do next, O'Neill hurled the baseball directly at him.

The ball hit Menendez squarely in the chest. Losing his footing, he slid off the roof, banged against a drainage pipe, and tumbled into some bushes below. O'Neill heard a yelp and rushed towards the suspect.

Meanwhile, Mulroy and Barnett had figured out the ruse. While Barnett guarded Alamazan inside, Mulroy rushed outside. What she saw brought a smile to her face. O'Neill was Mirandizing and cuffing Menendez. Like a pro.

Chapter Fifty-Three: The Persuasive Power of Coffee

At Radic's suggestion, he and Fred Vinson from Internal Affairs met for breakfast at Commonplace Coffee in Squirrel Hill. Radic believed in the persuasive power of good coffee. At least, it was worth a shot.

Although they arrived at 7:30 a.m., the café was already brimming with customers. Radic snagged a window table and suggested that Vinson remain there while he placed an order for both of them.

Ten minutes later, Radic returned with two fragrant cups of coffee (one from Ethiopia, one from Papua New Guinea), two breakfast burritos, and two muffins. Vinson's smile after the first sip of the Ethiopian coffee was encouraging.

Radic decided to begin with new information. "We apprehended a suspect at Gary's apartment the other day."

"I heard something about that."

"Just so you know, we didn't initiate this. A Mexican national rode to Pittsburgh on a towboat and headed straight for Gary's apartment after being dropped off. Turley simply followed him there."

"I believe you."

"Now here's the funny part. Our burglar encountered another burglar while he was there. The first burglar was disguised to look like me."

"Did you catch the first burglar?"

"He got away. But he shot the second burglar before he did."

Vinson shook his head in disbelief.

"Can you think of anyone who might want to discredit me by burgling Gary's apartment pretending to be me?" Radic asked.

"I can think of two people."

"Frenchy Frobisher and Mark Atwood?"

"Those are the two."

"Are you ready to file charges against them?"

Vinson hesitated. "We're close."

"Well, let me tell you something in confidence that might make a difference. Sometime over the next few days, the *Post-Gazette* is going to publish a story. They will present evidence showing that Gardenia, Frobisher, and Atwood extorted money from Gary Mabry's organization for the past five years."

"What evidence do they have?"

"A comprehensive list of payments, recipients, and dates. Most of the transactions were at Muscle Mania in East Liberty; some of them were at other venues."

"Any canceled checks?"

"All in cash, but well documented."

"That gives us pause. If it's cash, it's one man's word against another."

"I hear you. But there's other evidence."

"What other evidence?"

"Audio recordings."

"From whom?"

"Gary Mabry."

"Have you heard them?"

"No. But the word is that they're incriminating beyond a shadow of a doubt."

"What does that mean exactly?" Vinson asked.

"It means that Gary says to Gardenia, 'I'm going to give you ten thousand dollars, as requested, but after this, it's gotta stop.' Then Gino tells him no, it's not going to stop."

Vinson tilted his coffee mug a couple of times, as he considered this.

"How about Frobisher and Atwood?"

"The same stuff. Gary knew what he was doing, and it never occurred to these clowns that he might be recording them. As they saw it, Gary was in too deep. He wouldn't want to incriminate himself."

Vinson gazed out the window for a few seconds, collecting his thoughts. "Can we get the audio recordings?"

"The *Post-Gazette* might resist. But their resistance is likely to be perfunctory."

"What makes you think that?"

"Their confidential source is dead. Confidentiality still matters beyond the grave, but not as much."

"Do Stilton and Reilly know about the audio recordings?"

"I'm telling you first."

"Thank you. I appreciate that."

Radic turned to his own coffee, still plenty warm. He wolfed down one of the breakfast burritos.

"So, what do you suggest?" Vinson asked.

"I suggest that we both visit Gary's apartment this morning at nine o'clock. I've invited Mulroy to join us. Maybe something will turn up. But even if it doesn't, the *Post-Gazette* story is going to put intense pressure on Reilly to do something.

"If you're on board, you and I can meet with Reilly and Stilton this afternoon. Give them a heads-up. Urge them to sic our lawyers on the *Post-Gazette*. And recommend that the D.A. indict Frobisher and Atwood on charges of extortion, based on the evidence you've gathered."

"Just out of curiosity, how does this advance your murder investigation? Or is it personal?"

Radic paused before responding. "I care about the department and its reputation, just as you do, Fred. If the *Post-Gazette* uncovers flagrant corruption within the department and we're still dotting the i's and crossing the t's, it's just not going to look good. If, on the other hand, the *Post-Gazette* reports that the D.A. is about to indict two bad apples based on a careful in-house investigation by Internal Affairs, then we're all doing the right thing, except for Frenchy and Atwood."

Vinson nodded slowly.

"As for the murder investigation, we think we know who killed Gardenia, but we still don't know who killed Gary Mabry. Maybe that one is personal for me, because I know his family. But it's also a high priority for the department and for Reilly, given the growing discontent within the Black community.

"I don't know exactly how this will play out. Anything could happen. But I'm a great believer in shining a light on the cockroaches on the kitchen floor after dark. See them scamper. Watch where they go. It might give us some leads. People say and do strange things when you put them on the spot."

Chapter Fifty-Four: A Motley Crew

True to his promise, Radic convened a second brainstorming session in Scuglia's home. Radic, Mulroy, and Turley participated, along with Scuglia. Stilton had also been invited, but he preferred to be briefed after the meeting.

The setting was Scuglia's living room. Scuglia was sitting comfortably on a worn Barcalounger, his left leg outstretched.

To Radic, Scuglia looked good and seemed much more mobile than on their previous visit. Louise also reported that he was in good spirits. "Keep giving him work to do," she whispered to Radic in the hallway. "It distracts him from his leg."

Scuglia was very appreciative when Radic produced some apricot nut bread, baked by Lexie. "You have a winner there, Radic," Scuglia said, munching on a slice. "I hope you realize that."

"I do."

"She's beautiful and smart and fun. A fine baker, too. What are you waiting for?"

Radic squirmed. "We have our own timetable."

"Just don't wait too long. She's a gem."

"I know it."

Eager to move to another topic, any other topic, Radic called the meeting to order: "Okay, folks, our focus today is Gary's Army. Who are they? How did he recruit them? What did he tell them? How did he pay them? And do any of them know anything about Gary's murder?

"We're interested in those who were paid to give blood. But we're especially interested in those who were paid to give money to help re-elect the mayor. Gary's money, as it turns out. Getting paid to give blood is not a crime. Getting paid for making a campaign contribution with someone else's money is a crime. Mulroy, care to explain?"

"Sure. Let's begin with the blood donors. According to the Red Cross, it's okay for people to get paid for donating blood, but they shouldn't conceal it. The FDA requires the Red Cross and other organizations that handle blood to distinguish clearly between blood that was donated voluntarily and blood that was traded for money. Members of Gary's Army violated that rule, knowingly or unknowingly. They screwed up. Gary screwed up."

"How about the campaign donors?" Scuglia asked. "Did they break any laws?"

"At first glance, it appeared that campaign donors might be off the hook, because the three thousand three hundred dollar ceiling on individual contributions applies to federal campaigns, not state and local campaigns. BUT the Pittsburgh Ethics Board recently decided to adopt the federal government's campaign finance rules for local elections. So, in practice, the rules for federal and local campaign contributions are now one and the same."

"Did Gary's Army violate the law?" Scuglia asked.

"Yes, they did. Members of Gary's Army are considered to be straw donors. They're the nominal donors, but it's a fraud because the actual donor is Gary. When Gary gave thirty-three hundred dollars each to members of his army, with the understanding that the money go to the mayor's re-election campaign, he was violating the law."

"And the donors themselves?"

"I did some digging," Mulroy replied. "The person who starts the straw donor scheme by giving the cash to an intermediary is violating the law. And the person who takes the cash and funnels it to the political campaign is also violating the law. There are precedents for prosecutions."

"Why would someone agree to be a straw donor? What's in it for them?" Scuglia asked.

At this point, Radic jumped in. "Many of the campaign donors were also blood donors. They didn't benefit from the campaign funding, but they definitely benefited from the blood donor funding. Also, some of them may have received a payment in kind after agreeing to be straw donors. Subsidized housing at Bigelow Towers."

"So are we going to recommend that the DA prosecute these guys?" Scuglia asked.

"We're not particularly interested in enforcing Pittsburgh's campaign finance laws," Radic replied. "But the fact that many of these young men committed a crime gives us some leverage to try to convince them to tell us what they know.

"So, question number one. How many of these young men are in our database? Tony?"

"Okay, that's what I've been working on. Out of twenty-four guys who donated to the Mayor's PAC, presumably with funds provided by Gary, fifteen have a criminal record."

"Big stuff? Little stuff?" Mulroy asked.

"It's a mix. But eight of them have committed at least one felony."

"What can you tell us about those eight?" Radic asked.

"Well, they're not choir boys, but they're not murderers either. At any rate, they don't fit the usual profile. Two of them were involved in a carjacking. Three of them committed a robbery or a burglary. A gun was involved in two of the three cases. One of them was found guilty of embezzlement."

"What can you tell us about the two who used a gun to rob someone?" Radic asked.

"Well, the first guy with a gun was Bradley Gibbons. The second guy with a gun was Marvin Casper."

"Hold on a second," Mulroy said. "I know both of those guys. They were at the Mayor's re-election fundraiser at Phipps Conservatory. At least one of them is a blood donor. In fact, he passed out at the reception because he had just given blood."

"Very interesting," Radic said. "What can you tell us about them, Tony?"

"Well, they were arrested for breaking and entering twice. The first time, they burgled a well-known drug dealer—the guy who ran the roost until

Gary came along. They spent twenty-five days in jail, then agreed to a plea bargain and went home."

"And the second time?"

"The second time, they burgled a prominent politician. Joey Fantuzzo."

"The city councilman?"

"Yep."

"Whatever happened to him?" Scuglia asked.

"He left under a cloud," Radic said. "He resigned from the City Council as part of a plea deal with the DA."

Chapter Fifty-Five: An Earful of Complaints

Father Buckley limped across the living room and sat down in his favorite chair with a sigh. His knee was still painful after the baton beating he received from Detective Atwood in Market Square. His head ached, and his stomach growled in frustration. It was 10:00 p.m. and he had yet to eat dinner.

His favorite part of his job was pastoral care. Comforting those who were sick, disaffected, or alone. Persuading a parishioner not to do something rash or foolish. Letting a forgotten soul know that others cared.

But sometimes it could be overwhelming. Like today. It all began with a phone call from the Red Cross. Patiently, he had done his best to answer all their questions and to allay their fears.

Yes, the donors had been paid. No, he didn't know they were supposed to disclose the payments. Yes, they would continue to donate blood. Yes, they would identify everyone who was paid. And yes, the Red Cross was due to receive one million dollars from Gary Mabry, as soon as the estate was settled.

Next came a surprise visit from Wanda Charles, who was very upset and peppered him with pointed questions and bitter complaints. Her ex-mother-in-law, Ernestine Mabry, had mentioned the generous gift to Dorothy, and she wanted to know why no one had spoken to her. "Am I the mother or am I not the mother?" she had asked.

"You're the mother, Wanda."

"Is Larry trying to stop the payments to his own daughter?"

"No, he's not. Larry has left those decisions to me. And I will do my very best to follow Gary's wishes to the letter. He wanted Dorothy to have the money."

"But it has to go to education? Are you kidding me? A million dollars for an education? We could send her to Harvard and there'd still be a shitload of money left over."

"I'm sorry, Wanda, but our hands are tied by what's in the will."

"How about me? I got bills to pay. I'm a working mom. I should be getting money for rent, for groceries, to buy gasoline, to service the car."

"I'm afraid we can't do that."

"You can't? Or you won't?"

"Let me try to explain, Wanda. Until Dorothy turns twenty-one, the money can only be spent on Dorothy's education. I'm willing to define that as broadly as I can. Piano lessons, violin lessons, art camp. Maybe you want to take her on a trip, a nice trip. So long as it's educational, we can do that."

"What happens to the money when Dorothy turns twenty-one?"

"At that point, she gets what's left. Once she's an adult, she can spend it as she likes."

"And me? Her mother? The single mom who raised her? What do I get? You tell me that."

"What you get, Wanda, is the knowledge that Dorothy is getting a chance that you and I and most people never had. It also means that you don't have to pay a penny to put her through college. You don't have to pay to fill out the application forms. You don't have to pay to take her on a college tour. If she goes away to school, you don't have to pay to fly her back home."

"Who came up with these rules anyway?"

"It was Gary. And it will be up to the lawyers to interpret them."

"Well, fuck Gary, and fuck you. What kind of a priest are you, anyway? Aren't you supposed to be helping your parishioners? Well, I'm a parishioner. And I need help."

Father Buckley winced as he recalled the exchange. Wanda had slammed the door on her way out—a fitting ending to a very painful conversation.

After Wanda, and a brief lunch, it had been one thing after another. Phil Hodges, from the Mayor's re-election committee, dropped by and was anything but cordial. He had received a visit from the Pittsburgh police and wanted to know how much they knew about Gary's finances.

Father Buckley responded that they knew about the contents of the will. He simply confirmed the specifics.

"Did they ask any questions about Gary's Army?"

"I told them that Gary has helped pay the bills for some young men who live in Bigelow Towers."

"Did they ask you whether these young men have contributed to the Mayor's Re-election Campaign?"

"I know that some of them support Mayor Graham. Do some of them also contribute to the campaign?"

"Well, that's none of your business, and none of the police's business either. If the police contact you again, Padre, I want you to say nothing about contributions to the Mayor's re-election campaign. Don't reveal anything. Don't speculate about anything. Capiche?"

Father Buckley almost objected to being ordered about, but held his tongue instead. This was a man he didn't want to cross. A powerful man, a well-connected man, someone who was unlikely to forgive and forget if things didn't work out.

Then, moments after Hodges departed, he got a call from the bishop's office. What's this we hear about a big contribution from the drug dealer? One million dollars for the church? Will some of this be going to the diocese?

Father Buckley fielded these questions as gracefully as he could. He emphasized that each of the bequests was quite specific. Very little wiggle room. He was the executor, but that meant he was to execute the will, not rewrite it. The bishop's aide sounded disappointed, said he would confer with the bishop and be back in touch.

Two members of Gary's Army had visited him at seven o'clock, just as he was about to fix dinner. Bradley and Marvin. Two of his favorites. At one point in time, he had thought of them as future priests. That hadn't panned out, but they were still good, decent young men with lots of potential.

Hodges had tracked them down at Bigelow Towers and had frightened them half to death. What kind of person would do that?

Putting the pieces of the puzzle together, it appeared that some members of Gary's Army got money for donating blood *and* money for political campaign contributions. They were free to keep the Red Cross money but were expected to give the other money to the Mayor's Re-election Committee.

Father Buckley didn't know much about campaign finance, but the whole thing was starting to sound pretty fishy.

Why had they done it? In a nutshell, because Gary asked them to. If Gary asked them to jump, their only question was: how high? Gary had that kind of power over people, especially two insecure young men.

Father Buckley wished he had known about this. Had he known, he would have taken Gary aside and reasoned with him. Too late for that now. So, what could be done?

Clearly, the laundering of political campaign money had to stop. That was plainly illegal. If Marvin and Bradley kept doing that, they could end up in jail.

But maybe the one million dollar donation from Gary's estate to the Mayor's re-election campaign offered a way out. Assuming it was legal, of course.

Hodges would not be happy if the gravy train were to grind to a halt. But one million dollars could heal a lot of wounds, even if it was the end of the line.

Tomorrow, Father Buckley would contact Gary's lawyer and get her to confirm that the one million dollar payment to the mayor's campaign could proceed. Then he would contact Hodges, assuring him that the one million dollars would be his soon, but insisting that the other payments must stop.

Father Buckley turned on his CD player. He chose a recording by Larry and the Rough Riders. He should call Larry, to see how things were going in New York.

Sitting in his favorite chair, listening to Larry's rendition of "Song for

My Father," by Horace Silver, he started feeling drowsy. Time for bed.

As a priest, Father Buckley saw people at their best and at their worst. In his opinion, most folks were just trying to get by. If they behaved inappropriately or said something spiteful, they were probably stressed out. It didn't make them bad people.

The key was to find a path out of a sticky situation. Light that path, and most people will follow the light. He firmly believed that. Tomorrow was another day. He would clear things up. And he would reschedule that PT appointment.

Father Buckley put on some pajamas and fell asleep.

Chapter Fifty-Six: Constitutional Rights

As the member of the Homicide squad who knew the most about Menendez, Mulroy had a special interest in the drug trafficker's case. On her way to work, she dropped by Mercy Hospital to see how he was doing.

"I don't want to see you, you gringa bitch! I only want to see my lawyer."

"I'm sorry, Mr. Menendez, but your lawyer hasn't arrived yet."

"I don't believe you, you lying pig."

Mulroy scrolled through her e-mails and produced one from the legal department: "Mr. Suarez will be representing Jorge Menendez, but not until he concludes a trial, currently underway in Tampa. We expect the trial to end later this week."

"Chinga tu culo."

"What did you say?"

"Fuck your ass, lady."

Mulroy sighed. "Would you like to be represented by someone from the Public Defender's Office until Mr. Suarez arrives?"

"I don't want to be represented by some loser who represents losers. I want Suarez."

"Well, that's entirely up to you. But with or without counsel, I have some questions for you, and I think it's to your advantage to answer them."

Menendez scowled. "Well, I think it's my advantage to say nothing at all. Nada."

"Your call. But let me explain how a case like yours works. We need to obtain some information, and we're willing to bargain to get that information. Whoever talks to us first gets special consideration."

"No one else knows what I know."

"I'm not so sure. We're talking to your landlord. We're talking to Jose Castillo, the man that you shot."

"The man you *say* that I shot."

"We're also talking to Carlos Almazan."

"You can't talk to Carlos."

"We can and we are."

"Carlos won't talk."

"Maybe, maybe not. We're going to make him a very generous offer. A get out of jail free card in return for telling us what brought you to Gary Mabry's apartment the other night."

"You're bluffing."

"No, I'm being perfectly honest with you. Also, we're having conversations with people at Muscle Mania. Many of them remember you quite well."

"Like who?"

"I'd prefer not to share those names with you. Some of them say you're a very scary man."

"Yeah, right. You're blowing smoke."

"We're also going to take a very close look at your locker at Muscle Mania."

"You can't do that. I have my constitutional rights."

"Yes, you do. But they're not identical to those of a U.S. citizen. In fact, the Supreme Court has held that the police can search and seize a foreign national's property without a search warrant."

"I don't believe you."

"Ask Mr. Suarez when he arrives. U.S. v Verdugo-Erquidez. He'll confirm it."

Menendez thought for a moment. "Nurse!" he yelled. He pressed a buzzer. Within a minute, a nurse arrived. Stout, worldly-wise, battle-tested. Named Rhonda.

"Nurse, this woman is bothering me," Menendez complained. "I want her to go away. And I want my lawyer."

"I don't know anything about a lawyer," Rhonda replied.

"I want my fucking lawyer."

"Watch your language, Mr. Menendez. We've spoken to you about that."

"Okay, I want my goddamn lawyer."

"Detective, have you concluded your business here?"

"For the time being," Mulroy replied. "But Mr. Menendez, I hope you'll think about what I've said. If you'd like to talk, I'm just a phone call away."

Menendez gave Mulroy the sourest expression he could muster and also gave her the finger as she exited.

"Is he always this way?" Mulroy asked the nurse.

"I'd say you caught him on a good day."

"Has he had any visitors?"

"Not to my knowledge. But your babysitter would know for sure."

Mulroy asked the babysitter, an Officer Gomez.

"No visitors. Lots of complaints."

"Like what?"

"Bad food. No HBO. No magazines. And there are people he wants to contact. He offered me cash if I'd deliver some private messages."

"Who does he want to contact?"

"His lawyer, Suarez. And a guy named Almazan."

"What did you say?"

"I said no outside communications unless you or Radic approve it."

"Good man. But you know, Gomez, we just might want you to deliver those messages. Or to say you'll deliver them."

"Whatever you say, Detective."

"Let me check with Radic. We'd like to know what Menendez is thinking. It might be worth a shot."

Chapter Fifty-Seven: A Fiery Message

Radic was fast asleep when he got a call on his cell phone. 2:30 a.m. He answered quickly and took the phone into the kitchen, to avoid disturbing Lexie.

Detective Ken Syrzicki from the Arson Squad was calling to let him know that a suspicious fire had taken place at the St. Martin de Porres rectory. Father Cyrus Buckley had been rescued by a concerned neighbor, just in the nick of time. The priest was groggy, suffering from significant smoke inhalation, but no visible burns. He was rushed to Mercy Hospital. No other victims.

"The rectory?"

"It will have to be totally rebuilt."

"Arson?"

"Almost certainly. The scene reeks of kerosene. It was sloppily done."

"Was the intent to kill or to send a message?"

"Hard to say. We'll know more within the next few days."

Radic thanked Syrzicki for the call, asked him to keep in touch, and went back to bed, after reassuring Ralph that everything would be okay. Amazingly, Lexie was still fast asleep. Within minutes, he was asleep too.

* * *

Larry recognized the phone number instantly. "Hi, Mama. How are you doing?"

"I'm fine, Larry. But I'm calling about something serious."

"Is it Dee, Mama? Is she okay?"

"Dee is fine, honey. Though she misses you. Badly."

"I know, Mama. I miss her too."

"But Father Buckley is not fine. Someone burned down the rectory, while he was inside it."

"So he's…he's…"

"No, he survived. He's at Mercy Hospital, and they're going to release him soon."

"Hallelujah! But where's he going to stay if there's no rectory?"

"Some of Gary's friends who live at Bigelow Towers have rented him a room. They're going to look after him while he recovers."

"I can't believe it, Mama. Was it an accident?"

"I spoke with Detective Radic yesterday. He says it was deliberate. They found a can of kerosene in the living room."

"But who? And why?"

"The police don't know. They're investigating. On top of everything else."

Larry was silent.

"Are you still there, son?"

"I'm just trying to think, Mama. Could there be a connection between Gary's will and what happened to Father Buckley? I know it's been in the news."

"I don't know, son. It could be."

Larry paused again. "Do you think Father Buckley is having second thoughts about being the executor for the estate?"

"I don't know, Larry. He has a lot of things on his mind."

"Mama, I have a gig tonight. But tomorrow's a free day. Maybe I could fly to Pittsburgh tomorrow. See you, see Dee. Talk with Father Buckley, talk with Radic."

"That would be very nice, Larry. We'd all love to see you."

"Okay, let me see what I can do. Don't tell Dee yet, or Wanda. I'll call you back in half an hour."

"I'll be right here."

"Love you, Mama."

"Love you too."

* * *

The arson squad reached a quick verdict: The rectory fire that nearly cost Father Buckley his life was deliberate. Someone had gained access to the rectory, left a can of kerosene in the living room, lit a fuse from the front door, fled, and pretty much guaranteed an explosion and a fire. The gash on Father Buckley's head was probably, though not definitely, from a painting at the head of the bed that fell on the priest when the rectory shook from the explosion.

Beyond that, little was known. The rectory had no surveillance system. Given the devastating damage to windows, doors, and everything else, it was probably impossible to determine how the arsonist had gained access to the building.

Door-to-door canvassing yielded next to nothing. Neighbors were so accustomed to the steady flow of traffic in and out of the church and a smaller but still significant amount of traffic in and out of the rectory that they largely stopped noticing individual faces.

To a person, every neighbor had something nice to say about Father Buckley, supporting the view that he was the rare soul who "had no enemies."

Except for one, of course. Could the arsonist also be Gary's murderer? Although Father Buckley professed ignorance, Radic suspected that he knew more than he was divulging about Gary's complicated life and death. The question was, how to get him to spit it out?

As Radic thought about the situation, he decided that Father Buckley was unlikely to volunteer anything but equally unlikely to lie. The key was to ask the right questions and make the most of the answers.

But if Radic was to coax Father Buckley to speak honestly about suspects for the murder and the arson, he needed a short list of suspects to discuss. Instead, he had a long laundry list.

For starters, the Pittsburgh drug network, including Khalif and other locals, plus Frenchy and Atwood. Or perhaps someone from the cartel. It couldn't have been Menendez because he was in jail. It might have been Almazan, but he didn't seem vicious or violent. Perhaps a rival network.

Next, people who benefited from Gary's estate but didn't like the fine print. People who thought they should have benefited from Gary's estate, like Wanda Charles, who was reported to be unhappy with the specifics. Members of Gary's Army. People whose campaign contributions might have violated the law.

Finally, the mayor's re-election committee, the mayor's drug task force, maybe even the mayor's opponents. Community activists who viewed Father Buckley as too soft on police and too committed to non-violence.

Whatever Father Buckley's neighbors and parishioners might say, he was not a man without enemies. But would he identify them? At a more basic level, did he even think of them as enemies? Unlike some Christians Radic knew, Father Buckley genuinely seemed to believe in forgiveness, charity, and redemption.

Well, if Father Buckley couldn't or wouldn't protect himself, what about the young men he was so devoted to and who were so devoted to him? If Father Buckley wouldn't point the finger at anyone, maybe they would. Even if they themselves might pay a price for identifying an arsonist and a possible murderer.

Chapter Fifty-Eight: Costumes to Spare

As tension mounted over the Mabry case, Mulroy decided that a good movie might be a welcome diversion. Then again, a bad movie might be even better — a chance to be snarky and to unload pent-up frustrations on Hollywood's elite.

With that in mind, Mulroy and Jake settled in to watch the latest incarnation of Spider-Man. As bad movies go, this one was actually pretty good. Smart, suspenseful, with lots of birdlike human beings defying gravity. Still, Mulroy and Jake found plenty of cringeworthy moments that made them laugh.

"Have you ever been tempted to go to one of the comic-con conventions?" Jake asked, as they munched on some chips and dip.

"You mean for people who write comic books?" Mulroy asked.

"No, for people who are hooked on comic book characters. They do these things all across the country."

"Including here in Pittsburgh?"

"Absolutely. It's called Steel-City Con."

"Have you ever been?"

"Once. Last year."

"Did you dress up?"

"Of course. Can you guess who I was?"

"Han Solo?"

"Close. Darth Vader."

"Get out. Did you have a voice box to make your voice all gravelly?"

"Yep, it was pretty cool. People kept coming up to me claiming to be my long-lost son or daughter."

"What did you say?"

"I usually said, 'I'm very proud of you,' unless they had an earring in their nose and henna-colored hair, in which case I'd say, 'Are you absolutely sure?'"

"Nice. Did you have a date?"

Jake fidgeted.

"Come on, Jake, you can tell me."

"Well, I don't like to talk about people I used to date."

"What's the big deal? You dated people, I dated people. Who was she?"

"Her name was Virginia."

"And?"

"And what?"

"Who did she dress up as?"

Jake squirmed. "Lady Octopus."

"Lady Octopus?"

"It was a disaster. I was driving a Toyota Corolla at the time. We had trouble squeezing her into the car."

"I can imagine."

"Then at the conference, she broke a bunch of glasses next to a punch bowl."

"In a fit of rage?"

"No, it was an accident. She didn't have total control of her arms."

"Did they make her pay for the damage?"

"No, they were pretty understanding. Until the incident on the dance floor."

"You went dancing with Lady Octopus?"

"Well, not for long. One of her tentacles latched onto Snow White's dress and destroyed her costume."

"Snow White must have been pretty mad."

"She used language she would never have used with the dwarfs. Then she attacked Virginia with Little Bo Peep's cane."

"Uh-oh."

"It wasn't pretty. They both drew blood."

"I didn't know that octopuses bleed."

"Ha, ha. Well, I can tell you that Virginia was bleeding, because there were blood splotches and tentacle scraps all over the back seat of my car."

"She sat in the back seat?"

"That's the only way we could fit her into the car."

"Well, at least you went out with a bang. And you got to meet some kinfolk."

In bed that night, Mulroy chuckled over Jake's brief moment of fame. As she drifted into sleep, she thought of something and made a mental note to check in with O'Neill.

*　*　*

The following morning, Mulroy was able to locate O'Neill at a Zone Two police station in Lawrenceville. "O'Neill, what are you working on today?"

"Neighborhood patrols, Lawrenceville."

"How about the rest of the week?"

"The same."

"Nothing special?"

"Is that a trick question, Detective? If I'm serving the community, then it's already special, right?"

"Don't give me that crap, O'Neill. I just want to see if you'd like to help us out with our murder investigation."

"For real?"

"I'll need to clear it with Stilton first, but I'm pretty sure he'll say yes."

"Will I have to throw any baseballs?"

"No more target practice, O'Neill. Just investigative work."

"Who will I be investigating, if I may ask?"

"Well, in a nutshell, super-heroes. Or people who dress up like super-heroes."

"You mean like at comic-con conventions?"

"Why does everybody know about these things but me?"

"I actually went to one a couple years ago."

"You didn't by any chance go to the one where Lady Octopus and Snow White got into a fistfight, did you?"

"No, but I heard about that. I heard that Darth Vader was involved."

"Well, it just so happens that I've spoken with Darth himself. He denies responsibility."

"And you believe him?"

"Darth Vader has been unfairly maligned. He's actually a very nice guy."

"Sometimes you worry me, Detective. But I'm willing to help."

* * *

After checking first with Radic, Mulroy contacted Stilton, who agreed that O'Neill could work on a special assignment with Homicide for one week. His mission—to ask if the comic-con organizers remembered any guests dressed as Spider-Man, and to screen footage from the organizers, in search of a lethal Spider-Man. It might be time-consuming. Better O'Neill than one of his senior detectives.

Mulroy accompanied O'Neill on the initial interview, in case someone needed to play the homicide card.

In fact, the organizer of the event, Nathan Hornbeeck, was more than happy to talk about the conference and to share footage.

"Do you have a list of everyone who attended the conference?" Mulroy asked.

"Hmm. We should have a list of everyone who registered in advance and paid by credit card. But not people who paid cash at the door."

"How long a list?"

"Last year, we had eleven thousand people overall. I'm gonna say, two-thirds of them probably paid in advance. So we can probably get you about eight thousand names."

Mulroy turned to O'Neill. "You up for this, O'Neill?"

"Piece of cake."

"Could you give us a list of attendees for the past four or five years?"

273

"Sure, except when we didn't meet during COVID."

* * *

O'Neill had enough programming skills that he considered writing code to match names from the two lists. Instead, he looked through the list Mulroy gave him and then looked through it a second time. Then he started running through the much longer list from Steel City.

If a name rang a bell, he checked the list Mulroy had given him: blood donors paid by Gary, campaign donors paid by Gary, and persons of special interest to the murder investigation. Occasionally, the names coincided, and he circled the name on the master list.

After doing this once, he did it all a second time, picking up a few more names along the way. Imperfect, perhaps, but he was confident that he had produced a list with at least eighty percent of the names that matched.

Mulroy reviewed his handiwork and grunted appreciatively a few times, which O'Neill took to be a good sign. Finally, she set the list down and spoke. "Good work, O'Neill, very good work."

"Did I come up with a good list?"

"You came up with a very good list. Any of these gentlemen could be our Spider-Man, but three names jump out: Bradley Gibbons, Phil Hodges, and Khalif Wilson."

"Who are they exactly?"

"Bradley Gibbons is a blood donor and a campaign donor, though he donates other people's money and pretends that it's his. He has a criminal record and just managed to avoid serious time by the skin of his teeth. I met him at Phipps Conservatory at a fundraiser for the Mayor. He's devoted to Father Buckley. In fact, he's one of two men who arranged to get Father Buckley a room at Bigelow Towers while he recovers from the rectory fire."

"I'd say he makes the cut."

"Phil Hodges is the head of the Mayor's re-election campaign. He was also at the Phipps reception. A friendly guy, but kind of creepy. I can't quite put my finger on it. Just my intuition. Still, if you don't trust your own intuition, who will?"

"I gotta agree with that."

"Finally, Khalif Wilson. The heir to Gary's drug empire and, as far as we know, one of Gary's closest friends. Charming but maybe ruthless. He's very smart. Maybe he didn't like Gary's decisions, which may have cost him a fair amount of money. He has as good a motive as anyone."

"You've convinced me."

"I want you to go back to Hornbeeck and give him photographs of these three gentlemen. See if he recognizes them. If he does, maybe he can suggest where to look for them in the convention videos. If you find them, see what they're wearing, who they talk to, how they behave. If one of them is dressed as Spider-Man or a ninja warrior, I want to know about it ASAP."

"Will do."

"Meanwhile, I'll tell Radic what you've come up with. I know he'll be very pleased."

"Happy to help, Detective. This is good stuff."

Chapter Fifty-Nine: Advice from the Feds

Now that the DEA was officially involved in the Gardenia murder case, Radic decided to solicit inside information from them on the complex, byzantine world of Mexican drug cartels. Ed Harkin, who would be heading up the delegation to Pittsburgh, instantly agreed to a quick tutorial. In fact, he volunteered to do it in Scuglia's living room after hearing what happened in Charleroi. "When a fellow officer takes a hit in the line of duty, I'm more than happy to accommodate them," he explained.

Before beginning, Harkin distributed maps of Mexico with the names of drug cartels dominant in each region in red, in caps, and in boldface.

"Let's begin with the big picture. Mexico's drug cartels are vicious, brutal, and all-powerful. They have close ties with the government, the police, and the military. They routinely bribe these officials to look the other way or to commit crimes themselves.

"In recent years, their power has only grown. The number of homicides continues to climb, thanks mostly to drug wars. The number of young people who've disappeared without a trace is close to a hundred thousand. It's reached the point where groups of mothers with shovels and hoes visit makeshift graves in the desperate hope of uncovering the remains of their missing children.

"If you look at your maps, you'll see that different cartels dominate different regions of Mexico. Some are more powerful than others. We can get into that if you like. But what really matters to you, I imagine, is which cartels have an active, ongoing interest in Pittsburgh's drug traffic.

"For years, the leading cartel in the Pittsburgh area has been Costa a Costa, which is based in Oaxaca and which does its dirty work through a dummy corporation known as Comerciantes al Mundo. In recent years, their local rep has been Jorge Menendez. Nice work tracking him down and incarcerating him, by the way."

"How about other drug cartels?" Scuglia asked. "Have they been active in the Pittsburgh area? And are any of them linked to Exportaciones Internacionales?"

"Exportaciones Internacionales is a dummy corporation with close ties to Empresas de Tabasco. That's your second cartel. Those are the guys you arrested in Charleroi, I believe."

"That's right," Radic said.

"They've been eager to make a bid for Pittsburgh's drug traffic, and there's been enough upheaval lately that they may see this as their big chance."

"Because of Gary Mabry's murder?" Scuglia asked.

"Yes, for sure. But even before that, the word was out that Mabry was itching to retire. Anytime that happens, wannabe cartels show up like vultures awaiting a tasty carcass."

"Is that why Detective Gardenia was trying to track drug shipments via the barges?" Mulroy asked.

"I can't speak to Detective Gardenia's motives. You folks know far more about that than I do. But if Gardenia was on the take and had a longstanding relationship with the dominant cartel, then activity by a rival cartel could easily make him nervous."

"We have a prisoner in custody, who has just been charged with the murder of Detective Gardenia," Radic said. "His name is Jose Castillo. Is there any way to confirm that he's employed by Empresas de Tabasco?"

"Is he being represented by counsel?"

"Yes. The name is—"

"Don't tell me. Someone from Miami?"

"How did you know?" Radic asked.

"Noonan and Garcia?"

"That's the name of the firm," Radic replied. "The lawyer's name is Armando Garcia."

"The big cheese himself. I'd say the chances are extremely high that your guy is working for Empresas de Tabasco."

"How about Redding and Suarez?" Mulroy asked.

"Why do you care about them?"

"They're representing Jorge Menendez," Mulroy replied.

"Ah, ha. Well, they're based in Tampa. And they are well known as the law firm that represents Costa a Costa when they get in a jam. Who's the lawyer?"

"He hasn't arrived yet, but I believe it's Pedro Suarez," Mulroy replied.

"He's bad news. Wily and mean."

"So we have two legal heavyweights from Florida representing two different drug cartels in Pittsburgh," Radic observed. "Is there any way to play the two lawyers against each other?"

"That's not a crazy idea," Harkin replied.

"What might convince Garcia to incriminate Costa a Costa, Menendez, or both?" Radic asked.

"Well, the obvious answer is if you're willing to reduce the sentence for his client."

"Any other approach?" Radic asked.

"He might be willing to implicate Menendez out of pure spite."

"Why's that?" Mulroy asked.

"Have you interviewed Menendez?"

"Yep," Mulroy replied.

"Nobody likes Menendez. He's scary. He's hateful. And he's a pain in the ass."

"So someone might serve him up on a silver platter?" Mulroy asked.

"As a public service. In a business dominated by assholes, Menendez easily qualifies for the Assholes Hall of Fame. I'd throw him to the wolves in a New York minute. And I hardly know the guy."

Chapter Sixty: An Overdose of Politics

Radic read the unexpected text from a phone number he had not seen before. Then he read it again, more carefully: Detective Radic—Can we meet, privately, sometime soon? I have information that may be useful to your investigation. Ceci

Radic shared the text with Mulroy, who was in the squad room at the time.

"Should we speak with Stilton?" Mulroy asked.

"And tell him what?" Radic replied.

"That the Mayor's wife wants to speak with us."

"I'd rather speak with Ceci first. If we speak with Stilton, he may take it upstairs to Reilly. It could take days. Let's hear her out. Then we speak with Stilton."

Ceci Arceneaux proposed meeting Radic at the Red Cross. She was a frequent visitor, and no one would be suspicious if she went there. She had arranged for the office manager to set aside a private room.

Radic okayed this, adding that Mulroy would be joining him.

* * *

Unlike Mulroy, Radic had not visited the Red Cross in years. As he entered the waiting room, he sensed a lot of tension. Long faces, worried looks. He and Mulroy spoke quietly to someone at the front desk, who promptly escorted them to Conference Room B.

Ceci Arceneaux looked more like the grief-stricken mourner at Gary's funeral than the charming hostess at home the week before. There were bags under her eyes, and her smile seemed forced. She was clutching a tissue.

"Nice to see you again, Detective Radic," she said. "And nice to meet you, Detective Mulroy. I saw what you did at my husband's fundraiser at Phipps Conservatory. Quick thinking on your part. You may have saved a young man's life."

Mulroy nodded, appreciatively.

Ceci Arceneaux turned to Radic. "Detective Radic, the last time we talked, I asked you if we could keep our conversation confidential. I'd like to make the same request today."

"Ms. Arceneaux," Radic began.

"Please, call me Ceci."

"Okay, Ceci, we have no idea what you are about to tell us. Given that, I can't offer any assurances."

"Let me try a different tack, Detective. The subject of today's conversation is blackmail. If I confide in you, my husband's campaign for re-election could be doomed. If we have an honest conversation, as I propose, I hope that you will at least brainstorm a bit, to see if there's a way to handle some delicate facts without ending a promising political career."

"Again, Ceci, I don't mean to be uncooperative, but I just can't make any promises. I have no wish to jeopardize your husband's campaign or anyone else's campaign. We're in business to protect people. But we're not in business to protect people's reputations."

"Very well, Detectives. I'm going to trust both of you and hope for the best. At this point, I don't think I have a choice."

"Before we begin," Mulroy interjected, "may I ask whether your husband knows that you are meeting with us today?"

Arceneaux was silent at first. "No, Detective, he does not. I hope that he would approve of what I'm going to say. I've thought about it a lot. But I can't be absolutely sure."

Mulroy produced a notebook. "Ceci, we're not proposing to record this conversation, but one of us will need to take some notes."

Arceneaux nodded slowly and then began:

"A week ago, my husband and I learned about some irregularities and perhaps some illegalities in the financing of his re-election campaign."

"Who informed you of these irregularities?" Radic asked.

"For the time being, let's just say a friend of Gary's. Someone we are inclined to believe."

"And what were these irregularities?"

"Without putting too fine a point on it, some campaign donors were making donations with money supplied by someone else."

"And that someone else was Gary?"

"Yes."

"Do you know how many donors were doing this and what the dollar amounts were?"

"A substantial amount of money. Perhaps one hundred and fifty thousand dollars."

"Have you gone to the city's Ethics Hearing Board with this information?"

"Not yet. Walt decided to speak with his campaign manager, Phil Hodges, first."

"And what did Mr. Hodges say?"

"Initially, he tried to deny it. But eventually, after Walt laid out the evidence, he agreed. He said he didn't know it was illegal at first. He blamed Gary. He said he himself was in the dark."

"Do you and the Mayor believe him?"

"No, we do not."

"So, what did your husband tell Hodges?"

"He told him that what he did was wrong and that he should resign immediately. Walt would do his best to undo the damage."

"And did he? Resign immediately? We've seen nothing about it in the press."

"No, he did not. He said that he would not resign and that if Walt tried to fire him, he would say publicly that Walt knew about the illegal payments and authorized them months ago."

"Did he know?"

"Absolutely not."

"Can he prove it?"

"How do you prove a negative?"

"So, if your husband takes down Hodges, Hodges will take down your husband."

"Precisely."

"Is that the gist of what you want to tell us?"

"It's only the beginning."

"There's more?"

"We have reason to believe that Hodges was involved in the burning of the rectory that almost cost Father Buckley his life."

"That's a serious charge. What's the evidence?"

"In addition to threatening us, Hodges has been threatening two young men who were involved in the campaign finance scheme and who have misgivings about it. And he has threatened Father Buckley himself."

"Who's your source?"

"The two young men."

"Ceci, we think you may be on to something here, but do you have any eyewitness evidence linking Phil Hodges to the arson at the rectory?"

"He threatened the two young men and Father Buckley the very day before the rectory was torched."

"Circumstantial evidence, I'm afraid."

"He visited Father Buckley at the rectory, which gave him an opportunity to 'case the joint' as you might say."

"Again, suspicious but circumstantial."

Ceci gathered her thoughts. "He threatened our family as well."

"What? What exactly did he say?"

"When he spoke with Walt, he threatened to harm me and our children. He said accidents happen all the time. He said that even if we left politics, even if Walt resigned as mayor, we would never be safe. He said we were in this together, like it or not."

"What did your husband say?"

"He was badly shaken. And he may have punched him."

"He MAY have punched him?"

"He DID punch him."

"Did Hodges punch back?"

"I don't think he had a chance. Walt buzzed his secretary and told Hodges that the meeting was over."

"Do you know if they've had any words since then?"

"Not in person. A couple of texts. A couple of calls."

Radic sighed. "Ceci, from what you've told us, Hodges is a bad egg, and he's out of control. It sounds like Hodges is an accomplished liar who will do whatever it takes to advance his career and to protect his reputation."

"That's about the size of it."

"Based on what you've said, we could call Hodges in and have a little talk with him. Do you think that would do any good?"

"Probably not."

"The best evidence in a case like this would be for Hodges to confess."

"Unlikely."

"But he might confess privately to you."

"What are you saying?"

"Would you be willing to wear a wire and talk with Hodges yourself?"

Arceneaux seemed shocked by the suggestion. She said nothing for a long time.

"It's potentially dangerous," Radic conceded. "But the dangers of doing nothing are just as great, if not greater."

Finally, Arceneaux spoke. "I don't know if I have the courage to do that, Detective."

"I understand," Radic said.

"Where would we have this conversation?" Arceneaux asked.

"Does he ever visit your husband at your home?"

"He used to. After this, that's doubtful. Walt wouldn't want to see him."

"But perhaps *you* would want to see him."

"Wouldn't he get suspicious?"

"If the mayor called him into his office, he might be suspicious. But if you were to intervene as the peacemaker, and offer to meet him at your home, he might be willing to come."

"I'm conflicted, Detective. I want the blackmail to stop. I want the threats against my family to stop. Even if it means that we lose the election."

"Does your husband feel the same way?"

Arceneaux paused for a long time. "Walt is a good man, an honorable man. But he's also a good politician and a fine public servant. Politics has been his life for a long time. I don't think he's there yet. Maybe it's up to me to take the first step. Walt will get there eventually."

Chapter Sixty-One: Bait and Switch

After the meeting with Ceci, Radic and Mulroy went to a coffee shop in Polish Hill for a chat.

"I noticed that you didn't ask Ceci whether Hodges might have had something to do with Gary's murder," Mulroy said.

"That's right."

"Why not?"

"Lots of reasons. I didn't want to freak her out. She's scared enough as it is. Also, she might leak that information to Hodges, to convince him to leave Pittsburgh forever. That would be unfortunate. If he committed murder or arson or both, we want him to be right here where we can grab him when we have the evidence we need."

"It just seems to me that the wiretap idea puts Ceci at great risk."

"Some risk. But you and I would be there."

"Okay, but wouldn't it be better to determine whether Hodges killed Gary before inviting him to meet with the mayor's wife?"

"We need to find out who Spider-Man was and fast. If it was Hodges, we need to put him behind bars. If it was someone else, God help us, because we've been barking up the wrong tree."

"Will Stilton approve the wire?"

"I think so."

"Which judge are you thinking? Federal or state?"

"We have lots of evidence that Hodges has violated state campaign finance laws. Everything else is hearsay. So, I say we ask Judge Belsky to authorize the wiretap."

"Do you want me to handle it? I just worked with her on the snake stuff."

"Yeah, it would be great if you dealt with Judge Belsky. I'll pave the way with Stilton first."

* * *

Stilton instantly agreed to having Ceci Arceneaux wear a wire. In fact, he thought it was a splendid idea.

Mulroy had a much harder time convincing Judge Belsky. "Are you kidding me, Detective? The mayor's wife? If something goes south, there goes my reputation, there goes your job, and there goes your department's budget. What does her husband, the Mayor, think about all this?"

"Well, to be honest, your honor, she hasn't told him."

"She hasn't told him? She hasn't told him? Are we living on the same planet, Detective?"

"I believe so, your honor."

"Well, let me tell you, on planet Earth, this would be a non-starter. If you come back and tell me that the Mayor himself approves of this tactic or that the Mayor himself is willing to wear the wire, then I'm willing to consider your request, subject to lots of limitations. Until then, I suggest that you try other avenues to solve your murder cases and your arson case. Which, incidentally, raises the question: Aren't there other homicide detectives besides you and Radic in the PBP?"

"Well, Detective Scuglia is also part of the team, your honor."

"Detective Scuglia. Isn't he the one who was badly injured in a gunfight on the Mon?"

"Yes, your honor."

"He's now skipping rope with the best of them?"

"No, your honor, he's working out of his living room."

"Then how is he going to help you, Radic, and the Mayor's wife if something goes wrong with the wired conversation?"

"He does a lot of behind-the-scenes work that's invaluable to the investigation."

"I don't doubt it, but is he going to spring from the closet if Mr. Hodges pulls a weapon on the Mayor's wife?"

"No, your honor, but he'll be in telephone contact."

"Well, that's reassuring. If something goes wrong, you can send him a text message, then he can send your boss a text message, and then fifteen minutes later someone will arrive on the scene, to ship the Mayor's wife's dead body to the M.E.'s office without delay."

"Your honor…"

"Enough said. Come up with a different plan. I'm saving you and Detective Radic from a caper that only the Three Stooges could have come up with."

Radic winced when he heard these words, or their rough equivalents, back at the office. "I guess she has a point," he conceded. "We need to go back to the drawing board. My bad. I wasn't thinking straight."

* * *

Radic took the lead in the conversation with Stilton, after Mulroy explained that Judge Belsky had put the kibosh on their initial plan to broker a conversation between the Mayor's wife and Hodges. Mulroy made it clear that the idea was a non-starter.

"But we have a new plan that we think would get Judge Belsky's approval," Radic said. "A direct conversation between Hodges and the Mayor, in the Mayor's office, with the Mayor wearing a wire."

"Would the Mayor do it?" Stilton asked.

"We think he would."

"Does he know about the conversations you've had with his wife? Isn't he likely to be angry at you? At us?"

"We have no way of knowing until we ask him," Radic said. "But we believe Ceci will make a strong case for doing something and doing it now."

Stilton thought for a moment. "How do you lure Hodges into the Mayor's office when Hodges has already tried to fire him and punched him in the nose?"

287

"There is that," Radic admitted. "But the first rule of politics is survival. Hodges gets that for sure. We think he would understand that the Mayor gets it too."

"What exactly do you have in mind?"

"We want the Mayor to tease Hodges with the rough outlines of a plan—a plan that enables both of them to keep their jobs."

"What are you thinking?"

"The Mayor and Hodges can say they both knew that a bunch of young Black men were making donations to the Mayor's campaign. But a number of these young men were also being paid to give blood to the Red Cross. The Mayor and Hodges can say that they thought the young men were flush with cash because of the blood payments, and they were essentially using their own money. They can also say that they investigated it and confirmed that there was nothing illegal about Gary's paying blood donors. They exercised due diligence. They just neglected to take the crucial step of matching the blood donor list and the campaign donation list."

"Okay, I think I get it."

"It doesn't have to be airtight," Radic said. "It just has to be plausible. Plausible enough for Hodges to believe that they might get away with it."

"Okay, I like the idea. Let me see if Reilly likes it too. If he does, we'll take it to the Mayor."

"Thank you, sir."

"Is there a Plan B if the Mayor won't do it?"

"We're still wading through video footage from the comic con to see whether Hodges was wearing a Spider-Man outfit."

"Any luck?"

"There's a lot of footage for the most recent year. Three days, multiple cameras. O'Neill is about a quarter of the way through."

"Then get him some support. Whatever you need. Does Hodges know we're looking at him for the murder?"

"Not yet, sir."

"Let's keep it that way, then. And find out whether Hodges was Spider-Man for at least three days."

* * *

It didn't take long. Stilton called Radic that evening to report that the Mayor himself was willing to wear a wire and meet Hodges in his office, in the hope of putting this ordeal to an end. If it meant resigning or losing the election, so be it.

"Wow!" Mulroy said when Radic called with the news. "I guess I underestimated him."

"Stilton says he was losing sleep over the situation anyway. Ceci's conversation with us helped him to do the right thing."

"What's our timetable?"

"Wednesday."

"Two days. Will we be there?"

"You and me in an adjacent room. Two or three undercover agents elsewhere in case Hodges tries to flee."

"Will he be checked for weapons before seeing the Mayor?"

"Unless he has a way of bypassing security, I'd say the answer is yes."

"We should probably check."

"Good idea."

"Will we be carrying weapons?"

"No one wants a shoot-out at the O.K. Corral. But yes."

Chapter Sixty-Two: What Did I Do to be so Black and Blue?

Although normally an optimist and a man of faith, Father Buckley felt dispirited and anxious. Part of it was physical. His lungs still hurt whenever he breathed, as if he had swallowed a hot coal. And his knee was sore most of the time. He needed to get some rehab for that.

The events of the last few days had jarred him more than the injuries themselves. The community Gary had created, known loosely as Gary's Army, was on life support. Gary's heart was in the right place, but he had not bargained for the close scrutiny that followed his death.

At this point, direct donations to the Mayor's campaign were probably out of the question. Blood donations to the Red Cross could probably continue, but he wondered whether they would continue if the young men were not being paid.

The one million dollars contribution to St. Martin de Porres seemed like a lot of cash a couple weeks ago, but now that the rectory would have to be rebuilt, it seemed woefully inadequate.

Larry was still on the fence about whether to accept a payment for Dorothy's education. Father Buckley felt confident that he would come around, but maybe not. Gary's house of cards was toppling before his very eyes.

Yet there were signs of hope. The young men he had nurtured and mentored and sheltered in Bigelow Towers had rallied magnificently in his hour of need. Not just Bradley and Marvin but more than two dozen others.

They had organized shifts to watch over him, to take care of his medical needs, his physical needs, and his security needs. An armed guard was just outside his new apartment at all times.

At the same time, these young men were doing vital parish work that he himself was unable to do. They held a bake sale on schedule, recruited a deacon to conduct a Tuesday prayer meeting, and arranged for another Pittsburgh priest to say Sunday Mass.

Members of the community had also responded. The Mayor and members of the City Council had vowed to donate some of their own money towards rebuilding the rectory, and at least two private foundations had stepped forward to express their support.

As Father Buckley wrestled with conflicting feelings—hope and despair—the one thing that nagged at him was the possibility that Gary's killer would not be brought to justice. Though Father Buckley was not a vengeful person, he decided to make this a high priority, even if it meant breaking some confidences and even if it thrust him squarely into the maelstrom of local politics.

* * *

While fretting about these issues, Father Buckley heard a knock on the door. It was his bodyguard. He wanted to know if the priest was willing to receive a guest. A gentleman by the name of Larry Mabry. Father Buckley smiled and nodded. "With pleasure."

"How are you feeling, Father?" Larry asked, after giving the priest a warm but gentle embrace. "We're not ready to lose you yet. A lot of people think of you as irreplaceable. And that includes my mother and me."

"It's very nice of you to say that, Larry," Father Buckley said. "But I hope you didn't come all the way from New York City just to say that in person. Don't you have a month-long gig up there?

"I do, Father, but I wanted to see Mom, I wanted to see Dee, and I wanted to see you. New York City can wait."

Larry took a seat in a stuffed chair, close to the priest, who sat on the sofa.

"I'm sorry that I can't offer you a hot beverage," Father Buckley said. "My throat isn't ready for that just yet. But would you like some apricot juice? It's a kind of medicine for my throat. And it tastes really good."

Larry cheerfully accepted but offered to pour the drinks for both of them. After a few more pleasantries, Larry came directly to the point. "Father, I understand that Gary's will has been getting a lot of attention in the news media. I hope that hasn't made things too difficult for you, as executor of the estate."

Father Buckley dismissed the concern with a wave of his hand. "If I didn't have problems to deal with, I wouldn't know what to do with myself. It hasn't been that bad."

"Honestly, Father, I feel guilty about all this. And I just want to tell you, if it's too much, I'm willing to do the executor thing. Gary was my brother. That matters more than whatever reservations I have about the specifics."

"Larry, that's very generous of you. It really is. But you and your mother both had good reasons to say no. I respect those reasons. And I don't want to burden either one of you more than is absolutely necessary. I may be feeling a little weak at the moment. But I'm getting P.T. and my knee is on the mend. In a couple of weeks, I'll be doing cartwheels in front of the church."

"I'd pay to see that, Father," said Larry, with a laugh.

"So how long are you in town?"

"Well, only for a day, Father. I still have a commitment for one more week in New York. I'm going to honor that commitment. Then I'm coming home for good."

Father Buckley looked up in surprise. "Really, Larry? Your mother said that you received an offer to go on a world tour next month. An offer you couldn't refuse."

"That's right, Father. It was a very tempting offer. I almost signed on the dotted line."

"Why didn't you?"

"Well, here's the thing. A lot of people depend on me. Dee, my band members, my mom. I just didn't feel I could abandon them. It didn't seem right."

Father Buckley was silent for quite a while. "Does that mean you're giving up your dream, Larry? Your dream of being the best trumpet player since Clifford Brown?"

"No, Father, I can be a great trumpet player right here in Pittsburgh. That's what I finally realized. Don't get me wrong, New York City is amazing. When I'm performing there, it's almost like an out-of-body experience. Exhilarating. Intoxicating. Kind of spiritual, if you know what I mean."

"I think I do. Music often brings us closer to God."

"We're using different words, Father, but I think we're saying the same thing."

"You're willing to give that up?"

"Well, the way I see it, I can give the New York part up without abandoning the jazz part. In return, I get to see Dee grow up with a strong father in her life. Me. I get to see my Mom grow old with a strong son in her life. Me. I get to work my musical magic with my own band, not someone else's band. Doesn't that seem like a win-win to you?"

"I like the way you think, Larry. Pittsburgh will be a stronger, more vibrant community if you're part of it. And who knows? Maybe you'll find a way to squeeze in a bit of Gary's vision too. If you have the time, Westinghouse High could reach new heights with you as one of their instructors."

"I've thought about that, too, Father. If they give me enough freedom, that could be a hoot. But one thing at a time. Let me get my feet on the ground first. Then I can think about being a teacher too. Besides, I've already signed up to be a private tutor for a young lady who has a lot of potential."

"Who's that, Larry?"

"Dee."

Father Buckley laughed. "I'd love to be a fly on the wall for that. Teaching is hard. Teaching kinfolk is harder."

"We'll see, Father. I think I'm up for it. And it means a lot to Dee."

"It'll be fine, Larry. Good for both of you. It'll bring you together."

294

Chapter Sixty-Three: The Trap is Sprung

Ceci's lips were trembling as she kissed her husband goodbye, just before his scheduled meeting with Phil Hodges downtown. She knew just how much was riding on that conversation.

If the meeting went well, they could sack a corrupt and dangerous staffer and let the criminal justice system do its work. If the meeting went poorly, her husband's political career could come crashing down with a thud.

With the children at school, Ceci decided that gardening was her best bet to relax. She had been meaning to plant some nasturtiums and Gerbera daisies in the back yard. But first she needed to do some weeding and lay down some mulch.

As soon as the Mayor left, Ceci put on some overalls and a long-sleeved work shirt, slipped into a pair of tennis shoes, and headed to the shed for supplies. She found some thick gloves, a wide-brim hat, a trowel, a hoe, and some weed-killer.

Near her chosen spot of turf, weeds were sprouting like whiskers on an old man's face. Ceci hadn't done any garden work since late March, and it showed. This was shaping up like a day-long project, which was just fine. A lot of sweat and a few aches and pains were just what she needed.

A half hour into the gardening, Ceci was so absorbed in her work that she didn't hear the soft footsteps of a guest. When she finally noticed her visitor, she gasped.

"Phil, you startled me. What are you doing here? I thought …"

"You thought what?"

Ceci noticed an ugly purple bruise on Hodges' right cheek, a reminder of his altercation with her husband. "I thought you were meeting with Walt today."

"Well, I changed my mind. It just didn't feel right."

"What do you mean?"

"How much do you know?"

Ceci hesitated, trying to decide what to say. "I know that you and Walt have had some disagreements, and that he's hoping to patch things up. That's why he wanted to talk with you today."

Hodges scratched his chin and smiled. "Well, that's a possibility. But in politics, I've learned to think in terms of probabilities, not possibilities. The man who punched me in the face the other day didn't seem like a man who was trying to kiss and make up."

Just uncomfortable at first, Ceci was now starting to feel afraid. The man in front of her played hardball. He was corrupt. Unreliable. According to the rumor mill, he might even be an arsonist or a murderer. And no one knew he was here. All of a sudden, Ceci wanted to be somewhere else. Anywhere else.

"Phil, I really think you should talk with Walt. Tell him you're running late. Go downtown and have a conversation with him."

Hodges scratched his chin again. "I don't think so, Ceci. Something doesn't feel right."

"What doesn't feel right?"

"Well, I checked with Walt's secretary to make sure our appointment was for ten o'clock. She said he has no other appointments for the rest of the day. Now what might that mean? He *always* has appointments, especially in the middle of an election campaign."

Ceci thought quickly. "Well, I can explain that, Phil. He and I are taking the rest of the day off."

"Is that right? Where are you going?"

"We thought we'd take a break and go hiking in the Laurel Highlands."

Hodges laughed. "Nice try, Ceci. But that can't possibly be true. You and I both know that Walt injured his ankle the other day. The last thing he'd want to do is go for a hike."

"He's feeling better," Ceci said, trying to think of a way out.

"I think a better idea is for you and me to go for a hike."

Ceci turned pale. "What do you mean by that, Phil?"

"I mean, you and I need to talk. And not here, where our conversation might be interrupted. What do you say?"

"I'm not going to do that, Phil."

Hodges pulled a gun out. Ceci tried to swallow but couldn't.

"I don't want to use this," Hodges said. "But I will if I have to. Now put down that trowel and come with me. You have nothing to worry about if you do as I say."

* * *

Scuglia really wanted to be in the vicinity when the Mayor spoke with Hodges. But Stilton had vetoed the idea, due to Scuglia's bum leg. Radic and Mulroy promised to text him in real time, as a consolation prize. Not the real thing, but he appreciated the gesture.

At 9:50 a.m., he received a text from Radic: "The stage is set. Wish us luck!"

At 10:05 a.m., he received a text from Mulroy: "No sign of H yet. Must be caught in traffic."

At 10:20 a.m., he received another text: "Still no sign of H."

Scuglia thought for a moment about their carefully laid plans. Suddenly, a possibility occurred to him.

"Louise, we need to take a little trip."

"What kind of a trip? You don't have P.T. until this afternoon."

"Just humor me. It won't take long."

Scuglia went to the bathroom, then fetched a satchel from the safe in his study. With a cane for support, he walked slowly with Louise to the garage.

Louise drove to Shadyside, with Scuglia navigating. Fifteen minutes later, they pulled into the driveway of a gorgeous home with a gazebo. Two cars were parked there: a Lexus and a Volvo.

"Where are we, Tony?" Louise asked.

"This is the Mayor's home."

"What in God's name are we doing here?"

"I need to check on something."

"Are you sure this is a good idea? Shouldn't you call Radic?"

"He's not available right now. I'm the only one who can do this."

"What do you want me to do, Tony?"

"I want you to wait right here. Lock the doors. If I'm not back in ten minutes, then text Radic and tell him to come here right away."

"I don't like the sound of that, Tony."

"Don't worry. Everything will be okay."

Scuglia reached into the back seat, extracted his satchel and his cane, and got out of the car. He closed the door as quietly as he could and walked as fast as he could to the front door. Then he heard voices from behind the house. One was a man's voice. The other was Ceci Arceneaux. They were screaming at each other.

Scuglia hugged the front of the house as best he could and walked slowly towards the far end. He reached into his satchel and pulled out a gun. The screaming worsened. Then silence, followed by screams from the man only.

Scuglia peeked into the back yard. Ceci Arceneaux lay prone on the ground, motionless. Hodges was running around in circles, rubbing his eyes and wailing, as if attacked by a swarm of bees.

"Down on the ground," Scuglia ordered. Hodges didn't obey.

"Down on the ground, or I'll shoot," Scuglia said.

This time, Hodges obeyed, more or less, though he continued to wail and flail, as he rubbed his eyes against the grass.

Scuglia moved to Hodges as quickly as he could, extracted handcuffs from his satchel, and cuffed him.

"What happened?"

"She sprayed me."

"What did you do to her?"

"I just pushed her."

Leaving Hodges for a moment, Scuglia shuffled over to Ceci Arceneaux.

Her eyes were closed, but she was still breathing.

Out of the corner of his eye, Scuglia spotted Louise, who had ignored his orders and come into the back yard. He was glad of it.

"Louise, call 911 and get someone here immediately, for both of them. Then text Radic and tell him that Hodges is here. Make sure you say that. Hodges is here. He'll want to come out as well."

"Got it," Louise said, as she pulled out her phone.

Scuglia returned to Ceci. He felt underneath her head for blood. Detecting none, he elevated her head and gave her left cheek a gentle pat. No response. He gave her cheek a firmer pat.

This time, she stirred. A good sign.

"Ceci? Can you hear me? Ceci?"

Scuglia decided to kill two birds with one stone. Spotting a hose near the back of the house, he turned on the water and extended the hose. After elevating Ceci's head again, he sprayed some water on her face. This produced some eye movements. He sprayed her again, and this time she looked up.

"Ceci? I'm Detective Scuglia. Say yes if you understand."

Ceci nodded her head.

Louise had finished her phone calls. Hodges was still groaning and complaining. Scuglia motioned for Louise to join him and Ceci. While Louise looked after Ceci for a few moments, Scuglia sprayed Hodges in the face, first a small blast, then a big blast.

Hodges seemed to benefit from this, judging from fewer screams and complaints. But his eyes remained closed, which was just fine with Scuglia. He located Hodges' gun and placed it in a clean bag after donning gloves.

An ambulance arrived just two minutes later. Scuglia identified himself and the injured parties and explained what he knew. The medics quickly took both Ceci and Hodges to Shadyside Hospital, in separate vehicles.

Scuglia called Radic. Getting no reply, he called Mulroy. They were on their way. Scuglia redirected both of them to Shadyside Hospital, telling Mulroy what she needed to know. He would remain behind to protect the crime scene.

Louise approached her husband and gave him a big hug. "How are you doing, hon? Is your leg okay?"

Scuglia smiled. "You know, for the first time in weeks, I didn't even notice it was hurting."

"That's because you love your job, Tony. Your job is better medicine than anything the docs have prescribed."

"Maybe, maybe not," Scuglia said, "but I feel good about what we did today."

"You're a hero, dear," Louise said.

"I don't know about that."

"You did more with a gimpy leg than most people would do with two good legs. I just hope they appreciate you."

"I just hope they let me go back to work."

Chapter Sixty-Four: An Enigma

Eager to talk with Phil Hodges, Radic secured the consent of the District Attorney's office and a local judge to do precisely that.

While Mulroy waited in the foyer, Radic was led to the prisoner's cell. Arriving quietly, Radic took the measure of the man inside the cell. To the casual observer, he didn't fit the image of a villain. He looked dapper, not sinister, mild-mannered, not mean. He had shaved and showered. He was now doing pushups. Clearly, this was someone who cared about his appearance.

What else did he care about? Politics? That seemed obvious. But what about politics? Was it public policy or electioneering? Was it issues or people? And who were his role models? Anyone who won elections?

Radic vowed to do additional research on this strange man who might very well be responsible for the murder of Gary Mabry. He cleared his throat, alerting Hodges to his presence. Surprisingly, Hodges smiled, instead of scowling. Now, why would he do that?

Radic explained that he and Mulroy would be escorting Hodges to headquarters for an interview. After he was cuffed and shackled, the two detectives placed him in a police car and drove across the Duquesne Bridge to Western Avenue.

They set Hodges up in an interrogation room, fetched some water, turned on the recorder, and commenced the interview.

"I understand you're waiving your rights to a lawyer," Radic began.

"That's right," Hodges said, with a cough.

"You know the city will provide you with a public defender, if you like."

"I'll pass."

"I've also been told that you intend to plead guilty."

"To certain charges."

"To attempted kidnapping?"

"Guilty as charged. What do you think the sentence will be?"

Radic was surprised by the question. "I'm not a lawyer. But you tried to kidnap the Mayor's wife. Any judge would view that as a serious offense."

"So fifteen years? Twenty years?"

"I really couldn't say."

Hodges nodded.

"Will you be pleading guilty to arson?"

Hodges shook his head, then started coughing, convulsively. "Allergies," he explained, gulping down a glass of water. "To answer your question, I don't think so."

"Will you be pleading guilty to murder?"

"No to that, too."

Radic nodded to Mulroy, passing the baton to her.

"You've been known to dress up as a superhero," Mulroy said.

Hodges looked up. "It's true. I attended a comic-con convention here in Pittsburgh. But so too did thousands of other people. Are you accusing them of murder, too? That's a pretty slender reed."

"Perhaps. But on arson, the evidence is more compelling. We have a witness who will testify that you threatened him if he revealed the campaign finance scheme you and Gary Mabry cooked up."

"Father Buckley?"

Mulroy refused to confirm or deny.

"A threat is one thing. An action is another."

"Are you saying you didn't commit arson?" Radic asked.

"I wouldn't even know how to do it."

"Then why did you threaten Father Buckley?"

"I told him to be careful. Nothing more than that."

Radic snorted. "I don't know whether to laugh or to cry."

"Suit yourself. You know, they said you were different. But I don't see it.

You're like all the other cops I've known."

"How's that?"

"You're so busy going after the minnows that you ignore the piranhas."

Radic was shocked. He had heard that phrase before. "Could you repeat that?"

"I think I've said enough. I'd like to go now."

Radic stopped the interview, and he and Mulroy returned Hodges to the county jail. Radic asked Mulroy to drive because he was deeply troubled by Hodges's remarks. He was beginning to look at the case differently, and he didn't like the conclusions he was drawing.

He and Mulroy needed to have a serious conversation, but it would have to wait. They were already running late for a meeting at the Mabry home.

* * *

Radic and Mulroy received a warm welcome from Ernestine Mabry and from Larry, who had agreed to join his mother at their family home. They both seemed relieved and relaxed.

"Detectives, how nice to see both of you," Mrs. Mabry said, inviting them into the living room. "Larry and I are both very grateful for all that you've done."

"Well, the case isn't closed yet, Mrs. Mabry," Radic said. "Don't thank us until someone has been arrested, tried, and convicted."

"You know the expression, Mama," Larry chimed in. "The opera ain't over till the fat lady sings. Right, Radic?"

"That's exactly right."

"But the newspaper said you have someone in custody, a Mr. Hodges."

"That's right, Ma'am, we do. Has either of you met Mr. Hodges?"

They both shook their heads.

"Do you recall if Gary ever mentioned Mr. Hodges?"

Mrs. Mabry shook her head, but Larry responded, "Gary worked with Hodges on the blood donations, and he worked with him on the campaign contributions. He mentioned him now and then."

"What did he think of Hodges? Do you recall?"

Larry grew pensive. "He didn't talk that much about him. I think he viewed him as a … well, as a go-fer."

"As *his* go-fer?"

"Well, to some extent. But mainly the Mayor's go-fer."

"Would you say that he liked Hodges?"

"Not particularly."

"Would you say that he feared Hodges?"

"Not really. Then again, Gary was pretty fearless."

"Did he ever mention Hodges cutting corners or engaging in illegal acts?"

Larry laughed. "That's not the way Gary looked at the world. Good and bad, yes. Right and wrong, yes. But leegal and illegal? Those words were not in Gary's vocabulary."

Radic decided to switch topics.

"Mrs. Mabry, we've talked with you before about Gary's experiences as an adult, but not that much about his high school years. You've told us that he was a football star."

"That's right."

"And he won some trophies."

"That's right. All of them are right here on that shelf." She motioned to a trophy case brimming with awards.

"Did Gary have any special friends when he was in high school?"

"Gary had lots of friends. Athletes mostly. Right, Larry?"

"That's right, Mama."

"How about Khalif Wilson? Was Gary friendly with Khalif in those days?"

"I wasn't around much back then, Mama," Larry said. "What would you say?"

"Khalif was definitely one of his buddies."

"What would they do together?"

"They would jog together. I approved of that. Good wholesome fun."

"Where would they jog?"

"In the neighborhood, I suppose. But also at Westinghouse High School. Khalif was on the track team, I believe."

"I didn't know that. So he was a good runner?"

"A very good runner, as I recall. He won some trophies, I think."

Radic nodded. "How about Halloween?"

"Halloween?"

"Would Gary and Khalif go trick-or-treating together?"

Larry laughed. "Man, you ask some funny questions. Is that what they train you to do at the Police Academy? Toss a few softballs before you throw the fastball down the middle of the plate?"

Radic turned serious. "Indulge me, Mrs. Mabry, just for a moment. I'm genuinely interested in whether Gary and Khalif went trick-or-treating together."

She paused and closed her eyes. "Well, in my mind's eye, I think I can visualize that. It was many years ago, of course. But I think that's right. I can see pumpkins, candy bars, Gary, and Khalif."

"Keep your eyes closed for just a moment, Mrs. Mabry," Radic advised. "It's Halloween night. Gary and Khalif are about to go trick-or-treating. Is Gary wearing a costume?"

"He was a ghost. I believe he was a ghost. Cause he cut up one of my sheets without asking permission."

"Excellent," Radic said. "Now, Khalif. He was there too. What kind of a costume was he wearing?"

Mrs. Mabry struggled. Then she opened her eyes. "Superman. He was dressed as Superman."

"Something homemade? Or an honest-to-goodness Superman suit?"

"An honest-to-goodness suit. I don't know where he got the money for it."

"Thank you, Mrs. Mabry. You've been a big help."

"I can't see how. But if you say so, Detective."

Larry was suddenly quiet. "I'll walk the detectives to the door, Mama."

"Okay, well, thank you for coming. It was nice to see both of you."

Larry walked outside with Radic and Mulroy and stood on the front stoop. "What was going on in there, man?"

Radic said nothing.

"I know you, Radic, and you always have a plan. Are you going after Khalif for the drugs? Or is it something more than that?"

"It's just a hunch, Larry. Being a detective, you come up with hunches. Some of them pan out, most of them deflate like a punctured balloon."

"I don't know, man. From the expression on your face, the balloon was inflating, not deflating."

Larry looked at Mulroy. She said nothing.

"Okay, okay, if that's how you want to play it. But promise me this. Keep me in the loop. If Hodges isn't the guy, I want to know who is the guy. You read me?"

"I read you, Larry. But let us do our work as police officers. That's what we're paid to do. If the evidence leads somewhere else, you'll be the first to know."

"I'm counting on that, man. I'm counting on that. Whoever did Gary is going to pay for what he did. Whether it's you or me holding him to account."

* * *

After leaving the Mabry home, Radic turned to Mulroy. "What were your impressions of Khalif the one time we met him?"

Mulroy thought for a moment. "Smoother than silk."

"What else?"

"Smart."

"How did he seem when we asked about Gary?"

"At ease. Comfortable. Like he and Gary were two peas in a pod."

"Did he seem like he was putting on an act?"

"If so, it was a darn good one. We showed up unannounced. He had no time to prepare."

"Who might know him well?"

"Hodges."

"He's not talking."

"Menendez."

"He's not our biggest fan. Unlikely to cooperate."

"Where does that leave us?"

"Maybe the DEA can help. They've been really cooperative."

"I agree. Let's touch base with Scuglia. Let's sift and winnow. Then we need to dig deeper."

* * *

Over the next two days, the Homicide Squad put almost everything else on hold, while they investigated the past and current activities of Khalif Wilson. They reached the following conclusions:

1. Khalif had been an outstanding track star at Westinghouse High School. He majored in Business at Pitt but left after two years without finishing his degree.

2. On social media, Khalif identified himself as an international trade specialist. He listed no official business address other than his home address. And there were no photos of him dressed as Superman, Spider-Man, or a ninja warrior.

3. The burgled documents from Gary Mabry's apartment had not yet surfaced. None of the documents obtained from Gary's lockers at Muscle Mania mentioned Khalif.

Having learned very little from Hodges during his interrogation, Radic was surprised when a sergeant from the county jail indicated that Hodges would like to talk again. The request was conditional, though. Hodges would talk with Radic and Mulroy and try to answer their questions, but only if he could speak with the mayor first. He said he wanted to clarify with the mayor what he could properly divulge and what he should not. He owed him that much.

This last-minute burst of ethics struck Radic as disingenuous. After all, Hodges had tried to kidnap the Mayor's wife! The time for scruples should have come much earlier. Nevertheless, he took the request to Stilton.

Stilton's advice, after thinking it over: Don't look a gift horse in the mouth. If the mayor is willing to talk with Hodges, we should be willing to talk with him as well.

Radic was fine with that, so he spoke directly with the mayor, who seemed eager to help. He was willing to have a private conversation with Hodges if Radic thought it would help to close the Gary Mabry case. Radic told him that it might.

To finalize arrangements, Hodges asked that the mayor bring him some personal effects from campaign headquarters, including an inhaler and allergy medications. The mayor agreed to serve as courier, provided that the guards were okay with this.

Two days later, the mayor himself arrived at the county jail. He was taken to a private room, where Hodges, in handcuffs, was sitting and waiting. By prior agreement, the mayor and Hodges would talk privately. No surveillance, no video recording, no observers.

A half hour later, the mayor left, apparently satisfied with the conversation. At some point, the mayor relinquished the medicine and received a letter in a sealed envelope from Hodges. After the mayor's departure, Radic learned that Hodges was ready for another conversation with Pittsburgh police. Radic and Mulroy picked him up and escorted him to the interrogation room at headquarters.

* * *

Hodges' body language was different than it had been three days earlier. He seemed less at ease, less self-assured. He smiled less. Also, his cough was worse. "I just need my allergy pills," he told them. "I'm supposed to get them later today."

After being stonewalled for two to three weeks, Radic decided to cut to the chase.

"Mr. Hodges, where were you on May 13, the day of Gary Mabry's murder?"

"I don't have access to my diary, Detective, but from memory, I'd say that

I was out meeting with donors that day. In Washington, D.C."

"So you're saying that you were not in Pittsburgh during the day of May 13?"

"No, I didn't say that. I'm saying that I was not in Pittsburgh when Gary Mabry was shot. I know that because I heard about the shooting as soon as I returned to Pittsburgh. It had happened earlier in the day."

"Okay, we'll investigate that, I assure you. But let's say you're telling the truth …"

"I am."

"Okay, let's assume that. Do you have any first-hand knowledge of who shot and killed Gary Mabry?"

Hodges sighed. "Detective, I've thought about that long and hard. I do have some information that might be useful to you, and I've reevaluated my situation. I've decided that I will tell you what I know, but I wish to speak with an attorney before I do that."

Radic was stunned. "So you've changed your mind about legal representation?"

"Yes, I have."

"Do you have a particular attorney in mind?"

"Yes, I do. With your permission, I'd like to call him this afternoon. If he agrees to represent me, then I'm prepared to tell you what I know with him at my side."

Radic concluded the interview. Two other officers returned Hodges to the county jail."

What do you make of that, Mulroy?"

"I'd say he's toying with us. Didn't you say he seemed fine with a prison sentence the other day?"

"For kidnapping, yes, that was my strong impression."

"So, is he no longer fine with that?"

"It's hard to say. Maybe he wants an attorney to protect him from the other charges."

"Does he really have something useful to tell us?"

"I don't know, Mulroy. So far, it's been bullshit. Except the comment about the minnows and the piranhas."

"Do you think he's going to finger Khalif?"

"I honestly don't know. Maybe the mayor knows more. I'd love to know what they talked about."

"Should we ask the mayor?"

"Well, why not?"

Radic called the mayor's office and was told that the mayor would meet with them the following morning at 10:00 a.m. Radic left for home early. He needed Lexie time, Ralph time. Above all, he needed time to figure out the truth.

Chapter Sixty-Five: Spring Can Really Hang You Up the Most

The first sound that Radic heard, through the mist of sleep, was that of Ralph barking loudly. Next, he heard Lexie speaking, softly, with the landline in her hand.

"Branko, honey. You need to take this."

Radic noticed the time. 4:10 a.m. He was in a barking mood himself, but managed to control his frustration. His eyes still closed, he grasped the phone that Lexie placed in his right hand.

"Radic."

He listened groggily, then grew alert, his eyes wide open. He asked a few questions.

"I'll be right there."

Radic turned to Lexie, with a look of deep pain. "Did they tell you?"

Lexie nodded.

Radic dressed quickly, kissed Lexie, and told her to try to get some sleep. He gave Ralph a treat, hoping it would suffice until breakfast time. Then he was out the door.

Despite the early hour, there was considerable activity at the City-County Building when he arrived. Three ambulances, two fire trucks. Multiple police cars parked hastily, their rear bumpers pointing in different directions.

Radic was greeted at the door to the jail by Sergeant Herb Dillard of the Allegheny County Sheriff's Office, a former PBP colleague who had always been a good cop.

"What do we know?" he asked.

"At about 3:30 a.m., as Officer Bernard Lanley was making his rounds, he noticed that Hodges was sprawled on the floor. He checked his pulse and determined that he was dead."

"Suicide?"

"That seems like the only possibility."

"Did he hang himself?"

"It was pills. He had a container with pills near his cot."

"Has anyone touched the container?"

"Lanley was the intermediary. Unless he put on gloves, his prints are probably there."

"Have you called the M.E.?"

"She's on her way."

Radic nodded and walked with Dillard to the cell. With all the lights on, some inmates were grousing about interrupted sleep. Others looked worried or concerned.

The scene was pretty much as described. Hodges was curled into a fetal position, a pool of vomit near his face. The pills were near the cot. Wearing gloves, Radic checked the prescription. Pseudoephedrine. Harmless stuff, unless taken in exceptionally large quantities. Yet the bottle was nearly full. The M.E. would have to sort it out.

"No note?" he asked.

Sergeant Dillard shook his head. "Not as far as we can tell. But he gave the Mayor some sort of letter yesterday."

Radic nodded and did some rummaging. Nothing under the pillow. Nothing under the bed except dirty socks. A notebook that seemed like a makeshift diary. He leafed to the last page. No entry over the past twenty-four hours.

Fifteen minutes later, Saroja Prakash arrived, wearing scrubs. She was accompanied by a technician and by Mulroy. "We just ran into each other," Mulroy explained.

"What do you make of this?" Prakash asked.

"You'll want to do a tox screen on the pills," Radic said. "Supposedly allergy medicine. But I'm betting you'll find something else."

"Suicide?"

"Or murder."

"Where did he get the pills?"

Radic paused. "From the mayor. The mayor of Pittsburgh."

***

Some news stories ricochet across the community with lightning-like speed, even if the evidence is fragmentary. This was one of them.

The inescapable fact was that a murder suspect was dead. By his own hand? Perhaps. But the murder weapon was supplied by the mayor. The same mayor who had punched him in the face in his office. The same mayor whose wife had been targeted for kidnapping by the dead man.

Gary Mabry's messy murder case had become even messier. And the man who was in the best position to connect the dots—Hodges —was now dead.

After a brief phone conversation with Stilton, it was agreed that Radic and Mulroy would meet with the mayor, as scheduled, at 10:00 a.m. They ate a quick breakfast, with plenty of coffee, and braced themselves for what lay ahead. The man they were about to interview could be a material witness to a murder. He was also a murder suspect himself.

"How do we treat him?" Mulroy asked.

"Respectfully, but not with kid gloves."

"Do you think he's involved?"

"Not necessarily. But we can't cut him any slack."

At 10:00 a.m., Radic and Mulroy were escorted into the mayor's office. His assistant, Regina, was polite enough but subdued.

The mayor's mood was worse. He seemed shaken and upset. Radic noticed a bottle of Maalox on his desk.

"Mr. Mayor," Radic began, "I need you to walk us through your visit with Phil Hodges. Let's begin with the pills you delivered. What kinds of pills were they, and where did you get them?"

"According to Phil, they were allergy pills. He said we could find them in his desk drawer at campaign headquarters. An inhaler, too."

"Did you pick those items up before your visit?"

"Not personally. I had one of my staffers do it. Jane Sheehy. Very reliable."

"Did you deliver those pills to Mr. Hodges?"

"Yes, I did."

"Did anyone else touch the pills besides you and Ms. Sheehy?"

"Well, yes, when I entered the jail, the guard, an Officer Lanley, said that Sergeant Dillard needed to look at anything I proposed to give Hodges. So the guard and the sergeant would have handled the pills and the inhaler."

"Alright. Can we fast-forward to when you left the jail? Did Mr. Hodges give you a letter to read?"

"He gave me a letter, but I haven't opened it. It's for you, not me."

Startled, Radic accepted a letter from the mayor and took a close look. Sure enough, the envelope, in printed letters, said: "Detective Raditch, PBP." Radic opened the letter, also in printed letters, and read it aloud:

"Dear Detective Raditch, I cannot bear the guilt over what I have done. And I don't want to go to prison. So, I've decided to take my own life, with a suicide pill I included in my allergy meds.

"I confess that I did it all. I killed Gary Mabry. I burned down the rectory. I kidnapped the Mayor's wife.

"I apologize to the Mayor and to the Mabry family. I'm a bad person. I don't deserve to live.

"Yours, Phil Hodges."

No one said anything for a while.

Finally, Radic addressed the mayor. "What's your reaction? Is this consistent with what Hodges said to you?"

The mayor paused. "I'm surprised, Detective. Very surprised. When we spoke yesterday, Phil had a very different message."

"And what was that?"

"He told me that someone else was behind the whole thing and that he was ready to identify that person as soon as he spoke with a lawyer."

"Did he say who that person was?"

The Mayor shook his head.

Radic thought for a moment, then handed the note to the mayor. "Mr. Mayor, have you ever received handwritten notes from Hodges?"

"Maybe once or twice, at a campaign rally."

"Was the writing in print or in cursive?"

"In cursive."

Radic nodded. "His cell diary writing is also in cursive."

"What are you saying, Branko?" Mulroy asked.

"I'm saying that I have some doubts that this letter was written by Phil Hodges."

"But who could have written it?" Mulroy asked.

"Mr. Mayor, can you excuse me for five minutes?"

The mayor nodded, and Radic left the room, taking the letter with him.

When he returned, Radic resumed his questioning. "Mr. Mayor, did Phil Hodges hand this letter to you?"

"Yes."

"So you are the only person to have touched it, other than Hodges?"

"Actually, no. The same protocol applied when entering and leaving the jail. The guard had to show it to his sergeant before I could take it with me."

"So they would have handled it?"

"That's right."

"Did you speak with the sergeant personally about this?"

"No. The guard spoke with him."

"How long did it take?"

"Well, it wasn't instantaneous. Maybe ten minutes."

"Mr. Mayor, please excuse me, but Detective Mulroy and I need to return to the jail immediately."

"I feel terrible about this, Radic. Despite what Phil did, I did not wish him ill."

"We'll try to get to the bottom of this. We appreciate your time and your help."

As Radic and Mulroy left, Radic picked up the pace. "What's going on, Branko?" Mulroy asked.

"I don't know for sure, but I have a hunch. We need to hurry back to the City-County Building, or some crucial evidence might be destroyed."

When Radic and Mulroy arrived, Sergeant Dillard was waiting at the front door.

"Did you do what I said?"

Dillard nodded.

"What was Lanley's reaction?"

"Indignant."

"And his locker?"

"It's under surveillance, with orders that no one may touch it."

"Good man," Radic said. "Mulroy, how would you like to visit your friend Judge Belsky again?"

"Always a pleasure," she said.

"I need you to prepare a search warrant for Officer Lanley's locker, the clothing he's wearing, and his apartment. But first, let me tell you what I think is going on."

A half hour later, Mulroy was on her way to Judge Belsky's chambers.

* * *

One of Judge Belsky's best qualities was her honesty. If she hated a warrant request, she said so. If she loved a warrant request, she said so. Luckily, she loved this one and approved it without a single editorial suggestion.

"You're getting better at this, Detective," she said.

"I've gotten lots of good advice along the way," Mulroy replied.

"And nice work with the snakes, by the way. I couldn't give you a warrant, but I'm glad you solved the problem. I live in Mt. Lebanon, not far from Brookline, where you discovered the snakes. I'm sleeping soundly again, thanks to you."

"Thank you, your honor."

Mulroy arrived at the City-County Building ten minutes later, after telling Radic that they were good to go.

Radic showed the warrant to Sergeant Dillard, who walked him to

Lanley's locker and explained to the guard that a judge had approved a search.

One by one, Radic and Mulroy removed every item, including civilian clothing, sundries, and papers. Inside the sheaf of papers was the letter Radic had hoped to find, written in cursive. After processing some paperwork, he and Mulroy repaired to a private office.

After assuring himself that no one was listening, Radic read the letter out loud:

"Dear Detective Radic:

"Khalif Wilson is trying to kill me, and my guard, Officer Lanley, is working for Khalif. They have threatened to kill me in jail unless I remain silent. But if I remain silent, I will go to prison for crimes I did not commit. Here are the facts:

"1. Yes, I threatened Father Buckley. But I did not burn down the rectory. That was Khalif, who also ordered me to threaten Father Buckley. I regret that. But Khalif has been blackmailing me for some time. Within limits, I must do what he tells me to do.

"2. Yes, I kidnapped Ceci Arceneaux. I assure you that I would not have harmed her. I am ashamed of what I did. But Khalif insisted. He would kill me if I didn't do it.

"3. Yes, I helped Gary Mabry channel funds from drug sales to the Mayor's campaign. In retrospect, that was not smart. We thought it was legal, but I guess it was not.

"4. No, I did not kill Gary Mabry. That was Khalif. I know he killed Gary because he bragged about it. He said, I killed Gary. And if you don't do what I say, I will kill you, too.

"I am writing to beg for your help. I know that I will be sent to prison for my role in the kidnapping. I accept that. But I do not deserve to die. Please transfer me to another jail or arrest Officer Lanley. He is a corrupt, dangerous man.

"Yours, Phil Hodges."

Chapter Sixty-Six: Scuglia Reports on the Stock Market

Radic and Mulroy were in the enviable position of having broken the case wide open. At the same time, they were in the unenviable position of not having the evidence to bring Gary's killer to justice. And there were loose ends begging to be addressed. Was the mayor an unwitting accomplice in a jail inmate's suicide? Or was it murder, orchestrated by Khalif, executed by Lanley? If so, what poison was used and how was it obtained?

Radic groaned out loud as he contemplated the latest developments. His headache had gotten worse, despite six Tylenols. He and Mulroy needed sleep, but they also needed to take stock. Louise Scuglia had invited them over for dinner. Well, they needed a break. Radic took a shower at work, then hopped into his car and headed to Scuglia's. Mulroy was already there.

Radic smelled something wonderful emanating from the kitchen. Salmon perhaps. He also detected olive oil, garlic, onions, and rosemary. He had expected take-out. But Louise had risen to the occasion.

At Louise's suggestion, they avoided discussing the case while eating dinner. "You need a fresh perspective. Enjoy the meal. Have a glass of wine. Then you can tear your hair out. Tony's as upset as you are. But no shop talk until after dessert."

Louise was right. The conversation felt strained at first. It's hard to discuss sports when a Level-4 Hurricane is heading your way. But somehow they managed to talk about baseball, snakes, and washing machines.

"Why can't they make better washing machines?" Scuglia complained.

"They can make them," Mulroy argued. "They just don't want to. It's like with umbrellas. The technology is there. But if you make umbrellas that actually work, where's the profit in that? Instead, they make umbrellas that fold up on you and collapse whenever the wind exceeds fifteen mph. Which forces you to go out and buy another one that's equally bad. It's a disgrace."

After a delicious dinner and two bottles of Pinot Grigio, everyone was feeling much better. Radic and Mulroy started to clear the dishes, but Louise shooed them away. "You all go into the living room and get set up in there. I know that Tony has something to tell you."

Radic thanked Louise profusely for a lovely dinner, but secretly his heart was aching. It seemed obvious to him that Scuglia was going to turn in his badge. Radic had seen it again and again, and with much younger cops. The stress and strain got to be too much, even without a serious injury.

Scuglia found his seat on the Barcalounger. He had made remarkable progress since the shooting on the Mon. And his mood was upbeat. When you're ready to lay your burden down, Radic thought, it must be a huge weight off your shoulders.

The crew switched from wine to water and soft drinks. It was time to get down to business.

"But first, guys, I have something to say," Scuglia began.

Radic braced himself, waiting for the other shoe to fall.

"When you're confined to quarters, as I've been for the past few weeks, you start thinking about your future. I mean, seriously thinking about your future. In my case, I've been focusing on finances, more than ever before. Will Louise and I be able to make ends meet when I eventually retire from the force? That's been on my mind since the shooting.

"So, for the past couple of weeks, I've been following the stock market closely. We have a couple of money market accounts. I've zeroed in on the riskiest stocks in our portfolio, to see how they're doing. After a while, it gets to be kind of obsessive.

"And after a while, you need a break. So the other day, just for fun, I checked the stock for Exportaciones Internacionales. It seems that their stock is up, noticeably. I don't mean like ten percent. I mean like seventy percent. So, I've done some investigating and talked to our financial advisor, just to satisfy my curiosity.

"It turns out that the reason for the surge in prices is quite simple. They recently bought out another Mexican company. It's called Comerciantes al Mundo, and it's a front for…"

"Costa a Costa," Radic said, excitedly. "I remember seeing the two linked in a DEA report on drug cartels."

"You have a fine eye for detail, my friend," Scuglia said with a smile.

"So what does this mean?" Mulroy asked.

"Unless I'm mistaken," Radic said, "it means that Avis just purchased Hertz. Or to put it another way, the betta fish just swallowed the piranhas."

"Okay, okay," Mulroy said. "It sounds like a big deal. But what does this mean for our case?"

"That remains to be seen," Radic said. "But when something like this happens, it's a game-changer. Whoever sees it coming and repositions himself accordingly, that guy comes out on top. Whoever backs the losing side, well, that guy is expendable."

"You mean Gary?" Mulroy asked.

"That's what I'm thinking," Radic said. "How about you, Tony?"

"We're just speculating, of course," Scuglia said. "But I'd say we need to take a close look at Khalif's finances and/or his telephone logs."

"How do we get a warrant to do that?" Mulroy asked.

"That's the catch," Radic responded. "We have accusations from a dead man, but that alone won't get us a warrant from Judge Belsky."

"Can we at least show some contact between Khalif and Hodges?" Scuglia asked.

"They both spent time at Muscle Mania," Mulroy said. "Maybe Denise can confirm seeing them together. Or even Fielding."

"I don't see Fielding volunteering any information," Radic said.

"He doesn't like bad publicity," Mulroy observed. "If we frame it as a way to avoid yet additional bad publicity in the wake of another high-profile death, maybe he'll say yes."

Chapter Sixty-Seven: Mixed Bags

Agent Harkin was excited when Radic told him the news of Scuglia's surprise discovery. He said it explained something that had been puzzling him after sifting through the confiscated drugs.

"Every major cartel has a logo, and that logo appears on their shipments, more often than not. The shipments you confiscated in Charleroi featured a Mexican wolf or the lobo mexicano. That's the logo for E.I.'s drug cartel, Empresas de Tabasco. Which makes sense.

"But some of the drug shipments you seized featured a jaguar. That's the logo for Costa a Costa. Do you follow?"

"What are you saying?"

"Originally, I thought that our friends from Cartel number two had stolen some drugs from Cartel number one. That's still a possibility. But from what Scuglia says about the cartel reorganization, I have a different hypothesis: that the two cartels are now blended and acting as one. If so, this is the first concrete manifestation of the new world order."

"So how will that work? Will they continue to use their respective brands indefinitely? Or will Cartel number one's products eventually get re-branded?"

"I don't know. It remains to be seen. But there will be winners and losers. Cartel number two is riding high. They're making a bid for international preeminence. Cartel number one is on the ropes. When you're on the ropes, you lash out. Or you get liquidated."

"Will these battles spill over into Pittsburgh? Or will they play out in Mexico?"

"I'd say the battles already have spilled over into Pittsburgh. And Gary Mabry was the latest casualty."

* * *

Attorney Pedro Suarez strutted to the front of the federal district courtroom like an alpha rooster at the top of the pecking order. His pomaded hair glistened, his gold cuff links sparkled, and his Bruno Magli shoes looked freshly polished. As he sashayed towards the bench, he looked more like a flamenco dancer than a defense attorney. But when he spoke, he exuded confidence.

"Your honor, I intend to show that the Pittsburgh Bureau of Police has behaved lawlessly, capriciously, and with discriminatory intent. They violated my client's constitutional rights when they arrested him for drug trafficking and burglary and held him in custody without any evidence that he had committed a crime. We will also show that they demonstrated racial prejudice against my client."

As Suarez continued, the smirk on Menendez's face flowered into a full-blown grin. At one point, he turned to Radic, pointed to his attorney with pride, and mouthed the words, "Fuck you."

The hearing didn't last long. The judge announced that he would take the case under advisement. The following morning, he issued a decision from the bench:

"The district attorney alleges that Mr. Menendez burgled an apartment and that while he was there, he shot another man who was coincidentally burgling the same apartment. On the surface, this seems very hard to believe. What are the odds of that? More importantly, where is the evidence? The police have no video footage to link Mr. Menendez to this alleged burglary, they have no fingerprint evidence to suggest that he was there, they have no weapon linked to Mr. Menendez, and they have not recovered the valuables he is said to have stolen.

"On one point, we do agree with the district attorney. The defense argues that the police have discriminated against Mr. Menendez because he is

Latino and because he is a foreign national. The court finds no evidence to support these particular charges. What seems to have motivated the police is haste and corner-cutting, not racial discrimination or a hatred for foreign nationals.

"So, we have an unjustifiable arrest, which violated the suspect's constitutional rights and which resulted in an injury, after a remarkable throw of a baseball by a police officer masquerading as a baseball player or a baseball player moonlighting as a police officer. I'm still trying to figure that part out.

"Mr. Menendez, you are free to go. Mr. District Attorney, you have no case. Detectives Radic and Mulroy, frankly, I expected better of you. You're trying to catch a murderer. I get that. But you need to respect the rights of all of Allegheny County's residents as you try to solve the crime."

* * *

Although Jorge Menendez had a good deal of business to attend to, he couldn't resist the urge to take a few parting shots at the police and the D.A. as he left the federal courthouse. A cluster of reporters was only too happy to oblige.

"Mr. Menendez, how do you feel about your release from prison?"

"The police fucked me over, man. I should never have been arrested in the first place."

"So you believe the police were out to get you?"

"Fuck yeah, man. They discriminated against me because I'm not a U.S. citizen. Well, I have news for you. I pay taxes. I pay rent. I'm not on the dole. I'm part of the solution, not part of the problem."

"What do you plan to do, now that you're a free man?"

"I have some business to take care of. Then I'm gonna find me the sandiest beach in Mexico, get myself a couple bottles of tequila, and enjoy the sunset for a couple of weeks. After that, we'll see. I might move to Miami, where they know how to treat immigrants. I might run for office in my own country. Don't be surprised if I'm the next President of Mexico. People have told me I should run. They say, Jorge, you have what it takes. You're a man of the people."

"Is it true that you're employed by the drug cartel, Costa a Costa?"

Menendez took umbrage at the question. "Who the fuck asked that question?"

A female reporter raised her hand, her expression a half-smile.

"Let me tell you, lady, I don't do drugs, I don't approve of drugs. Whoever said that is a lying son of a bitch."

"A member of the Mayor's Drug Task Force said that," the reporter countered.

"You gonna give me the bastard's name?"

"He'd prefer to remain anonymous."

"He'd prefer to remain anonymous," he repeated in a sing-songy voice. "Well, you tell Mr. Anonymous I'd like to see him say that to my face. Will you tell him that for me?"

"I'll tell him."

"Pendeja."

"What did he just say?" the female reporter asked another reporter.

"I think he just called you an asshole."

"Okay, I've had enough of this bullshit. Goodbye, Pittsburgh! Excuse me if I don't say it's been fun. Cause it hasn't. Pittsburgh sucks."

With that, Menendez headed toward the parking garage. He found his Alfa Romeo there, exited, and headed straight for Muscle Mania.

Despite what he had said about Pittsburgh, Jorge had a soft spot for some places in Pittsburgh, like Muscle Mania. He loved their equipment, especially the glute machine, which kept his butt muscles tight. He liked being able to chat up the chicas, even if they didn't always reciprocate. Above all, he liked the steady flow of cash into locker number ninety-three. Ka-ching. Ka-ching. His locker. His retirement fund.

Menendez brought a gym bag with him. He grinned, opened up the locker, and then stared in disbelief.

"Mierda!"

Locker number ninety-three was empty. Menendez was furious.

Slamming the locker door shut, he stormed into Fielding's office, grabbed the manager by his shirt collar, positioned his face one inch away from Fielding's, and growled, "Where the fuck is my money?"

* * *

Fielding shook loose of Menendez's grip, glared at the man who had disrupted his peaceful morning, and wiped his shirt to remove some spittle.

The altercation was so fierce, and Menendez's reputation as a hothead was so secure, that Fielding's secretary appeared out of nowhere. "Is there a problem, Mr. Fielding? Do you want me to call security? Do you want me to call the police?"

Fielding turned to Menendez, who suddenly seemed to realize that escalating this conflict, after just leaving the federal courthouse, was not in his best interest. A look passed between the two men.

"No, Gloria, that won't be necessary. Mr. Menendez and I just had a misunderstanding. I think we can clear it up if we adjourn to the diner across the street. Is that good with you, Jorge?"

Menendez nodded.

"I'll be over there for less than a half-hour. Remind me on my cell phone if I'm not back by then."

"Understood, Mr. Fielding."

With that, Fielding and Menendez exited the gym and headed to the diner across the street. The two men found a corner booth, ordered coffee, and spoke in soft tones.

"I swear to God, Jorge, this comes as a total surprise to me. And in case you're thinking it was me, I wouldn't do that to you. We've had a good arrangement. Why would I want to mess that up?"

Menendez gazed intently at Fielding. "Who's been here since I've been away?" he asked.

Fielding thought for a moment. "The police cleared out Gary's locker. Two lockers, in fact."

"Two lockers?"

"That's what they said. He had two lockers—one for cash, the other for documents."

"Did they mess with any of the other lockers?"

"I swear to God, they didn't. I had someone watch them. Plus, how would they know which locker was yours?"

Menendez paused to think for a few moments. "Who else?"

Fielding considered the matter. "Your guy was here."

"Almazan?"

"No. Khalif."

"I didn't send Khalif."

"You didn't? Doesn't he have a key to your locker?"

Menendez nodded.

"I thought you two were tight."

Menendez gritted his teeth.

"Oh."

Menendez stood up. If looks could kill. At least Fielding was safe. Menendez's hatred was focused on someone else now.

With fury in his eyes, Menendez left the diner. Fielding returned to Muscle Mania. He heard the screeching of tires in the background. Menendez was out for blood, and Fielding did not want to be on the receiving end. When Menendez was angry, he was volcanic. The molten lava would extend to anyone who had the misfortune of being nearby.

Chapter Sixty-Eight: Feeding Time

Menendez was no stranger to Khalif's apartment, but he usually entered through the front door. This time, he chose an upstairs window, accessible through a rickety fire escape. Despite his injury in Altoona, he was able to ease his six-foot frame through an open window into what appeared to be a guest bedroom.

He removed his shoes and proceeded slowly down the carpeted staircase to the first floor, a gun in hand. Khalif was busy feeding his betta fish. From previous visits, Menendez knew that the food consisted of live insects—bloodworm, brine shrimp, micro-worms. "Only the best for my boys," Khalif liked to say.

"Nice to see you, Jorge," Khalif said, not looking up. "How's it feel to be free?"

Menendez grunted, while pointing his gun directly at Khalif.

"I saw you come in through the upstairs window," he said. "You could have come in through the front door, you know. You're still welcome here." Menendez noticed video footage from four security cameras in the living room. Either this was new, or the cameras had been hidden before.

"What kind of game are you playing, man? I want my money!"

"Give me a minute to finish up, Jorge, and then you'll have my undivided attention. Help yourself to a beer, if you like."

Menendez was thirsty, and he needed time to think anyway. So that's what he did. He retrieved a Dos Equis from the refrigerator and rejoined Khalif in the living room.

"What did you do with my money, man?"

Khalif adjourned to the kitchen to wash his hands, then returned with a hand towel. "Are you going to put that gun down so we can talk?"

"You give me my money, then I'll put the gun down."

"Have a seat, then, with or without the gun. And let me explain the A, B, Cs of the new regime."

"What new regime? Mexico has a new president?"

Khalif laughed. "No, not that regime. You already got yourselves a new president, not much different from the old president, or so I hear. I'm talking about the world of cartels. While you were watching baseball games in Altoona and hanging out with the pretty nurses at Mercy Hospital, a revolution occurred. I hate to be the one to tell you, Jorge, but you're unemployed."

"What the fuck are you talking about, man?"

"Costa a Costa agreed to a merger with Empresas de Tabasco. Empresas is now the dominant partner. And they're none too happy with you for having shot one of their top traficantes."

"What makes you think it was me who shot him?"

"Everyone knows it was you who shot him, Jorge. You were the first burglar. The bosses in Tabasco know. The police in Pittsburgh know. And I know because that was my gig you took on. Frenchy asked me to do it. I asked your homie to do it. Imagine my surprise when you decided to take it on yourself. Why did you do that, Jorge? You're usually more careful than that."

"I wanted to make sure the job was done right."

"I get that impulse, I really do. But what you didn't realize is that the people from the cartel who wanted those papers cared enough about it to send one of their best operatives—Jose Castillo. They're really pissed off that their favorite fixer is likely to spend a lifetime in federal prison in the United States."

"Who is this *they* you keep talking about, man?"

"I don't think you need to know their names, Jorge. In fact, I'd say you're better off not knowing their names. That would be one more reason for them to kill you."

"I want my money, man. I want my eight hundred K."

Khalif laughed. "What you don't understand, Jorge, is that your liquid assets stopped being *your* liquid assets when the merger took place. As far as Empresas is concerned, the eight hundred K is *their* money now. The only open question is whether they're going to let you work for them or not. And, frankly, what they decide is going to depend on what I tell them to do."

All of a sudden, the doorbell rang. The video screen revealed two police detectives at the front door—Radic and Mulroy. "I wasn't expecting company," Khalif said. "Are you here or not?"

"Not," Menendez said.

Khalif motioned for him to step into the kitchen. He covered up the video screens with a curtain and strode to the front door.

Chapter Sixty-Nine: A Tough Conversation

Radic heard some scurrying inside as he and Mulroy waited for Khalif to open the door. He checked his right ankle to make sure his gun was accessible if needed.

"How can I help you, detectives?"

"May we come in?" Radic asked.

Khalif motioned for the two detectives to enter his living room.

"We're looking for Jorge Menendez," Radic said.

"What makes you think he's here?"

"A reliable source said that he was coming this way, and that he intended to do you bodily harm."

Khalif laughed. "I appreciate the concern, detectives, but I can take care of myself."

"We're here for two other reasons," Mulroy said.

"And what are those?"

"We have some questions about Gary Mabry's murder. We'd like you to come down to headquarters to answer them."

"I've already answered your questions to the best of my ability, Detective. I don't see how a visit to police headquarters would serve any useful purpose."

"We also have some questions about an arson that took place at the St. Martin de Porres Church rectory."

"I was sorry to hear about that. But what makes you think that I can help your inquiry?"

"Because we have reason to believe that you committed the arson."

"Well, I can't imagine where you got that idea."

"From Phil Hodges."

"You mean the mayor's aide who took his own life? Too bad he's not around to testify about that."

"Well, that is unfortunate. But luckily, he left behind a letter in which he made it crystal clear that you told him to threaten Father Buckley and that you actually committed the arson."

"The man was delusional and desperate. Would a jury believe an accusation from someone who tried to kidnap the Mayor's wife? Someone who was so unhinged that he wound up killing himself?"

"Nevertheless, we'd like to have a conversation, at the police station."

"And if I refuse?"

Without warning, Menendez emerged from the kitchen with a gun in hand.

"Enough is enough," Menendez said. "I say let's get rid of these guys once and for all."

"I'm sorry you did that, Jorge," Khalif said.

"I'm sorry, too," Radic said, "because backup is just minutes away."

"You're bluffing," Jorge said.

Radic was bluffing. And his options were limited. Jorge's gun was drawn, and he wouldn't hesitate to shoot if Radic were to reach for his own weapon, a Glock 27, in an ankle holster. His best chance was that Khalif would talk Menendez down and de-escalate the situation. But whose side was Khalif on?

Remembering the affection with which Khalif had spoken about his betta fish, Radic grabbed Mulroy by the hand and pulled both of them to the ground, directly behind the fish tank.

"Don't shoot, Jorge!" Khalif warned.

Enraged, Menendez fired at the top of Radic's head, but hit the fish tank instead. The tank exploded with a deafening blast, and fifty gallons of water and four betta fish emptied out onto the living room rug.

The explosion gave Radic time to withdraw his gun, but Khalif was quicker. Producing a small pistol from inside his waistband, he shot Menendez once in the chest. Menendez gasped, a look of betrayal on his face, and collapsed on the floor with a thud.

Radic aimed his revolver at Khalif. "Drop it, Khalif."

Khalif paused for a moment. Then he dropped his gun and raised his hands. "You win," he said.

Radic kicked the gun farther away and motioned to Mulroy. "Cuff him."

"What's the charge?" Khalif asked.

Radic thought quickly. "Unauthorized discharge of a deadly weapon."

Khalif laughed. "Lots of luck with that. My unauthorized discharge just saved your life."

Radic said nothing, because, truthfully, he thought that Khalif was right.

Once Khalif was cuffed, Radic checked Menendez's condition. He felt no pulse, turned to Mulroy, and shook his head.

Khalif was silent for a moment. Then he turned to Radic: "I have a request."

"What's that?"

"Help me to save the fish."

Radic considered the matter. "What would you like us to do?"

"There are four plastic water basins in the kitchen that we use when the fish are being cleaned," Khalif said. "There's distilled water, too. Do it quickly. Please."

After a nod from Radic, Mulroy entered the kitchen and began pouring water into the basins. Meanwhile, Radic picked up Khalif's gun with a handkerchief and examined it. A Ruger LCP, about five inches in length. The same kind of pistol that shot Gary Mabry.

Radic viewed Khalif once again, with renewed interest. The man he saw was tall and lean, like Spider-Man. He moved quickly and gracefully, like Spider-Man. Radic was convinced that, at long last, they had found Gary's killer.

But there was still much to be learned. Did the bullets in the gun match the bullets obtained from Gary's autopsy? What caused the falling out between the two former friends? And why did Hodges have to die?

As Mulroy plopped the betta fish into separate basins of water, each with perforated holes at the top, Radic noticed Khalif's expression ease. Once the fish were restored to water, Khalif was looking more relaxed.

Radic couldn't understand why a man who found human life so expendable could get so worked up over four betta fish. But he remembered something a CMU psychology professor once said: "Everyone cares about someone or something. Even a serial killer."

There was a question he was dying to ask, so he asked it. "Does it bother you that you've made a living by killing young men and women who get hooked on fentanyl and can't kick the habit?"

Khalif paused. "Aren't you going to read me my Miranda rights?"

Radic read him his rights. "Now answer my question."

"No comment."

"Have you ever lost a friend or a relative who died of a fentanyl overdose?"

"No comment."

"Do you still run?"

"Yeah, I still run."

"I'm guessing that you can't run well if you're using fentanyl."

"You guess correctly."

"So you don't use fentanyl?"

"That's correct."

"Yet you encourage other people to use it."

"I don't encourage anyone to do anything, man. People are going to do what they're going to do. Gary's idea was that if he stopped selling drugs, people would stop buying them. But the world doesn't work that way. If you stand up to the drug traffickers, you're not going to stop drug use, you're just going to make some powerful people very unhappy."

"So that's why you killed him?"

"That's why *someone* killed him. Gary was my friend."

Chapter Seventy: Seeking Spider-Man

Despite his initial enthusiasm, O'Neill was reaching the conclusion that sifting through endless video clips of super-hero wannabes was his worst assignment yet. Only Mulroy's encouragement kept him going. "You're the right guy for this job, O'Neill," she said. "You're a keen observer and you have a good eye for detail. You'll come up with something."

Mulroy herself had pitched in for several hours, getting a taste of O'Neill's frustration. She made one useful suggestion—focus on the cameras near a bathroom, because that's where civilians were likely to change into their costumes.

With permission to focus on the cameras near bathrooms, O'Neill was getting more good looks at costumed performers and their fans. He saw Remy the rat, from Ratatouille, adjusting his incisors to make sure that they did justice to his overbite. He saw Gollum from *The Lord of the Rings*, doing leg stretches before slinking towards the main walkway. He saw Darth Vader, adjusting his voice box and rehearsing his lines. I am your *father*. I am *your* father. I *am* your father.

Several superheroes popped Tic Tacs into their mouths, eager to make a favorable impression on their fans. In contrast, a vampire chomped on a raw onion until tears came to his eyes. He seemed determined to have bad breath, whatever the cost. Another vampire drank some tomato juice before mingling with the fans. Well, O'Neill hoped it was tomato juice.

By the end of Day Two, O'Neill had little to show for his efforts. And he was only a third of the way through the footage. Locking the door, O'Neill noticed the manager, Hornbeeck, who was also preparing to head home. Hornbeeck was sympathetic when O'Neill expressed frustration over all the video footage he had examined, with little to show for it.

"Were there any Spider-Men who stood out at your last convention?" O'Neill asked.

"Well, Spider-Man always stands out. People notice him. They want a selfie with him. They want his autograph. They want to dance with him."

"I don't think of Spider-Man as being much of a dancer."

"Well, in the movies, you're right. But we end our conventions with a dance or a costume ball. Spider-Man is always in great demand on the dance floor. He's kind of a babe magnet."

"Do you have any footage of the dance?"

Hoornbeeck looked at his watch. "Give me fifteen minutes and I'll get it to you. Then I'm outta here."

A half hour later, O'Neill had banished thoughts of going home and was looking through the new footage, fueled by a fresh cup of coffee. As Hornbeeck had predicted, two or three Spider-Men could be seen on the dance floor. One of them was a pretty nimble dancer. Tall, graceful, athletic, and strong.

Spider-Man took a turn on the dance floor with Little Bo Peep, who had some pretty good moves of her own, once she got rid of her cane. He also danced with a couple civilians and with Snow White, who was so cute you just wanted to squeeze her.

The most exotic of Spider-Man's dance partners was Lady Octopus. She was, in a word, a handful. Yet, somehow, Spider-Man managed to spin her around the floor, avoiding other dancers with ease.

The situation deteriorated, though, when Lady Octopus changed partners. Her next partner, Darth Vader, didn't seem to know what he was doing. Within seconds, Lady Octopus crashed into Snow White and one of the dwarfs, sending both to the floor with a thud.

Remembering a fleeting conversation with Mulroy about this, O'Neill stopped the video and gave her a call, describing the scene.

Mulroy got very excited and told him to stay put. She added a warning:

"Whatever you do, O'Neill, don't erase that video."

After watching the dance scene, it didn't take Mulroy long to decide that they had hit pay dirt. She instructed O'Neill to make a copy. Then she called Jake. O'Neill was surprised that Jake seemed reluctant to help, but eventually Mulroy got what she wanted. A meeting with someone named Virginia.

* * *

Virginia Wickstrom was not quite what Mulroy expected, which, she hated to admit, was a buxom bimbo with no brains. Instead, she found a tall, slender woman with good manners and an assortment of high-brow books in her bookcase. She also found her to be disarmingly friendly.

"I made the octopus costume myself," Virginia recalled. "It took months but it was worth the trouble. At the convention, everyone looked at me with admiration, even awe. Until I started stumbling and running into folks. Frankly, I was out of control. An uncoordinated, undisciplined bundle of arms and legs. I crashed into a bunch of people, including Snow White and Little Bo Peep."

"Do you remember dancing with Spider-Man?"

"How could I forget? He was an awfully good dancer."

"I could tell from the video. Did you by any chance catch his name?"

"He didn't volunteer it. And I didn't volunteer mine. As far as I was concerned, he was Spider-Man. As far as he was concerned, I was Lady Octopus."

"Did he say anything memorable?"

"Not exactly, but he was a smooth talker. And he seemed to know a lot about fish."

"How so?"

"Well, I said I had always wanted to dress up as a fish. Then he said, but that's not who you are, because an octopus is not a fish."

"What did he mean by that?"

"According to Spider-Man, an octopus is a mollusk, not a fish. I didn't believe him at the time, but I looked it up later and he was right. He knew a lot about fish."

"Did he explain how he got to know so much about fish?"

"He said that he owned some. He had a proper aquarium."

"Did he by any chance say what kind of fish he owned?"

"You're testing the limits of my memory. Um, alpha fish? Is there such a thing?"

"Betta fish?"

"That's it."

"He said he owned betta fish?"

"Yep."

"Virginia, I'm going to have to call this in. Then let's sit down and have a proper chat. You've already been a big help."

* * *

Radic had no wish to speak with Frenchy Frobisher, alone or otherwise. But that was the deal. Frenchy wanted to speak with Radic alone. No taping. No notes. No lawyers. That conversation would determine whether he offered something up to the District Attorney.

Radic objected, and Internal Affairs objected even more. At the very least, they demanded to be present. That demand was emphatically rejected by Frobisher and his attorney.

In the end, Frobisher got his wish. Chief Reilly himself insisted that Frenchy and Radic should hold a private meeting. It was time to bring the Mabry murder case to a close.

The man who sat before Radic at the county jail was still the same old Frenchy. Despite his suspension, his arrest, and the prosecutor's charges, he remained cocky, defiant, disrespectful, and annoying.

"Radic."

"Frenchy."

"Thank you for coming."

"I didn't have a choice."

"Do you want to solve your murder case?"

"Of course."

"I think I can help."

"I'm willing to listen."

"You probably think of Gary Mabry as the top drug dealer in Pittsburgh."

Radic nodded.

"Which he was. But not for the past few months. Ever since December, Khalif Wilson has been in charge."

Radic nodded.

"How much do you know about Khalif?"

Radic said nothing.

"Okay, if that's how you want to play it. Well, let me fill in the blanks. Khalif is tougher than Gary. Smarter than Gary. Meaner than Gary. They were pals, from way back. But they had a falling out. Khalif didn't like the deals Gary was negotiating. Khalif's your man. He shot Gary."

"That's an interesting theory. What's your evidence?"

Frenchy laughed. "I'm willing to point you in the right direction. But I need assurances from the DA that I will not be prosecuted. A free ride. Those are my terms."

Now it was Radic's turn to laugh. "Do you honestly believe that the D.A. and the PBP will allow you to get off scot-free?"

Frenchy moved forward, so that his face was inches away from Radic's, so close that Radic could see the stains on his teeth and smell the coffee on his breath. "I honestly believe that the D.A. and the PBP want to put Gary Mabry's murderer behind bars. And I'm the one who can make that happen."

"What do you know that's so incriminating?"

"I'm no fool, Radic. I'm not going to be specific with you here today. But I will tell you two things to whet your appetite.

"First, I can reveal where to look for Khalif's valuables. I don't mean money or trinkets. I mean drugs.

"Second, I can get you video footage of Khalif wearing a Spider-Man costume on the morning of the murder."

Radic squirmed, reluctant to engage with Frenchy but also curious to know exactly what Frenchy knew. "What makes you think we haven't discovered Khalif's special place?"

Frenchy smirked. "Radic, take a good look at your situation. According to my sources, you've examined Khalif's locker at Muscle Mania. Did you get what you needed there?"

Radic said nothing.

"Just as I thought. Close but no cigar. Well, I know where you can find evidence that will clinch your case. So I ask you this: Would you rather see me behind bars for five to ten? Or Khalif behind bars for life?"

Radic thought for a moment. "You haven't mentioned Atwood."

"Fuck Atwood. It's every man for himself."

Radic stood up. "Let me talk with Stilton and the D.A."

"That's all I ask. Oh, and Radic?"

"What?"

"What's the deal with that earring?"

Radic winced and said nothing. Frenchy was the last person on earth he would tell that story to.

* * *

Having informed Radic of Lady Octopus' initial recollections, Mulroy was eager to learn more. It felt odd to be interviewing one of Jake's former girlfriends. She was sorely tempted to ask her what went wrong. But Mulroy did her best to put Jake out of her mind.

While Mulroy had been on the phone, Virginia fixed some lemonade and a couple of fruit plates. Mulroy hadn't eaten dinner yet, so she was grateful for something to eat.

A few minutes later, Mulroy got out her notepad and resumed the interview. "Virginia, I'd like to know more about the man you know as Spider-Man. What did he look like?"

"Well, he was tall. Taller than six feet. He was wearing a mask, so I couldn't see his face. But he had pearly white teeth. And his breath was fresh. Maybe a little minty. Unlike some of the other guys I danced with that night, who smelled like booze."

"How would you describe his personality?"

"He was charming, dashing, funny. More so than the Spider-Man you see in the movies, who is quite serious."

"Did he hit on you?"

Virginia laughed. "It's pretty hard to hit on an octopus."

Mulroy laughed as well. "I get that. So you didn't exchange phone numbers?"

"No. Remember, I was seeing Jake at the time."

"Did he say anything about what he did for a living?"

"He was pretty vague about that. International trade or something like that."

"Did he say who he worked for or where he worked?"

"He didn't name a company, if that's what you mean. But he said he worked in Bakery Square, near Mellon Park."

"You're sure of that? He said Bakery Square?"

Virginia thought for a moment. "Yep. He said his office is right where the old Nabisco plant used to be."

"Great! That's really helpful."

Chapter Seventy-One: A Race Against Time

Stilton called Radic with two bits of news. First, community activists were growing restless over the unsolved Mabry murder and were planning another demonstration to demand justice for Gary Mabry. Father Buckley was counseling patience, but was too hobbled by his injuries to play much of a leadership role. More protests and violence seemed inevitable. Second, Chief Reilly had decided to accept Frenchy's offer. No prison time if he produced evidence that would put Khalif Wilson in prison for life. Radic was to make a strong case to the D.A. and arrange to meet with Frenchy's lawyer no later than Wednesday morning. Stilton's advice to Radic: "Hold your nose and do it."

Radic was disheartened, but at least he knew where things stood. The clock was ticking. They had forty-eight hours to make the case against Khalif Wilson, or Frenchy Frobisher was going to make the case for them. The very idea stuck in his craw.

Radic didn't even have to look up Fred Vinson's number at Internal Affairs. He was getting to be a frequent caller. They weren't exactly pals at this point, but he thought they had turned a corner.

Radic summarized his conversation with Frenchy, emphasizing that this was hush-hush for the time being. "When you were tracking Gino and Frenchy and Atwood, was the warehouse on the North Side where Gino was killed on your radar screen?"

"Yes. We knew it's where they often met."

"Just the cops? Or cops and drug dealers?"

"Just the cops."

"Did you identify any other venues where the cops met with drug dealers?"

"Muscle Mania."

"Anywhere else?"

"That was the main meeting place."

"Is there a warehouse or retail establishment where Gary stashed his drugs?"

"Yes. It was in East Liberty."

"Where exactly?"

"Bakery Square."

"Do you have an address?"

"I can get you that. What's up?"

"We think Khalif Wilson may be using the same warehouse. And if there are drugs there, there may also be evidence relating to the murder."

"I'll get you that address ASAP."

* * *

A raid on a drug warehouse raised all sorts of jurisdictional issues. Having reached a détente with Internal Affairs, Radic now faced a new battle with Narcotics. He knew that some Narcotics detectives believed that the suspension of Frenchy and Atwood was long overdue. But others thought the two officers were being hung out to dry.

Stilton went straight to Reilly, who approved the raid instantly. Narcotics would be there as well, but Radic would have access to everything at the scene, except for drugs and cash, which would be handled by Narcotics.

Time was of the essence, not just because of Frenchy's time-limited offer but also because Khalif was likely to be released soon. His high-priced lawyers ridiculed the charges against him as shaky at best, and they threatened to go to the press if the charge of discharging a firearm wasn't dropped. How would it look if the police were to charge a citizen with a crime for saving the lives of two police officers?

It was important to get to the warehouse before Khalif did. If vital evidence was there, and Khalif knew the police were hot on his trail, he could easily store contraband elsewhere.

***

As plans for the raid were crystallizing, Radic got word that Khalif and his two lawyers were stirring up a new controversy, maybe real, maybe fake. They charged that the police had tapped into one of Khalif's bank accounts and that the funds had mysteriously disappeared.

This was above Radic's pay grade, so he sought out Stilton as soon as possible. Stilton had already spoken to Fred Vinson and to Chief Reilly. Some kind of financial theft had happened, but no one in the PBP knew who was behind it.

The quickly-drafted complaint against the PBP made the allegations clear: Khalif had a bank account in the Cayman Islands that he intended to use to pay his legal fees. Two days earlier, the entire bank account had disappeared, to the tune of two point eight million dollars.

Technicians were hard at work to determine who had masterminded the plot. Thus far, there were no good answers, not even good hypotheses.

As he was puzzling over this, Radic got a call from the manager at the Red Cross. He remembered her from their conversation about Gary's Army.

"Detective, I'm reaching out to you because I didn't know who else to call. We have some good news. At least, I think it's good news. But I don't know who to thank or how to explain it."

"Okay, let's hear what you have to say."

"Yesterday afternoon, one of our accountants reported a highly unusual increase in one of our bank accounts. The one that is used to pay for blood storage. It was a *very* large amount of money."

"How large?"

"Two point eight million dollars."

"I'm sorry, could you repeat that, please?"

"We have an unexplained bulge in our bank account, to the tune of two point eight million dollars."

"Where did it come from?"

"That's just it. We don't know. An unknown benefactor."

"An unknown benefactor," Radic repeated.

"We've gotten gifts before, but never anything this big. And never from someone who is completely anonymous."

"An unknown benefactor," Radic repeated.

"Yes, you said that before."

"I'm sorry, I'm still processing what you said. I'll tell you what. Let me call someone. When I get to the bottom of this, I'll call you back."

"But, but ..."

"I promise to be back in touch."

Instead of placing a call, Radic decided to pay a visit. He hopped into his car and drove the short distance to St. Martin de Porres Church. He entered the church, took a moment to get his bearings, and then entered the sacristy.

Usually filled with clerical garb, candles, incense, hymnals, and other devotional materials, the sacristy had been transformed into a bachelor's apartment, complete with a couch, two chairs, a table, a microwave, and a mini-refrigerator. Judging from the smell, Father Buckley had just made himself a grilled cheese sandwich.

"Detective Radic, welcome to my humble abode. Care to join me for lunch?"

"No thanks, Father. But if it's okay, I will pull up a chair."

Father Buckley nodded, and Radic made himself at home.

"I've just come from the Red Cross, Father. They're two point eight million dollars richer today than they were yesterday. I'm guessing that you know something about that."

Father Buckley smiled. "As a matter of fact, I do."

"Do you want to tell me about it? Or does the seal of the confessional apply to what you know?"

"There are gray areas, Detective, and this is one of them. So let's try a hypothetical. Imagine a man who thought that someone might be trying to kill him. Not just someone, but a business partner. Not just a business partner but a friend. A close friend.

"At first, he didn't want to believe it. But there were signs that his business partnership was moving in a new direction, and that the bonds of friendship were wearing thin. Very thin.

"He and his friend had joint access to a foreign banking account that was unreachable by U.S. regulators and law enforcement officials. Although it was a joint account, he had set it up, and he knew the protocol that was necessary to withdraw funds in case of an emergency.

"Unfortunately, he couldn't decide whether an emergency existed. And he suspected that he might be dead before that became clear. So he did something creative. He transferred the funds to another account, not immediately but thirty days after his death."

"But he wasn't dead."

"He anticipated that he might be."

"Didn't he need the co-signature of his business partner?"

"Not really. The fine print said that if the person who created the account should die, the right to transfer or withdraw funds from the account would revert to the executor of his estate."

"And the executor of the estate decided that the Red Cross would be a fitting beneficiary?"

"Exactly."

"So in your hypothetical scenario, what did the creator of this account hope to accomplish?"

"Well, I think his position was that if his business partner stabbed him in the back, so to speak, he should be punished for that treacherous act."

"Isn't that up to our legal system to determine, Father?"

"Well, when it comes to determining the guilt of someone accused of committing a horrible crime, the answer is yes. But when it comes to determining whether certain funds should transfer from a murder victim to his murderer, the anticipated victim felt that it was *his* right to make that decision."

"Unilaterally?"

"Subject to the approval of the executor of his estate."

"You believe this will hold up in court?"

"I do."

"For what reason?"

"Because in my hypothetical scenario, I believe the victim would have consulted a very good lawyer before drafting the language. I also believe the victim would have made it clear to the executor of his estate that it was his intent for the money in question to save lives through blood transfusions rather than to destroy lives through the sale of dangerous drugs."

"Very interesting, Father. But was the victim sure who the executor would be?"

"In my hypothetical scenario, Detective, the victim was pretty confident that the ultimate executor would be someone who shared his values and who knew his intent."

"In other words, someone trustworthy. Like a priest, for example."

"That would be one possibility."

"So this is a done deal?"

"I expect there will be legal skirmishes. But one thing is crystal clear: these funds cannot be accessed by the person accused of murder, nor can they be accessed by this person's lawyer or lawyers."

"So if the lawyers pursue this...?"

"They will do so at their own risk, knowing that they may never receive any legal fees."

"In which case...?"

"In which case, they may choose not to pursue it at all."

"Which leaves the person accused of murder...?"

"Up the creek without a paddle."

Chapter Seventy-Two: A Bad Day for Lawyers

On Wednesday morning, Radic and Mulroy met with Frenchy Frobisher and his lawyer, John Danko. Despite the solemnity of the occasion, Frenchy was as obnoxious as ever. "Hey, Mulroy, how's tricks?" he asked.

Mulroy said nothing, then sat down next to Radic.

"Cat got your tongue? Or maybe a snake? Hisssssssssssss!" He laughed, but was the only one who did so.

Radic took the lead, summarizing the time, date, and participants before commencing. He turned to Frenchy's lawyer. "Mr. Danko, I have good news and bad news. The good news is that our meeting can be brief. The bad news is that the District Attorney has decided not to accept your client's offer."

Judging from the sour expressions on their faces, Frenchy and his lawyer were both surprised. "Did I hear you correctly?" Danko asked.

"Yes, you did."

"Are you saying you want to negotiate the terms on the table?"

"No, I'm saying that there's nothing to negotiate. We're not interested in what your client has to say. We will see you in court." With that, Radic and Mulroy left the room, while a uniformed officer escorted Frenchy back to his cell.

"You'll be sorry, Radic!" Frenchy yelled as they headed in different directions. "You'll be sorry. Just you wait."

* * *

Their next stop was a different interview room, where Khalif Wilson and his two attorneys awaited them. Unlike Frenchy, Khalif looked serious, curious. He was also more respectful, nodding politely to Radic and Mulroy as they entered the room.

After the preliminaries, Radic asked which lawyer would be representing Khalif. "Both of us," they replied in unison.

"I'm sorry, gentlemen, but you should save that act for the courtroom. Here, different ground rules apply. I need one of you to be the official spokesperson for Mr. Wilson today."

Khalif intervened. "For today's purposes, I'm content with representing myself."

Both attorneys objected, but Khalif was adamant. "I know what I'm doing. Your day will come."

Radic shrugged, then spoke. "For the record, Mr. Wilson will be representing himself. Detective Mulroy, would you like to begin the questioning?"

Mulroy nodded. "Yes, I would. Mr. Wilson, are you familiar with a woman named Virginia Wickstrom?"

Khalif raised his eyes a bit, then answered. "No, I'm not."

"She also goes by another name. Lady Octopus."

Both attorneys objected, but Radic reminded them that Khalif had decided to represent himself.

"I don't remember meeting a Lady Octopus."

"Well, that's funny, because she clearly remembers meeting you. In fact, she remembers dancing with you at the comic-con convention last year. And we have video footage of you dancing with her."

"Video footage of me? Or footage of some costumed character?"

"Both, because they're one and the same. You dressed up as Spider-Man at the Steel City Comic-Con Convention last year. We have you on tape. I must say, you're quite the hoofer."

"You must be confusing me with someone else."

"I think not. Let's move on. Mr. Wilson, where is your place of work?"

"I work at home."

"Five days a week?"

"Five days a week or more."

"So you have no office?"

"I have a home office that's very convenient. Working at home makes it easier for me to feed my fish."

"What if I were to tell you that we have video footage of you entering your office at Number 62 Bakery Square?"

"That address means nothing to me."

"We also have video footage of you entering your office building dressed as Spider-Man, on May 13 of this year."

"What you're saying, Detective, is that you apparently have video footage of someone dressed as Spider-Man entering a building that has no connection to me."

"But that's where you're wrong. Video footage in our possession shows that on the morning of May 13, someone dressed as Spider-Man approached Number 62 Bakery Square. That person then removed the upper portion of his costume to reveal a real live human being. That human being is clearly, unmistakably you."

One of the attorneys had had enough. "This meeting is over, Detectives. And we demand that you share these videos with us, so we can show to everyone what they are—fabrications aimed at discrediting the good name and reputation of our client."

"Hold on," Khalif said. "Hold on."

"Mr. Wilson, do you wish to terminate this conversation or do you wish to continue?"

"I agree with my attorneys that this charge is an outrage. But before we terminate this meeting, I'd like to know what happened to my money, my two point eight million dollars."

"A perfectly reasonable question," Radic agreed. "Well, Mr. Wilson, I'm sorry to have to tell you this, but your bank account is no more. The money has been transferred to the Red Cross of Pittsburgh, which is where it will stay until they decide how they're going to spend it."

"You can't do that!" Khalif cried. "They can't do that!"

"We can and they can," Radic replied. "You see, when Gary Mabry set up the account, he included an escape hatch. Under normal circumstances, withdrawals from that account would require two signatures: yours and Gary's. But if the person who established the account should die, his rights revert to the executor of his estate, and no co-signature is required. The executor has decided that all the funds should be transferred to the Pittsburgh chapter of the Red Cross. I have copies of the bank account protocols right here. A copy for each of you. Gentlemen, this meeting is adjourned."

With that, Radic and Mulroy exited the room. A uniformed officer escorted Khalif back to his cell, while his attorneys squawked. There would undoubtedly be a lot of huffing and puffing at press conferences and in the courtroom in the days to come. But as far as Radic was concerned, the case was closed.

In all likelihood, Khalif Wilson would be sentenced to life in prison. The M.E. had confirmed that a Ruger LCP pistol registered to Khalif was used to kill Gary Mabry and, weeks later, Jorge Menendez. A video expert confirmed that the man wearing a Spider-Man costume at Bakery Square, just minutes after Gary Mabry was shot, was Khalif. If necessary, Officer Lanley could be plea bargained into revealing that the order to poison Hodges came directly from Khalif.

Radic looked forward to telling Larry Mabry that his brother's killer would be locked up for years to come. He would tell Ernestine Mabry the same thing, but he doubted that this would provide true closure for her. Gary's death left a hole in her heart that would be very difficult to repair.

The D.A.'s case against Jose Castillo for murdering Gino Gardenia was equally strong. The M.E. concluded that Gino had been bludgeoned to death by binoculars left in a North Side warehouse. Castillo's DNA and Gardenia's DNA commingled on the binoculars. Castillo had an expensive lawyer in his corner, but the D.A. had the evidence on his side.

As for Frenchy Frobisher and Mark Atwood, Internal Affairs had ably documented their corruption. Audio tapes left behind by Gary Mabry were icing on the cake. Radic expected the two officers to spend as much as twenty years behind bars for crimes that included bribery, perjury, and falsifying evidence.

For the PBP, these were major victories. Reilly, Stilton, and others would be pleased. Radic, Mulroy, Scuglia, and Fred Vinson could all expect praise and maybe even a pay hike. There was also talk about putting O'Neill on the fast track to detective.

As for the Mayor, his campaign, and his family, Radic wondered if their ordeal was over. The Mayor had announced a press conference for the following day. Rumors swirled. According to one, the Mayor would distance himself from Hodges, declare his innocence, and double down on his re-election campaign. According to another, the Mayor would withdraw from the race and leave politics for good. Though generally wary of press conferences, this was one that Radic intended to attend. If the moment was right, he would also have a private word with Ceci, to apologize for having put her at risk.

And what about Father Buckley? The saintly priest was more cunning and worldly-wise than Radic had ever imagined. In fact, Radic was beginning to wonder whether Gary's master scheme had been accepted by Father Buckley or whether Father Buckley's master scheme had been accepted by Gary. It was said that Gary's acolytes would do anything that Gary said. But what if Gary was one of Father Buckley's acolytes? In truth, they would probably never know.

Radic pulled into his driveway and heard the familiar sound of Ralph barking and whining. Something had given Radic away. The purring of his engine? The color of his car? His scent? Whatever it was, Radic looked forward to spending the evening with Lexie and Ralph, with nothing to worry about but where to take a walk, what to watch on TV, and when to go to bed. Radic could already feel the tension draining from his limbs.

Chapter Seventy-Three: Piano Lessons

With Gary's killer in custody, Larry resolved to move forward with his life. His first step was to teach Dee how to play the piano.

Larry knew what it took to be a good teacher, and he knew what it took to be a good dad. He just wasn't sure he knew how to combine the two.

One easy decision was to designate his mother's piano as Dee's rehearsal piano. If Dee was to make progress, she would need to practice daily, on a piano that she could access easily. Larry wouldn't always be around to supervise her in his apartment, but his Mom would gladly play that role at home, with milk and cookies afterwards.

A harder decision was to choose a couple of books for Dee's musical education. His own path had been quite different—listening to a record and replicating some version of it, or listening to his Uncle Hal, who then taught him how to produce ii-V-I progressions in multiple keys.

Much as he would have preferred that approach, he sensed that Dee was more likely to flourish with a traditional music education. So he bought a couple of books and decided to give them a try.

Dee appeared punctually at her grandma's doorstep at 3:00 p.m., just after school. She looked adorable in pig-tails and seemed eager to begin.

"Okay, babe, let's start with clefs. Do you know what a clef is?"

Dee shook her head.

Larry drew a treble clef on some musical notepaper. "This here is a treble clef. The notes tell you what to do with your right hand. Most of the time, that is."

Dee nodded.

"Now, see if you can draw one."

Dee did a respectable job.

"Very good. Now this one here is what's called a bass clef. The notes tell you what to do with your left hand. See if you can draw one of these."

Dee reproduced one admirably, even placing the dots exactly where they belonged.

"Very good. Now let's go back to the treble clef. The notes you're gonna play today are either inside the lines or on the lines. There's an easy way to remember which notes are which. Inside the lines of the treble clef, you have F-A-C-E. What's that spell?"

"Face."

"Very good." Larry drew a smiley face.

"Okay, now let's tackle the notes on the lines. There's an easy way to remember that. Every Good Boy Does Fine. That's E-G-B-D-F."

Dee seemed puzzled. "Why is it Every Good BOY Does Fine? That seems kind of sex-twist, Dad."

"Where did you learn that word, honey?"

"From Mama."

Larry sighed. "Dee, baby, I'm not being sex-twist, as you say. It's just an easy way to remember the notes on the lines."

"I think it should be Every Good Girl Does Fine."

"No, honey, that just doesn't work. Cause you'd be repeating a note."

"Is there something wrong with repeating a note?"

"No, not necessarily. Sometimes it's good to repeat a note when you're performing. But when you're trying to remember the notes on the lines of the treble clef, you don't want to repeat the note."

"I don't think I'm going to remember it if it's all about boys."

Larry rolled his eyes. "Okay, I'll tell you what. Our next one will be about girls. Let's look at the bass clef. Inside the lines first. All Cows Eat Girls. A-C-E-G. How's that?"

"All cows eat girls? Are you kidding me?"

"Well, it's actually All Cows Eat Grass. But you said you wanted one about girls."

"I wanted one that makes sense, Dad. All cows eat girls is just plain silly. And kind of gross."

"Okay, bear with me for a minute, Dee. Take a look at the lines for the bass clef. That's Good Boys Do Fine Always. G-B-D-F-A."

"Seriously, Dad? Now that's REALLY sex-twist."

Larry, perspiring badly, sensed that things were spinning out of control. "Dee, honey, maybe we should take a break."

Ernestine arrived with some milk and cookies. Larry appreciated the interruption. He needed to reboot.

While Dee chomped on some cookies, Ernestine motioned to Larry to join her in the kitchen. "Larry, honey, I don't mean to be a buttinsky, but are you sure you're going about this the right way?"

"What do you mean, Mom?"

"Well, maybe you need to teach Dee the basics, the A-B-Cs. But that's not what's drawing Dee to the piano, hon. It's the music. Your music. Why not start with that?"

"I'd like to do that, Ma, but Dee's not ready for my music."

"I'm not so sure. Ask her to play one of your songs."

"One of my songs? What do you mean?"

Ernestine took Larry by the hand and rejoined Dee in the living room. "Dee, honey, why don't you play one of your Daddy's songs?"

"Is that okay, Dad?"

Larry looked at his daughter. "Show me what you got, Dee."

Dee wiped her lips and fingers with a napkin. Then she proceeded to play a tune with her right hand, smiling beatifically as she did.

Larry was astonished. Dee had just produced a perfectly credible version of "Blue Skies" by Irving Berlin.

Larry beamed. "Where did you learn that, sweetheart?"

Ernestine intervened. "By listening to you, Larry. By listening to one of your CDs."

Larry joined Dee on the piano bench. "Move over a bit, hon. Now I want you to play exactly what you just played. Don't mind what I might be doing.

Focus on your own stuff. You got that?"

Dee nodded. Then she began playing again.

After allowing Dee to play a few bars by herself, Larry joined in with a few bass chords. E minor 7th, B7, E minor 7th, A7, G major, A7, D7, G major.

"Let's do it again, babe." This time, Larry introduced a walking bass, using the same chords. He sensed Dee's excitement as they produced some beautiful music together.

Ernestine applauded when they finished and wiped a tear from her eye. "Dee, honey, I'd say you have a bright future as a jazz musician. What do you think, Larry?"

Larry gave his daughter a big hug, then some noogies, as she squealed. "I'd say you're right, Ma. We're gonna have to sign her up before one of the other bands does."

Chapter Seventy-Four: Loose Ends

Radic felt a strong sense of déjà vu as he retraced his steps to the Bigelow Towers. Once again, he smelled urine, laced with weed, in one of the hallways. He also noticed a Coke bottle and a beer bottle. Thankfully, no rats.

He marched up to 2D and rang the buzzer for M. Casper. The man who answered the door was Black, of medium height, wearing black slacks, a black photo shirt, and open-toe sandals.

"Good morning, Detective," he said, ushering him inside. "I appreciate your meeting me here rather than at police headquarters. That place gives me the creeps. No offense intended."

"None taken."

The apartment was simply furnished, with a sofa, a dining room table, and chairs. A crucifix adorned the living room wall, and a statue of the Blessed Virgin Mary graced an alcove in the corner.

Casper invited Radic to sit on the couch, while he pulled up a chair for himself.

"As you've probably heard, we've arrested Khalif Wilson for the murder of Gary Mabry," Radic began.

Casper nodded.

"Does that sit well with you?"

Casper nodded again, this time more emphatically.

"At this point, we have enough evidence to convict Khalif," Radic explained. "His gun matches the gun used to kill Gary at Mellon Square Park. We have a video of a man dressed as Spider-Man ten minutes after the murder. He removes his mask before entering a building in Bakery Square. It's clearly Khalif. We also have accusations from Phil Hodges, in writing, just before he was murdered. He explicitly said that Khalif killed Gary and that Khalif was plotting to kill him too."

Casper digested all of this. "Why are you here, Detective? You obviously don't need my help."

"Well, I'm here to ask a simple question. Why? We thought that Gary and Khalif were friends. What went wrong?"

Casper sighed, stood up, and wandered over to the window, where you could glimpse PPG Paints Arena, home of the Pittsburgh Penguins.

"At this point, Detective, you've probably figured out that Gary was not your typical drug dealer. He was a good man, a caring man, a compassionate man, a religious man."

"I've spoken with Father Buckley about all this."

"I know, and I can guess what Father Buckley told you. Gary made some very bad decisions. And then he saw the light. After that, he made some very good decisions."

Radic nodded. "That's basically what Father Buckley said." He noticed that Casper was looking at the floor. "But you disagree?"

"It's a good story," Casper said. "And it's true, to a degree."

"But not entirely?"

"I see more consistency in Gary's life than Father Buckley does. Gary devoted himself to ending or reducing pain. Initially, the pain he fought was his own, rooted in deep grief over his father's death. As that pain diminished and Gary healed, he continued to fight pain, but this time it was the pain of other members of the community. At first, Gary thought that drugs were the answer, especially for people whose pain was deep. Over time, he came to conclude that drugs were the problem, or a way of substituting one problem for another."

"Khalif didn't see it that way?"

"Definitely not. Khalif is basically a businessman with a strong work ethic. He helped Gary make his business a big success. And he expected when Gary retired back in December, that Gary would step aside and let him call all the shots."

"But Gary didn't do that?"

"Gary wouldn't be Gary if he just walked away. He spoke out against drugs. He became a member of the Mayor's Drug Task Force. He fought against the police gravy train. He talked to the press. He made some enemies along the way."

"Understood. But what's in it for Khalif? Is it just about money? He has hobbies, friends. Does he have debts to pay? Why would he kill his closest friend?"

Casper sighed. "I think it's pretty simple, Detective. Khalif was the loyal deputy for several years, and he did an excellent job. Now it was his turn. He expected some reciprocity. He felt he had earned it. Gary was raining on his parade."

"So you don't blame him for what he did?"

"I DO blame him. Very much so. It wasn't right. It wasn't necessary. It wasn't cool. But I also understand what can happen inside your brain when you lose your moral compass. A few years ago, I made some big mistakes. Poor judgment. Selfish behavior. Sometimes it's harder to take a broader view. In my case, my faith has helped me. And Father Buckley, who nurtures my faith every day. In Khalif's case, he didn't have that guidance or support."

Radic thanked Casper for his help and stood to leave. "Did you know Phil Hodges?"

Casper nodded.

"He said that Khalif was blackmailing him. Any thoughts on that?"

Casper paused before answering. "Phil Hodges wasn't always Phil Hodges."

"Okay," Radic said.

"Phil Hodges used to be Phil Fantuzzo."

"As in Joey Fantuzzo?"

"Joey was his uncle."

"Phil changed his name?"

Casper nodded. "Joey resigned from the City Council in disgrace, as part of a plea agreement with the D.A. After that, the Fantuzzo name was mud. At least in Pittsburgh. Phil left town, changed his name, and came back ten years later. Gary knew. Khalif knew. I knew. But no one in the power structure made the connection between the pimply-faced teenager who worked as an intern for his corrupt uncle and the smooth college grad from the Midwest who helped draft campaign finance reform legislation in Minnesota."

"He did for a fact?"

"Yep."

"But he returned to his corrupt ways?"

"Once a Fantuzzo, always a Fantuzzo."

"Did the Mayor know?"

"Mayor Graham? If he knew any of that, he wouldn't have hired Phil."

"A straight arrow?"

"No one straighter."

"What's next for you, Marvin?"

Casper smiled for the first time. "I'm going back to school. A special school."

Radic put two and two together. "You're going to become a priest!"

Casper laughed. "They don't call you a detective for nothing."

Radic shook his hand. "I wish you luck, man."

"I don't need luck, Detective." Casper gazed at the crucifix. "I have something stronger than luck on my side."

Chapter Seventy-Five: A Busman's Holiday

For weeks, Jake had been talking about taking Mulroy on a school bus ride once the case was closed. Just for fun, he said. She was to meet him at 4:30 p.m., at the Lincoln-Larimer Elementary School, where he finished up.

Mulroy arrived more or less on time, but didn't see a school bus, or Jake, or Jake's car, for that matter. She checked her phone. No last-minute texts.

Just when she was getting exasperated, a little girl with a ponytail emerged from the school and walked up to her. "Excuse me," she said, "are you Detective Mulroy?"

"Yes," she said.

"Mr. Jacoby said you should come with me."

"Okay," Mulroy said, as the girl took her hand and guided her to a smaller parking lot, where Mulroy saw a school bus with a sign noting their destination, "Kennywood Park."

Mulroy grinned. Kennywood Park was where she and Jake had first met, while working on a case. Suddenly, Jake emerged from behind the bus. He wore his usual attire—khaki pants and a crisp blue shirt—plus a chauffeur's cap. He was grinning too.

"Thank you, Dorothy," he said, patting the little girl on the head. "I'll take you back in just a moment."

Then he turned to Mulroy. "Nice to see you, Kathleen," he said, giving Mulroy a big kiss on the lips.

"Are you taking me to Kennywood?" she asked.

"That's the idea. Do you mind?"

"No, that sounds great. After all, it's where we met."

"How could I forget?"

"Did you buy tickets?"

"Wait and see."

"Oh, I get it. You don't need to buy tickets, do you? Because you still work there."

Mulroy sat up front and buckled up, after letting the seatbelt out several inches. "This seatbelt is making me feel fat," she said.

"Never," Jake said. "As Goldilocks would say, you're just right."

Jake started up the bus, dropped Dorothy off at the front entrance, and headed into traffic.

After settling in, Mulroy took time to admire the special touches that Jake had added to make the bus fun for young kids. Behind the bus driver's seat was a huge blown-up poster of a Mo Willems book cover, "Don't Let the Pigeon Drive the Bus!" Directly underneath was a smaller, subversive sign that said, "Don't Let Mr. Jacoby Drive the Bus Either!" With a smiley face.

If you looked down at the floor, you immediately noticed big paw prints leading towards a reserved seat near the exit door. Buckled into that seat was none other than Paddington Bear, wearing a floppy red bucket hat. The seat next to Paddington was so coveted that kids signed up in advance for the privilege of sitting next to the most beloved bear on the planet.

Each window seat included a small pillow so that kids could lean their faces against the window if they were feeling sleepy.

Mulroy loved the way that Jake took a ho-hum chore and transformed it into something special, something magical.

The traffic was pretty slow, as the bus proceeded from Forbes Avenue to Braddock Avenue, then across the Rankin Bridge, and finally to River Road. But this gave Mulroy and Jake a chance to catch up on the events of the day.

When they arrived at the main parking lot, Jake parked and gallantly escorted Mulroy off the bus with a tip of his chauffeur's cap.

"I hope you don't expect a tip," Mulroy said.

"A kiss will do."

Mulroy was happy to oblige. They walked hand and hand into the park.

Although school had not yet officially ended, many kids and their parents seemed already to be in vacation mode. They were everywhere, hustling to their favorite rides. Those already riding on the Steel Curtain or the Phantom's Revenge could be heard screaming with delight, horror, or perhaps a little bit of both.

Jake and Mulroy proceeded to the Administration Building, which Mulroy remembered fondly enough. It was here that she and Jake had discovered a clue that helped her and Radic to solve a murder case.

On her previous visit, the Administration Building had been cluttered with boats, resting indoors to avoid the ravages of winter weather. This time, in late May, the main area was remarkably clean, except for a big table that seemed ready for a fancy dinner.

"Is there some sort of shindig tonight?"

"I don't know," he said. "Let's ask. But first, can I get you a drink?"

"Sure, water's fine."

"I think we can do better than that." Jake opened the door to the kitchen and yelled, "Waiter, could you get us a drink?"

Moments later, a waiter appeared, with a bottle of champagne. Except it wasn't just any waiter.

"Radic? What the hell are you doing here?"

"Would you like a glass of champagne, miss?"

Mulroy didn't know what to say, so she accepted a glass of champagne and sat down, befuddled. "Who's the dinner for, Jake?"

"It's for us," he replied. "Depending on what you say."

"What I say to what?"

Jake reached into his pocket and produced a small black box. Inside was a beautiful diamond ring. "Kathleen, I know I'm just a humble bus driver, but there's no one who could love you more than I do. And there's no one I could love more than you. Will you marry me?"

Mulroy had not expected this. She started to blubber. On cue, Jake produced a handkerchief. "Since when do you carry a handkerchief?" Mulroy asked, between sobs.

"Since today. I thought one might come in handy. So, what do you say?"

Mulroy bent forward and gave Jake a big, salty kiss. "Of course, I'll marry you, you silly goose! I'm glad you finally got around to asking me."

"It's a yes!" Jake said to Radic, who was standing discreetly nearby.

"It's a yes!" Radic repeated. With that, the celebration began. Inside the kitchen, a handful of Irish-American musicians struck up a chorus of "When Irish Eyes are Smiling."

On cue, the musicians streamed into the main room—a fiddler, an accordion player, a banjo player, and someone with a percussion instrument that Mulroy couldn't put a name to (it turned out to be a bodhran).

After the musicians came a lot of familiar faces, including Lexie, Volcker, Lucas Renfert, a handful of Mulroy's college friends, and several of Jake's friends from Kennywood and from school. They greeted Mulroy and Jake with hugs, kisses, and pats on the back.

"Are you ready for the first course?" Radic asked, after giving Mulroy a big hug and kisses himself.

"I hope you're not the chef too," Mulroy exclaimed.

"Mulroy, you cut me to the quick," he said.

"No offense, Radic, but you're not exactly chef material. At least that's what Lexie tells me."

Radic smiled. "Don't worry, Mulroy. We've hired a master chef for the occasion. He opened the kitchen door. "Chef, could you join us for a minute?"

Moments later, the chef appeared, wearing a double-breasted jacket, an apron, and a toque.

"O'Neill?"

"At your service, Detective. Congratulations!" O'Neill gave her a peck on the cheek.

"What the hell? Are you sure you're a proper chef?"

"I got a degree from the Pennsylvania Culinary Institute. In between baseball and the PBP. I was a short-order cook for the Harp and Fiddle for a few months."

"O'Neill, you never cease to amaze me."

"Please, no compliments until you've tried the food. We're going to begin with a potato salad, followed by corned beef and potatoes. Every Irish meal must have at least two potato dishes, right?"

"I'd say that's a requirement."

"Relax and enjoy."

"But I have to work…"

Radic interrupted. "Stilton knows all about this. He sends his best wishes and says you don't have to report to work tomorrow."

"Okay, then," Mulroy said. "Who's hogging the champagne?"

Acknowledgments

The jazz musician who inspired the opening to this book was Miles Davis, who was physically accosted by a police officer outside the famous jazz club Birdland in downtown Manhattan. I thought it would be interesting to imagine how a similar incident might unfold today in my hometown, the city of Pittsburgh.

I visited Con Alma, Pittsburgh's fine version of Birdland, while doing research for this book. I was also lucky enough to visit the Allegheny County Medical Examiner's Office, the Pittsburgh Bureau of Police (as a guest, not a suspect), and other venues featured in this book.

This book was a labor of love but also a team effort. I would like to thank Delia Pitts, John DeDakis, and Nancy and Frank Pfenning for providing detailed critiques of an initial draft. I would also like to thank Jessie Chandler, Alice Honeywell, Martha Reed, and Susie Hogan for critiquing selected chapters. Perceptive comments and suggestions from this distinguished group helped me to sharpen my plot and reimagine some of my characters.

When doing research for this book, I turned to friends and others with special expertise. For insights into the care and feeding of trumpets, campaign finance, blood donations, and locks and dams, I would like to thank Dick Stark, John Pachter, Clyde Wilcox, Dr. Dan Bursick, Jorge Martinez, and Rod Mackler. A special shout-out to Carlos Suarez for helping me out with Spanish cuss words!

To understand police practices and procedures, I have benefited from conversations with Dave O'Neil, Sergeant, Pittsburgh PBP, and Bruce Coffin, former Detective Sergeant with the Portland Maine Police. Retired law enforcement officers with Cops and Writers have also offered good advice.

For lots of good insights into the craft of mystery writing, I would like to thank my fellow Sisters in Crime, Pittsburgh Chapter, especially its President, Annette Dashofy. I would also like to thank my brother Ken Gormley for lots of great advice on how to promote a book once you've written it.

From the very beginning, it has been a pleasure to work with the team at Level Best Books, my publisher. I am especially grateful to Shawn Reilly Simmons for her excellent criticisms and suggestions of a full draft. Deb Well has also been very helpful. Hooray for the Dames of Detection!

The jazz scenes in the book come from years of visiting jazz clubs in many different cities, including New York City. More personally, I have benefited from countless jam sessions with some wonderful amateur musicians, whom I met through Paul Pieper's Jazz Workshop in Tyson's Corner, VA.

While writing this book, I have learned more from jazz than just musical knowledge. Improvisation – the key to every jazz musician's tool kit – is a valuable skill for writers as well.

Finally, I would like to thank Rosie and Angela for supporting my foray into the wild and wonderful world of fiction writing. It's been a hoot!

# About the Author

Bill Gormley is Distinguished University Professor Emeritus at Georgetown University.This is his second murder mystery.

AUTHOR WEBSITE:

https: //billgormley.com/

Podcast: Profs on Cops, available through Apple and Spotify

SOCIAL MEDIA HANDLES:

Facebook: https://www.facebook.com/profile.php?id=1000866819904 85

Also by Bill Gormley

Too Many Bridges (Level Best Books, August 2024)

Also books on public policy and bureaucratic politics published by the Brookings Institution Press, the Harvard University Press, the Harvard Education Press, Princeton University Press and others.

For example:

Everybody's Children: Child Care as a Public Problem

Organizational Report Cards, with David L. Weimer

The Critical Advantage: Developing Critical Thinking Skills in School

Taming the Bureaucracy: Muscles, Prayers, and Other Strategies